NOVCHOK

THE NOVICE ASSASSIN

Ray Torbiak

◆ FriesenPress

One Printers Way
Altona, MB R0G 0B0
Canada

www.friesenpress.com

Disclaimer: In these days of plausible denial, the author allows that this story is based on real-life events. The Project is fictitious (to his knowledge) and there is only one character in this story who is known, however unfortunately, to exist.

Acknowledgments: The menacing cover art was created by my friend Eduardo Melendez Cerda. He has read my mind. John Carter provided expert editing service while teaching me to think while I write.

About the author: Ray Torbiak is a physician living in Canada with his family. He enjoys a good story over a coffee. This is his first novel.

Editor: John Carter
Illustrator: Eduardo Melendez Cerda

ISBN
978-1-03-918608-8 (Hardcover)
978-1-03-918607-1 (Paperback)
978-1-03-918609-5 (eBook)

1. FICTION, WAR & MILITARY

Distributed to the trade by The Ingram Book Company

Enjoy this story with coffee.

Best,

Ray T.

Enjoy this story
with coffee.
Best
Ralph.

2024

At sunrise the train slowed, then clanked noisily along on a side track. The train was surrounded by low buildings rather than tents; a huge military base from the look of it. Novi felt Father Boris's elbow on his ribs and started awake. The rest of the carriage was still asleep. Novi looked at Boris and saw him sending and reading messages from his phone, a burner that Miroslav had given him at the last moment.

Boris spoke nonchalantly, as if remarking on the weather. "We have accommodation in the city for a few days. We're to meet Father Maxim in Gorky Park this afternoon. An Army vehicle will take us there. Luchenkov can't accompany us from here. He's connected us with a driver. We'll tell him we have two days off as tourists until our next assignment. No deviation. We need to stay in uniform. When the train stops, we go straight to the latrines, then get some water or tea, and go to the motor pool. I know the way. Follow me and don't say anything unless you're directly asked. We want to get out of here fast." He muttered all this in tense, clipped syllables, but softly enough that nobody else could hear him. His black beard hid his lips; anyone more than a metre away wouldn't even know he was speaking.

Novi asked him if he'd slept at all. Boris grinned and shook his head. They moved to the rack and retrieved their duffel bags as the train slowed to a crawl and then stopped with a jerk. The wounded man at the back of the carriage was fully awake and groaning again. His face was flushed, and shiny with sweat. Novi could guess from the other end of the carriage that he was sliding into sepsis. Nothing Novi could do about it now. Boris and Novi slipped quietly out the doorway and stepped onto the platform.

Boris's newest contact was waiting at the motor pool. They had to clear out of the encampment. They walked briskly to the right, showed their badges to a hungover-looking young recruit, and were directed to the third truck in a long line. At the wheel was an impatient middle-aged man in camo gear. He looked as though he'd been recycled and thrown right back into duty. He had a cheap glass eye that stared straight ahead and the left hand gripping the wheel was missing two fingers, the remains stained yellow.

"Luchenkov said I was to get you to Gorky Park. He didn't say what for. I trust him but I don't know your asses from Adam. I owe him one, that's all. Let's get out of here!"

They said nothing. They took their seats, bags on their laps. The driver backed out and took off at speed toward the front gate. He waved his badge at the surprised guard at the gate. The guard cranked up a wooden gate, adorned with the orange and black letter Z, and they were on the road away from the base. Novi reached into his pocket, found a tablet of comfort, and surreptitiously slipped it under his tongue as Boris, riding shotgun, tried to make small talk with the driver.

"The camp looks bigger than the last time we came through here. New men?" He asked innocently. He held out his packet of cigarettes; the driver took one without looking down and lit it with Boris's lighter.

"Yeah. More big plans. We don't know anything. It's the mushroom treatment. Keep us all in the dark and feed us bullshit. I don't think even the officers know what they're doing around here. New guys keep coming, they get on the trains, load up with ammo and food, and disappear. The COs tell us how everything is just great, but we never see those guys again." He puffed hard on the cigarette and relaxed somewhat. "So, what's in Gorky Park that you need to see so damn urgently, huh? Are you guys tourists or what?"

Boris spoke for them both. "We're chaplains, that's all. Not cut out for fighting. Our boys came back for medical help. A fellow priest said he'd show us around the big city, get us places to stay in a monastery here. We're tight for time. Our next train to the south leaves in 48 hours. My buddy here, he's a bit spooked by all this. We need some rest."

The driver seemed satisfied by this and finished his cigarette in silence, flinging his butt out the window. He turned onto a larger road, then again onto a ramp, and then the A101 going toward the city. Novi decided to try for sleep and soon dozed off. The wakefulness after taking the memory drug had faded days ago; he would soon need to repeat the procedure. The tablets in his pocket were few, and he needed to open both his surgically implanted pouches soon. Their driver woke him after a half hour or so, proud to show them sights as they advanced further into the historic central city. The sky had clouded over, and soon a light rain began.

They passed dense forests of apartment blocks, bright cafes, and stores. The driver took a short detour to show them Novy Arbat, then turned away from the deeper city core to avoid traffic. They could see the huge glass towers of the International Business Centre a few kilometres ahead. Novi listened with his language ears tuned to pick up the man's accent and casual phrases, sifting for mannerisms of speech he could use if needed. His map memory was perfect; he recognized the Garden Ring Road as they turned south. One more bridge, another turn, and they were at one of the great park's many gates. Boris gave the driver another cigarette. They pulled out their duffel bags and the Army truck drove away.

The rain had increased. They walked hurriedly into a small shop just outside the park entrance, a tourist trap displaying umbrellas in the window. A middle-aged woman behind the counter saw their uniforms and badges. She immediately came out to greet them, asking what they needed. Novi and Boris pointed to the array of umbrellas beside the postcards, T-shirts, candy, and knickknacks. They both selected dark blue. Novi paid with his stack of rubles while Boris tapped at his phone. The woman tried to refuse payment, calling them heroes and thanking them profusely. If she only knew, thought Novi.

They crossed the street and entered the famous park, headed west toward the river. Father Maxim would meet them at the Rosary Garden in the park in ten minutes. He was watching for two men with blue umbrellas. Novi knew it was time for goodbyes, and suddenly he felt an awkward rush of emotion.

Novi spoke, his Russian fluent and rapid: "I need to thank you for everything you've done to get me here. You gave me the moral okay to do this, you connected me to the team in Canada. They gave me back my memory, my mind, my life. This has been the scariest experience I've had since I don't know, maybe ever. You got me across countries, over the hurdle of my faith in myself, and now here. I feel alive. I can't repay you, only thank you.

"If this goes wrong, it won't be any fault of yours. And I'll do my very best to succeed. I want to survive this if I can. Survive and go home to my family. Only right now do I understand how I miss them. I appreciate the fact..."

He began to cry.

"...The fact that you saw my potential and brought me back to life."

The rain was coming down harder now, and Novi was relieved to have an excuse for his wet face as they passed a few strolling people along the path.

"I'll never forget you, Father Boris. In case this doesn't go as planned, please tell my family that I loved them, and that I really wanted the best for them. My poor wife especially." He paused and collected himself, then asked, "Now what about you? Where do you go from here?"

Boris smiled and gazed across the river. "I have other business in this city before I go home. I have people to meet here, locals who are sympathetic. They don't know of you or our Project. I have other plans to work on with them. You don't need to know. I hope we will meet again, back home. Promise me you'll start going to church!"

As they walked into the garden, a stocky man in black priest's clothes approached from across a circular path. He carried a blue umbrella too. He wore a broad smile, and his bright eyes twinkled over a bristly grey beard. He stuck out his hand and greeted them cheerfully, "I'm Father Maxim. Welcome to Moscow."

PART I

1

—

2016

The old lady in section 106 never saw the puck coming. It was a fluke bounce off a second player's stick and it caught her on the right cheekbone. She stood up briefly while the whole arena, a sellout crowd, gasped their concern. Her adrenaline evaporated then, and she half-fell back into her seat.

Joe Danko, five rows back and directly behind the victim, bolted to the aisle and down the stairs to her side before her family could react. She'd just begun bleeding when he told her, calmly but firmly, "Hi. I'm Joe, and I'm a surgeon. You're gonna be all right. Do you take any blood thinners?"

She looked dazed but shook her head; she understood. Her eyes moved synchronously, and the cut on her cheek would need a few sutures. No bony asymmetry. The blood flowing from her right nostril might settle with ice, positioning and gentle compression. She would need a CT scan to be sure there was no serious unseen injury. He held her wrist gently, finding a brisk radial pulse. *Good, a systolic over 100,* he thought. *Decent rate; she's not a fainter.*

The house medic and security team arrived just then. The medic, a friend from work, smiled at Joe. "Thanks for this. We'll take her from here. Go enjoy the game. Your family looks worried."

Joe glanced up at the big screen and saw himself briefly displayed under the Jets' team logo and the score. 1-1 tie, halfway through the second period. He felt a rush, a brief tingle, at the electronic salute for his help. A crackle of applause followed him back to his seat.

"Wow, Dad! Is she gonna be okay?" Asked Will, his eight-year-old son.

"Does she have to go to your hospital, Daddy? Do we have to go? I don't wanna go! It's not even half over! And it's our first game ever!" pleaded Sam, his daughter, a six-year-old whirlwind.

Sara, his wife, let the kids have their reactions first. Joe glanced half-apologetically at her. She simmered silently, used to it and years past being impressed. It never failed to fire the kids up, but Joe doing his "surgical hero" thing irked her more as time went on. Someone always needed his help, his second opinion, his talented hands. It never stopped.

To everybody else in that cavernous building, this was an ideal portrait of Canadian wholesomeness. But Joe, and his attention, were pulled in so many directions by his work that Sara was now indifferent to his career triumphs and the high regard of his colleagues. Ten years of this was a long time. She longed for the earlier days when he really saw her, when their souls followed the same path, when he didn't opt for the first medical distraction. His talented hands did little for her now. His mind was always elsewhere.

The game ended with the Jets winning, 6-4. Walking through the overpasses above the winter streets, a young man wearing team colors stopped them. "Doctor Danko? You might not remember me. You did my mom's cancer operation two years ago. Rosa DiBiagio? She's all better now, off chemo and everything. Thanks for doing such a great job! We're all really grateful to you and the hospital. My family made a big donation; we were so impressed with how you all worked so hard for her. And the whole city.

Anyway, have a great night! This your family? He's amazing! Look after him! Bye!"

From the edge of his vision, Joe saw the little sparks of irritation in Sara's eyes.

Back home after the game, they teamed up to put the children to bed. "No stories tonight, sorry. Tomorrow's a school day. So, sleep! Stat, as your father says."

The protests were weak, and the kids fell asleep promptly. Sara was ready with Joe's instructions. "Okay, Will has two hockey practices this week again and a game on Saturday. Sam wants to start jazz dance, so that's an extra evening, Tuesdays after dinner. Most of her dance classes will coincide with Will's hockey, so we have less driving to do, and I'm exploring options for carpooling too."

"What about my on-call nights, Sara? What if I get called in?"

Sara was still smarting from the "hero-Joe" show at the arena.

"Is that surgeon-speak for 'Thank you, Sara'? It takes me hours every month to line these things up. Every month, Joe! Whether you're involved or not, someone has to do this. Same with your conferences, the family birthdays, Christmas, vacations. Your income tax! I swear you need a degree in math just for that."

"But Honey, you're so good at organizing things, and you know when everyone's available, what plans people will enjoy..."

"Don't 'Honey' me, Joe. When was the last time we got away on our own? Or just went to a show or dinner without the kids or your boring surgical buddies? Their wives are full of Botox and full of shit too. I have a brain, and I had a life once." Sara was a recognized expert in health care communication, particularly focused on the inequities of access for racialized groups. Her intellect was a pure force that on good days inspired and energized Joe.

Her hazel eyes flashed a warning even as Joe's eyes traveled to her full lips and lower. "Hey Joe! Up here! Looking at my boobs will *not* improve your hopes of getting me off this channel. I know your career is the one that makes the bigger difference and supports the family. The patients love you; you sing them corny old songs. The hospital depends on you and your team. Blah blah blah. I've heard it all. But you've managed to subordinate everything to your work. It's not healthy for you, and it's definitely not good for us. I keep waiting for the day when you'll see the rest of your life to be just as important as your work!"

In spite of his clinical acumen, his command of the OR, and his technical brilliance, Joe never stood a chance in these discussions because he knew that Sara was absolutely right. Every losing battle nudged him imperceptibly farther away and closer to the hospital. His comfort zone.

Joe had never even had stitches, never mind surgery. He'd seen all sorts of health problems. Always other people's, not his own. In his line of work, he didn't take his own good luck for granted. But he had an old injury, a sore knee that locked, made grinding noises, and kept him awake at night.

How would it feel to wake up with an intentional cut in his own body? To know that one of his colleagues had literally seen into him, made alterations, cut away pieces of his flesh, improved him? What must it be like for someone who's not in the trade? Who doesn't know the kibbitzing, the symphonic perfection of teamwork, the truth about what a surgical team does while the patient sleeps? He knew that his own dreaded day of reckoning wasn't far off.

The nurse checked his ID bracelet strictly for the record. Everyone in this hospital and a few other hospitals in the region knew who Joe Danko was.

"Wow! I never thought I'd see you sampling our services, Dr. Danko. I'm feeling the pressure here."

They both laughed. Ella, her name tag said. He noticed her hands shaking as she started an IV on his right hand. They would be working on his left knee. Less chance of getting the tubing tangled up. The room felt too cold, the lights too bright. A pale green tint of fluorescence. Joe fidgeted with the ties of his blue hospital gown, tying and untying them. Left hand, right hand, one-hand tie. Four, six, eight. He blushed when he knocked the clear plastic bag of his bundled clothes to the floor, his spilled underwear on display.

"Calvin Klein," Ella commented. "I can pick that stuff up. You look a little worried. How are you doing?"

"Been better, Ella. I'd rather drive the bus than ride in it. I don't think I'll be a model patient, but we'll find out soon." He'd sent hundreds of patients here to rest after he'd finished doing things to them. Ella and her team made sure these people were fit to go home and then sent them on their way.

Now Ella teased him again. "It says here you don't need a catheter for your bladder. I'm really good at it. Are you sure?" There was a hint of lewd animal interest in her eyes.

Joe shuddered. "Sorry Ella. I'm kinda freaked out here. Can we just stick to the plan? My humor's at low tide."

"Got it. Sorry." She took out an indelible marker and wrote her initials on his left knee. She didn't try anything cute. Joe settled back and fiddled with his phone. He'd done all the hardest puzzles already. He'd caught up on the hockey, the politics, the music news. The Hip were touring again. The Jets were playing cohesively under Paul Maurice. Great news!

Half an hour later he lay in a gurney outside the OR. Accidentally or not, the orderly had parked him directly under a crucifix and casually warned Joe, "Are you getting that knee thing from Dr. Byron? I hear that's a painful surgery." He vanished down the hall before Joe had time to respond. Joe looked at the forlorn crowned face staring back straight at him and reflexively began to pray, trying to melt the solid iceberg of his terror. Adept at inflicting and alleviating pain, he was not at all keen on receiving any.

Garry the anaesthesiologist was a friend from hockey, a former military medic who'd succeeded in leaving that world behind without being deployed to any hot zones. He greeted Joe with a broad grin. "Morning, Big Shooter! Heard you had a hat trick last week. Too bad you'll be missing the tournament this year. When did you get so good?"

"I really don't know. I have my lucky nights when everything clicks. But you know my baseline; it's nothing like most of the guys. I'm just happy to go out on a high note. My season's over."

Garry switched to professional mode, describing the process of putting Joe to sleep and keeping him there. He couldn't remain serious for long. "Any questions, Joe? Last words? Confessions?" He chuckled at his own gallows humor.

Something the hockey guys told him about, rumors on social media, came to mind. Joe was curious about his own subconscious thoughts. What would they reveal about him? Would he surprise himself? "Yeah, just one thing, Garry. If I say anything weird as I'm waking up, can you write it down?"

"Sure! I think I've heard it all. No problem."

Joe the general surgeon was into his third decade in the trade. He'd taught this craft for twenty years, selected and rejected students for the medical school, written cranky letters of complaint about the state of health care. To the Dean, the Chancellor, the Minister of Health, the Royal College. He had Experience. He'd Been There. They should fuckin' well listen to him.

Joe believed in breaking down barriers between neighboring segments of the healthcare world. He'd tried orthopedics, OR nursing, NICU, and the weird quasi-surgical approach of the radiologists to minimally invasive treatments. He could read images and use them to perform procedures just like his colleagues in X Ray. He could do decent grief counseling and change a premature baby's diaper inside the isolette.

His patients loved him. They were filmmakers, great-grandmothers, teachers, poets. Holocaust survivors, assembly-line and sheet-metal workers. He alleviated their pain and fear with a carefully titrated mix of skill, medicines, and humor. Many became repeat customers. They relied on his lame jokes and off-key Johnny Cash songs. Joe and his team in the room knew something these people didn't yet know: they had crossed an invisible barrier into a twilight zone of fear and pain. They were *patients*.

He took comfort in believing, however unscientifically, in some sort of higher creative force. He empathized with his patients, even prayed with them (and for himself if a case started going awry). He grew less sure every year about where those prayers went. The hand of Fate seemed to be guided by a whim. Still, the habit of sending his hopes into the universe comforted him; it was difficult to give up.

In Joe's worldview, it was far too scary to imagine that there was nothing at the controls, just an empty void. He'd seen too many unlucky souls: Kids with cancer, drunk driving victim injuries, that forty-year-old woman with five kinds of cancer. War and famine on TV. The world's alpha-humans blithely ran things into the ground while lining their pockets with something that would ultimately prove to be useless. He retaught himself gratitude every time he saw someone else receive bad news.

They wheeled Joe into the OR, and he shuffled sideways onto the table. A scrub nurse called the team to attention and read out the checklist: Name, planned surgery, correct side identified, last blood results. Someone put an oxygen mask on him. She asked him to breathe deeply. Joe heard a soft hiss, then his pulse speeding up, little beeps somewhere behind his head. Joe stared straight up at the ceiling. Garry injected a drug down the IV tubing. He told Joe to count down from ten. Joe made it to eight.

Garry met him afterwards in the Recovery Room. He chuckled, "You were raving about the president of some foreign country. You said there would be a war soon. I didn't catch it all, but it sounded pretty far out there. You must read too much news. We've called your wife. You can go when the Recovery nurse clears you. You're fine from my side."

Joe dozed off.

A pretty woman in workout gear waited nervously at the foot of the bed. Joe woke up again, thirsty and foggy. Relieved, she tapped his free hand. From inside his drowsy state, he relished her touch. "Joe, it's Sara. How do you feel? Your surgeon said he was really happy with his work. When they clear you, I can take you home." She checked her watch, pulled out her phone and started sorting emails. Joe mumbled something and drifted back into light sleep.

An orderly arrived an hour later with a wheelchair and showed Joe how to transfer properly, Sara on the other side. "Not bad for first timers. I'll walk you down. Dr. Danko, do you remember when you did my gallbladder? And my daughter's appendix the next week! We never really said thanks. So, thanks now."

"Sure, Dave. No problem. Thanks for the ride."

Sara watched, her brow furrowed, as the porter carefully deposited Joe in the passenger seat. She put the crutches on the back seat, hopped in, and started the car. "I sure hope this helps you. That knee has bugged you for years. It'll be great if it doesn't limit you anymore."

"I have my hopes too. I hope for a lot of things." Joe chanced a glimpse; she was focused straight ahead.

"Let's get you settled. I've made up a bed on the couch in the family room. That can be your headquarters until you figure out the crutches. Remember, the doctor said no stairs until you're steady, and even then, only with crutches and some help."

Joe's knee had been so painful at night before the operation that the surgeon's little green pain pills weren't really necessary once the insides were scraped and stitched, cleaned out and rinsed. Instead, he made a surprising discovery: the little pills took him away from his worries. The nagging anxiety that he was letting his wife down, the neglect of his kids that he whitewashed over with gifts. The spark of apprehension at the start of a twenty-four-hour shift—wasn't he getting a little old for this?

"Hey, anyone? Can you get me an apple and some water? Hello?" He'd awakened in the middle of the day, a week post-op. No one answered. He tried again. "Hello…" His opiated brain forgot the time. Everyone was at school or work. He zoned out again, carried gently on the soft cotton breeze of his pain pills. Some indefinite time later he heard the front door open and close, then, "Dad, can you go upstairs? Our friends want to come over."

Another week later Joe saw the surgeon for his post-op checkup. "Any new problems? Does this hurt? Or here? It looks fine, no swelling. Your range of motion will take some time to come back, but that's normal." Dr. Byron prodded and stretched Joe's knee, feeling for clicks, looking for problems. Joe had exhausted his supply of little green pills and asked for a repeat. His colleague was puzzled, but grudgingly complied, offering half the previous number of pills. Another month on, Joe was back in the surgeon's office and again asked for another repeat. The surgeon looked at him strangely—a mixture of familiarity and contempt. He said no. Joe flushed, felt suddenly nauseous and left in a hurry.

The rest of the hockey season passed him by. The other guys made the annual road trip to a tournament in cottage country. Joe resumed full medical duties, staying late for physio right inside the hospital, doing extra on-call coverage to compensate his colleagues for his time away from full duty.

One such evening, his phone pinged—a text message from another colleague. Jill needed his help with a complicated patient. Could he drop by to talk for a minute? Jill's office was around the corner from the only coffee shop in the building. He brought over two cups and opened the door with his elbow.

Jill was scrawny, birdlike, and terrified Joe with her ferocious, combative intellect. Today she seemed more conciliatory than usual and accepted his coffee offering gratefully. On her desk were rows of the little green pills and an open bottle of more. A huge bottle. She blushed, stammering out, "I get really bad menstrual pain. My husband's a pharmacist. He has a way to get them. Nothing else has worked."

Joe's gaze was fixed on the desk. Her eyes narrowed suddenly. It took one to know one. "I bet you could use some of these too, Joe?" Her tone answered its own question. She was all business now. "A mutual friend said I might expect a visit from you sometime."

Joe's hungry eyes darted between Jill and the table. "Uh, Jill… You said you wanted to talk about a complicated patient?"

"That's you, Joe." She softened her voice. A kind, maternal tone replaced her usual brusqueness. "You're one of the most valued team players we have in this hospital. You never turn down a patient. Your outcomes are way better than average. You always show up and do your best.

"But right now you're hurting, Joe. You need these. I have them. Here, you take a hundred."

Joe felt that curious hunger coming on—a craving for the soft oblivion he'd fallen into after his surgery. "What do I do if I want more?"

"Text me through the hospital app. Just say 'ready' and nothing else. But never more often than once a month. Ever. And if anyone asks where they come from, I'll deny this happened."

"What about losing my hospital appointment?" His voice faltered. His eyes caught something in the fine tremor of her hands. Fear? "Or yours, Jill? Doesn't it worry you?"

Her voice firmed up again to the nasal twang he was more accustomed to. "You'd be surprised if you knew how many of our colleagues I provide for. If you keep this between us, it'll never be a problem. But if anyone suddenly finds out and I run into any trouble, I'll assume it was you. And needless to say, I'll turn off your supply. Right?"

She said it all with a humorless smile, leaving him no option but to nod silently. His mouth was dry, his palms sweaty. He wanted to grab two pills and down them right there.

"They say the first time's free. For me, it's two bucks a pill. After this, it's five. Cash only. For the risk, right?"

The deal was sealed. Now Joe looked her squarely in the eyes. Her pupils were pinpoints.

2

Joe coasted back to the bench, his repaired knee holding up well enough for the new fall season of old-timers' hockey with the doctors' group. Garry the anaesthesiologist ribbed him, "Hey, slow down there, bud. Do you wanna blow the other knee?" They both knew Joe to be among the slower, older guys, and thus fair game for jokes. "You'd be faster if you came out more than once a month, you know. Even you surgical types can improve."

This was a sore point for Joe. "Hey, I don't get to make the OR schedule. Or the Day Surgery, or the postop clinic, or my office. You've been lucky and smart. Military career, part-time medic at fifty. Full pension."

Dave One, the nighthawk ER doc, chimed in, "Yeah, Garry. We don't all get to arrange our lives around rink time like Lou and Santosh. Erectile dysfunction as a specialty? Give me a break! The limpest dicks in town are right here! Plastics? Santosh makes more for a pair of boobs than I do in three ER shifts."

Kheo, a serious jock, added, "I have four kids in hockey. The only way to be satisfied with the coaching is to do it myself. I'm lucky to get here at all. Can't wait 'til they grow up!" He was an orthopedic surgeon, former Olympian, and usually ready to drop the gloves if one of the shrinks or the younger guys wanted to scrap.

Taras chipped in, "Everyone potentially has a choice. How much work and hospital status do you want to give up to chase the puck around? I took a month off in 2014 during the Maidan uprising to serve as a volunteer medic. Went to Kyiv and helped treat sniper victims. Best thing I ever did—to help my cousins make history. A lot of people died, but we saved a lot more. It was something I'll never forget."

Taras wore his ethnicity proudly and often ribbed Joe about the poor quality of his childhood Ukrainian language skills. All Joe could recall were the swear words, prayers, Christmas carols, and foods. "Plus, my wife said it was okay. She still lets me go volunteering there every year. I hope it's not so Dave Two can sneak in the back door!" Taras tapped Dave Two, divorced four times and on the prowl again, on the helmet with his stick.

Dave Two grinned wickedly. "I don't hunt in my friends' backyards."

The puck flew over the boards, bounced off Garry's helmet and back onto the ice.

Dave One laughed, "Best play you'll make today I bet!"

Joe had arrived late to the game by decades. His colleagues and his wife had told him he really needed to do something outside of his comfort zone. He fell in love with it—making a decent pass at the right time, foiling the other side's efforts, trying to perfect his skills. Most of the group were good-natured. Fighting was rare and mainly limited to the younger, faster, and more competitive types—the orthopedics guys, the psychiatrists, one unhinged cosmetic surgeon. There was unspoken respect for the oldest players, guys still lacing up at seventy. Nobody took a run at them or got close enough for accidental contact. Joe kept his head up; he wasn't in that age bracket just yet.

Joe listened more than he talked. The changing room remained a strange space for him, being literally decades late to the game. The better, more experienced players dominated the banter. Did he know these guys well, as friends? Sure, a few of them. Did he ever stay for a beer after the game? No. There was work to do.

"Let's go, Dad! You promised."

Joe was nearly through his pile of Saturday homework: billing, discharge summaries, a new clinical trial. A beautiful autumn day beckoned. Sara and the kids stood by the front door, helmets on. The bikes were outside the front window and the majestic colors of early sunset glowed overhead. The kids could rely on him only sporadically, for math help, a movie or a trip to the ice cream parlor. Sara would prod Joe out of the home office to make these things happen. Joe was safe, a known but dull quantity. Better than being on her own? Sometimes, she mused.

Joe logged off with an inward sigh and put on his most convincing cheerful smile. This would cost him sleep later. "Okay, everybody! Ice cream at the Bridge, or the bike trails? Your call."

"Come on, Dad, you know the answer to that one." Will teased.

"It's *both!*" screamed the kids in unison, as they always did.

A lace network of unofficial trails ran alongside the riverbanks throughout the city. Every kid who was able knew the trails in their own neighborhood. In their earlier days, Joe and Sara had met here with school friends. After dark, the teenage parties took over, but in the daylight hours, the trails remained safe for everyone. Even as Joe's career intruded into family time, he took pride in his familiarity with the riverbank trails and taught bits and pieces to the kids.

Now they waved to him from the overhead branches of an oak tree. Sara laughed and pulled out her phone for a picture. "Nobody falls out of there, right? You know the rules. We need to go home in one piece, not to the hospital all banged up!"

Joe admired her wistfully, her relaxed features in profile against the sun, raven hair tossed on the breeze. Times of grace like this pinched at his conscience. His childhood of scholarships, medals, and awards hadn't prepared him for a lifetime of taking turns and being present with his family. Patients and colleagues were so much easier for him than the emotional Snakes and Ladders of the real life he avoided at home. He'd always chosen work. He plowed the seeds of emotional support under and just bought the family stuff instead.

Joe's phone pinged on a frosty winter afternoon, the sort of day that made him appreciate working indoors. The hospital app again. That goddamn thing had become the bane of his life. The hospital Chief of Staff insisted that all pings be answered no matter when or where they were received. Now he was directly messaging Joe. This was an unwelcome first. Joe scowled at the message: Please come to my office ASAP. *Fuck's sake,* he muttered inwardly. Having just finished a short case, he had about ten minutes of option time, usually reserved for emptying his bladder or eating lunch while reviewing requests for consultation.

The admin wing straddled the corridor just past the coffee shop, beside Jill's office. Joe shuddered. The bird-woman had become a two-edged sword. Joe's dealings with her remained strictly a matter of commerce. But it gave her leverage. Now she asked Joe for help with every complex patient under her care, even though she was rightly respected for her own acumen. She made other, subtler requests for help of a more personal sort. Joe blithely ignored these as politely as he could.

The Chief of Staff's office looked out on fifty metres of river-bank park. A uniformed maintenance man drove a German-made cleaning machine silently over the floor. The carpeted corridor here was kept meticulously clean even in winter. A.Y. Jackson prints adorned the walls. Allan, the Chief of Staff, was two rungs higher than Joe on the hospital food chain. He offered Joe an espresso; Joe gratefully accepted. A Miele purred for a minute while Joe sized up the room and the unfamiliar face at one end of the table. Allan closed the door. He made a lame joke. "There are no microphones in here. We're not recording. This time." He waited for smiles and seeing none, continued. "As we know, we have some very highly skilled and highly regarded physicians among our professional staff. Many of us have contributed years to the university as mentors, instructors, researchers, or all three."

A slender, wraith-like shadow glided past the frosted-glass door. Joe felt her presence as a shiver, goosebumps on his arms. How many of the people in the hospital did she provide for? What was this meeting about anyway? His pulse began to quicken.

"Joe, this is Jim Carter, from the Ministry of Trade." He indicated a tall man wearing an expensive blue suit, sitting at the end of the oversized table. "Jim, I'll let you explain this."

The tall man cleared his throat and began his pitch. A faint British accent. He glanced briefly, disapprovingly, at Allan. "It's Carter. No Jim. We have a problem you can help us with, Joe. The Ministry is aware of certain skills you have that could help a foreign patient. A biochemist from outside Canada is staying in the city as a guest. He's been instrumental in developing toxic materials for military applications. His specialty is in neurochemistry. He's worked in the Russian system and possesses knowledge of their programs, including their nerve agents and their production." He paused. "Sarin, VX, ricin, Novichok. His conscience has gotten the better of him now. He wants to spill, and we have people ready to listen."

Joe's phone pinged. Next patient. His face soured. "How can I help you? I need to get back to my room."

Carter glared briefly at Joe's phone and resumed. "This scientist is a wanted man back home. He moved from Moscow to Kyiv but he's a sitting duck there. He can't go back. He and his family are guests while we sort out a new identity. But he's having a medical issue. He needs a house call off the record. Some of your hockey friends report that you're better with needles and knives than with a puck and indicate to us that you can help him. This is a favor to several other countries as well as our own."

Allan took over. "His gallbladder is rotten. Ideally it would have been dealt with back home, but he and his family were under watch. There was very real concern that he'd be abducted out of the hospital there. They came here via British military plane. Your friend Taras was visiting overseas and happened upon this whole thing. He called our consulate. They evacuated the scientist and his family. I know Taras likes to rag on you about heritage patriotism. You can do him one better now. We want you to drain his gallbladder and put in a secure IV line for antibiotics and hydration."

Joe glared at his phone as it pinged again. "When do I do this? I've still got a list going on. Why isn't he at the military hospital? It's just a few kilometres away."

Carter started to tense up; it seemed to be his state of comfort. "His identity is classified, with a capital C. Nobody in the military or security service can know where he is, who he is, beyond us here in this room. We're not even telling you his name, for your safety and his. He has intel that Russia would kill to silence. Admittedly, our own backyard isn't as secure as we need it to be. So, it has to be a house call. Some doctors still do them, you know."

Joe considered this for a minute and chanced another question. "How do a community hospital and a Chief of Staff figure into doing pro bono work for endangered foreigners? I'm not objecting, just curious. Does this put me at any risk? My family?"

Allan, the Chief of Staff, spoke in his softest voice. Joe had heard this tone in general meetings before. The voice usually hinted at vague threats, but this time it was fully direct. "That query is offside. Jill thought this might be a great way to show the hospital how much you enjoy working with her. And how much you appreciate your colleagues, your place among them. As she has done by putting your name forward for this. It's just another procedure to you, but it's so much more than that."

Behind him, as he spoke, Joe was sure he saw her shape darken the frosted window again. He felt his vision narrowing. His breathing seemed insufficient as his situation began to sink in. Carter's eyes took Joe's vitals every few seconds. Joe counted to ten while considering any small chance that he had options. "Okay, can I tell you what I need? Ideally, he'd be skinny, able to cooperate, hold his breath for a few seconds at a time. Does he speak English? And it hasn't happened to me with a patient yet, but I could kill him doing this just through straight bad luck. What happens then?"

It was Carter who replied. "He hasn't eaten in three days. He's had a fever for a week before that. English is not bad; he's studied in the UK. He's skinny as a rake; smokes too much. No allergies to morphine or any antibiotics. His wife is hysterical, and his kids are tearing up the house. They'll be removed and you'll have no distractions. We've heard you're pretty good at this stuff. And we know you can keep it quiet. I believe your membership in the hospital family depends on it." His eyes traveled from Joe to Allan and back. There was a glimmer of threat; Joe sensed that Allan owed something to this stranger, and Joe's service was the price tag. "Just don't kill him."

Joe saw the inevitability before him and switched into working mode, suddenly all business with the briskness he employed in the room when a patient's situation was difficult. "Okay, first thing is a portable ultrasound unit. Allan, can you get the nice one from ER?"

Yes, he could.

"And a sterile laceration tray, bottle of prep, size 7½ gloves, 20 ml 1% xylocaine, 2.0 silk suture. Ten milligrams morphine, at least five days' worth of Pip/Taz. I'll get the rest after everyone goes home. Please get me two of everything in case anything gets dropped."

Joe texted Sara. He'd be late getting home from work. He had plenty of well-used excuses to choose from, usually a late added emergency procedure. Tonight would surely qualify.

Nobody noticed Joe holding bitter green paste under his tongue, walking toward a rusty Chrysler parked outside the shipping door behind the hospital building, his backpack bulging with supplies Carter drove like a professional racer. A silent guy in fatigues rode shotgun. His uniform bore no badges, but he was heavily armed. Near the edge of town, the houses thinned out and shafts of wheat poked through the snow in dormant fields.

"Okay, Joe, I'm sorry about this, but you need to put on this blindfold now." Carter nodded to his seatmate. The silent companion handed Joe a strip of black cloth with a menacing glare. "Fifteen minutes and we're there."

Joe knew only that they were east of the city, maybe approaching Anola. He listened to the wind, the CBC on the radio, the tires crunching into ice on a farm road. After a short interval the car stopped briefly, then moved forward again.

"You can look now, Joe. Same thing again in reverse when we leave."

"Right", Joe replied. They were in a heated single garage. Through a side door they entered a modest house decorated at least forty years ago. Some of the furniture seemed to come straight from Joe's own childhood living room. All the drapes were closed. Harvest Gold. Avocado Green. He stifled the urge to laugh while Carter's helper gathered up all the gear Joe and Allan had assembled.

The ultrasound machine was state-of-the-art, the size of a large laptop. Joe had used it once or twice before. He powered it up, then entered his name as a patient to enable it. He poured some blue acoustic gel on his own neck, looking at his right carotid artery while he adjusted the settings. Then he pulled up his shirt and changed the settings while he scanned his own gallbladder. He smiled at the sharpness of the image. He looked around at his own insides for a while and pronounced it sufficient. "Where's our first contestant?" he asked.

The rest of the house was silent. The family had been taken to McDonald's in town. No complaint from the kids or the exhausted wife. Up a short staircase, with two doors on each side under a dim hallway bulb, a blue camera ball in the ceiling winked at him knowingly, once per second. Joe knocked on the second door on the right and opened it. A pale, skinny man in his mid-forties lay on his side, eyes sunken and skin as dry as his bones. He was obviously in a state of severe dehydration and probably impending septic shock to boot.

Joe forgot his professionalism completely. "Holy shit!"

The patient's gaze fixed Joe dully. "Thanks you for coming so far to see me, doctor. Please help to me."

Dim lighting came from a desk lamp behind Joe's shoulder. The military assistant became Joe's nurse. He poured the sterile prep while Joe opened up a PICC line kit—a long central IV line that would extend from above the elbow to a large central vein above the heart. Joe tied a tourniquet around the man's upper arm. He opened and donned a pair of gloves, painted the patient's arm three times with iodine cleanser, and with help, covered the ultrasound probe with a sterile plastic sheath. With the tourniquet on for the last few minutes, a basilic vein rose as a black circle on the screen. Joe raised a bubble of local anaesthetic in the skin over the vein and made a small cut with a steel blade. He entered the vein with a thin needle, threaded a metal wire 40 centimetres in, and snapped off the tourniquet. He enlarged the entry with a plastic dilator and cut the line down to 42 centimetres—guesswork based on experience. He fed the line down the sheath toward the patient's central circulation and tested it by drawing back until he saw blood in his syringe. No resistance. He flushed the line with saline. Good to go.

The silent assistant handed Joe dressing materials in series as Joe asked for them and then hooked up a litre of sterile saline solution from Allan's supplied gear.

"Good," smiled Joe at the patient. "Sleep now".

The assistant opened a vial of morphine. Ten milligrams. Joe drew it all up and injected four into one of the ports on the line. He then hung up a smaller bag, the antibiotic Allan had provided and opened the roller to let it drain into the man's sunken body. The saline ran full blast into the other port.

"Excuse me, sir." Joe felt around the thin torso and pulled the garments up over the man's chest. He spread blue gel on the sick man's upper belly, under the right rib line. The probe found the swollen gallbladder easily enough. Its wall was thick, angry with inflammation. The man groaned slightly with the pressure. There was no dominant stone, just gravel. Joe wiped away the excess gel and donned a second pair of gloves. His assistant refilled the cup of iodine and Joe began painting again, over the belly and lower ribs. Three coats. Joe laid down towels to outline his field of interest. The patient slept now, the morphine doing its job.

He jabbed the man's skin with the local anaesthetic. Seeing only a trace of discomfort he probed deeper, adding more local as he went, right up to the wall of the angry gallbladder. He watched the screen, judging carefully, planning his next approach. He cut the man's skin with a fresh blade, and with a bigger needle, entered the gallbladder itself easily, with a perfect ultrasound view in real time. He pulled back on the syringe and was rewarded with thick green pus. "Bingo" he said softly, almost to himself. The assistant handed Joe a sterile metal wire with a J-shaped tip to avoid injury. Joe could see it curl up inside the inflamed chamber. He eyeballed the depth, enlarged the entry to four millimetres with a plastic dilator, and finally, threaded a drain of the same size into place.

Joe drew out another 50 ml of pus and sutured the drain to the man's skin. He flushed the drain with 10 ml saline and connected it to a small empty plastic IV bag to catch whatever might return over the next day or two. He snapped off the gloves. "Billions and billions served."

Now he could relax. He looked at the sick man, now awake, showing him the nasty fluid he'd withdrawn. "I think you'll start to feel a lot better soon. But you'll have to wear this thing for at least six weeks. Or sooner, if there's somewhere to take out that gallbladder before then."

"*Spasibo*. Thank you." Came a feeble reply.

Joe conferred with Carter and the assistant. "Don't let him eat any high fat foods for at least a week. He can drink clear liquids from now, low fat foods starting in the morning. Bed rest for four hours. Here's the rest of the morphine. He can have a third of it at a time, three doses, three or four hours apart. Get him some Tylenol for when this runs out. The antibiotics are one bag every eight hours. Keep him hydrated. Run this saline bag in over the next two hours and another bag over the next eight. Then put this cap on the end. Keep it clean. Don't lose it."

To the patient he said, "Good luck with this. I hope you feel better soon." And to Carter, who'd watched silently from the corner of the room, he said, "Now I need to go back to the hospital. Enough fooling around; I have work to do."

The assistant took Joe back to the car, Carter staying behind with the new patient. Joe sat up front, wearing the blindfold and attempting small talk.

"Hey, Wheelman. Is this routine for you guys? What if I'd fucked it up? Would I still be wearing a blindfold? Tell me about Carter. Are you guys spies? Am I one of you now?" He was wired, buzzing on the ego boost of another successful case—this one spiced with a sense of adventure and the kick of an extra green pill.

But the military man grunted only one-word answers. Joe's adrenaline dissipated like clouds in the silence. The man's refusal to speak became unnerving. "Hey, Buddy, you *are* taking me back to the hospital, right? I mean, I'm not gonna tell anyone about this. I've been put on the leash by my boss. You know that, yeah?" Blindfolded, alone in the car with this stranger, and unsure of his safety, Joe was suddenly onto a fearful tangent that swamped his euphoria. *What if I'm disposable?*

The man drove on as the silence thickened. Joe could feel the sweat forming inside his winter clothes, started to feel carsick for the first time since childhood. Another agonizing ten minutes went by, and the car stopped suddenly.

"Your bike's in the back yard. You can look now." They were stopped outside Joe's house. He shuddered. "You unlocked my bike? You know where I live? Who are you guys anyway?"

For the first time, the silent man smiled and spoke. "Nice work back there. Thanks. Have a good night."

The next week went by in a blur, the usual work to do at night while his kids slept. Sara watched something interesting on TV; Joe had to beg off and catch up. There was no one he could talk with about his house call. He couldn't forget the fear on the sick man's face, or his own sudden terror that he was an expendable part of the scientist's recovery. So, Joe did what he'd been taught to do as a child. He prayed daily for the man's health and his own safety. It was a reflex.

A month later Joe's phone pinged again with a message from Allan. Joe sighed; what now?

"Patient did well, in Germany and GB removed. Thanks. Got 5 for annual review?"

Highly unusual; in every other year of his career Joe's annual review was conducted by his own department chief and took about two minutes, a formality. They met in Joe's office, a space large enough for a computer desk and a chair to sit on while working or changing clothes. Allan closed the door and kept his position beside it; Joe had no way to escape.

"Thank you for helping our international patient. I realize that we didn't offer you a choice, but you were apparently a total pro."

Allan often began with a sweetener before conveying his real message. He had perfected the delivery of the shit sandwich. Joe braced himself as he heard Allan's voice dropping into that reptilian register that he used for threats.

"Obviously there's more to your health status than you've disclosed in your annual reapplication for hospital privileges. I want to emphasize that word for you. Privileges."

"Aw, come on, Allan. Has anybody said anything about my work in these last few months? Any differences? No. And I seriously doubt they ever will. Because my work is a sacred thing to me."

"Fortunately, you and your work are both well-regarded. We can provide a little, uh, latitude in select cases. But it means me sticking my own neck out for you. Is there any reason I shouldn't do that for you? We're friends, right Joe?"

Joe felt the squeeze somewhere between his balls and his chest. Or maybe both. He thought quickly, and settled on, "I'm one hundred percent behind this hospital and what we all stand for, Allan. As I have been since I arrived here. Yes, I have my 'health issues,' but I can count on one hand the times I've ever missed work for an unscheduled absence. Has the hospital ever been sued because of my behavior, or my incompetence? No? Good. Let's leave it there."

Allan regarded Joe as one would a disobedient child, then decided to let it drop. "Okay, Joe. But it's a short leash and my head will roll with yours if anything untoward were to happen. I'm charged with maintaining the quality and competence of our care providers. Short leash. Right, Buddy?"

Joe detested this false equality. They were no more buddies than sharks and swimmers. But he caved and put out his hand. "Right, Chief."

He knew what Allan wanted to hear. They shook hands and Allan opened the door. He was gone without a word. Then and there, Joe resolved to wean himself away from the grip of the bird-woman and Allan the extortionist. *What might they ask me to do next?* he mused. Over the next few months he gradually reduced his intake of the little green pills, but continued to order Jill's limit of a hundred a month. Joe kept them in a desk drawer at home where nobody else ventured. Within two months he'd saved a full bottle. What would he do with them? He had no idea. That bottle comforted him somehow, proof that he had strength even within his weakness. And a supply. Always keep a supply. You never know.

3

—

2018

Boris the Priest sat uneasily in the private room at the back of a Knightsbridge coffee bar with a group of three men, each in their mid-fifties. They were unremarkable aside from their high-end wristwatches. His eyes shifted furtively between them, studying their unease. If any one of them knew anything about their missing comrade, they concealed it well. Oleg checked his Patek Philippe constantly, the others kept glancing at their phones or the door. Demitasse espressos cooled on the small marble table. The ashtray overflowed, the air was thick with smoke and nervous silence. The waitress rang a bell from outside. Boris, nearest to the door, looked through the peephole and opened the door. She brought them refills and a new ashtray, retreating silently with her eyes lowered.

Boris shuffled his feet under the table, looked at his watch when they did, and puffed on his Gauloise cigarette—a luxury he granted himself for the danger he lived every day. He mimicked their discomfort without overdoing it. He wondered what the others thought of him; he had found and recruited these oligarchs for their connections and their staggering wealth.

"It's unlike Semyon to be late," Boris offered at last. Someone had to say something. The men spoke quietly, their Russian tongue an unwelcome sound to the British ear. "Car trouble?" His Russian was perfect, remarkable for a Westerner.

"Not likely," said Oleg, tugging heavily on his cigarette. "Semyon has eight vehicles in London. Unfortunately, he isn't shy about flaunting his wealth." It was true; he'd even showed up to one of their meetings in a new Lambo.

"Could he have been found out?" Ivan the quiet one rasped.

"Then he'd better not roll on us! Not if he values his friends," replied Oleg. They all knew the rules and had sworn to stay in the game.

"Boris! You know everything. Where's our friend? You wanted us all so badly to join your little church choir. So, we've joined! Where's the safety guarantee?" Igor was the argumentative one, but valuable for his links to businessmen still living and operating inside Russia.

"I know what you might be thinking. Have I not been absolutely up front with all of you? We all want the same thing. It comes with hazards, and these are greater for me than for any of you, believe it my brothers.

"I must congratulate all of you on your perfect attendance and your dedication so far. We grow closer to resolving our problem every month. Tonight, I fear we must assume the worst. I pray for Semyon's safety, as we all should. This meeting is adjourned. I have two new members for your consideration. But we need Semyon, all of us, to be here for that approval. Remember, also, I'm just a middleman. Watch your secondary phones and keep an eye on the news. Be careful my friends. Next month, same time, next location."

This group met every month, sometimes virtually. It was a rare event to have them all in one country. Out of necessity they had all learned how to use VPNs and burner phones. These were some of the president's former best friends, businessmen who had assumed control of most of the Motherland's biggest companies. Their freedom to operate had once been limitless, but in recent years, each had come to the conclusion that there was no hope of a permanent future back home. The president took a healthy slice from their profits and never failed to mention their indebtedness. They had no nostalgia for the old days: bread lineups, inferior clothes, travel restrictions, mandatory Party membership and expensive bribery structure. The President's enthusiasm was his alone.

These men savored the good life. Their families had estates in Spain, Italy, Switzerland. Lavish homes in London and Dubai, ski chalets in France. They had worked hard for these luxuries. Why risk it all for the president's dream of a united, rebuilt Soviet Union? Little by little, they'd found each other and found ways to hide chunks of their massive fortunes outside the Motherland and out of the President's reach.

Semyon was the local leader strictly based on his financial status, but it was Boris who had the Western connections that they could only dream of. They called him "the Priest" out of respect; he'd once told them he was ordained but none of them really believed it. Men like Boris weren't close to God; they joked when he wasn't around or was late to a VPN call. More like the opposite, they said. Still, he inspired their confidence and kept them motivated.

Boris knew there were other groups of men with tension headaches, wearing sweaty blazers or high-end track suits, meeting at other coffee houses, pubs, and parks. Some met in Moscow, others in Manchester, Washington, Dubai, or Berlin. Boris met with men in Newark, Philadelphia, and Winnipeg in addition to his visits to Europe. They met to share information and concerns, sometimes to consider new recruits. The leaders met to generate operation plans and approve budget plans. Theirs was an expensive line of business.

As always, the group disbanded in pairs. Semyon would have departed with two of the others, had he shown up. No one ever left alone, for reasons of both trust and safety. Two of the men left together, then the remaining pair five minutes later. Boris drove an old Fiat that he wove through the alleys with the skill of a local. "It's a strange way to do God's work," he mused aloud to Ivan, his carpool partner. "Robin Hood never had to go so far to reach his merry men. Jesus said that people of such immense wealth and power could never enter the kingdom of heaven. I disagree."

Ivan defended himself. "Being wealthy doesn't always equate to having no soul, Father Boris. You've given us a direction to follow, but we could have ignored your call. We could have turned a blind eye to you, gone on our way and been no wiser. Or better.

I still trust you, but this kind of thing with Semyon makes me wonder how safe this Project is."

"I understand how this could cause us all some concern. We need to keep focused and pray for Semyon's safety and our own. Is our cause just? Absolutely! Remember that whenever your courage wavers. Good night, Ivan."

They stopped outside the gates of a mansion not far from the coffee shop. A uniformed security guard opened Ivan's door. A light rain fell. The guard held his umbrella over the car as Ivan alighted. "I know you're right, Boris. Pray for me, or something." He shook the Priest's hand and went through the heavy iron gate with his guard.

"Where would I be right now, if not here? Thanks, Father, for bringing me to Your service in this way. Please keep me and these men I've found safe while we help them reclaim their country for their people." Boris prayed out loud as he drove south over the river. He arrived at his walk-up flat, nodded to the neighbors, an older couple who rented him their upper floor. He retrieved his Glock from under the seat, hung it in the holster under his left armpit while they opened their own front door to go inside after an evening at the pub. Something told him to keep it ready. He'd learned to trust his intuition. His sleep was light and uneasy.

Boris's phone pinged an hour before the news outlets released the story the next morning. "Brace yourself," he said to no one else, instantly wide awake. A Russian national had been found alongside his wife in their Tuscan villa. Their throats had been cut, there was blood everywhere, and an unbelievably clumsy suicide note written in Russian, Italian, and English had been left on the floor near the front door. The corpses couldn't possibly have carried it that far. Semyon was the third oligarch to die in Europe in the past year.

"Holy shit," he said softly, "better get to work." He slid a fire-proof metal box from under his single bed. The box itself was installed on rails and couldn't be easily removed. The lock on the lid was a combination in Cyrillic letters. Boris took no chances with the contents. There were several burner phones, all on a battery pack charger. The cord trailed out the back of the box to a wall plug covered by the bed. A stack of twenty-pound notes, two credit cards, two passports each for the UK, USA, Russian Federation, Ukraine, Canada, and the EU. One of each was under a false name. All were in waterproof plastic pouches.

Now Boris had to move quickly. He selected a locally enabled burner phone and alerted one of his co-conspirators, a Ukrainian national who lived in Zurich, explaining the problem in terse sentences. His IT colleague, an expert financial hacker, grasped the urgency of this request before Boris had finished.

"So, you need the assets moved," the colleague stated. He never asked a question.

"Yes, and fast. The other side will find out very soon where everything is. I'm guessing Semyon's visitors had half a night to get into his account numbers, computer, and house safe. There was no mention of torture, but I'm sure they wouldn't have hesitated to pull a few teeth."

Boris had played this particular game a few times before, with results any master thief would be proud of. This time the payoff was an order of magnitude larger. He'd coaxed the banking information from Semyon two years ago in case of exactly this eventuality. Prudent financial planning for a man with no interest in money. Semyon had played it back in turn, giving Boris decoy account numbers with smaller balances. Boris had never tried to go after that money—millions of euros. Semyon had gone on to trust the Priest with the real thing: Swiss accounts worth over three billion euros.

Boris's financial colleague knew his way around the banks he raided. This was a routine situation for one of Ukraine's best IT expats, one with finely crafted high-level clearances and unparalleled abilities. Semyon had moved his assets to an account outside the bank's mainframe the previous year. Boris knew the passwords, numbers, and balance. The cash would be moved twice that day by Boris's colleague, arriving in 24 hours—half in the Bahamas and half in the Caymans.

This was just one of dozens of similar accounts known to the Project. This bank was large enough that even the disappearance of an account of this size wouldn't attract immediate attention. Someone's head would eventually roll, but the bank would never publicly admit to clients like Semyon, much less own up to losing the handle on such an account. The IT man who had created the account knew why Semyon needed to hide his main assets, and they both knew what would happen to the money in this event. Semyon's former benefactor would be enraged. The arrangement satisfied all the other parties.

Boris made his next call from another one of his burner phones, labeled with a Canadian flag. "Operative Three, a man is overboard but the fish are in the net. At least three Bees. Usual arrangements have been made. It's all set. There may be others to follow. I trust this news will find you well. Have a great day."

Carter stood in his kitchen in a suburb of Ottawa, making a pot of tea and listening to voice mails while his family readied themselves for the day. He listened silently, hung up, and took the dog outside. From the backyard he rang the next Project member on the list. "Raj, Three here. Remember the Priest? The one you weren't so sure about? Yes. He works really well with your banker friend; I'll give you that.

"I've been told three Bees. We can operate unhindered for about five years minimum. Yes, fully funded. Thought you'd like to know. He has also told me to be prepared for more similar scores. This is exactly why we needed to be who we are. Non-government, quick on our feet. Do we want that inertia? The deadwood, the dead weight? Those nabobs! We're so much more nimble. Yes, have a fine day. Thank you. Cheerio."

He kept his jubilation, his sense of vindication, well under wraps. He was a very hands-on director, but he'd made an exception in the case of Boris. The priest had shown himself to be absolutely reliable, motivated, and trustworthy, even with access to undreamed-of wealth. The MI6 people, the CIA, CSIS—all those government-affiliated orgs—fought for funding, and here was this upstart bunch getting it done in a fraction of the time with much smaller resources.

Carter had survived a successful career as a field agent for MI6 but left the party after a dispute with his direct supervisor that resulted in his being deployed into ever-hotter environments. He'd packed up his family and decamped to Canada, first as a legitimate government trade representative. His old life followed him, as so often happened in these circles. He found himself co-creating the Project. His family were blissfully unaware of his new career. He was an expert in keeping such things hidden from those he loved most. Such knowledge could be fatal.

Former field agents and directors like Carter had grown disillusioned with the lack of will to get things done in a more direct, old-school way. Far too much appeasement policy ran amok in the free world. Compromise never worked when playing cards against murderers in suits and generals' uniforms. Carter knew that the adversaries were streetfighters like himself, who understood the language of force to be the real lingua franca that made history.

Carter had helped will the Project into being as his answer. And if one knew where to look, plenty of potential partners merely needed a little guidance, a nudge onto the dance floor of treachery and death for the cause of freedom and a stable world. Semyon had been a prime example, and Carter allowed himself a pang of grief at losing such a trusting ally. No room for guilt though.

4

—

2020

The young man on the table was so covered with tape, his face so swollen, that his mother didn't recognize him at the bedside. The ventilator tube was double secured. A feeding tube occupied his other nostril. A suction device was taped to the pillow beside his iodine-brown shaved head. A baseball seam of staples curved over his temple. His eyelids were taped over so that they didn't relax open while he was in medical coma and allow his eyes to dry out. He'd been fitted with a central intravenous line, a bladder catheter, and a diaper. Oxygenation and ECG monitors completed the attachments. IV pumps rose like cell relay towers from the top corners of his bed. Everything beeped intermittently.

Garry was working ICU that week. He had two layers of bags under his eyes, visible above his N95 mask. "Let's make this quick, Joe. This one's barely stable enough for the elevator ride."

The whole world had seen the videos from China of families being welded into their apartment buildings, of exhausted nurses sleeping on the floor outside the ICU in Italy, of mass graves being dug by prison inmates in New York City, funeral pyres in India. There was no escape, only zones of lesser risk. The curve now rose like a cobra's head in Joe's part of the world.

It was 0930h on a Monday. Before stepping to the scrub sink, Joe looked around. All eyes were focused on transferring the young man and his support equipment to the OR table. A lot of hardware needed to be protected besides the patient himself. Joe slid a small round green pill under his N95 and chewed it while he cleansed his hands. He held the dissolving paste under his tongue, where the vessels were rich, and the mucosal surface was thin. The drug arrived quicker, the blood levels spiked higher this way. He savored the bitter chemical taste, an old friend returning to his life in this terrifying time. The delicious secrecy, the sense of getting away with something he shouldn't, was its own guilty pleasure. It hit him every time before the drug did.

Between cases on a day like this, Joe would be locked in the only bathroom for fifty staff, trying to slow down his breathing. The four rounds of handwashing before and after each patient exposure gave him time to imagine all sorts of dire outcomes. For his patients, his team, and himself. All that extra preparation, times six patients a day, lengthened his workdays and stripped layers of skin off his forearms and hands as the disinfectant burned him.

Here and now, in the autumn of 2020, work dominated his life in ways it never had before. His hospital lost workers to burnout and retirement. As the pandemic stretched them on the rack of fear and overtime, the comforts of the hospital-being the guy in charge, making a great save, being wanted and needed—wore thin, and then wore through.

Gyms and hockey rinks were closed, playgrounds taped off with public health notices. Joe replaced exercise with beer as a quick substitute to keep his mood in balance. Knowing, of course, how stupid and counterproductive it was. Sara went into self-preservation mode but still sent out brief radio pulses of warmth, advice, even tenderness sometimes. He clung to these, an astronaut adrift in his own universe.

Joe practiced fear the way saner people might practice yoga, flower arranging, or their tennis serve. He awoke many nights to an anime vision of a railway platform in the rain, late at night. His family, his dreams, his love, his future, were aboard. Against the darkness the lights inside the train were bright and the music was lively. It was a terrific party, but he was uninvited. The lights and music receded into the far distance and were gone. His sodden bags were heavy with all his pain and fear.

Now, at the leading edge of the worst pandemic in over a century, Joe was obsessed with how it would end for him. He'd already lost several friends. Aneurysms, suicide, heart attacks, brain cancers. He couldn't understand why he was being spared only to worry about when his turn would come.

The pandemic raged on and eventually found its way through Joe's home, and those of everyone he knew. Work from home lived up to its promise and its threats. Joe could manage paperwork at half-speed while he coughed; it was better than nothing.

The hospital took whatever time and energy it could from its servants.

"Hey, Joe, that pass was for you, eh? Both hands on the stick, Bud. And the beers are *after* the game, not before." Taras and Garry ribbed Joe at the bench. Something about his coordination seemed off, magnified during games. A new season had just begun with pandemic rules in place. Physical distancing, no showers, handwash bottles everywhere. Still, it felt better, almost normal, to be back playing.

Another red flag went up over the winter as his memory began to develop a Swiss-cheese porosity: some events and conversations were recalled in crystalline, minute detail. Others were lost entirely and randomly. The missing pieces were increasingly important—annual dues to maintain his medical license, a Zoom work meeting, paying the monthly bills. Joe knew, in cold certainty, that he had a problem. The holes in his Swiss cheese felt larger every month.

In embarrassed trepidation, he asked a buddy at work, a neurologist for whom he'd done many patient favors, to check him over off the meter. He was completely transparent with his friend Krishna, a trusted old-school colleague. He told all his secrets, past concussions, past and present medications both licit and not. Krishna drew Joe's blood himself and sent it to a genetics lab through a research side channel.

"Can you come to the office tomorrow?" Krishna asked into the phone a week later. "I have your results. Last appointment of the day. Wear your mask." His tone was off, quiet and guarded.

The last snow of a long winter still decorated the spruces outside the clinic. Joe went in just after closing; the receptionist had been sent home, and he caught her eye as she closed her car door; he'd coincidentally parked beside her. She looked away and he knew.

Krishna went over a brief preamble but then smiled thinly and his eyes welled up. "I'm really sorry it's you, Joe. I'm pretty sure it's an ALS variant with dementia."

Krishna looked at a coffee stain on the desk between them. "You could have a few years of good time. It isn't always a rapidly progressive thing. You can try taking fewer pain pills; I know it's a habit for you, but this is different. Taking them or not won't make much difference.

"Your variant gives you five years max. The first one to two years will be mostly memory deficits and minor motor issues. It'll get worse from then. There are treatments that help some patients keep the symptoms down and might even prolong your life. I'll give you a prescription. You can read up on it and then start it if you want to. Let me know either way. If there's any good news here, it's that this is a rare recessive gene. Your kids aren't at any risk. I know this is tough to hear. Call me anytime you need to."

Joe went into a fog. He could hear his friend's voice, understand the carefully chosen words, attach meaning to them. But the experience was happening to someone else. *A patient!* Nobody he knew well.

He didn't react until he had left the parking lot and pulled the car over halfway home. He pounded the steering wheel, jumped and strained in his seat, hit himself in the head with a coffee mug. He was outraged. This didn't happen to *him*! To the patients, sure. To ordinary people! He stopped and laughed at the absurdity of what he'd just heard.

Joe took a long drive to the riverside, a park outside the city. He sat on a bench and watched the snow sparkle under a rising full moon. Chilled, Joe retreated to the car and tried the voice-command feature. He needed to ground himself in some familiar comfort music. Moonlight Sonata. Nothing. Elgar's cello concerto. Same thing. The Clash, The Weakerthans, The Beatles. Buddy Guy, Louis Armstrong, Suzanne Vega. After several more tries, Joe realized that his hands were bleeding. The music had stopped playing too.

Fuck me. My hands. Joe glared at his reflection in the rear-view mirror of the car. He got out of the car and put his hands into the snow to clean the cuts, then wiped them with more snow. His knuckles oozed, so he took a glove and pressed it to one hand at a time, basic first aid. *All bleeding eventually stops*, he thought grimly. An old surgeons' joke. He got back in the car.

Joe glared into the rearview mirror. "You fuckin' idiot. Feel better now? What about your hands? Who did you think you were? Special? Get the fuck over yourself, bud. Something had to happen. This is your share. You're ordinary. Not Mozart, not Da Vinci, not Einstein. Average height and weight, brown and brown. Can't even sing. They bought that radio for the OR cuz they couldn't stand it anymore! Think you were gonna get discovered or something? Fuck. Your DNA's no good. Guess what? You're a *patient* now! Eat that! Five years! Get your shit together cuz after the first two, Krishna says it'll just get worse. And don't fuck around with your hands like that again. You'll need them until one day when you won't."

Joe's only solution was to do what he knew best—to work harder. Work in and of itself remained his lodestone, his anchor. He was still unaware that his career was pulling him under. For now, best to keep this quiet. Make sure the insurance covers it. Don't change anything just yet; change causes stress. Any more stress might make him burst into flames.

He needed to go see his mother—a visit through the side window of her seniors' apartment. He stood in the snow outside, wearing two masks and shouting a greeting through the mosquito screen on her bedroom window.

"Joe, what are you doing out there in the snow? Why don't you come inside? We can get a coffee from the dining room."

"Uh, no, sorry, Ma. I'm not allowed in the building yet. The house rules, remember? But I wanted to drop by and say hello—see how you're doing. Do you want anything from the store? Apples, or chocolate, or anything like that?"

"I don't need anything, thanks. Why can't you come in?"

"Ma, the pandemic rules say no visitors. Not even me!" Joe was patient; the pandemic isolation stressed her badly. Even with her repetitive questions and total lack of short-term memory, her voice soothed his anxiety in a way he couldn't explain. It was enough. Joe knew that this visit would be the last for a long while, as seniors' residences tightened rules to keep the virus out. They talked about old memories, friends of the family, and shared a few inside jokes, and then he was off. She was asleep by 6 PM most days. She would forget this visit. He knew that one day he would too.

Downtown was slushy, salt and sand clinging to his boots. Faces were covered and masks leaked snot that froze and stuck them in place. Discarded masks littered the sidewalk. The pandemic crushed people's jobs and livelihoods like empty cigarette packs. Everyone struggled with the virus in their own way. Seniors, the poor, racialized and disadvantaged were crammed together in their apartments, public transit, and at work. They were sitting ducks and took the heaviest burden of illness and death. The policies weren't written for them but for those who had better options and deeper pockets. Anyone who could afford to escaped the cities, worked from home, moved away, started new lives.

A tsunami of drug use washed over the city. Crystal meth was freely available and provided a cheap escape from the boredom and misery of people's amputated lives. Many took the bait and then couldn't disgorge the hook. They asked for spare change, shoplifted, sold their possessions one by one. Crime rose. This was just one of many cities in a wealthy, privileged country.

Joe went into a coffee shop at the riverside Forks market. A favorite place, usually vibrant and alive with activity in defiance of even the coldest prairie winters. A few skaters glided past on the still-frozen river. Several food vendors were closed, put out of business by the pandemic. Joe watched the high clouds gliding on the wind, drank his coffee, brooded some more. His thoughts spun uselessly in the background. A roulette wheel with no ball. He hadn't found the solace he'd hoped for. Even the luxury of a day of spare time, a rare treat, had turned against him.

Joe ruminated on his diagnosis at night as a solitary pastime. How could he explain this to Sara? He tried to imagine the conversation and saw only tears. He'd definitely blow it, scare the hell out of her, and create a mess he couldn't undo. He'd tell her when the time was right, when he was stabilized on Krishna's treatment and improvements in his lifestyle. When he'd had time to fully absorb what Krishna had told him.

Joe's diagnosis made him acutely aware of the coming time when he wouldn't be able to support the family. He called a meeting one evening at the dinner table. "Everyone, I have a chance to work up north once a month, for a few days at a time. They pay really well, and the hospital is desperate for help. Because of COVID, there's some free time opening up there in the OR."

He saw the storm clouds building in Sara's eyes and the questions forming on her thinned lips. "Where are you getting this spare time all of a sudden, Joe? Why would you want to work harder?"

"I knew you'd ask. I can earn myself extra time off. I'm barely here when I'm on an on-call week, right? They have all these incentive payments to go there. I can buy time off with the extra money. I'll be able to help with the kids' schoolwork, or take them to the park, or whatever's open, so you can work from here with less distraction. Win-win."

They all regarded him dubiously. "When COVID ends, we'll even have some extra money. We can take a nice trip somewhere. The way families should enjoy time together. Disney World, anybody?" He knew he might not get there himself, but it was an effective bribe. Sara's eyes softened, and he knew he was on the right track.

"How does it work, Joe? They line up elective cases for you, or consultations? Where do you stay? What do you eat?"

"The government pays all the travel expenses, a meal allowance, rental car. It's a plane ride away, and the climate is harsh. But a lot of people need the kind of help I can give them. The hospital collects lists of people for the OR, day clinic, follow-ups on other surgeons' work. The food is very good, I'm told. Great pizza, poke bowls and burgers. The hospital staff are really talented and dedicated, again as I hear it from friends who've been there. The work is intense though—about a hundred hours a week. That's why it pays so well, I guess. Anyway, I'd like to try it out for a few months and see if I can bank us a nice vacation. At least while COVID is still a problem. We can't do much of anything until then anyway. So, what do you think?"

Sam went first. "How many nights will you be away, Dad?"

"Never more than five at a time, and I'll try to make my away time shorter."

Sara went next. "Are you really sure you want to spend your off weeks doing more work? Explain again how this will turn into more time off."

"Okay, so if I earn twice the money in a week as I do here, I can use the spare cash to hire another surgeon to take my practice for two weeks. I can trade my OR day to someone else, and the locum I hire can mind my clinics and the inpatients."

Will added, "Does this mean you can't help me with math? You're my good luck charm! And grade eight is *way* harder than baby math!" He cast a smug big-brother look at Sam.

"Actually, Will, your mom is the good luck charm. I just show you how things work. She makes sure you do it over and over." The boy's face fell, just for an instant, but it was enough for Joe to feel a pang of guilt. "But I get to see the report cards, right? So, let's focus on the positive! When you need urgent help, we can do a remote lesson. And this isn't forever." *At least not for you guys, he reminded himself.*

Patients continued to arrive gasping for breath and coughing viruses through paper layers into the air they all shared. The hospital remained a teeming Petri dish.

Then came the vaccines. Most embraced the chance to protect themselves, and their contacts, from the virus.

There were doubters, outliers, skeptics. Families argued, friendships dissolved. The social fabric frayed, tore, and flapped in the wind. Protesters blocked the streets to demand their freedom from what they saw as tyrannical control by government and health agencies. The airport, masked faces everywhere, the tang of hand sanitizer in the air, was tense. Every few flights, some rebel or other would refuse to keep a mask on and get a lecture from the lone flight attendant, or a threat of bodily harm from another passenger.

The plane was a twin-prop Dash 8, holding about forty people. It was small enough that winter clothing added to the claustrophobia. "They should give out Ativan and Tylenol for these rides," Joe joked to the attendant one day. He was regular enough that soon the local airline staff knew him by name and often thanked him for coming to their community.

"The employees would have taken it all home by now, Dr. Danko. This job isn't as much fun as it used to be."

"No job is, I guess. Have a good one." Joe replied and went out to take his seat.

5

—

2022

In late February 2022, Joe sat in the northern airport departure lounge with the rest of the masked passengers, eyes glued to the CBC news. After a gradual accumulation of men and machinery over several weeks, open warfare had returned to Europe. The images of dead and wounded, explosions, and destruction circled the globe in the ether, descended to these screens, and horrified a world still burying its pandemic victims. He called Sara, anxious to feel some grounded connection before the lightning in his mind fried all his circuits.

"Is everything all right, Joe? Will your plane be on time?" It was unusual for Joe to call before returning home; Sara could access flight information anywhere.

"Yeah, I'm fine. We'll leave on time. I, uh, just wanted to hear your voice and know you're okay. Sounds corny, I know."

"Well, yeah, we're all good here. The kids are looking forward to seeing you. It's report card week and they're proud of their results. They're making you a pizza too."

That plane ride home seemed to last forever. "Dad! Welcome home!" the kids hollered, always delighted at his return. "Did you bring us hockey cards? And junk food? Remember, you promised!" Rides home with his family never failed to give Joe a sense of deep satisfaction; he loved seeing Sara at the wheel, smiles all around, and felt pride in his ability to support them. *For how long?* He wondered inwardly.

"You guys never forget the good stuff. Of course I did! How about the school work? I'll trade you hockey cards for report cards. Good deal?"

In the late evening with the kids asleep, Joe fired up the home office computer for a head start before Monday. Sara lingered in the doorway at the edge of his view. Joe offered an icebreaker from inside his own wheelhouse.

"So, pretty scary war news, isn't it? I hope this isn't some kind of effort to shuffle the deck, create a new world order. I suppose we're safe here." World events, a hobby for Joe, were an unwelcome intrusion for Sara. Her battles were daily, right here. Her work with the racially disadvantaged, the disabled and marginalized, flew under Joe's radar.

She sighed, "I don't know, Joe. I'm sure there's somebody more interested in debating this with you. Did you check the kids' report cards?"

No, he'd forgotten.

He won't change, she sighed inwardly and went upstairs to sleep.

"Why are you riding your bike to work, Dad? Isn't it too cold?" asked his daughter Sam the next morning.

"More like too slippery. Your helmet won't stop you from breaking your neck, right?" Sara teased without a smile. Her eyes were on the sandwiches under construction on the kitchen counter.

Joe fastened his strap, pulled up his gloves, and opened the front door. His twenty-minute pandemic commute was often the best thing to happen all day, a focal point and something he needed today more than usual.

The bare branches of a few weeks earlier now showed the promise of renewal. A few cardinals called to each other from between houses as Joe headed toward Riverside Drive. He could see past the slushy streets, the waterproof plastic pants and the biting wind. The fresh air, movement and bright blue sky urged him onward.

Joe locked up his bike outside the front door of the hospital. His last two had been stolen over the past year from the rack beside the Security door. This spot seemed safer so far. Hand spray, mask, ID badge, phone, lunch in his backpack. The final ingredient in his morning routine was coffee. He joined the queue just inside the main door, near the admin wing and Jill's office. A few waves to colleagues and friends passing by, smiling eyes above his mask for the coffee ladies, both at least fifteen years older than Joe and unable to retire.

The seating area remained roped off, but a middle-aged man in a blue overcoat stood just outside the margin, glancing up from his device screen. His eyes met Joe's briefly. Familiar? Joe wasn't sure. He'd never been much good with faces and names. Song lyrics, an interesting medical image, sports trivia—no problem. Joe collected his coffee and headed "backstage," as he called his office, to get ready for the day.

On a busy day like this one, 1700h rolled around quickly. The team closed up the room, cleaners came in, and Joe put his bike clothes back on. Beside his bike stood the blue suit man. In the half-shadows of late winter and early sunset, Joe recalled suddenly. Carter. A night-time blindfold car ride, the off-the-record house call for a desperately sick foreign scientist on the run.

"How was your day, Dr. Danko?" Outdoors, his face was bare. Bland features but hard eyes.

"Pretty good, actually. Routine stuff, no hiccups. Can I help you?" Joe searched the brick wall of Carter's face for clues.

Carter was looking up, scanning for cameras. Finding one under the roof peak he kept himself out of view, turned toward Joe, his overcoat collar up. "Can we go somewhere to talk? Some people are very interested in speaking with you further. Not your typical government types, but related. They have a job offer that might interest you."

Joe regarded him curiously. "First aid for foreign agents and scientists? Tell me more. Does it pay well?" He was only half joking.

"What we're after is someone with no footprint in social media. A total newcomer, a rookie. No history in the military or security field. Aptitude and motivation count. I understand that you've had some, let's call them, life and health challenges."

Joe nodded wearily. "Things could be better. A lot of things could be better."

They hiked along the riverbank trail, away from the hospital. The sunset spread itself majestically across the western sky; the trail and park were otherwise deserted. Their boots crunched through the hardening crust of ice.

Carter continued. "Suppose a program existed that allowed for the use of your talents and included a heavy insurance policy. In case of any mishaps. This kind of work doesn't always go according to plan. About 50% of the time, in fact. Your family would be taken care of. Relocation if they want it, education for the children, job training for your wife."

"You mean like the veterans' families? No thanks."

"I'm talking about a different source of funding. This isn't the government. Let me sweeten the pot here. These trips you make on your vacation time? You go to the far north in winter for the scenery? Come on. I know the money's good there. We'll double it. Watch your bank balance over the next two months and see if I can't make good on that."

Carter saw the surprise on Joe's face. "We have your banking information. I know about the speeding tickets you rack up. I know your fireplace needs fixing, your mom has some health—" The sudden indignant, surprised violation on Joe's face stopped him cold.

"Okay that's enough. So, you know me and my life well. Do I get to insist on some security for my family too? It sounds like they could use some protection from you people for starters," Joe snapped.

Carter pretended not to hear. "We also have access to some of the best research in dementia treatments anywhere. Yes, I've seen your other chart. A lot of this research is Canadian, some from Europe and the US. Really positive results, I'm told. I don't have that sort of background, so I can't say I'm any kind of expert. But they have trials that would interest you. Maybe turn back the clock or stop it altogether for a while."

He studied Joe's reaction. Any sign of fatigue was gone.

"No side effects? No problems?" Joe asked, a cautious note in his question.

"Nothing I've heard about, but I'm happy to put you in touch with the research team. First thing is they'd have to run your baseline, see if you're a candidate, and tell you more about the treatments they're using. Pre-clinical trials is all I can say."

Carter pulled out a phone with unusual screens, like nothing Joe had ever seen. He put his eye to the camera. Four small windows opened, and he selected one. It enlarged as the others faded. He already had Joe's contact info, last blood tests, driver's license—everything.

"No doubt you're aware of the events in eastern Europe this past month. Western militaries, intelligence, and heads of state are trying to find the best way forward before this gets too far out of control. This isn't Canada versus Quebec. It's a sovereign nation being attacked by a larger, powerful, and aggressive neighbor. With nuclear capabilities.

"NATO can and will provide assistance, but only for self-defence. No soldiers on the ground, no air force. Anything more risks being taken as a major provocation. And we don't know yet just how far the enemy is willing to go. I work with a multinational intel service. We aren't related to NATO or any government. Our analysis is that the instigator needs to be taken out if at all possible. The security is massive. It's a dangerous task."

As Carter spoke, Joe guided them into a small diner across the street. It stayed open until 2 AM every night to catch the closing time trade. The owner allowed the place to function as a warming shelter on nights like these. Carter and Danko settled into two hard wooden benches. A girl of late high-school age stirred herself, put down her phone, and poured them each a coffee. On the far side of the diner sat a pathetically scrawny man of about thirty, surrounded by shopping bags and warming his hands on his coffee mug before he began to drink it. Next to his table was a trucker plowing through a bowl of poutine, eyes glued to the news on his phone. Two more tables were occupied by street people grateful for warmth. The girl at the counter came back with menus, but Carter pointed at the trucker's poutine and said, "We'll have two of those."

Carter resumed his pitch. "There are many behind the scenes who see this as a major retrograde step in the fight between free countries and dictatorships, whatever you want to call it. There are countries on the sidelines who don't know which side to back or want to remain neutral. The aggressor has allies and so does the defender. Our sources indicate that the general population of the invading side is evenly split between support and opposition to this Special Military Operation.

"There are opponents right in his own government and military who must remain silent for fear of losing their positions, or worse. These are our potential friends. We are actively cultivating that garden, and the work is bearing fruit. There are other countries who are watching this play out with interest, to see whether this aggression will be countered successfully or not. Some are our potential future adversaries.

"Every time your family thinks you're going north to work, we'd take you straight to the Air Force base here in town. We're not partnered with the military in any way beyond renting space in their facilities, right out the back door from the commercial airport terminal. You would need thorough testing first. If you meet our physical standards, you would return every month until you are fully trained for deployment to Poland, and then across the eastern border into Ukraine. Our field people provide help all along the way. You would be a houseguest in Kyiv for a short while, get your memory boosted, and then continue on toward the goal."

"'Goal? What exactly is this goal? It sounds a bit different from saving a scientist with a minor procedure. If you're looking for a trauma surgeon, and it's a well-paid gig, that's one thing." He lowered his voice almost to a whisper. "You said 'taken out.' I'm guessing you don't mean dinner and a show? I'm not exactly qualified for that."

Carter dropped into a lower register of voice himself. "Come on, doctor. We both know your pressure points. Your dreams of glory. Your ego, your shortcomings. Everyone has them. Yours are outsized. Your whole life has been processed by our systems. If you could have just *one* wish, achieve *one* thing, what would it be? With the cards you hold, I mean. You can't be John Lennon, or Antonin Dvorak, or Einstein, or Wayne Gretzky. You've done a pretty fair job as a doctor. This is bigger. I'm offering the chance to make history. To really leave a lasting gift to the world. And a fifty-fifty chance to survive it, a boosted memory, maybe more quality time with your family. Before it's too late for that. Right now, all you do is work. And in a few short years, what happens?"

Carter paused to let the words sink in.

"Doesn't the Special Military Operation worry you? It does me. I know you have a nerd's interest in the old homeland, the place of your ancestors. I know you despise communism and dictators in general. Don't look so surprised. I know every book you've ever read, the movies you want to see but haven't yet. Now you have a dictator invading that homeland. It's deeply unsettling, isn't it? What will they do next? Do you think for one second that the general population, or the entire Russian military and ruling class, really want this?"

Joe felt his pulse quickening, the blood rushing in his ears. This man's words struck a gong deep in Joe's soul. His initial indignation at being so thoroughly examined and dissected by this stranger gave way to thirst. He felt a sudden rush of adrenaline and was instantly transported to the place a killer must enter—no right or wrong, only predator and prey.

"Your family would be told that you are doing relief medical or nursing border work. We already know of one colleague of yours who has made that trip. We know that it's not a stretch for you to follow suit. You'd inform your base hospital that you need time off for burnout. COVID. We've seen the stats on healthcare workers, and it's a plausible story. You would also tell the north that you can't return for a while. Your base hospital needs you more. I've seen their schedule, and it doesn't look like a problem for them. Everything I'm telling you now is strictly confidential, of course. You can't talk it over with your wife or anyone else. Time is tight on this. We've tried it once already. It failed. I need to repeat: the fatality rate for this sort of work is about fifty percent."

Here he paused. The server placed two bowls of poutine in front of them. "Think about it. But not for too long. Let's eat. I'm starving."

Joe's mind hummed as he ate his poutine in silence. He looked up periodically from his plate to see the other man studying him like a schematic diagram. He felt the cold nakedness of being appraised, compared against the data this man had accumulated and sculpted into a facsimile of the person Joe was. Or could become. He veered between a rush of excitement and suspicious, stony disbelief. Were this conversation, the man and the offer before him, real? With genuine effort he maintained an outward calm.

After several minutes of silence, between slurps of coffee Joe said, with exaggerated nonchalance, "I'll need a while to think through how this really feels. You're telling me I might be granted a huge final wish, but that wish itself might be fatal. It's not a decision I can reach immediately. How and when will I let you know?"

They agreed that future communication between them would be via Joe's hospital Webmail. It was secured from both hackers and his family. Joe was not to leave any written notes to himself about any related matters, no matter how bad a day his fickle memory was having. The emails, in case they went to junk mail, would come from gordiehowe@project.ca

6

The first email arrived the next day. Joe's trembling hand shook so badly he nearly missed the email icon. In the junk folder he found it—an invitation to participate in a clinical trial under the supervision of a Dr. L. Young and his team, evaluating a new anti-dementia drug. Joe opened a search in a private window. Dr. Young was a big name in the field of memory research, and he was a superb talent scout for promising new researchers.

The drug was ridiculously expensive, price explained as usual by the cost of research. For every drug that survived lab trials, and became commercially viable, there would be 200 others that didn't. Joe read the words several times, his disbelief melting slowly. He would receive this elixir *at no cost*.

Now Joe calculated mentally. A healthy bank balance. A chance to make history. Possibly die doing it. Travel and adventure. Danger and uncertainty. Financial security for his family. A chance to keep his mind alive past the expiry date he'd been given. Past the expiry date... Joe wrestled inwardly with the pros and cons. He asked for time to think about it. "Gordie Howe" agreed. One week.

Joe stopped in the front entrance of the hospital the next morning. Magazines had long ago been replaced by screens in all waiting areas. The news channel beamed images from Bucha. People entering the building were shocked into silence by what they saw. Mass graves, burned bodies, hazmat suits. The lobby was full, but the air went still. *I could do something about that,* he thought.

Joe racked his frontal lobes for guidance. He imagined himself in various scenarios: How would it feel to take a life? Could he remain silent? Would his outsized ego get him into any trouble? Now suppose he played it safe, stayed home. Inevitable slow decay. A wheelchair, feeding tube. Diaper, catheter. *A patient.* He didn't want to be remembered that way. He'd seen way too much of that at work.

He sketched Cartesian what-ifs on sheets of paper late at night while the family slept, then fed them into the paper shredder along with the bills and mortgage statements. After a few sleepless nights, he was getting nowhere.

Joe rode his bike past the local Ukrainian parish church every in-hospital day for years, in all seasons, without giving it any thought. The bike path was well-tended and enjoyed by people of all ages. It meandered through groves of trees, past community gardens, historic plaques, and a children's playground that was busy all year. The street at the end of this path was quiet, just a short stroll to the river. The church stood beside the end of the path like a sentry with a gold-painted eight-sided dome and a cross on top made of cast iron. The lot was full on summer Sundays when he happened by for a coffee at the farmers' market in a vacant lot across the street.

The sight of this solid, squat brick fortress never failed to send Joe back in time. In his childhood, church meant a long hour of boredom, stuffed into a winter coat and herded among the other families into the basement of the church in the neighborhood of his youth. The community hadn't yet raised the money for the main floor, the church proper, so they adapted the completed basement level, using the same large room for parties, banquets, and worship. For twenty years they scrimped, held dinners, banquets, and bingo games.

The folding chairs and wooden kneeling boards were moved into place in the basement banquet hall every Sunday morning by stern, silent church men with help from the altar boys. For three years, Joe had been one of those altar boys; it was a good way for his parents to keep him engaged when he'd rather watch the sparrows outside the windows. The birds changed color as they flitted over the stained glass high up, above their subterranean makeshift church. Joe admired their swiftness and envied their freedom. They didn't have to listen to Father Isidore's rambling sermons or go through the motions of standing, chanting, singing on cue.

One time, he'd fainted in the middle of the service, too overheated in his winter coat and not yet over the flu. It was a silent church man, not his own father, who'd rushed him out the door into the cold, revitalizing winter air.

He handed Joe, a sweating bundle of bewilderment, to his father with words of advice. "This one should stay home until he's well. We don't want the whole congregation getting sick. Of course, you know better. I'm sure he'll get stronger someday."

Joe's father blushed under the other man's criticism. What sort of man doesn't know how to look after his own children? The dads were in an unspoken competition. Demonstrating control of their families was part of membership. Some were more rigid than others; Joe's father insisted on some things, relented on some others. A real dad could show off his sons' polished black shoes; the superstar dads would, none too subtly, show the others how clean their sons' fingernails were. They'd done their shoes the previous night and had time to properly remove the polish from their hands before Mass. Straight parts in the boys' hair, pretty dresses for the girls. All a show. Status and ranking.

Joe's father told him once about going to church as a kid in his day. Every adult ruled every kid. If some other parent saw a child misbehaving, it was fair game to take that child by the ear and deposit them beside the altar along with the altar boys. The shamed child would probably get a good strapping at home after church and spend the afternoon picking rocks from the fields (they damaged the plow) until dinner. Respect and order were major ingredients in the whole town's survival. God, the parents, and the community were all in agreement on this.

Joe wasn't the God-fearing type as a kid. Why did God let kids starve in Africa? Why did He allow war? Or Satan? Why didn't God just beat Satan up and send him packing back to the underworld? Where was hell, and why didn't God just close it down, or blow it up with dynamite or something? What if people grew up somewhere where they'd never heard of Jesus and all His miracles? It didn't seem fair that they'd go to hell just because they weren't informed. How do we know we're right and some other religion is wrong? If those other people, the Jewish kids a few streets over or the newcomers from the Far East, Africa, and the Caribbean, had a faith, any faith, wasn't that just as good? Didn't it count?

Joe had a child's strong sense of fairness, and an even stronger sense of unfairness. The small boy of 8 years asked these questions relentlessly. Of his parents on the way to church in the car, and of the Catechism teachers, who had no easy reply.

In April 2022, melting snow revealed fresh buds in carefully tended gardens along the bike path. Green grass poked through, and birds sang everywhere. Days were warming up, spring arriving earlier than usual this year. Joe drifted through the days in a strange state of animation, Carter's offer percolating in the back of his mind. A spring rain had cleansed the air and the streets. The short commute by bike remained the best part of most days. As he passed the church, a pedestrian crossed his path, and he was obliged to stop and wait. The old man looked familiar. When he spoke, Joe nearly jumped out of his skin.

The man said, "You should go to church. They'll tell you what to do next." He looked about eighty years old, wore a blue windbreaker and hat like any other senior around town. He was solidly built and looked like he had held up his side of many fights over his years. He pointed at the bilingual sign beside the front entrance to the Church of the Resurrection.

Joe replied, "Hey, Mister. What do you mean?"

The old man shook his head, answered, "*Ide Tserkva!* Go to church. It's good for your soul," and kept walking on his way. He didn't turn around and vanished around a corner. Now Joe wondered: was this one of those coincidences that are too weird to believe? Was he being watched? What about his family? Why did the old man look familiar? Joe had never been much good with recognizing people. He racked his brain, had no revelation, and carried on to work.

Midway through the workday, it struck him forcibly: the old man was Father Isidore from his childhood church. Why would he spot him here, on the other side of the city, forty years later? And why would he direct Joe to the church?

The following Sunday, Joe got off his bike, locked up next to the building with its shiny faux gold dome, and took a deep breath. He went in and took a seat in a pew near the back. A stern churchman, seemingly frozen in time, beelined straight toward Joe and whispered, "Father wants to see you after mass." Joe had never seen him before, but the churchman seemed to know exactly who he was talking to.

The priest was a tall man of perhaps forty years. He had a few streaks of gray in a black beard that gave him a look of ferocity and command. He moved briskly through the mass, carried the gospel with energy and reverence. The service hadn't changed in all that time. It was a warm blanket of memory—the chanting, the faithful repeating the old prayers: "I will love you, my Lord and my strength. The Lord is my strength and my refuge. Thy kingdom come, thy will be done, on earth as it is in heaven." But then the blanket was torn and thrown to one side.

"My brothers and sisters, everyone who has seen the news of the past few weeks knows what's happening to our homeland. A homicidal dictator has made a unilateral decision to upend millions of lives, to rampage and murder his way back to a mythologized empire. Women raped, children kidnapped, men tortured and mutilated. For what? Greed and hate. It's inexcusable, it's medieval, it's against every ethical code of right and wrong.

"There is no God anywhere that would condone this! Thousands are dead already. We must remain brave. Strong. Connected. Please get in touch with your families if you have relatives back in Ukraine. Find out what they need. Make lists, bring in your unused clothing. Shoes, eyeglasses. Non-perishable food, hygiene items, diapers. We will store your donations in the church basement. We need volunteers to sort and pack these donated goods for shipment. There's a sign-up sheet at the back of the church. Do whatever you can to help. If you have nothing at home to give, send money to the Red Cross as soon as possible. This isn't the fight of our friends and family back home. This is the fight of everyone who loves freedom, who opposes tyranny, cruelty, dictatorship. Give your support, your love, your pride. Our people are trapped in basements and bunkers. Help them now!"

This sermon was not like anything he'd heard in the old days; it was galvanic, stirring, energizing. More than once the priest stared straight into Joe's eyes as he sat alone, pinned to a pew near the back row. He tried to evade the exploratory glare, looking anywhere else. His eyes landed on Father Isidore sitting beside the altar, dressed in plain black vestments. The old man's eyes also locked onto Joe; he wore a satisfied smile. The priest continued his fiery sermon about war, death, and the price for sins of aggression. It was a stirring antithesis of "turn the other cheek."

"Who appointed this one man and gave him the power of life and death over so many? Is he God? No! Why is he doing this? To recreate something that was evil to begin with. Thousands are dead already. What sin are they being punished for? For no crime other than their proximity to an aggressive neighbor, and their wish to live under the same freedom that we enjoy here in this country without a second thought.

"Has our family back home been perfect? No. The government has had troubles with trust, corruption, inefficiency. There have been stories of racism, abuse, preferential access to jobs, and now, to exit from the country. We must admit that those people, *our* people, are not perfect. And are we? Has Canada, the West, solved these problems so completely that we can sit back and be critical? Can we cast the first stone?

"But which direction was Ukraine headed before the war started? Lives, schools, businesses were thriving. Ukraine, the country that nourished our ancestors and relatives, is a nation of great accomplishments. A major exporter of foods—sunflower oil, grain, eggs. Technology—software and IT professionals, the largest airplane in the world. Beautiful Scythian art. History, poetry, music, dance. And there was increasing acceptance of differences among people. Less hate for its own sake. They were well on the path to a bright future."

Here the priest paused to collect himself. He took a deep breath and resumed. "There's an old Russian story about two farmers. One brings home a new cow one day. He's excited about how calm this cow is, how she gives more milk, and is content eating hay, grass, anything. How patient she is, even a child can milk her without fear! The other farmer is jealous. He lies awake at night, thinking about his neighbor's cow, and how happy he is with the new addition to his farm. In his anguish, his envy, the jealous farmer prays to God. And of course, God hears our prayers. He says to the man,

'My son, I see that you are in distress about your neighbor's new cow. I don't want you to suffer like this. How can I help you?'"

"And without hesitation, the man says, 'I want you to kill that cow.'"

The priest paused. "Unfortunately, envy and greed exist everywhere, my brothers and sisters. They poison families, they destroy friendships, they lead to war, to killing. It has happened in too many places, for far too long. I ask you to pray with me now for the people of both Ukraine and Russia. Pray for an end to the destruction, the suffering, and violence. Pray that righteousness will prevail over sin. Pray that the other farmer eventually also has a new cow, that there is no longer a reason for this irrational jealousy. Pray."

The rest of the service proceeded as usual. The congregation lined up to receive Communion. Joe, a newcomer, didn't queue up but remained kneeling, then sat through the rest of the service. The priest was at the door, greeting the parishioners as they filed past to go out into the sunny midday. Joe was led into the sacristy after the Mass by two of the silent churchmen. He crossed himself as he passed by the altar, his old childhood habits hard-wired across decades. One of the stern-faced ushers said, "Give me your phone. We'll give it back when you leave." Another patted him down for weapons. The sun beamed down on them through the scenes displayed in stained glass. Joe gazed up at the Stations of the Cross. Beside "Jesus is condemned to death" shone "Jesus takes up his cross."

I'm no Jesus, thought Joe. *I just hope this is the right thing.* He averted his eyes from the twelfth station: "Jesus dies on the cross."

An open laptop sat on a small side table beside a burning candle in a red glass cylinder. Joe could see the latest news from Europe, but the script was in Cyrillic alphabet, and although he could read the letters slowly, he didn't understand their meaning.

The priest strode in at a brisk pace. "I'm Father Boris. You're Doctor Joe." He extended his hand. "I'm a visiting priest here this week. I have affiliations with several parishes in Ukraine and elsewhere. It's no accident that we're meeting today. You can ask or tell me anything you wish. I've heard a lot about you, and you must be curious as to how. Carter has recently reached out to you. We work together for an NGO you've never heard of. We keep it that way. My help and connections have, unfortunately, become necessary to several countries because of recent events.

"People have been watching you for some time. Your particular skill set lends itself to working in our field. You were put on their radar several years ago, when you performed a procedure outside the hospital on a foreign national. I apologize for the pressure that was applied to persuade you to help. That patient—his contacts and his intel have been invaluable in helping us to develop friendly contacts inside the Kremlin's scientific and security communities. Our organization is grateful to you for saving him. Back then it was precautionary, but now it's all too clear that our preparation was prescient.

"You met Father Isidore on the street the other day. He was sent to direct you here. To meet me. To find out whether you have what it takes to become a vital part of the solution to a major security problem. Motivation, skill, willpower. The capacity to keep a secret. Courage most of all. We are in dire need of brave, serious people to assist us in restoring the balance of good against evil. It is becoming clearer every day that our people's situation is desperate, and that greater sins can only be prevented by committing grievous sins ourselves."

Again, Joe took in the priest's youth, about forty. Big black beard, solid build, piercing eyes. A look of dawning realization passed over the doctor's face. "You're CSIS?"

"Not really, but something similar. We're more specific, and right now our attention is focused entirely on the war in Ukraine.

A few priests were recruited because of our contacts, our motivation, and we're all bilingual or more.

"You would take the memory drug. Assuming no adverse event, the science team would calibrate your dosage. We would feed you intel like candy. Train you into better fitness, able to withstand some degree of hardship. Fasting, thirst, heat and cold. Weapons training, basic martial arts. Once fully prepared, you would go overseas for a month. The cover story is that you're going to perform relief work at the border between Ukraine and Poland. We would arrange transit into Russia, and other contacts in the Project would house you in Moscow. At the right time, you would be deployed, delivered unto evil.

"There's a lot of time, money, and thought behind this. The variables have been considered, the risks mitigated as much as possible. But we know it's a war zone, and anything can happen. We have some redundancy, but not too much. The more people know, the greater the chance that one of them can go rotten, get cold feet at the wrong time, or be found out. First thing for you to consider is: Are you okay with the possibility of this being a one-way trip? There is unheard of security around the target. You may not get close enough, or you might be killed. We have inside people willing to die for this. You would meet them in Moscow. If anyone is found out, we stop and reassess. And if you are found out…"

Joe swallowed. "I've thought about it. You know my medical history, right?"

The priest nodded.

Joe paused, took a deep breath, then confided. "To be honest, the last few years have been difficult for me to the point that I've sometimes felt that living and dying are about the same thing. I'll die from the virus, or too much work, or the dementia I'm told is waiting for me. On top of that, I know I'm better off than ninety-nine percent of people. I still *have* my job. So, I feel guilty, and I make myself worse just thinking too much.

"I know time's running out for me. Life ends for all of us, but it feels more urgent since I got this diagnosis. I wake up in the morning and wonder what I'll lose or forget next. Maybe I'm depressed, or bored, or I don't know what. Maybe it's the beginning of dementia. Crazy, or I'm just an asshole who can't appreciate anything. Sorry, pardon my language, Father.

"I can accept the risk of this assignment if my family are properly taken care of. As for motivation, the world is in a bigger mess than before because of one man's homicidal greed. I can't stop looking at the news, it's so upsetting. I've nothing to lose in trying your drug. Whether it works or not, I'd love to help stop this war."

Father Boris smiled. "So, you don't need any persuasion then? That makes my task much simpler. You will submit your list of weeks away from your day job. We will make introductions to the research team that administers the newest memory drug. You will undergo rigorous testing of your health and your psychology. They will not spend the drug on you if you fail these tests, and they don't want the drug somehow compromising the testing process itself. They need someone whose body won't fail and who has the mindset to kill when necessary."

Joe replied, "I understand." His vanity began to take control; here was a chance to make an impression on the future. How many people could claim such a thing? How could he turn it down? For an ego like his, this was a winning lottery ticket.

Father Boris said, "I have to be honest with you. You must realize that while we can guarantee your family's safety and income, we cannot do the same for you. We will have help available and close to you at all points until your deployment, but your odds of coming back are fifty percent from what we know about the target's security apparatus. Many candidates, more suitable than yourself perhaps, have been considered and rejected.

"Your medical situation, ironically, makes you a better fit for this. I have grappled with the ethics of sending a sick man to perform this task. And I have made peace with it. That's easy for me to say, but you're the one who would make the commitment. And possibly, the sacrifice. I ask you to trust all of us who are part of this enterprise. I don't need your answer immediately, but time is not with us. Ask your questions now or within the next few days. 'No greater love than this: to lay down one's life for one's fellow man.' John 15:13. One of my favorites."

As they talked, Joe felt the growing sense of trust that this man, and the organization around him, could accomplish what was being presented. The priest's conviction and enthusiasm were infectious. Joe felt his trepidation melting and replaced by calm.

Father Boris added one last thing. "And obviously, this is highly sensitive subject matter. There is nobody you can talk to about it, aside from me and Gordie Howe. We keep it tight. Right?"

Joe nodded. "Yes, of course. Right. I have to ask, though: I have two brothers. If this is a recessive gene, they're each at a one in four risk of having this dementia happen to them. They live in other parts of Canada. We talk every few weeks but don't see each other more than once or twice a year. I haven't told them about this dementia stuff and don't know how."

Father Boris held up his hand. "You mean Tom in Montreal and Theo in Vancouver. We've already tested them. They're okay, they're negative for the gene. They don't know any differently. You don't need to know how we got their genetic samples, just trust that we've done our homework."

Joe's surprise at the reach of Boris's team was visible. So was his relief that his brothers were unaffected. "I'm reassured that your people are so thorough, and they think ahead. It gives me comfort, if that's the right word. Please give me a week to think. It's a huge decision, and I'm honestly not sure if I know myself well enough to be certain I have the resolve to do what you need."

The priest asked Joe to kneel on the floor. He put his left hand on Joe's head, made the sign of the cross with his right, and said something in rapid-fire Ukrainian. A blessing—something Joe had heard many years ago. Joe rose and they walked together past the altar and the empty pews. The sun beamed down on them through the scenes displayed in stained glass.

He paused for a few seconds to admire the beauty of the vivid patterned colors splashed across the pews and the floor, the sun brought to life by the work of an unknown artist. Fragrant myrtle incense still hung in the air; the smoke created slanted shafts of colored light. For an instant, Joe experienced something akin to grace.

The bike ride home was a time of rare, silent reflection. The sun lit up the edges of trees and buildings; the retreating snow left promising green shoots at the margins of the path. On this quiet ride, there was no external distraction. He let the conversation replay itself slowly, absorbing the substance of the offer before him, and feeling his reaction for tension, for pressure points. The sun winked down on him as he rode under the bare branches, the spring sky a brilliant prairie blue. He was trying to scare himself out of it and found that he felt no fear, only the rushing tingle of vanity.

Joe parked his bike along the backyard fence line and went in the back door. Sara called out, "Oh good, Joe, you're back. Remember, the barbecue needs to be cleaned out and the kids have homework. My family will be here at four."

Joe headed straight for the coffee maker, pausing to give her a squeeze as he passed by. "How was church? It's a bit of a departure for you, isn't it?"

For an instant Joe wondered—*how could she know?*—before realizing that she was just curious, making conversation. "It was fine. Nothing seems to have changed. It's a comfortable constant. I'm not sure if or when I'll go back." He replied with an attempt at offhand nonchalance. "Ah! Coffee's ready. Want one?" Sara shook her head.

"Okay, who wants to have some math fun?" The groans from the TV room were genuine. "Sam, it's decimals, right? And Will, exponentials? Grab your books. Pencils, not pens. I'll see you in the office in two minutes." He picked up the TV remote and shut off the fun. "I'll hold on to this for the next hour. I promise to give it back if you give me a decent effort. Deal?" He felt Sara's smile, the radiant heat, as much as he saw it.

Math class lasted until the kids' patience ran out. Half an hour, better than usual. "Okay, I'll go clean up the barbecue." He hoped his relief to get outside didn't show.

Scrubbing and scraping, Joe went over his choices repeatedly. *Plan A: Stay home, play it safe. Tell Sara and the family and await the inevitable. It sounds so defeatist, so resigned. Is that even natural for me? Plan B: Accept their assignment. Take their miracle drug. Live an adventure. See what's down the rabbit hole.* The priest's offer and the urgency of his sermon echoed in Joe's memory. The news images of the last few weeks stung him. *There will be a lot worse if they don't get help soon. Yes or no?*

"Hey young man, How ya doin'? It's been a long time!" Joe looked up from the blackened metal to see his father-in-law's broad smile. "Sara tells me you went to church! Are you in trouble with God?" He joked. "Better Him than me at least."

"Hi Pops! Great to see you too. Nothing serious. I've been reading the news too much maybe, a bit on edge about this war stuff. I wanted to see what the local Ukie community is doing about it, how they're feeling. I donated a day's wages. I'd like to do more but haven't figured out exactly what to do." *That much is true,* he told himself.

Joe felt tremendous fondness for his father-in-law, a scrappy immigrant with a huge work ethic and a big heart. The old man leaned close. "I'm worried about Mother though, jokes aside. She's

forgetting where she is. She lost the car last week at the super-
market. When she figured out where it was, she left the groceries
behind and came home without anything. And there have been
other things. Walking around the house at 4 AM, making a pot of
coffee and forgetting to drink it. Seems like she can't hear well all
of a sudden. And you know how she is; she won't go to the doctor
to get checked out. I haven't told Sara yet. I know she'll worry, and
I don't want that."

"Damn, that's hard to hear, Pops. It's really tough if she won't
get evaluated."

Joe's mother-in-law had a legendary fear of the medical estab-
lishment and hadn't seen a doctor in decades. She enjoyed Joe's
company but not his medical advice. His inner soundtrack was
blaring now: *Dementia! This will be you sooner than you think!*
The two men went inside to get a glass of whiskey; it was cold out
beside the barbecue.

Joe greeted Rose, Sara's mother, with a kiss. "How have you
been? You look lovely as always!"

Her gaze was just a bit distant, and Joe realized that she didn't
recognize him immediately. He'd seen it enough with his older
patients. It was just a brief spell of neutrality, a puzzled wrinkle
of her forehead and question marks in her eyes, but then she
retrieved his face from her memory file and recovered herself. In
that moment Joe glanced at Sara. She saw it too.

The doorbell rang again, and Joe's brother-in-law Kenny strode
in, wife and son in tow. "Joe! You're slipping! Usually, you'd have a
beer in each hand by now. One for me, right?" Kenny had become
Joe's closest confidant and an irreplaceable friend over the years,
both men being married to brilliant, strong-willed sisters.

"Ah, just the guy I was looking for. Your team lost to mine last
night, you know. You owe me a coffee. Maybe in New York, or
Santorini, or Tokyo. I'll let you decide."

Joe kept up the banter while an inner track spooled constantly. Inwardly the tension was pulling his mind apart.

"What's on your mind, Joe? You look like you're somewhere else." *Kenny and I know each other too well sometimes. Can't let on about this shit,* Joe reminded himself.

"Aw, just tired. Work's been a little much these days. Still hangin' over from COVID. Some people in my hospital are never satisfied. Let's forget that. How's the family?"

Kenny enthused about a coming trip to Florida, his favorite place to visit. Joe half-listened, his thoughts far away. In a long-term bed? On a plane over Europe? Crossing a border in the shadows of a foggy night, a gun hidden under his coat? Reading coded messages by flashlight? Lying in a wet diaper in a room smelling of antiseptic and his own waste? Bedsores, a feeding tube, finally choking and dying alone at night? Using his wits to evade capture? Getting into position to take a critical shot for freedom, for history? For his ego. Or handcuffed to a bedframe, interrogated for days and then executed, dumped on a roadside where the message of his death would be clear to his co-conspirators?

With an effort Joe pulled himself into the present. Kenny was saying, "Of course, they have guns there but if you're a good guest, nobody will get crazy, right? Speaking of which, how about another beer? Or a whiskey, if that's what you and Pops are havin'. And let's get out the backgammon board. I wanna win back some of my money!"

They found everyone in the kitchen. Joe automatically picked up a knife and started chopping vegetables to grill. Sara, Rose and Kenny's wife Maria had enlisted the kids to set and decorate the table, fill water glasses, and feed the dogs. *My hands are still fine,* Joe noted with relief.

Kenny had gone outside on a ruse and started cooking without Joe, a prank he enjoyed playing. "Hey, get away from my grill you sneaky bastard!" Joe pretended to be upset. Kenny could cook anything. Pops laughed at the mock battle for the tongs.

The three men stood out in the cold, ice cubes rattling in their tumblers. Pops leaned in

to the others. "Watch Mama. She's not right. Kenny, I was telling Joe about it. She's forgetting where she is, losing things, has to be reminded about everything. Keep an eye on her over dinner. Tell me later on what you think."

Joe saw the concerned look, heard the fear in the older man's voice. *Do I want to go through that, or put my own family in that place?* He asked himself.

It became obvious at the dinner table that Rose was losing her faculties.

Maria recounted a problem customer who demanded free service for the third time in a week at her tailoring shop. "So, I've told him not to come back, and then he brings his friends too."

"Well, Dear, tell him to get his groceries somewhere else!"

"Groceries, Ma? It's a tailor shop, right? You got all your fancy dresses from me."

"Oh no, I'm sure they're all from Hudson Bay." She stood up and began removing her sweater. "Here, I can show you the label on this one."

"Ma, sit down. Don't worry about it, it's not a big deal."

The kids and their cousin George smirked at each other over their grandmother's odd behavior. Joe shot a warning glare to their end of the table. "Okay, who's hungry?"

The dishes were passed, and everyone loaded their plates. Rose's was nearly empty. Joe saw Sara's worry as their eyes met for a moment. Pops joked, "So Joe, you're all holy now. How about saying a grace?"

Joe was off guard but thought quickly. "Heavenly Creator, please remind us all to be grateful for the good things we have. For our health, for this food, for the blessing of each other's company.

For peace and freedom in our part of the world." He looked out the window, facing east toward Europe thousands of kilometres away. "Help us all to be good, to be kind, and to make your world a better place. Amen."

Later that evening, he was alone again. Sara was upstairs already, either reading or asleep. He decided to play some music while he reviewed charts for the week ahead. Grieg, Peer Gynt. A favorite, part folksy and part desolate. With a start, he realized that it struck his ears as noise. No feeling; he couldn't connect with it. He tried something else. Dvorak. Punk, metal, jazz. It was neutral; it could have been the coffee maker. Music had been a pillar in every time of strength and weakness, joy and sorrow. Now his numbness terrified him as it had when he'd received his diagnosis.

The next morning, Joe heard his family whirling through the daily blur of preparation while his coffee cooled. Sara called out, "Okay, any homework you need to pack up? Who's ready for something to eat? Will, you're on lunches today, Sam tomorrow. Let's get going! Don't expect Dad and me to do it all the time."

He was struck forcefully by the realization that he filled no irreplaceable, essential role here. The sudden attack of loneliness, in a room full of his dearest people, shook him again. He retreated into a bathroom to collect himself, and then quietly left for work.

The bike ride calmed Joe's nerves. He weighed Plan A versus Plan B. He felt calmest when he envisioned accepting the Project, seeing how far it would take him. His indifference to the music he loved the previous night and his detachment from his family weighed heavily for the next few days. He began to bargain with himself: *Suppose the memory drug doesn't work for me. Suppose they choose someone else. Suppose the war gets worse faster than anyone expected. Then I'd be out of their Project anyway. And they'd need me to keep quiet. Might I already be in danger of being kept silent?* His mind spun like a roulette wheel—*Russian roulette*, he thought, grinning inwardly. Three days later, Joe sent a one-word note to gordiehowe@project.ca: Yes.

That weekend, Joe tackled his monthly online banking. While paying bills and coordinating his next tax instalment he discovered a deposit of almost $50,000 from G Howe.

7

Joe had a chance to see his mother, coinciding with his first appointment at the nearby military base. It was hard enough to witness her decay happening remotely on a screen. Close up, sitting on her flowery sofa, her decline came into painfully sharp focus. A year of nearly complete isolation had chewed relentlessly at her formerly sharp edges. Her voice and facial recognition declined every month. The whole family used cues to remind her of who was calling or visiting. Joe knew the outcome, and that her time would be limited. He wondered idly if he could barter with the spy people for some extra doses for her.

Lately Joe had felt the changes coming on inside his own head. Trouble finding the proper word. Nonsensical typing errors. Terrible facial recognition, never one of his strengths, but now almost as bad as his mother's. He'd figured out some tricks to keep his deficits hidden but a dim awareness of his fading acuity crept into bed some nights to keep him awake. So far, the essential faculties of rote memory and repetition had kept him under the radar at work, but one day those would fail too. His working abilities were so grooved that he sensed that they would be the last thing to go. How would it feel? Would he even know? An earthworm, blind, deaf, no past, no awareness. He shuddered.

His mom knew him too well, even from inside the fog of her own decline. "What are you thinking about so hard, Joe? Is everything alright? Are your family okay?"

Her concerned tone gave him a sharp pang, but he deflected gamely. "Come on, Ma. What's there to worry about? I don't play enough hockey, maybe? We eat too much pizza? Everything is going well now that this pandemic stuff is receding. I'll admit that it's been hard for the kids, and for Sara looking after home school. Nobody enjoyed that, but we did okay considering."

She had always seemed almost psychic, able to read her children's states of mind. She was barely 50 kilos, 150 cm, wobbly on her feet, and deep lines of both worry and laughter were etched in her face. Her cardigan sweater engulfed her. Knobby arthritic hands gripped his tightly while her eyes focused sharply and drilled into him for clues about the state of his life.

He needed a diversion. "Hey, Ma, I have some news for you about my job. You know how I've been complaining about working too hard? I have an option to go part-time, starting really soon. If it goes according to plan, I'll be able to visit every week." It was perfect: she'd never remember what he was saying anyway.

"That's terrific, Joe!" She beamed. "Starting when? Maybe you'll bring your mother some borsch! Or sushi!"

He waved another goodbye as he drove past her window. She didn't see his hand shaking.

Joe had emailed ahead to Gordie Howe and received a map of the base, a photo of the clinic/lab building, and an electronic pass sent to his phone. He drove slowly through a short series of pylons that forced his speed down, stopping in front of a small guardhouse. A woman in uniform approached as he lowered his window. A blue hemisphere on the roof watched them both, winking once per second. He felt his pulse rise as she asked him his business at the base. "Who are you here to see? Can I see two pieces of ID please?" She was all business, perhaps thirty, and reminded Joe of every female Customs agent who'd given him a hard time over the years.

He showed her his phone. "I'm here for the clinic. They didn't give me a person's name."

She glanced at his phone screen. Something on it, or something he said, brought her eyebrows up sharply. The metal arm went up and she waved him through, pointing to his right.

Joe sat in the waiting room of an infirmary building. The chipped paint, rusty steam radiators and worn terrazolite floors seemed more like a low-budget prison than a place to receive care. The late afternoon sun slanted in through the window. Alternate chairs were taped off to maintain distance. There were no other patients in sight. Aside from the buzzing of old fluorescent fixtures, the place was silent. A harsh hand-sanitizer scent hung in the air. He was apparently the only patient being seen in person. After a few minutes of silence, Joe decided to poke around. He entered a chilly exam room and found a flimsy, neatly folded gown on a wooden chair.

Joe changed into the gown, piled his own clothes on the chair, and waited. He had a brief flashback to Krishna's office and hearing his worst fears confirmed. A vague, creeping unease sidled up and settled down next to him as he leaned on the examining table. He reminded himself reluctantly that he was a patient. In the cool still air his skin tightened and goosebumps rose.

A bank of machinery stood opposite and filled up a third of the room. The naked navy blue eye of a video recorder bulged from each corner of the ceiling. Most of the devices here were familiar. Ophthalmoscope, tuning forks, ECG, EEG tracers, exercise bike, BP cuff and monitor. An eye exam system with slotted cases of lenses. Audiometer. There were several others he couldn't fathom. After a few more minutes, the door opened. A man and a woman in lab coats, and a guy in a nice suit. Carter.

Carter made introductions. "Good afternoon, Dr. Danko. Thank you for agreeing to some eligibility testing. My medical colleagues are Drs. Ginette Giguere and Lewis Young. Dr. Giguere has joined Dr. Young's team to lead investigations into the drug we're here to assess your suitability for. They will verify that we're handling you according to ethical and eligibility protocols.

Dr. Young spoke up, his voice a staccato burst of syllables. He wore a bowtie patterned with chemical symbols. He was tall, slim, and reminded Joe of Bill Nye the Science Guy. "My team has experience with medications that can reverse the effects of early dementia. Memory loss is our main focus, and we've had some great results in mammal studies. Dr. Giguere, my colleague, is a stellar researcher in this field. She's a world leader in the discovery of the chemical causes of dementia-related memory loss. I've watched her career from the sidelines and her momentum is steadily forward. I thought I was a big deal, but when I saw her work, I had to have her join my own research team. Most importantly, Ginette has developed all the main techniques in use now for replacement therapy. She'll tell you more in a minute."

He opened a laptop, and the screen lit up with graphs. "This is the main prize. I'll keep it short. The red tracing is baseline, time to complete tasks after repetition. We use rats in mazes, chimpanzees with complex use of tools to access a reward, and various other standard mammal lab procedures. We graduated to human trials two years ago."

Joe looked at the tracing, saw it slope down gradually to the right. "And the blue line? Looks steeper."

"Exactly," said Young. "We have almost one hundred percent agreement between species, and reproducibility within the same subjects. If we stop the drug for more than two weeks, we begin to see a return to baseline. The effectiveness vanishes exponentially and completely in six weeks."

"What happens to the subjects then? Have you observed anything else? Is there a withdrawal, or does their behavior change somehow?"

Carter interjected, "Let's not get too far ahead here, people. You have an evening of testing beginning now. And if you pass, there's a second round."

Dr. Giguere interrupted him, "Fair question, though, don't you think? *Informed* consent."

Dr. Young turned to her with a glance at Carter. "Ginette, this is your baby. Tell him anything you feel he should know. Full permission."

She turned to address Joe directly. She had a soft, almost hypnotic voice, and to Joe's ears, a noticeable Quebec French twang.

"You should know exactly what we're considering here for you. If I came to you for breast or colon surgery, you'd give me a full description of your treatment, its risks and benefits.

"I'm part of Dr. Young's overall team. My subspecialty is with RNA upregulation gateway peptides. You remember peptides from med school, right? Those long chains of amino acids. Some of the amino acids in the central nervous system are slightly modified to become neurotransmitters. When strung together in short chains of ten to fifteen, with neurotransmitters embedded midway along them, the peptides act to turn on RNA synthesis and enable the creation of new memories. A person with high concentrations will learn and retain new information much better than someone with fewer of these peptides. In large enough concentrations, they also prevent loss of both long term and short term memories in dementia sufferers. Still with me?" Her love of the subject was infectious; Joe and the others were fully attentive.

"So, we create these same peptides and get them into brain cells. It's analogous to insulin replacement therapy in diabetes. Initially we injected the test peptides into the spinal fluid space. That works really well but only in sedated lab animals. Human subjects don't like repeated spinal taps for some reason."

She smiled at them and blushed faintly at her own joke. "I've found that a larger dose injected intravenously is almost as effective. The peptide sequence has been shortened to allow the drug to cross the blood-brain barrier. There are mild side effects, none of which are anticipated to interfere with your function."

She paused, and Joe could see her choosing her next words carefully. He tended to over-inform his own patients about operative risks and appreciated this small detail in her own practice. "We have tested this medication on over one hundred human volunteers. Half are military, half are palliative care patients seeking better function in their last days. About ten percent have become impulsive, almost as if they're overconfident when they realize how much they can remember. How well they're functioning. None have been violent so far.

"Some lose the ability to experience strong emotions. We've had subjects complain that when they lost friends and loved ones over the pandemic, they couldn't properly grieve. Interesting," she mused, almost talking to herself. "Sleeplessness is observed in nearly all subjects. The average subject sleeps about five hours per twenty-four. As a side effect we actually like that one, as they get more hours of alertness per day. However, when they discontinue the medication, in week three, the subjects all basically go to sleep for about forty-eight continuous hours.

"Part of the molecule is also distantly related to amphetamines. Thus, there's a theoretical risk of psychosis from prolonged use. Our longest trial of this formulation in any subject is only six months. I am obliged to inform you also that this is the third iteration of the formula. We have had some negative outcomes in terms of mental health in the first two rounds of treatment. The current drug has been reconfigured, and we have seen no serious adverse events so far."

She added, "The peptide hormones are a tricky class of agents though. They require storage at body temperature and pH, since they're of similar composition to those already present in the body and become denatured in the wrong environment. That means the molecule itself changes shape. Imagine melting the key to your front door. It wouldn't fit anymore. I'm still trying different storage media, but the shelf life is only a few hours. I know time is tight, and my team is working around the clock to solve this issue."

Joe looked around at all of them. They were standing in a circle. Joe noticed, for the first time that he was visibly older than any of them. Ideas came to him in a rush: They weren't taking any of their experimental drugs, were they? Would any of them be along on the trip overseas? How would he ensure not to run out of this wonder drug before his errand was completed?

He took a chance. "Have any of you actually tried this stuff yourselves?"

Young spoke up. "Of course. In fact, I'm on it right now, this minute. It's an IV infusion, takes about half an hour. The first few days afterward, you can study and memorize like you did in med school. I've taught myself Spanish and did my tax return in two hours this year.

"I understand you have good hands, doc? Is that right? You'd have to give this to yourself unless you can enlist a travel companion who has IV skills and doesn't mind if it's a one-way trip." He glanced at Giguere. She reddened slightly again.

Carter cast a scowl at Dr. Young, and added, "Our intention is that you complete a task and return home safely. We know this is a dangerous idea, and security around the target will be intense. More intense than anything we've encountered anywhere. We have people in place along the way to support you with physical needs and intel as each step leads to another. But we're getting way ahead of ourselves right now. I suggest that we do all your medical and aptitude testing first; three days should do it. The rest of this is a moot point if you don't pass the physical." He gazed out the window. A small group of soldiers were marching in formation, rifles up. "Dr. Young gets excited about his work. But you don't get to that stage without doing the mundane stuff first."

They drew blood and fed him a standardized meal. Something like tofu, but Joe could taste the protein powder. Fake vanilla. A cube of some cake-like substance heavily sweetened and almost inedible. It made him appreciate the quality of the city's tap water as he rinsed his mouth. The lab had its own MRI unit-small bore, head only. An expensive research tool. A masked technologist scanned him with a functional technique. The team hooked him up with wires, tapped his knees and elbows, shone lights in his eyes. They ran him on a treadmill, measured his calorie burn, took all sorts of caliper measurements, drew more blood, took a urine sample, a cheek swab for DNA.

Joe was assigned a bunk in the barracks attached to the building. The monitor patches remained in place. He fell asleep then woke up with a start, thinking about the strange cube he ate for dinner. What exactly were they feeding him? Was there a drug test among all those vials of his blood? Joe suddenly realized: *Hey, I haven't signed anything!* Thoughts came to him in a rush: *How would he complain about these people anyway? To whom? This whole thing was one big secret.*

8

He was at the lab again at 0800h, fresh and rested. Giguere met him at the doorway. "Great performance so far, doctor. Today we'll see what makes you tick. Pop quiz time!" She applied wires to the patches the team had left in place the previous day. Her touch was gentle, her hands delicate but firm. She sat him down at a desk. "You have several hours of standardized personality inventory questions beginning now. The instructions are on the first page. There are two pencils and one eraser. This is deliberately low-tech analog. We will shred the result immediately after it's been evaluated. There will be no digital record linked to you, so be entirely honest in your responses."

Joe knew that buried in the mountains of questions, the ones that mattered were evaluating him for fitness to embark on a mission like this one.

"I could never kill an animal."

"In certain situations, it's okay to kill another human being."

"I am more comfortable taking instructions than directing others."

"I am more curious than the average person."

"I often have violent thoughts."

"I am creative under pressure."

His responses were graded one to five. He darkened the pink bubbles with a sharp pencil. He was careful; he'd been a stellar examination writer through all his years of school. He had a well-grooved system that served him well and resurfaced now, decades later. Sprint through the easiest questions, then return with more time per item for the rest. Questions like "I can tolerate physical discomfort better than others" made him pause to think about where his answers could lead him. He blocked out the direst thoughts and kept working.

By the end of the morning quiz the pencils were worn down. He realized that he hadn't moved for four hours. The examiners noticed it too. The afternoon session lasted six hours, the questions more subtly shaded, the heat in the room deliberately turned up to induce fatigue. Dr. Giguere fell asleep. A single washroom break. Water, no food. This testing process had many dimensions.

The team evaluated other physical attributes over the next two days. Some of the more concerning ones involved being closed in dark spaces, curled in fetal position. Cold or hot, hungry or thirsty. Reactions to loud noises. In the middle of the third day, a man in uniform came in and screamed at him in a foreign language then abruptly left the room. The wires attached to his body transmitted his reaction; his vital signs synced up to the video record. In the corners of the ceiling, the blue camera balls glowed like electric houseflies. These researchers and others offsite, he imagined in places like Washington and London, watched video into the night.

Late on the third day Carter met with his scientists and Joe. "We have a big problem here, people. Ginette, your team still hasn't found us an answer to the storage problem. Your drug does wonders for the mind, but it's of no use outside a lab. It can't be frozen, and an incubator box is too cumbersome to carry around. And what sort of battery, thermostat, and insulation would we need? If one of our people is in the field and depends on the drug, they have a time limit of a single dose interval—what's that, two weeks?—to get over there, into place, carry out a task, and return. I can't see how that's possible unless the other side lays out a welcome mat." Carter looked as though he was winding himself up, a coiled spring. The others could see his blood pressure rising.

Young and Giguere glanced at each other. He shrugged; her hands were out, palms up waiting for an answer to fall from the heavens.

Joe closed his eyes and thought back to a salvage operation he'd seen once. A colleague had used a plastic IV bag to close a gaping abdominal incision, leaving the patient's guts visible so fluid buildup or developing infection could be observed in real time. Soon after that, another surgeon had invented a sterile zipper, replacing sutures, for use in patients who needed frequent repeat surgeries. A breast reconstruction Joe had assisted with recently after cancer treatment popped into his head. The silicone tissue expander... "Hey, Mr. Carter. Can I have a pencil and paper?"

Joe drew the standard hexagon of a surgical diagram. His mind defaulted into the zone he enjoyed in his work, where ideas flowed, and answers came effortlessly. "Okay, body temperature, right? Suppose a subject like me has a small silicone bag with a zip-lock seal at the top implanted below the skin. One on each side, nice horizontal suture lines. Tunnel them backward away from the skin. They won't be visible or palpable. Close them with running subcuticular suture." He drew another diagram. "Like this. The scars are invisible. I do really nice ones. Use a tissue expander, basically a sterile plum, to create the space needed to hold, say, 50 ml per side. How big is a vial of this drug?"

"5 ml," replied Giguere.

"Okay, great. So, one pouch like this can carry the memory drug, the other for something to carry out the task." *Or green pills,* he thought to himself. Carter was nodding his head as a light seemed to flip on. Their eyes met and Carter took Joe's vitals again. *He knows,* Joe realized. *Of course he does, fool! How did they find you in the first place?*

Young chimed in. "Just one thing. Who's going to do this for you? Open and close the incisions? Who's going to start the IV and administer the drug?"

"It's not deep internal work," Joe observed. "I can access the pouches myself under local anesthesia." He paused and looked at the others squarely. Carter's eyes reflected equal parts curiosity and mild amusement. Joe took a deep breath and made his confession. "Provided I keep a supply of pain pills handy for before and after."

Dr. Giguere spoke gently. "I wondered when we'd have this discussion, Dr. Danko. Do you think your habit will compromise your abilities in any way?"

"No, actually. My intake is small, and it hasn't changed since the pandemic began. I don't get sleepy, just calm. If anything, I'll make a great smuggler. No metal, no lumps. Invisible stitches."

Dr. Young added, "We appreciate your being up front about this, doctor. You were originally identified to us because of your, uh, habit. So, of course, we knew all along. I'd like to interpret this conversation as a sign of trust."

Carter's eyes alternated between the two. He smiled as he saw Joe's shoulders relax. "It happens that Dr. Young has run several simulations of your capabilities both on and off your little pill. We've used the physical metrics you're providing via monitor, your career performance, and those boring questionnaires you've been doing these past few days."

"That's right, and our AI analysis is that if your brain and the memory drug are a good fit, your best option is actually to maintain your habit at a steady state. For our purposes, keeping you in the role without a reliable supply is far riskier than status quo. We can't have you jonesing in the middle of the mission. We've also learned something very important about you, Dr. Danko: you've been better than you think at keeping a secret. That could save someone's life. Or your own."

"Good. So, that's sorted out." Carter declared briskly. "Our next item is: What's our method of dispatch for the target? Any ideas?"

The researchers lowered their heads; Joe did the same unconsciously. They had taken the Hippocratic Oath, after all. Now they were looking for ways to contravene it. Joe hesitated a few beats, then began listing. "Gun? Pluses: effective if there's a clear shot. Minuses: metal, maybe difficult to carry in. Noisy. Easy to get caught. No thanks. 3D printed guns are possible but not perfect."

Young added, "Knife, box cutter, cord, hand-to-hand fighting. Pluses: possibly quieter if there's no screaming or shouting. Minuses: bodyguards. Uncertainty of success in close quarters."

Joe spoke up again. "I've seen the video of a young woman, a judoka, letting the president throw her. She had to jump up to get her feet off the floor so he could do it. I'd love to go one-on-one with him, but his entourage would probably be like a brick wall." There was a short silence while the team pondered ideas. Joe smiled, imagining throwing the president to the ground.

His eyes suddenly widened. "How about poison? It could fit in my pouches. Better yet, a drug overdose. Carfentanil! It's perfect!"

"Explain," said Carter.

"Let's say I have two of these kangaroo pouches. One holds the memory drug and a few pills in sterile containers. The other, at the right time, holds Carfentanil. I open the incision, take out the Carfentanil, and spray it into the air. But I wear a mask, and I prepare my brain for it."

Giguere and Young exchanged smiles. "That could work. How would you do it?"

Joe continued, "If someone maintains a consistent intake of an opioid their receptors will be reduced in number." He drew a brainstem in profile on another sheet of paper. "That's tolerance. On the big day, you block the remaining receptors with the antidote—Naloxone—and you're immunized for about an hour or so from Carfentanil." He drew Xs over the receptors on his diagram.

Carter put up his hand. "Excuse me. I'm a layman here. Please tell me what you're all on about."

Young was clearly excited by the idea. "Large animals occasionally require medical exams or surgery. Most medication dosages are based on body weight. Certain drugs used in animal medicine are much more potent than the human analogues. Carfentanil is one such example. Used in small amounts it can sedate a horse, camel, or elephant. Minute doses, a grain of sand, given to a human are lethal. This is why the overdose rates among drug users in North America have jumped, as the illegal trade in Carfentanil is booming. It's easy and comparatively cheap to synthesize. Dealers add it to regular Fentanyl for an extra kick, but this drug is so powerful that any mixing is dangerously unpredictable. A lot of it comes from China and Mexico, but gangs anywhere can produce it. A side effect of globalized commerce.

"Suppose we put it into the air where the target is located. Russia actually did the same thing in a theatre under attack about twenty years ago. We make Joe immune, first reduce and then block his receptors. All we need are trace amounts. A large animal veterinarian can probably stockpile it. At the Moscow Zoo?"

"Okay. This is good forward momentum! So, we need a zoo vet. Maybe a pharmacist or something, a nurse or some other hospital employee to get gear ready for Joe to open his pouches and run his IV. Every two weeks. Plan for three doses overseas." Carter was showing something almost close to excitement. "We have a method, we've solved the issue of keeping the drug warm, and we can smuggle the drug, Joe's little helper, and the Carfentanil in the kangaroo pouches. What else?"

"I need to talk to the surgeon who will do the work." Joe said. "The suture lines must be absolutely clean. There are news stories of people being stripped to search for tattoos. It's a big part of the prison and military culture in Russia. The refugees and soldiers are examined for any body art that might represent gang, military, or Nazi affiliation. If anyone strip searches me, and they're able to see the incisions, I'll tell them these were hernia repairs. The neater, the better. Maybe they'll be undetectable on a quick look.

"Your surgeon should remove my appendix too. They used to do that with explorers and astronauts. If I'm having an operation anyway; better to eliminate the risk of a preventable random illness."

Gordie Howe loved it. They were also pleased that Joe was bringing his own ideas to the table; it proved his commitment. Someone ran a simulation behind the scenes and calculated that a gram of 50% carfentanil could kill any adult human within 2.5 metres of the point of release.

Joe had been adjusting his own brain for years and worked out a plan for Showtime. He would run out of his pain pill supply about the time he arrived in Moscow, and trade over to Methadone. At Showtime he would block his remaining receptors with Naloxone. Withdrawal? So long as his supply wasn't interrupted, he would be fine. He might have an hour or two of shakes, runny nose, bone pain. Diarrhea? He hoped not. He would then add more Methadone and try to escape. If he hadn't already been caught or killed.

Joe's sense of time measured itself along several axes; one of these was his internal clock. Always counting down to the next dose of opioid, his brainstem was ruthlessly accurate. Methadone itself was a controlled drug and would certainly land him in jail if he were caught carrying it across borders. He would need an inside supplier for both Methadone and Carfentanil.

Back at home, he felt the giddy thrill of a roller-coaster ride build deep within. He wanted to shout his triumph out loud, but the family were in the next room. He logged off from Gordie Howe silently, shuffled his feet in a little dance of victory, and went to his family in the next room. "Hey, anybody! Who's up for a bike ride?"

9

A month later, with all his testing completed, he was back at the base. Joe's excuse for absence from home remained the same; only the nature and location of the work had changed. Every month Sara drove him to the airport. As soon as she rounded the curved facade to leave the terminal, he slipped out a side gate to a Project car reserved for him, regular plates and nothing conspicuous. Classified access to the base hospital, but not the rest of the facility. The team didn't want him seen by anyone outside the Project.

The Project paid fairly for the use of rented space here in the middle of the continent. The military appreciated any interest in their facility, which badly needed a coat of paint after decades of neglect as a side effect of peace. Here, far from the simmering conflict zones of the world, the Project could carry out its work without interference.

The base staff consisted of flight trainees, instructors, and maintenance crews. Their orders were to ignore the tenant scientists who used the main infirmary block. These guests were citizens of countries known to be trusted allies. The debacle with the Chinese virologists was fresh in the minds of many on the base. Pains had been taken to minimize qualms and curiosity so that the Project could conduct its drug research, surveillance, candidate testing and training, even its food services and banking, under complete security.

Loose-fitting clothes. Nothing to eat or drink for four hours. No more than two coffees in the preceding twenty-four hours. No vitamins. He skipped the other pills for three days ahead of his clinical trial introduction.

Carter beamed as he met Joe at the infirmary. "Today is a major milestone. We'll be evaluating your interaction with our memory augmentation formula, and its interaction with you. Both are important. We, uh, we've taken the liberty of awarding you a call sign. It's mostly an air force tradition, but nowadays individual fighters create their own *nom de guerre*. Yours is apt in several ways and we hope you'll like it. Novichok. The newcomer, the rookie. The nerve agent developed in Soviet times and used under the watch of your target. The scientist you saved had a hand in refining it. You are new to this world, an unknown quantity. It's a huge advantage for you and for us."

Joe rolled the word around on his tongue. "Novichok. *Novichok.* Yup. I like it. Thanks, Mr. Carter. I expect I'll wear it well. Novichok." He paused to look at the rest of them, hoping they couldn't see his ego inflating. "Okay, here we go. Let's get to work."

Giguere started his IV herself. She had good hands, thousands of IV starts and blood draws in her sixteen-year career so far. "Relax, Joe; little poke." She smiled at him shyly. She patted the dressing into place and squeezed his hand. "You will do great, I know it." She hung up his first bag of IV fluid, injected the drug into a side port, and opened the roller. His first dose was small, and he didn't notice any change in his level of alertness, concentration or recall. His memory testing was repeated, and his scores didn't budge. They brought him back the next day and doubled the dose. This time, he felt a chemical energy, an alert vibrancy, a sense of confidence that bordered on euphoria.

Giguere took his vitals every fifteen minutes, making notes on a little tablet computer she kept in her pocket. Joe recalled one like it—where? Carter. She opened it with a long look from her right eye. This team must have its own computer lab too. She tested him again twice in the next twenty-four hours, a full battery of memory, personality, ethics and some basic knowledge questions as controls. He flew through it all.

Her own vital signs hummed in harmonic response. Her baby was performing exactly as it should. There was no dysphoria, no long night of hallucinatory terrors, no hangover. His morning round of tests was as good as the first had been. He took another set of online tests every three days once he was back at his day job, the questions less personal. They wanted to map out the time when his performance dropped to baseline.

In Joe's case, the euphoria lasted three days, and his memory boost lasted three weeks. Dr. Giguere pointed out that his metabolism would clear the drug more rapidly with time. She settled on an interval of two weeks between doses. The mild tremor that had begun in his hands two years earlier was eliminated. At the same time, his ability to respond emotionally to stimuli became blunted. Things that would have irritated him in recent months— the politics at work, the ridiculous workload—all faded to a soft background hum. And he found that for the first few nights after a shot of the drug, he didn't need more than about four hours sleep per night. The spare time was spent keeping up to his workload, getting some exercise, learning his European geography, history, bits of languages.

And learning everything available about his target. A career secret police agent, he had seen the opportunity to enter politics when his beloved mother state's empire was dismantled. Power struggles ensued. He had learned all the important lessons. Control over information. Keeping his enemies close until they were no longer needed. Hiding his wealth (amassed through complex transactions with friends whose success he had enabled and whose loyalty he'd demanded in return) and personal life from public view. Providing enough positive image for the media to create a cult of personality. Ambiguity was a science for him; would he poison an opponent? Could he blow up a building to boost his approval ratings before an election? Would he use the nuclear weapons his military held? Did he have a secret illness? A secret lover? Sufficient material to blackmail other leaders, maintain their loyalty? Only one man on earth knew for sure.

Like Joe Danko, the President also wished to leave his imprint on the pages of history. The man who reassembled shattered parts into the greater empire of his youth. His mother country would return to her former glory as a force to be taken seriously by all. Especially those depraved, gender-fluid, morally slack Western countries, who had undoubtedly orchestrated his country's fall from superpower to a common state. He had revenge on his mind.

The pandemic had hobbled the world's economies. Millions had died. The President's key demographic of elders with long, bitter memories were aging and dying. Many of the older generation pined for the era of Great Power, in command of huge military resources, surrounded by fifteen other countries under its heavy-handed central rule. These elders were his core support, but their numbers and influence were diminishing. He needed to start his great project while he still had those supporters to back him. The rest could be influenced by the correct use of the media. Conscientious objectors could be silenced with the application of convenient laws and a loyal police system. He had several forms of policing at his disposal, not all of them public knowledge.

Mokroye delo, or wet work, was an integral part of the president's *modus operandi*, although he would never admit to direct participation. His security apparatus employed a large staff of experts in neurotoxins, radioisotopes, herbs and plants. There was also the more dramatic use of defenestration, both home and abroad, of opponents for emphasis when he felt it was needed. His security staff carried out these missions at a great distance, but the President relished tinkering with the details, the time, place and method. Other men of a certain age took long walks, learned gardening, golf, yoga or other harmless pastimes. Planning wet work was one of the most satisfying parts of his job.

For the faithful, he had nationalized religion. Rather than believe in the sacredness of life and love of one's fellow human beings, his adherents were instructed instead in the righteousness of the government and its divine right to redress historic grievances, portrayed now as sins. Joe felt a strange affinity for the president's dream of a place among the immortals. He understood the depth of the other man's commitment to his ideas, even if he felt the ideas themselves to be distorted almost beyond belief.

10

Joe paid an overnight visit to the base hospital beside the infirmary to undergo his surgical preparation. Joe had psyched himself up for this day, reminding himself that it was one more necessary step of many along this new path. His fear—of pain, the incisions, complications—receded as he repeated this mantra to himself. The whole building had been cleared of military personnel. As there were no injured air force staff, it was a simple matter of putting the facility on "bypass" for twenty-four hours, a routine civilian hospital practice during the pandemic. The commanding officer happily accepted the story that a TV series was being shot on location, and the hefty cheque for new medical equipment that accompanied it.

The surgeon was a contractor, a young woman with full credentials in plastics from Poland but none in Canada. The Project occasionally employed such people because of their high skill level, lack of full-time work, and willingness to take on unusual cases. She remained anonymous to Joe, having done enough facial alterations that being named could put her at risk. He had sent her a sketch of the intended result and a surgical approach through Gordie Howe.

He was wheeled into the OR for removal of his appendix and "hernia repair"—the official diagnosis for the record. The surgeon related the details: "I will install heavy-gauge silicone bags with zip-lock seals, capacity 50 ml each, one per side on your lower abdomen. Each will hold a tissue expander for one month. On your right side, I will also be leaving a sterile ampule containing a medication as I've been instructed to do. You will assume post-op wound care and arrange retrieval of the tissue expanders. Both incisions will be closed with running subcuticular suture.

"There will be local disruption of your abdominal wall on the deep aspect. This may predispose you to future hernias requiring further surgery. On the right side, I will perform a routine appendectomy. This is correct?"

Joe nodded. "Yes, and I know the risks of routine appendectomy."

She probed him with her eyes. "My orders are not to ask any questions about your need for these implanted pouches. Morally I need only to know that you're not part of a drug-dealing ring. I have done work for Carter and Boris in the past year. They assure me that you're a good man. I trust their judgment. The written procedure record will be destroyed once you have recovered and been discharged."

A second doctor appeared with two nurses, scrub and circulating. "I'm Tadeusz. I do some part-time work alongside your surgeon as her anaesthesiologist. Our nurses are Binh and Maria. We're all part of a group that work for Carter. Nice to meet you. Any questions before we start? I'll answer your first one: Yes, we're all fully certified, just not in Canada. Next question?"

Having survived surgery previously saved him considerable anxiety. The emotional blunting created by the new memory augmentation drug didn't hurt either. This time, when they placed the oxygen mask and asked him to count down, he went willingly into oblivion.

Joe recovered uneventfully, and he was home two days later. Sara would be away at a friend's cottage for a few days. They handed off the kids, car, and house keys with the usual ease. The kids were preoccupied with school, TikTok, and video games. They didn't notice that he skipped mowing the lawn. His incisions healed perfectly and the pouches, each filled with a silicone tissue expander, were painless.

In their rare spare time Joe and Sara reconnected in the way that fortunate couples do in mid-marriage. Both were a little wary, guarded and careful not to cause harm while sharing a dinner out or making wistful travel plans. Joe took pains not to let her see him in full light without a shirt. He casually broached the idea of going to the Polish border for a month to do relief work with a small NGO or something bigger like the Red Cross or Medecins Sans Frontieres. They both had friends who had made the trip to Warsaw, gratefully welcomed by the teams already there. While not exactly battlefront trauma surgery, it was necessary work— managing the untreated medical conditions, immunizations, and mental health issues of uprooted people. Several hundred passed through daily at each of four nursing stations. There was a constant need for replacement volunteers, as they were rotated in and out of duty. The work was strenuous but not medically demanding; he would be competent within a day or two.

As he painted the picture of his role at the Polish border, Sara saw flashes of the same passion and excitement that she'd seen in the better, earlier days. She felt a pang of jealousy that he could get this excited about strangers halfway around the planet. He'd taken the memory drug and had been digesting travel and contact instructions. At night he learned basic Polish phrases while the house slept. The insomnia helped with working and studying.

The team dosed him monthly when he attended for training. They had him on a program of workouts every other morning, a mix of balance, flexibility, and power. They took care not to let him injure himself while trying to speed up the process of getting fit. His periods after receiving the drug were recorded; the first few nights they had him stay at the base. They observed his sleep, appetite, reactions to small aggravations. They locked him into a cold room one night of each visit. He solved thought problems and puzzles, answered more questionnaires, and underwent another functional MRI while the drug was still fresh in his brain. He remained focused straight ahead; if anything, the drug improved his resolve and his endurance for more testing. The medical researchers met privately and were consistent in their appraisal. Their candidate was doing well from the side effects standpoint. Carter informed them that other pieces of the team were being assembled simultaneously. Once Joe had reached his sixth dose, at three months, he would meet his travel mates.

Because of the need to take the memory-boosting drug every two weeks, Joe would have to open the right sided incision two weeks after the surgery, close it up, and start an IV on himself. On the designated night he was on call, Sara stirred only for a minute when his phone rang at 0300h, overnight phone calls being a routine part of their life. He reviewed an old man's appendix CT scan in the hospital network while the green pill dissolved into paste under his tongue.

Joe rinsed his hands with sanitizer beside the kitchen sink and waved them until they dried. He donned a pair of gloves, painted his belly with prep solution, and held his breath while he sank a 25-gauge needle into the skin along his incision. His hands remained steady, but he silently ran through a litany of curses as the anaesthetic stung him. He used the scalpel in the kit to open the incision, unzipped the internal pouch to access the drug, and sealed the fresh cut with tissue adhesive. Finally, he added the vial of memory drug to an IV bag and wound a belt around his ankle. Starting the IV was no problem. Joe plugged the IV bag into a side port and turned on the infusion. He sat down at the desk and reviewed some more charts; he was awake anyway. The whole thing took him twenty minutes. He'd have to work on getting his time down. This would be a monthly necessity.

Four weeks later and well past midnight, Joe opened the bottom drawer of his desk and placed a green pill under his tongue. While it dissolved, he unlocked the filing cabinet and took out a wrapped sterile tray.

"Dad? I can't sleep. Can I hang out with you?" Joe nearly dropped everything in surprise. He hoped he didn't look suspect; Sam had huge antennae and a vivid imagination.

"No, sweetheart. This is nighttime, and you should be asleep."

"What's that big box? Is it hospital stuff? What's a sterile procedure tray?"

Joe felt like the Grinch being caught stealing a Christmas tree. "It's really nothing you need to know about. It's just something for my work."

Now Joe looked up and saw Sara in the office doorway too. "Joe, what's going on?"

"Nothing, really. They sent us these trays to evaluate. Sometimes they're pre-packaged with half the stuff missing, or wrong size needles, no gauze or whatever. They asked me to see whether this would be a good vendor. I put it in my backpack and forgot to look at it earlier."

"So, you're evaluating it now at 2 AM?"

"You know how sometimes you wake up suddenly, go O-M-G, and rush to your computer to send an email? Same thing. Don't worry about it. I'm sorry I woke you both up."

Joe was just barely convincing enough; they said goodnight and went back up to bed. He gave them twenty minutes and then performed his monthly ritual. From that night onward, he resolved to perform his self-surgery at the hospital instead.

The rest of the summer passed in a blur of work, family and kids' activities, his home hospital job and side trips to the base, still under the guise of work up north. With each passing month he felt fresher and stronger. His whole life became a new experience in mindfulness as the drug cleared the fog from his brain. He made a point of spending some of his new-found energy with the family.

"Dad, wait up. You're going too fast!" Sam protested Joe's speed as they rode through the trails beside the Red River. Sara was already half a kilometre ahead with Will.

"This is the Olympics, bud! Gotta ride hard. Or at least, let's catch up to Mom. She's got the frisbee. But wait, look at this! It's really beautiful. See how the termites have written their names on this tree? Isn't that like a picture?"

These small moments were precious. Inwardly Joe swallowed his sorrow for all the times he would miss in the future. He held a hundred conversations a day with himself. He watched his bank account, and money continued to appear as promised, on time and never less than what he would earn up north. Arguments against his new path became less frequent with each passing month.

He took each daily bike ride to work as a chance to sharpen his reflexes against the traffic. His senses became keener. He practiced people-watching with an interest he'd forgotten. Maybe it was the drug? The weather, the squirrels that darted into his path, the many moods of the rivers through town. Crows gathering over a field, coyotes celebrating a kill after midnight. He tried to soak it all in impartially. Were the crows an omen? No, don't be silly.

He stopped snacking when working late. He continually performed small memory tests on himself, some with Cyrillic letters, or memorized appointment times, patient problems, work meetings, his children's friends' names.

Joe caught himself almost ready to tell Sara what he was up to and had to discipline himself to keep this secret carefully wrapped and out of view. Instead, he became more attentive, approachable, and interested in her life and work outside the home. They went for walks and dinners. His memory was better than ever, and his minor tremor was completely gone. He saw no reason to tell her about his medical situation. It was well under control.

The travel plans would be laid out soon. He had his precious chance to be part of history, almost close enough to touch, and approaching nearer every day. On the nights leading up to the next dose, Joe slept soundly and rose with the sun. He offered a silent meditation of gratitude, did a round of stretches, and started his days with a smile.

For the first time in years, life was good.

11

It was now late summer. Joe had spent many of his drug-induced insomniac nights learning the homework Carter assigned. He took crash courses in conversational Polish and basic Ukrainian. He memorized the map and street views of central Warsaw, photographs and maps of the train station and environs. He repeated his work until he could draw the maps, even sketch the exterior of the train station and the refugee tents, outdoor toilets, and living quarters.

He did the same with the vicinities of train stations in Lviv, Kyiv, and smaller towns along the way where the train was known to stop. He learned all the streets and alleys of the Podil neighborhood in central Kyiv. He imprinted subway maps, street level, and aerial views of rows of apartment buildings into his visual catalog. Most importantly, he was introduced to his future Kyiv hosts.

Pavel and Iryna, he read in their file, were partisans who had gained underground fame during the Maidan uprising. Like many young adults of that time, they'd seen their hopes of a happier, more successful life evaporating under a president who took orders from outside. Such orders were never in the interest of ordinary people. During that crisis, they had helped create, intercept, and translate emails sent between various government and military agencies in both Russia and Ukraine. The puppet ruler installed by the much larger, more powerful neighbor to the north was forced out of power.

After the Maidan, Pavel and Iryna had again become regular civilians with busy careers. They had no children. Pavel's talents as a software engineer were always in high demand. Government and private interests sent him a steady stream of projects. Iryna was a skilled language instructor, fluent in German, French, Russian, Ukrainian, and English. She had been recruited immediately when the invasion became inevitable. Through Father Boris, they had been approached to participate in the Project. They were happy to be reactivated. This war was the most dire possible threat to the way of life they had fought to preserve.

The couple inhabited an active social sphere of like-minded friends and good neighbors in their building and along the avenue. They spent their spare time and money traveling to European destinations, soaking in the beauty and culture they admired. Occasionally, they had played host to some of the friends they made on these trips abroad. Even in wartime, it would be no great surprise to the neighbors if they had a visitor for a week or two.

The Project leaders had decided to introduce the travel companions after Joe was acclimatized to the drug and had received enough training to function as part of the group. At the base Carter sat at the reception desk and watched his team arrive. He looked like a new parent, proud of what he'd produced. Joe had been told to arrive at 0700h sharp and took a seat beside Carter.

"Morning, Joe. I hear you've made excellent progress. Drug working all right? Any problems at all?"

"Nothing I'd complain about. If anything, maybe too much energy right after an infusion. I use the time to study. So, it works out fine. Been getting fit too; look at this!" He flexed his arm, patted his belly. "I've lost five kilos over the past few months, and I haven't felt this good in years."

There was a tap on his shoulder. "Great to see you again, Dr. Danko."

"Father Boris!"

"Sometimes, you get the right feeling about someone. I prayed—no, really!—that you'd pass all the tests. Mr. Carter will tell you we went to great lengths to get this right. We wondered sometimes if this could work at all. You've pleasantly surprised everyone. Congratulations, Novichok!"

Two more men approached from the foyer. They were dressed in long black robes; Joe figured that they were also priests. He looked carefully at the man on the left and did a double-take: it was like looking into a mirror. Somehow the Project had found someone who looked very similar to him. He pointed quizzically at the man, who laughed right out loud.

"See, Mr. Carter, this is just the reaction I wanted. Joe, my name is Matt O'Shea. Call sign Gemini, your twin brother. Part of my job is to act as your body double. I'm ex-military, a former Army captain. I was selected by the Project partly for my, uh, physical attributes, and partly for my bodyguard experience. I've done two tours in Afghanistan. I'm happy to meet you."

The other man had been quiet to this point and now spoke up.

"Hello, Joe, I'm Bill Rudyk. The Weatherman. I'm also ex-Army, from Edmonton, and fluent in Russian, Ukrainian, Serbian, and Polish. I process news and the local environment intel where we're heading. I might come in handy ordering from the menus as we tour the sights. Great to meet you."

There were handshakes among the team of travelers, phones pinging as they synced up and absorbed each other's contact information. This would be fine here, dangerous later. Father Boris was a commanding presence even here among these seasoned fighting men.

"Travelers, let's all sit down and listen to Mr. Carter's itinerary for us. He's paying for the tickets, after all."

He was a natural leader; they silently took seats in the reception room's empty chairs.

Carter cleared his throat. "We've been given a reprieve. I apologize to any of you who were hoping to get this party started. There have been some developments. The Project has a chance very soon to achieve its objective. Our instructions are to wait and give the team already in place the time and space to perform their tasks."

Joe felt all eyes turn toward him.

"Am I the only one who's unaware?" His work schedule wouldn't need adjustment after all.

Boris volunteered, "I knew this was a possibility. There are other teams and different travelers assigned to this. We aren't able to say any more. On the plus side, we're all here and there's time to get to know each other better."

"Good point. We need a solid connection among our teammates." Carter added, "You'll bunk together here on training weeks for the next three months. We're creating a bio for Joe and Matt as Father Mike, a priest from Saskatchewan, going along with Boris to do relief work on the Polish side of the border. You will all learn the bio. We can't afford self-inflicted errors as a result of failure to keep in character. In the meantime, I want Joe and Matt to look and sound like identical twins. Matt, stick to him like glue. You pass the test when I can't tell you apart.

"To maintain numbers for a fighting force, the law requires Ukrainian men of eighteen to sixty years of age to stay in the country. We felt the priests' robes might limit the risk of traveling as men without families. On the other hand, they may draw attention. You'll have to make the call on the fly. Any adult male may be questioned as to why he is traveling in a given direction. Exemptions exist for care of elders or family members with disabilities. Soldiers, medical personnel, teachers, and the clergy are among those who do not require travel documents. Novichok will receive additional documents from his suppliers in Kyiv.

"I have been reassured that none of you have any tattoos or branding that could be interpreted by the other side as identifying you as members of any adversary groups. Am I correct? People are being detained for the wrong body art. Last chance." There were no takers.

"Novichok, I want you to make a list of whatever you need to open and close yourself up. That list will be sent ahead to a contact at each stop you're making. Kyiv and Moscow, basically. I need this to be absolutely specific. Err on the plus side if you err at all. Is anyone here having second thoughts, or any doubts that they can perform their functions? This is intended to be a round-trip ticket. Novi, I know your deeper trip will make the first part of it look like a honeymoon. Do you have any reservations at all?"

Joe shook his head. He was beginning to feel a jagged, strange fatigue. He knew the drug was due tomorrow. He'd feel better then.

The following morning, Joe demonstrated his kangaroo pouches for the team. Ahead of his performance he chewed up two tablets of his own favorite medication in the men's room around the corner.

Joe stood at the head of the row of chairs. "As you can see, I've nothing up my sleeve," he deadpanned.

A table was set with local anaesthetic, sterile swabs, prep solution, gloves, and a plastic blade. Tissue glue tubes lay to one side. Joe donned the gloves.

"This is how we put on our gloves without contaminating the outer surface. Now three coats of antiseptic..."

He swabbed his belly, drew a straight line along his right-side incision with a syringe full of local, the needle just beneath the surface of his own skin. It still burned, as it had the first time he'd done it, but he could talk himself through it more easily each time. He opened the incision directly on the thin white scar with the scalpel, careful not to go too deep. He put two fingers inside, felt for the top of the zip-lock seal and gently pulled the sides apart. He retrieved the memory drug, sealed in sterile wrap, deep in the pouch. Then he squeezed out some tissue glue and pinched the sides of his incision together for ten seconds, every centimetre.

The rest of the team sat masked a few metres away. These were battle-hardened guys. They watched in rapt fascination. None of them had ever tried to do minor surgery on themselves. The whole procedure took seven minutes. He pretended to take a bow. "I'll alternate sides to allow for healing between accesses. There's room for pain pills, Carfentanil and tissue glue, in addition to the memory drug."

Joe snapped off his gloves and opened an IV set. He applied a tourniquet to his ankle and swabbed the skin on the top of his foot. He started an IV, taped it down and connected it to a bag full of saline. Carter handed him the vial of the memory drug, and he added it to the bag. Then he opened the roller and let the bag deflate. The travel team sipped their coffees, chatted quietly about the coming trip, previous experiences traveling in Europe, the latest war news. Joe gradually felt his mind speeding up, alertness increasing and his perception becoming acute. Someone asked him a question; he answered in what he hoped was a normal voice but at double speed. His syllables were clipped, staccato, his speech like that of Dr. Young at the first meeting here, a few months earlier. He was high. Carter recognized it first and knew that what Joe needed was information to digest, process, absorb. He picked up a laptop, opened a file on Matt O'Shea. Class was in session.

12

O'Shea intrigued Joe. What fluke of genetics gave them each a near-identical twin?

"It's hard to get used to seeing myself without a mirror," Joe remarked one morning as he and Matt jogged on treadmills between wind-sprints. "Don't you find this strange?"

Matt puffed back, "Same here. I've seen your bio. We couldn't be more different in a lot of other ways. I grew up in Montreal. My mom was a single parent. I'm the youngest of four and she had a hard time keeping us in line. I learned most things the hard way. I'm a great mimic so I used imitations to keep the bullies entertained. That way they always bothered someone else. I got into photography in high school. Thought I'd meet more girls that way but no way! I still have a darkroom. It's my stress relief now."

The military beckoned as the quickest way out of his mother's fridge and toward his own independence. Thirty years of military life, absences, and relocations had been tough for his wife and two daughters. He was nearing fifty, had survived two overseas deployments to Afghanistan, and should have retired a year ago. On his last tour he'd lost contact with a scout group, and they'd been killed by an IED. It weighed on his memory, and he carried a burden of guilt. His marriage strained under his self-medication and bad habits, his wife always fearful when he received another assignment. His photography became therapy and he submitted many snaps to amateur contests, picking up honorable-mentions through local news outlets and such. It hadn't all been vanity, either, as some of his images, taken during deployment, had been instrumental in ops planning. Someone in the Project had used AI to spot the facial resemblance of Matt to Joe.

For the first training week or two after O'Shea's arrival, Joe found the man's constant presence jarring and intrusive. Even their voices were similar, and the other team members began having difficulty telling the two apart. As the time passed, both Joe and Matt became accustomed to having a "twin" present and began to prank their trainers and team members. For Matt, Joe was a figure to be admired—an academic type who'd been found by the Project, ready to roll up his sleeves. Joe admired Matt's own body of work but also saw a darker similarity: another ordinary man who did extraordinary things in his chosen profession, while the profession itself took over his life.

Bill Rudyk presented more of a puzzle to Joe. At first glance, the tall, skinny man looked as though he'd be most at home on a golf course. Seventy years old, his restless mind and visionary sense of momentum made him a legend in the shadowy world of intelligence gathering. Given the importance and audacity of this particular Project, the sources were classified; Joe knew instinctively not to ask too many questions about things not volunteered to him.

The team had no intention of traversing any active battle lines. Still, long-range attacks had occurred with varying frequency from the earliest days of the invasion, as far west as Lviv where the train station, an Art Nouveau masterpiece, had sustained significant damage. While the impossibility of perfect accuracy was understood, Bill was as good at predictive pattern recognition as anyone known to the Project. He tended toward shyness but spoke freely among the people he trusted. He explained his work, and his gift, to Joe one day.

"Remember Wayne Gretzky? He always said that the important thing was to know where the puck is going next, not where it is at the moment. So that's me. I'm Wayne for this team. The Weatherman, they call me. I translate between the relevant regional languages, I read satellite maps, I decode intel from the other side, I interpret troop and equipment movements. I've learned how to draw terrain maps from memory. I look for the "weather report" of hostile activity and make predictions about near-term future actions for the Project. I know how many patrol boats each side has on the Dniepr River, what airport our guys want to target next. Just one rule: don't ask me where my intel originates. If you don't know something, they can't extract it from you. Right?" He grinned and ambled away.

Father Boris had assumed his natural leadership role. As time went on, Joe saw firsthand the respect paid to the priest by the other Project team members, Carter included, and developed his own admiration. There seemed to be nothing Boris wouldn't try. He lifted more weight, ran faster on the treadmill (he *was* ten years younger) climbed the ropes course with ease. He often vanished, sometimes for days. Matt told Joe that the priest was in high demand and had duties in other aspects of the Project. All classified.

The team was gelling well under Carter's fatherly supervision. Joe and Matt's practical jokes broke the tension and served as opportunities for Matt to perfect his role. Bill and Boris crafted various travel plans, identity stories, routes and contingencies. Boris possessed his own mental Rolodex of contacts, many of them priests, imams, and rabbis he'd met in travels over the past ten years as a field agent. Others were locals: drivers, fixers, translators. Boris's specialty was, of course, Eastern Europe and thus he was actively recruited for this team. Not that he'd needed any persuasion.

Some elements of training required Joe to be brought rapidly up to speed. His test answers revealed more than even an experienced exam-writer could circumvent. Joe's phobias, anxieties, and dislikes bubbled to the surface, seen and known to Carter and his own concealed team of experts. Carter waited for a week between memory drug doses, when Joe's level had drifted into equilibrium, and called Joe outside for a walk.

"This is a midterm report card for you, Joe. First thing I'll say is that you're performing as expected, or better, in every metric so far. But we haven't begun to harden your mind yet. There are situations you may find yourself in, beyond your control, where you'll have to keep your cool no matter how hard that may be. Your life, and the whole Project, may be at risk if you can't handle something emotionally. Mentally. We've got you into reasonable shape physically. Now you need to learn how to hold down fear. I understand that you do it well already in a medical scenario. This is something different. We've analyzed the layers behind your responses to all those quizzes you took. We know your strengths and weaknesses. Fortunately for you, there are more of the former. However, we still see some room for improvement.

"Your profile shows us a strong tendency to impatience. Maybe that's an advantage when you need to do something surgical quickly or make a fast medical decision. But in our field, it can be fatal. Not only that, but we also see a strong aversion to discomfort, either physical or mental. If you combine these two traits, there is significant risk of, for example, poor tolerance for staying in cramped spaces, or inability to handle even the possibility of torture if you're captured.

"Next thing we'll need to do is reduce your responses to physical discomfort and stress. We're going to bring in a specialist in self-control, meditation, hypnosis, and other techniques. We will desensitize you against your phobias, anxiety, and impatience. Some of the best hunters in the wild are the most patient. Birds of prey, big cats—they can sit perfectly still for hours, waiting for their chance. Just when the prey relaxes—Boom! It's all over.

"I see that you're not a fan of spiders or mice. That's a great place for us to start, because you'll probably see plenty of both in the next few months. Imagine that you're in a closet or a basement somewhere. What will you do if a mouse runs across your shoe? That's what we want to minimize. Suppose the other side gets hold of you at a roadside checkpoint and you have to bluff your way through? Can you look a soldier in the eye while his buddy aims a rifle at you and tell a bald-faced lie?"

Joe arranged an extra few days away from work, created a cover story of an extra weekend where he'd be needed up north, and drove from the airport to the base three days early. It was at the nadir of his memory drug level, when he'd be most susceptible to fatigue, most in need of sleep, and least energetic. Carter had planned it this way for maximum effect. *I'm already getting good at lying*, he mused. His family, his wife… The truth was becoming something so far beyond his usual sphere that she'd never believe it anyway.

On the ride over, Joe recalled a psychology experiment he'd signed up to participate in as an undergrad. Students could earn an extra five percentage points by volunteering themselves as subjects. It was a crapshoot; one guy was injected with morphine and had blood taken every half hour. Several others viewed porno films, a rare commodity in those days, while their erectile responses were recorded. Joe, eighteen at the time, was envious. He didn't know any better back then.

Joe arrived at the University psych building at 0630 hours on a winter Saturday, was placed in a room, and given instructions to read. He was to insist that he hadn't taken the money that purportedly accompanied the written letter. As there was no money, it would be no problem. Two students wearing masks and white coats ushered him into a room and strapped him into a chair, something out of a dentist's office, and explained the nature of polygraph testing to Joe as they hooked him up. The last piece of hardware was a pair of leads connected to a car battery.

"Don't worry. If your reading shows no abnormality, we won't be forced to shock you," said one of the "investigators." Joe started to snicker; these guys were behaving so seriously. But suddenly the one holding the wires jumped and howled in pain. The other guy chided, "Don't touch the leads together! What do you expect?"

Now Joe began to doubt the wisdom of going after the extra marks. The white coats asked him repeatedly whether he'd taken twenty dollars from the envelope. Joe denied it each time. The pauses between questions grew longer. The questions changed. "Are you sure there isn't something you'd like to tell us? How long do you want to keep us all here?" An audible beep increased in tempo and volume. Joe braced himself as he felt the blood beginning to pound at his ears...

A lean, wiry middle-aged man introduced himself to Joe. "I'm Li Fu. I'm pleased to meet you; I've heard and read so much about you. We will train together in meditation and calming techniques, ones that can help you in times when you are under duress. Please don't tell me anything about your purpose here. My teaching is intended to cover any eventuality. We will do a combination of breathwork, hypnosis, and pure meditation. You will learn, to your best ability, to reduce your body's stress responses. Please sit with me." Joe, dressed in hospital scrubs, complied. Li Fu guided them both through a series of stretches over fifteen minutes.

"Feel the inside of your fingertips," intoned Li Fu slowly. Feel where you end and the outside begins. Keep breathing. Slowly. Smoothly. Feel the energy in your breath. It cools and warms us. It makes us part of everything."

Joe was in his third day of intensive sessions. Calming, stretching, meditation every morning. Two hours in the gym. Then came the afternoons and nights. Heat. cold, cramped positions. Thirst, hunger, denial of bathroom access. A diaper in a storage trunk with holes drilled for air. Sleep deprivation, but performed carefully, never longer than forty-eight hours. Then schooltime; images of dismembered children, fields of dead soldiers, homes on fire with weeping elders standing in the snow outside. Landmine injuries. The earphones screamed the pain of rape and torture into his ears and soul. All the while, the blue bulb in the ceiling blinked once per second. The monitor leads fed his vital signs to the Project leaders both on-and off-site.

At first, Joe lost his mental balance easily. His pulse rose, he felt himself sweating, his bowels clenched. His senses overloaded and he broke down several times, begging for a rest. The breaks lasted five minutes, never more or less. Joe had deliberately held off taking his little green pills for those three days at the base; he wanted to prove his endurance to himself and save the opiate as a safety valve. Now he felt every pressure point while lying in the box. His back complained bitterly, his operated knee began to throb.

Animal fear rose in his chest. He wanted to kick and lash out, strain the sides of the box and break loose. With a pure effort of will he pulled himself back from the edge of full-blown violent panic. He took a deep breath and held it, five seconds, and exhaled slowly. Count, breathe in… His lessons with Li Fu found their way to Joe's consciousness just as Joe thought he'd beg for another break. He flexed the muscles in one limb at a time, keeping his face near the air holes and reminding himself to regulate his breathing. The claustrophobic sense of stuffy confinement eased partially. The headphones continued to deliver their horrific soundtrack, but Joe found a way to focus his senses. He started with the inside of his pinky.

Young and Giguere—the medical team responsible for the drug, but more broadly for Joe's health—looked on like nervous parents, unable to help their protege so long as he passed the tests. They anxiously watched the tracings from his multiple wire leads, answered pings into their phones from offices and labs somewhere outside Washington and London. Yes, things were leveling off now. Give him a few more minutes. Gradually the readings settled into a gentler rhythm and the medical crew relaxed, their own inner tracings satisfied. Joe was asleep.

Joe sat upright on a wooden chair under a hot overhead light. The room was too warm; he hadn't had any food or water in a while. They'd skipped his midday meal and unexpectedly brought him here instead. He was naked aside from a blindfold and headphones. Electric leads trailed away from his chest and limbs. Early in this exercise, several hours ago, he panicked and lost control. A slipknot cord around his neck and a seatbelt at his waist prevented him from slumping forward to find a comfortable angle to catch some sleep. His wrists were duct-taped to the sides of the chair; his ankles zip-tied to the chair legs. Two flies (he guessed it was only two) buzzed lazily around the light bulb, occasionally venturing close enough to irritate Joe. They were the worst, he'd decided. A blue glass eye watched impassively from the corner of the ceiling, blinking once per second.

He was grateful for the insomnia of his drug weeks but now he craved sleep and he couldn't have it. The alternate weeks left him too many dream hours to replay the intensity of his daytime work. He discovered, quite by accident, how to trade his frightening visions for calm ones, and regain sleep. At times like these, strapped in and desperately learning to cast his mind elsewhere, he found himself vividly back in the past, before all this began. When life was unlimited and simple.

As the months wore on, the mental aspects of training became paramount. Nobody knew what might befall him when he reached the end of his European journey. He arranged to make his absences from home, and his base hospital, a few days longer. He had much to learn.

Whenever Joe went into an isolation exercise, interrogation room, or the ductwork full of spiders, Carter or one of the doctors held his phone and returned one-word responses only when necessary. In the Project's judgment, very few family issues were urgent enough to require his focus to be interrupted. He returned home from an extended week just in time to say goodnight to the children one Sunday night. As he turned on his home computer, Sara confronted him tearfully. "Joe, what's been going on with you lately? You're losing weight. You don't answer my messages for hours sometimes. Are you really working that much?"

Joe switched into his new gear. With a soldier's blank tone he replied, "There are a lot more sick people up there all the time. I sleep less than I used to, sometimes eat less too. Because it's just that busy now. But look at the money coming in. The kids can go to camp all summer or take any lessons they want. What else would I be doing besides working?"

Now her eyes welled up. "I don't know. You just seem really remote this past while. Is the north so much better for you? Don't you miss us? I feel like I'm on autopilot, just waiting for you to come home. Then you close yourself up and work your day job. It's too much for you, and it's definitely too much for me. So, I'll ask you only once, and I want a straight answer: do you have another woman up there?"

Joe had mastered his heart rate, his eye movements, his breathing. He knew, and had been warned repeatedly, that this conversation would happen one day soon and that he needed to have his response perfected. He looked at her squarely, eye to eye, and lightly held her shoulders. "I'm working really hard. I'd hoped it would settle down, but there aren't enough people interested, or capable, to go up there and handle it. The proof is in the bank account. There is no other woman. Please don't worry." He now could resist the urge to tell her what he was really up to. In the event of any breach, her innocence might save her life. Did she believe him now? Or when would she stop caring?

13

—

2023

Spring came late to Crimea in 2023. The paycheques for middle and junior officers also lagged. The front lines north of the peninsula remained static, stuck in the muddy soil. Restless officers and sailors of Russia's Black Sea Fleet crowded the bars and drank cheap vodka on their furlough time. Some of them became talkative when Oleg the bartender offered a few free rounds. He listened attentively with apparent sympathy. The sailors liked him; he really cared about what they had to say.

The bartender rode his bicycle past a news kiosk on the way to his shift at the harborside tavern. The street, a kilometre from Sevastopol harbor, looked like any other. Well kept low-rise blocks lined a brick sidewalk, with small shops at the ground floor of each. In his early twenties, he was dressed for the outdoors. A visiting priest had donated creative ideas and warm clothes to the group.

Oleg was a skilled cyclist; he'd never owned or driven a car. He needed a shave, a bath, and a warm meal, but these could wait. He parked and locked the bike. He bought a copy of *Argumenti i Fakti—Arguments and Facts,*a Russian government-owned newspaper—and a pack of cigarettes from the kiosk attendant. The attendant tucked a few folded sheets of marked-up newspaper into the current edition, and the young man cycled away. He would interpret the markings, letters yellowed with a high-lighter, later with his team of local partisans.

Atesh, the partisan group, had thousands of members, connected by an underground stream of communication among the civilians and the military of the Crimean cities. High quality information enabled them to time actions perfectly. A dark unpatrolled shoreline was ideal for landing Ukrainian Marines. A bachelor party for a radar unit's captain coincided with a new moon for a disabling attack on the radar relay station, and a blind spot in air surveillance. That blind spot created the opening for ships to resume the transport of grain to a world anxious about food security. The combined effect proved to be greater than the sum of its parts.

Increasingly, the families who had transferred their lives here since 2014 found themselves doubting the wisdom of their choice. Most just wanted a decent place to raise their kids, a stable job, a gentler climate. But with explosions visible from the beaches, frequent closures of the Kerch bridge, food shortages, and blackouts, it was proving not to be worth the original government incentive program's rewards. And Atesh was finding information easier to gather with each passing month.

A small group of university students stared into a computer screen in a dingy St Petersburg apartment. One of them snapped photos of the screen with her digital camera. They each copied instructions from the camera image onto paper. Their VPN connection lasted only a few seconds. This group had noticed their window shrinking with each use. It was a matter of time before the FSB caught them; time to subscribe to another service and create a new link. They had changed providers twice already this year. The girl with the camera deleted the image. All the while they made small talk as they decoded the report and instructions they were given.

One of the boys stowed the laptop in his backpack. They left in pairs, every five minutes, by different exits.

A soldier at the Russian Army base near Belgorod waited until his sergeant went back inside, then continued loosening lug nuts on the wheels of the officers' truck he hid behind. Three of his best friends and his only brother were already dead. He'd seen enough of this leadership.

Three months later a missile destroyed the Black Sea Headquarters of the Russian navy, killing several officers. At the funeral gathering, dozens were sickened and several killed by poisoned hors d'oeuvres.

Six months later, a large retail warehouse near St. Petersburg caught fire. Hundreds of millions of rubles worth of inventory was lost. The losses included food and winter clothing. Shortages began, and prices rose.

Nine months later, a group of soldiers beat their commanding officer to death when he refused to allow a retreat to safety.

Even the president's own allies began to question his grasp of the situation facing his military. A close advisor and friend who had once scored great victories for the Motherland had to be arrested and publicly tried for his public complaints. The people needed an example.

The president's favorite mercenary boss had seemingly gone off the rails, first privately criticizing the president's hand-picked generals and the Ministry of Defense. When he didn't see an improvement in the results on the ground, he took a run at the president's command chain on social media, airing his dissatisfaction to millions worldwide. His profane ranting was by turns humorous and scathing. His complaint? That the senior leadership group were ignorant sycophants, out of touch, incompetent, and wilfully sending large numbers of men to certain death in blunt frontal infantry assaults that carried a high mortality rate.

The spat culminated in an armed column advancing toward the capital, shooting down several aircraft and killing trained pilots in the process. There was confusion: does he support the Motherland or not? The answer: of course, but not the people or methods of the Special Military Operation. *I can do this better.*

The Project exulted from the sidelines.

There could be only one alpha on the playground. Even with his own billions of dollars, thousands of well-trained men, high-priced equipment, and a complete lack of regard for the rules of war, the mercenary signed his own death certificate by defying the president. Loyalty trumped bravery, skill, patriotism, and everything else. How could the president allow such a rebel, leading his own personal army, to survive unpunished? The mercenary's private jet crashed exactly two months after the insurrection.

The former primary opposition candidate had proven difficult to subdue, even surviving a serious poisoning with the president's favorite nerve agent. His doggedness and grit were such that he immediately returned to the motherland after recovering in Germany, where expert medical care had saved his life.

As expected, he was immediately arrested, locked away, and treated to a sham trial in one of the kangaroo courts the president favored to get the job done with emphasis and certainty. If anyone had failed somehow to get the message, he (again publicly) had his sentence lengthened before being moved to a prison at the edge of the planet, where even his most dedicated supporters and lawyers found access to him difficult. He died in captivity under shadowy circumstances. Mourners were given military summons papers and ordered to report for duty—to participate personally in the Special Military Operation.

The president was certain to be re-elected. Everyone who might be a serious opponent was now jailed, dead, exiled, or cowed into submission. The polls reflected not the people's will, but the president's mastery of media control and the psychology of learned helplessness.

But even in the president's own security apparatus there were cracks, well-concealed and whitewashed over to avoid detection. The Project had its own resources trained squarely at these healthy, dedicated young men (for they were almost all men). With the hundreds of thousands of other young men lost so far in the trenches, it was inevitable that the losses would begin to strike some of the president's guards personally; a dead or wounded brother or friend began to surface in discussion every few days in spite of the command structure's strict policy against delivering such bad personal news. Not all the president's guards were patriotic enough to accept such a deep loss as a necessary part of fighting a holy battle against the proxy of a satanic, imperial West. A slow drip of timely information, sent through VKontakte and Telegram, began to skew the opinions of these grieving guards and soldiers onto a different track. The Project, with its long reach, deep pockets, and access to technology, began sending images of dead faces, legless infantrymen, destroyed tanks and ships, to relatives known to be part of the official Guard. The accompanying messages offered the chance for revenge, large sums of money, the certainty that eventually the president must explain himself to all those ordinary Russian families who had lost their sons, brothers, husbands.

Invariably the recipients of such messages deleted them nervously. The Project's analytics predicted that after about the third delivery, up to fifty percent of these Guards would save the message and contact the sender via a burner phone message to a European VPN address. Some of these would later lose their nerve and others wouldn't. The contact information was changed frequently enough to avoid interception or investigation by loyalists. Predictably, the targets who lost their nerve had no desire to incriminate themselves by reporting anything amiss.

It was slow, painstaking work, but over several months, reliable groups of up to four members each were recruited and sworn to secrecy. The Project's AI established the numbers and limits to maximize secrecy while optimizing reach within the security force. In this manner, dozens of young men were enlisted to serve the Project. The higher the quality of information, the greater the payout. Such information, especially where it concerned the president's own movements, was analyzed and curated like the finest wine by Bill Rudyk and others of his rank within the Project. Knowing when the shifts would change, how many belonged to each level of security, how to obtain or block security passes, the shape and size of buildings where the president lived and worked.

Konstantin's phone pinged again. It was the third time since his brother Ilya had been killed, two months ago now. The first time, he'd been enraged by the photo of a naked, burned corpse sprawled on the snow beside a ruined truck. According to the accompanying text, the image had been taken by a comrade somewhere just behind the front line to the west of Donetsk. The news had first reached him in this way, not through his family or his section commander in the Guard.

It was the text below the image that had stuck to him like sand beneath an oyster's shell. *How can you accept this? Your president doesn't give a damn. Reply if you want to avenge your brother. Many others have already joined us.*

Konstantin typed: *How do you know this? What if it's a lie? Does our mother know?*

The reply was another question: *What could she do if she knew?*

He typed again: *Why should I believe you? Who are you?*

The reply: *How long before your "superiors" tell you? Weeks? Months? Never? They don't care about you. They want only your obedience.*

Two more weeks passed. He heard nothing from his senior officers. He typed into the burner phone he'd been instructed to buy. The man at the kiosk who gave it to him wouldn't accept his handful of rubles. Now he understood why. Konstantin went back to the kiosk several times, but the man was no longer there. A young woman with a long ponytail didn't know where the man had gone. She'd been given a few days off with pay. She didn't ask questions.

After he replied, he was connected to others in his brigade who were in the same boat. For them the game of cat-and-mouse became a vital means of revenge. Information trickled through the burner phones. Their families, some a few time zones distant, received food parcels, winter clothes, small stacks of rubles in their mailboxes. Konstantin and his new friends explained these surprises away to their families as the result of a raise in pay with promotion and a caution not to tell the neighbours of this good fortune.

Konstantin sat with his three new friends a month later. As instructed, they'd been introduced to each other via text message on their burner phones, the phones used only sparingly. Once acquainted, they wrote notes, met at the tea bistro near the HQ. They brainstormed for ways to get themselves promoted, to gain access to useful information to trade for family gifts.

One such night they were told to expect a new member to their circle. He'd been cleared; they could trust him. A tall, athletic young man walked straight to their table. "Hello brothers. My name's Dmitry." There were handshakes all around the table. He knew them all by name and rank, offering condolences to one of the group on the sudden loss of his own brother a week earlier—something nobody in HQ seemed to know about.

Dmitry spoke, "We all know why we're here. Let nobody else know of these meetings. We are instruments to end this madness as soon as possible. I'm two levels above you in the president's guard. I hope to be deployed to the Kremlin itself as one of the Central Team members. Any new information you can gather—maps, floor plans, schedules are especially helpful—please send to me straightaway and then delete. Here are new phones. Nice cameras. We've already populated them with the phone numbers you've stored. I'll wipe the old ones.

"In two weeks, when the work rotations change, we'll meet again here, and I'll bring fresh phones. Meanwhile, gather everything you can without contacting each other. Groups meeting outside their work unit may attract attention. Anything you hear that can't wait, send it in. You know the number; the one that's not in the phones. Otherwise, save it until ten days from now. My team will process it all before we meet next. Two of you can expect to be promoted by one rank within the next month. I can't say who just yet. All good?" They took their new phones quietly from his shopping bag.

Dmitry greeted the shop owner with a small wave and was gone. The others followed in pairs after five minutes. Only after they had left did the owner reach below the countertop and flip a switch. The camera over his little bistro resumed its blink, once per second.

"I miss my man, Officer. Maybe you can help me with something." The young woman at the window of the Regional Oblast offices smiled as she shivered. Light snow fell, whole flakes landing silently on her raven hair. She had removed her hat. He assumed that it was out of respect. They were in the decrepit central few blocks of a small city in Tuva Oblast. Such places were rapidly being hollowed out as their young men were lured away, many never to be seen whole again.

The officer was a pudgy middle-aged chair-filler. The Ministry employed thousands like him: too old and unfit for police or military work but entitled to a job after years of unremarkable service. Central Security shuffled these public servants to the far reaches of the Federation to keep office lights on. These days, with able-bodied men dying by the thousands, or coming home with missing limbs, officers like this one were kept busy scouring the far provinces for fresh meat to send to the front lines. Their limited creativity was well-suited to the bleakness of their own remaining years, the landscape, and the futures of the young men they harvested. Any diversion was welcome.

Today looked promising, thought the recruiting officer. He made no effort to hide his curiosity about the shape of the woman's body under her winter coat. She mirrored his interest, opening her top button and straightening her shoulders enough to give him a few square centimetres of smooth skin to rest his greedy eyes on.

He tried to maintain a composed, professional gruffness. "What's his name, Madam?"

"Ivan Fedorovich Letnikov, Officer"—she read his name on the shiny badge—"Fetyukov." She smiled shyly and flashed her teeth— surprisingly healthy for this district—between red-painted lips.

The old woman had coached her very well. She wasn't at all nervous, playing her part like a seasoned pro. The old woman had also taught her the importance of thorough homework. This recruiter lived alone. No family within a thousand kilometres, a recent arrival to the district with no friends to speak of. A few colleagues to drink vodka and trade stories with after work. A total of twelve staff in the whole place, including the four women who served as secretaries. Who had also lost loved ones to offices such as this. They had recently been hired, almost in the same week. No eyebrows had been raised. Their papers had passed a cursory check. They were busy right now, in the basement of this building.

The recruiting officer had heard rumors before. Women who would actually offer themselves for any news about their missing husband, brother, son. These local secretaries had been gossiping within his earshot for several weeks now. He was primed to believe that such a thing could happen to him. Today!

"Why don't you come in then? It's cold outside. Wait there, I'll let you in."

Half an hour later, he was dead. The building was catching fire, the cameras disabled and kerosene in the air. The rest of the recruiters, also term workers from the big cities to the west, were sedated and inhaling smoke in the basement.

The local firefighters were dismayed to find their tires flat, their canvas hoses slashed. The whole Ministry building was leveled. The "secretaries" were long gone. They had planted enough evidence against the local police deputy over the past few weeks to condemn him to trial as a partisan, a terrorist from the other side.

The Yenesei River hadn't frozen over yet. A small fast boat had taken them to a forest trail, and they were already on their way into the airspace over Kazakhstan.

This was the twenty-first reported attack against a recruiting office in the Federation. There had been several others, most less brazen and not necessarily involving homicide. It wasn't possible to stifle the news of so many such events.

An old babushka in Moscow read the daily papers with an inscrutable Mona Lisa smile. A single tear rolled down her cheek. She crossed herself with two fingers, in the manner of the Old Believers. Her tea kettle whistled cheerfully.

All over the Federation, thousands of wives, sisters, and mothers dried their tears and savored the bitter tea of revenge. Many banded together in silent resistance; others marched, chanted, and were detained. The babushka and her closest friends accessed those police records and used the information to recruit help, make introductions, and issue instructions. Gates were left open to factories, power plants, refineries. Kerosene was delivered in milk jugs. Train schedules were encoded and texted on burner phones. The babushka's friends had many skills; they deleted those marchers' police records.

The women's audacity reached new levels; they arranged air force base attacks while guards were distracted. Locations of vessels at sea, bomber flight paths transmitted almost in real time. The pace of materiel losses accelerated as the women of the Russian Federation voted in their own powerful ways.

PART II

PART II

1

The Project team was on ice. "What's really going on, Boris? We were ready over a year ago, and then it's radio silence. Everything was clicking into place. I feel okay, but what if that memory drug stopped working or caused some sort of bad side effect?" Joe and Boris pedalled side by side on stationary bikes in the Project's rented lab space in Winnipeg. They wore remote vital sign monitoring equipment; their data went into the cloud, and minders in the UK or New Jersey tracked their fitness.

Boris remained his usual imperturbable self. He smiled benignly. "Always remember, Novichok, that this Project, even with its own huge resources—contacts, money, great people with huge skills"—here he pointed at Joe—"must still answer to outside forces. Time, place, opportunity or not. Basically, it's like a traffic jam. We can't move until we have a clear green light. There's more to it, but for your sake I can't say anything more."

In-person meetings were infrequent now. Joe knew that Boris was in high demand and had responsibilities elsewhere much of the time. O'Shea was doing security detail for summit meetings, and Rudyk was surveying locations, checking contacts, ("sightseeing," he called it) in western Ukraine. Drs Young and Giguere were comfortable with Joe self-administering the memory drug most of the time, only requesting that he attend the lab every second month while the team hibernated. Joe had become proficient with his self-surgery, closing the incision either with running a subcuticular suture or glue. Carter was invisible except in the third person when Rudyk the Weatherman or Father Boris made an occasional announcement.

In spring 2024, Joe's hospital email finally showed an incoming message from Gordie Howe. His heart leaped.

"Apologize for short notice. Travel four weeks from date of this email. Medical volunteers to present at Red Cross tent 4 outside Warszawa Centralna station. 1000h local time. Travel separately. Use new passports."

Joe sat at the dinner table. He had no leftover urgent work, a rare evening off. His brain was at equilibrium, halfway between infusions of the wonder drug that had restored his memory.

He told his family, "I have an opportunity to go to Poland and do some relief work. It might be a month away, and I'll have to do some extra shifts up north to make up for lost time." He'd rehearsed this performance many times over the past eighteen months. With the help of the memory drug and his blunted emotional reactions, he had no problem getting the words out.

Easy for him, anyway. The children wailed. "Why do you have to go for so long? We'll miss you! Is it dangerous? What if we need help with school stuff?"

Sara was strictly even keel, as always. "I'm sure you'll be fine. Kids, Daddy will be fine. He's been away before, just not this long."

At least she'd have some time apart from his fretting, his stress, his complaining about the state of the world. His world. He sighed inwardly; he knew she would look forward to a rest.

Joe was still under the twilight glow of the drug's effects. His perception was sharper than normal, and he knew that in the near term of a few weeks, he wouldn't be missed. What if he didn't return? Different story. Either way, he could keep his reactions completely hidden. It was a game for him by now. He derived enjoyment from being so completely in control of his blunted emotions.

He pinched a few small things from the hospital—supplies for one open and close of his other pouch. He paid a visit to Jill, his colleague and source of oxycodone. He brought cash. He wondered to himself if he'd be purchasing again next month.

One night, between periods of a hockey game and patient charting, he opened the incision to the pouch on his right side and deposited sixty pills. His own personal bank. He used a running subcuticular suture to sew himself up these days, just to keep his hands nimble. He had the procedure down to seven minutes. *Like a vasectomy*, he thought absently. No showers for at least three days, and only with a dressing after that. Nowadays he always wore a T-shirt, even to bed. So far Sara hadn't noticed anything out of the ordinary. Any intimate contact was infrequent enough that a week without closeness wasn't obvious. He viewed the fact neutrally now. A pile of books on a chair blocked the door against any sudden and unexpected visits. He finished up the reports. The Jets won their game. He took himself up to bed.

The date of his departure approached, and Joe found himself less able to sleep than usual, even in the weeks when the drug level was at a low ebb.

"Dad, why do you have to go away so far? And for so long? You'll miss a lot of our practices! Can't you send someone else?"

Sam stood on his feet and pulled his arm with both hands, an old game from when she was smaller. Now she could take him off balance. The kids had grown and changed so fast.

"Don't worry, Big Girl. I'll be back before you have any dance competitions, and before your report cards come out. That's something I always look forward to. Same with you, Will. I hope I'll see great things. Maybe the Bank of Mom and Dad will pay off big time. It's up to you. Your main job while I'm away will be to listen to Mom and be helpful. I know you can do it."

He showed them the screen of his phone while Sara looked on from the kitchen.

"See? Air Canada. Return date from Warsaw is thirty days. So, no worries, okay?"

Inwardly, Joe wondered whether he'd be around to use the return ticket. The memory drug and Li Fu's teaching remained effective in helping him keep the mask over his emotions.

He went to work, riding his bike past the church where he'd first met Father Isidore. So much of this had been fluke, the Louis Pasteur adage that "Chance favors the prepared mind," omens, and coincidences. If not for his impending dementia, would he be on this path now? Joe thought now and then about his own diagnosis, but only fleetingly, and never in the way that made him internalize it, own it, suffer from it, or for it. He really had gone outside his relationship with disease and mortality. He was now fully trained and planning to kill a world leader. He would probably die in the attempt. And it didn't faze him at all.

Joe's wife and kids dropped him off at YWG as usual. There were a few tears, but his reassurance was so solid that no antennae were raised.

Sara told him, "Be sure you come home safe. Don't take any sort of silly risks. I don't know what their medical system is like but be careful. Don't eat anything weird. Call when you land." She hesitated a few beats, and added, "I love you. I hope this is good for you and gives you fulfillment."

The kids jumped all over him before he could give her a serious reply beyond "I love you too! I'll see you sooner than you think. Kids, listen to Mom and be helpful." He kissed them all, a brief peck on the cheek, and pulled up the handle on his single suitcase. He was gone before their tears began to flow. Inwardly, he savored his detachment, courtesy of the memory drug. His last dose was two days ago.

Joe sat in the international departure lounge, tasting a green tablet as it melted, and awaited his zone being called. A window seat helped him with sleep. Warsaw was mere hours away after all his soul-searching, his stresses through the pandemic, his diagnosis, his training. Joe was now Father Mike Kiriluk, a priest from Saskatchewan, listed date of birth five years and one day later than it actually was. Home parish in Yorkton, Saskatchewan. His family were farmers; a sister and brother still lived in the same area where they were born. The last few study sessions had been dedicated to absorbing the details of this fictitious life. It might be necessary, or not. But not knowing all these "facts" could spell the difference between success and death. The expressionless face on his passport gazed back at him. To Joe it looked like Matt O'Shea.

2

It was 1100h in Warsaw, a gloomy late summer day. The war further east rekindled and caught fire at the border between Ukraine and Belarus, directly north of Kyiv, where it had first begun. The flames were fanned by the draft from another thousand kilometres east, in the power seats of Moscow. Men and equipment stoked the blaze from both sides. Another wave of people streamed westward as the temperature rose.

Joe, Mike, Bill and Father Boris were shown into a huge tent set up as a reception and first aid centre. On one side, the queues stretched out into a soft rain. Those within fifty metres or so had the benefit of a plastic awning. Most stood exhausted, patiently soaking like cattle. Those with infants or small children were passed forward. These were the latest arrivals, not yet given temporary visas. Still unidentified and undocumented. Polish soldiers stood with rifles, flak armor, and nasty expressions at each opening, others walking in pairs between the queues outside.

On the other side, across a metal barrier, was the medical-care station. Introductions were made. Joe was stationed with Father Boris and two nurses from England and Poland. Masks were available but fewer than half the volunteers kept them in place. Joe and Boris wore theirs continuously. There were four such tents along the margin of the train station, each similarly laid out, staffed, and besieged by waves of desperate humanity.

The queues formed hours before dawn and lengthened with each arriving train. Many slept on the ground or sidewalks and began stirring before sunrise to claim places in line. They were mostly mothers with small frightened children or bewildered seniors who were still grasping the calamity that had befallen them. There were anxiety attacks and people sobbing with relief at having escaped the war zone.

The volunteers handed out food, water, menstrual kits, toothbrushes, diapers. The medications they dispensed were the typical crisis drugs: routine pain pills or liquids, insulin, Ativan, blood pressure remedies. Antibiotics for kids with earaches, bladder infections and such. This was simple but necessary stuff. These were people whose entire lives had been burned to the ground behind them. In their shocked states, there was no direction open to them except forward into Warsaw, to be absorbed into the generosity the citizens had extended to them with no thought about the payback.

The decency they witnessed over the next few days was at once heartbreaking and inspiring. Wheelchairs were dispatched to meet trains, greeters pointed exhausted travelers toward food, water, and portable toilets. Other volunteers worked phones constantly, moving the flood of refugees further away from the train station, and into the city itself. They belonged to multiple NGOs, tasked with preventing bottlenecks and logjams. Their efficiency and dedication were admirable.

Some refugees hadn't seen hot food for days. Hungry children's cries were soothed by full bellies. It was as magical as it was frenetic. Joe's team ate and slept in the volunteers' area, and each worked to the point of fatigue every day while they eased out of their jet lag and adopted the new hours of the place they were now immersed in.

He developed vigilance in his people-watching and lent an empathetic ear to hear their tragic stories. An old couple might need extra care; they'd been forced out of their house on the edge of Bucha, commandeered to help dig mass graves, and to fill them. They'd heard the screams of grown men—soldiers—having their fingers cut off, their kneecaps broken with rifle butts, and then killed anyway and clumsily cremated, battlefield style with flame-throwers. Or the women who had given birth in fields or cars, unable to use the destroyed hospital. Or the diabetics whose blood sugar levels ran away like wild horses, their metabolisms veering into shock. Joe took his cues from Boris. He listened patiently, filled whatever need arose, then moved along to the next refugee.

Some of the arrivals were hysterical when they disembarked; they'd left elderly parents, teenage sons, or lost younger children and couldn't be consoled. They were drained of everything but sorrow. Boris handled these with care and compassion, prayed silently with them, held their hands. Several times a day, Joe saw him in a new light: a healer of broken spirits, speaking words of hope into their shattered souls, giving them strength from his own seemingly bottomless reserves. His admiration for the spy priest grew by the hour.

One night Joe sat against a fence with the other three, bewildered and exhausted after a sixteen-hour shift. "So, this is what it's like? It's hard to keep track of how many shell-shocked, desperate people I've seen today. I tried this morning, but I gave up counting after an hour. How do all these aid workers handle it? Because I don't think I could do this every day. I just want to take them all home and put them in a warm bed with a cup of soup or something. The workers and the refugees both."

Rudyk answered, "This isn't routine, Joe. The maps and figures I've been watching for over two years puts this way, way beyond any war zone I've been to. This is really World War Two level, at least in terms of scale. This is Afghanistan, Vietnam, Rwanda, and Syria combined. And all at once. Over a hundred million people around the world are displaced from their homes now, this minute. And only a quarter of them are running from this war. It's really not hard to find misery in today's world. Plenty of shit to go around. And most of it is so totally unnecessary."

"We think we're so highly evolved. I disagree," O'Shea offered.

These were soldiers, hardened men who'd thought they'd seen it all. The sheer volume of misery and suffering brought each man to the same realization—that they were very small instruments in a grand play of something much greater than any of them. In spite of the effects of his memory drug and its ability to blunt his emotional reactions, Joe found himself near tears at least once daily as he tried, in his limited capacity, to bring a smile or a small measure of comfort to these struggling, displaced people. It had been many years since he'd felt so deeply, as though his training had a real ability to make a difference in someone's life. Here, he felt that his life's purpose was being achieved every hour. His teammates reported the same experience, the same sense of transformation to something better than they'd been on arrival. Joe slept like a baby every night. Of course it couldn't last.

3

"Bill has found us a break in the weather," Boris announced one morning. "The timing is good; we've been here a week, and it doesn't raise any eyebrows. We'll take the 0700 morning train to Lviv, stay on board, and ride to Kyiv. Father Mike, Novichok—you ride with me. Weatherman and Gemini, you'll ride in a separate car. I'll go in character. Everyone else will wear civvies. Four men in priests' robes may draw attention. Men traveling east in civvies won't be a problem.

"I have new phones for all of us. Take a minute to write down any contact numbers you absolutely need but haven't memorized. Don't add them to your new phones. We're leaving the old ones here in Warsaw. I have a friend waiting for them. Gemini, I know you like taking photos. These have nice cameras."

They signed out from their tent right after ladling out buckwheat porridge to the first wave of refugees and headed for Warszawa Centralna. Boris met a priest outside the station and handed over a shopping bag with their old phones. Each member boarded with his suitcase, went to his assigned seat, and pulled out a book, newspaper, or puzzle for the trip. The train moved slowly away from Warsaw station, headed southeast toward the Lviv Oblast of western Ukraine. They had nearly four hours to ride before the border.

Nobody on the train paid Novi or Boris any attention. Boris periodically checked his phone and keyed in messages. Novi began to take inventory of the other passengers, aware that they were all heading into a country at war. There were two men in blue uniforms and caps, rail employees on board as passengers, who seemed to be keeping an eye on things. Everyone else was preoccupied with their own problems. *How can I get Baba to leave with me? Who's watching the cats?* People carried plastic bags and suitcases with broken handles, their lives on their laps. Hungry babies shrieked for milk; at one moment, Novi saw three different mothers breastfeeding their infants. Many eyes were rimmed with red, faces drawn and exhausted. And these were the ones going back, having already escaped the hottest zones once. Could Novi do that for his loved ones? Several other mothers with young children sat in varying shades of weariness, trying to keep the small ones from wailing or squirming loose into the aisle. At each end of the car, a pair of Polish soldiers sat across from each other, spanning the aisle with their rifles. They looked twitchy, too alert. Novi looked down and away. He wondered what they knew. Two elderly couples sat in front of Novi and behind Boris. A good buffer. Novi picked up a discarded newspaper and silently began to practice his Polish.

The rhythmic motion of the train lulled the riders, and after an hour, most fell asleep. Novi looked ahead to Boris, who alternated between text messages and gazing at the fields of corn and ripening wheat outside. Little by little the fields were replaced by marshes and ponds. Families of ducks paddled the ponds looking for food. The sky brightened as the clouds broke up and were chased away on the wind. For a few minutes, Novi could have been anywhere. The placid scenery and rocking of the train gradually pulled him down into a light sleep.

Just beyond the border into Ukraine, the train slowed to a crawl. Novi started awake and looked anxiously ahead to Boris, who was now asleep. There was a series of loud metallic sounds. A row of soldiers appeared ahead of the train on each side. While

Novi slept, an old woman with a huge shopping bag had taken the seat next to him. She now blocked the aisle but didn't seem concerned by what looked to him like a hostage-taking about to happen.

Novi's new phone pinged; a text message.

> *Don't worry. They're changing the gauge of the*
> *wheels. We're on one of the modern lines. Fifteen*
> *minutes instead of three hours. :)*

Novi looked up to see Boris grinning in profile as he watched the procedure taking place outside his window. Novi heaved a sigh and studied his seatmate. She looked completely wrung out. Her clothes were for winter, and obviously too warm for today's early September weather. Her hair was snowy white and her face deeply lined, her skin brown from a lifetime working outdoors. Her bag was full of everything she couldn't part with. Most of her burden consisted of clothing. Novi also saw a photo album and a brown envelope stuffed fat with paper. In the middle of her load was a small kitten, only a few weeks old. The old woman stroked the spotted fur and allowed the kitten to gnaw on her thumb as she stared absently out the window. A rigidity in her posture seemed to relax as their train was adapted to the Ukraine rail gauge. Accepting her fate, or happy to be on home soil?

A hundred metres past the gauge-adjustment mechanism, the train pulled onto a siding and shuddered to a stop. The Polish soldiers stood and turned to address the passengers. The blue-suited rail staff stood beside them. In Polish, the soldiers barked out, "Passports, everyone. Have your passports ready for inspection now!"

This caught everyone by surprise. Novi saw even Boris scrambling for his passport, the falsified Ukrainian document. The mothers, the elderly, all hurriedly fished through their bags and pockets. The doors hissed open. A soldier and a customs agent climbed aboard. Blue and yellow patches were clearly visible on their shoulders. One carried an AK-47, the other a sheet of paper. The passenger manifest. Novi dove mentally into his memory and retrieved the file on himself as Father Mike Kiriluk, a Basilian priest from Canada going to Kyiv to help with relief work. His date and place of birth, Canadian passport expiry date, and passport number.

Even with the proper documentation, his inner tension rose. He recalled trying to smuggle T-shirts home for his brothers once, following his first trip alone to a big American city. He was still a student, sent as a Canadian representative to a major surgical conference. It was a prestigious honor and a great experience. The sales tags on his contraband T-shirts gave him away. The customs agent ordered him to remove his shoes and jacket and didn't stop there. Delighted with her position, she eventually had him standing in his underwear while the rest of the passengers filed by, amused at the free show. Novi had been phobic about border crossings ever since. And he'd never again tried bringing back any undeclared souvenirs.

The agent with the list studied the Father Mike passport carefully. Novi waited quietly, counting his pulse. The agent feigned putting the passport in his pocket, watching Novi's face for a reaction. He got what he wanted; Novi broke into a sudden sweat and turned beet-red. Then he relented, stamped Novi's passport and handed it back.

"How long will you be in Kyiv? Where are you staying?"

Novi gave the rehearsed answers. "Two weeks, maybe longer. My visa is good for a month, as you see. Staying at Vydubitsky Monastery. We are in pairs; my brother is up ahead. Father Boris."

The agent took the paper visa, noted the return date, and handed it back without comment. Novi's guts unclenched.

Just before he went on to the next row of passengers, the agent had one more question. "If you're a priest, why aren't you dressed like it?"

"We were advised not to both wear the cross and robes to avoid drawing attention to ourselves."

The agent seemed satisfied with this. At the same time, one of the babies further back in the carriage began howling for milk.

"I hope you can enjoy your stay. We appreciate your help."

"Bless you," said Novi in reply.

The agent glanced briefly at the old woman next to Novi, stamped her passport, and moved on. Through the window, Novi could see other agents standing on the platform, having finished their rounds. They traded stories, laughing and puffing on foul-smelling cigarettes. Another day at the office. A calm day, too. The train picked up speed and rolled further east.

Nearing Lviv, they slowed. The station was a masterpiece of architecture, a long arcade of white stone, columns and grace-ful domes in the French Art Nouveau style. In its one hundred twenty years the station had survived several attacks in WW2 and a bombing more recently, in 2022. Part of the facade was fenced off by hoarding as the local citizenry repaired the damage to this beloved landmark. One of the uniformed rail employees looked directly at Novi, then at the floor and pulled a mobile phone from his pocket. He turned to look out the window and began speaking in an animated voice while apparently trying to stay quiet.

Novi and Boris had agreed not to leave their car to avoid being separated or left behind in case the interior was barricaded, crowded, or otherwise difficult to navigate. O'Shea said he wanted to take a few photos of the station and send them to his cloud library, then delete them from his burner phone. The other, more pressing reason for his departure from the train was to sneak a cigarette. The habit resurfaced every time he found himself out-bound; it steadied his frayed nerves. He hadn't smoked around the refugee tent out of respect for the rules set out by the Red Cross and their associated relief agencies. He excused himself from the Weatherman and stepped off.

A border guard stopped him. O'Shea showed his passport and asked where he could go to smoke. The guard pointed down the main hallway and indicated a door on the right side. O'Shea started off, wondering absently why the guard had no badge or patches on his uniform.

The corridors were roped off for repair workers, who were in short supply. He was irked in the way only a desperate traveling smoker could be. Time was tight; they had perhaps a half hour before the train would pull out again. He found the side door, gave it a push, and stepped out into a small maintenance yard. Scaffolding and tools were strewn haphazardly around a statue on a pedestal. Two men in overalls approached him as he lit up. One asked, in Ukrainian, for a spare cigarette.

While O'Shea fished in his pockets, the other stepped behind him and pressed a gun into his back. He also spoke Ukrainian, but with a strong Russian accent. "Do you have another for me, friend? No, don't reach for it. I'll help myself." The first man approached again with a Taser. Matt O'Shea was down and paralyzed before he could think. They frisked him, took his cigarettes and lighter (first things first), then his money and burner phone. His ID and train ticket, like those of the others, were under his alias.

His new acquaintances handcuffed him, taped his mouth, and put him in the shed with their tools. They tied his ankles to a post inside, next to an unconscious man in a Customs uniform with blue-and-yellow Ukrainian flag shoulder patches. The other man was bleeding from a gash on his head. O'Shea tried to scream through the tape, his realization too late. The captors beat him roundly with their shovels but carefully, so as not to kill him. Just legs, back, arms. Make him weak, but don't endanger his health. The experts at local HQ would know how to learn more from this one. The "repairmen" were excited at the bonus they'd receive for such an easy catch.

Rudyk looked at O'Shea's empty seat, fidgeted with his watch, checking it every thirty seconds. He understood instinctively what O'Shea's absence meant but now was fearful about leaving the train himself. He texted Boris: *Gemini is down.*

Boris replied: *Sit tight. Depart Zhytomyr.*

The train pulled away from Lviv station and picked up speed as it traversed fields of growing wheat, passed forests, and crossed roads. Some fields were strewn with wrecked vehicles, both military and civilian, from earlier attacks.

Boris thought quickly, mentally spinning the Rolodex of contacts he'd memorized. There was a driver in Zhytomyr, a congregant of the largest synagogue in an ancient community that had lived peacefully through centuries.

Once they were clear of the station and the city, Boris texted Novi's new phone.

Don't react. Gemini is off the train. Watch your surroundings.

Novi became hyperalert, fear chilling him, studying every face in their car. The uniformed "train employees" had departed. He texted Boris, *There were two guys in railway uniforms. They're gone now too.*

Depart at Zhytomyr. I'll figure it out en route. Stay apart from me but keep within view.

No insurance for this on the train tickets, Novi mused. *Are we safe?* he texted.

We're never safe, Boris replied. A pause, then another text. *Get used to it.*

4

Zhytomyr was an important city, a renowned centre of Hasidic Judaism, Polish history and accomplishment, and birthplace of many famous musicians and artists. The war had shut down much of its once thriving culture. Soloists became soldiers, professors were now partisans. As in so many other parts of the country, survival took precedence over art these days. Father Boris, Novi, and Bill disembarked at dinnertime. Boris's contact was Anton the driver, a man he'd met several times before. They looked for a tall bald man of forty wearing a blue tracksuit and followed him to a waiting car. He was silent until they were all seated, and the door closed. Then he became talkative and energetic.

"Rabbi Lev called me and asked for a favor! *Him*, asking *me* for help. I'd cut off my right arm for him. A real hero, an inspiration, yet he has never held a weapon. He has told us so in his sermons. I myself was dying, you know, from too much drink. My family threw me away like so much trash. Rabbi Lev understood the sadness I had, how helpless I was. A grown man! With a family to feed. No job; I couldn't be reliable for more than a month.

"He rescued me from myself. He gave me a purpose. He says we all have a purpose even if we don't know what it is. Mine is to help him, to protect our people, and then rebuild my city. I look forward every day to seeing the end of this war. Their president thinks we want his way of life. He's lost touch with reality! I don't know anyone—and I know a lot of people—I mean *anyone* who wishes to live under someone else's heel. Especially his. Rabbi Lev will tell you himself; we haven't been perfect. But who has? Has America committed no sins? Slavery? Vietnam, Iraq, Central America? Afghanistan? I ask you: even with their past, would you rather live as the Americans do, or as the ordinary Russians do? That's our choice, here and now. Such a privilege to be living in this time and making it happen for all of history to witness.

"Is Zelensky not a wonderful man? See how he stands his ground! 'I need ammunition, not a ride.' Rabbi Lev has friends like him, leaders. Excuse my crudeness, but men with *balls*! And women with balls, too!" Anton chuckled at his joke. "His friends in the synagogues here, the university, the Jesuit seminary, they are like a piece of cloth. The weave is strong in all directions. They help each other, and the whole fabric, the whole community, is stronger. Try and tear that cloth. No man can do it. Shells and bullets can't do it. That's why we'll win this."

He ran out of breath and stopped long enough to light another cigarette. Boris tried to open a window discreetly; he was enjoying the driver's chatter immensely. "So, Rabbi Lev tells me you're going to Kyiv to do relief work with the church? Are you all priests?"

Father Boris spoke for them all. "These men are parishioners who came along to help me in Kyiv. We felt uneasy on the train. Maybe I read too many novels. Anyway, the guys humored me, and we got off. I know the rabbi from his time visiting a seminary in Canada. He impressed me deeply as a thinker, as a historian, and as a man of faith. He invited me to visit anytime. I asked him if you would mind giving us a ride because you were so helpful when I came through here last time. My friends and I appreciate your helping us out today."

Novi's mind had left the car. He wandered into a forest under a grey sky, a carpet of yellow leaves, soft footfalls. Occasional cool breezes, the birds chattering in nearby trees. He allowed himself to rest, to lean his mind against this soothing vision for a while.

The drug was at a point of equilibrium with his brain; its effects declining gradually.

His vision abruptly darkened. The wind in his virtual forest gusted harshly. Clouds of yellow leaves spun upward from the birches, then fell heavily and rained down as pregnant thunderclouds delivered their billions of offspring, pelting the earth below. A roll of thunder in the middle distance shook the air. Crows appeared in the hundreds, swooping through the falling leaves, shrieking into the sky. Peace had suddenly given way to chaos. Novi pushed his mind back from this unsettling reverie. It had been captured, turned back against him, no longer his to control. Now he went to the place he'd avoided so far: pondering the meaning of Matt O'Shea's disappearance, whose misfortune was to resemble another man too closely. He sent a positive thought, almost a prayer. He wondered whether it would reach O'Shea.

What would O'Shea do with that prayer? Would the blows, the shocks, the broken bones and teeth hurt any less? What would he confess to after a few days and nights of interrogation? How long would he last? When would they kill him? Where was he now, this second? How well did Novi really know him? His life might well depend on O'Shea's pain tolerance. He breathed deeply in the rhythm Li Fu had taught him.

Anton's voice brought him back. "Canada! Second-biggest home of Ukrainian emigres in the world. I've wondered why more who left here didn't go to America. Pretty much the same, from our point of view. I've heard that Canadians say differently. That's a whole other discussion I'll bet! Do any of you guys play hockey? I wish I'd been alive to see the 1972 series against the Soviet Union! Nyet, Nyet, Soviet! Da, Da, Canada! I saw a TV show about it once. Your guys beat those bastards too."

Anton had brought two cartons of cigarettes and two spare bags of fruit. The boys would appreciate such gifts if they were stopped at a roadblock. They readied their nicely counterfeited Ukrainian passports, rehearsing their lines and personal data. They drove a short distance out of the city, and then onto a side road off the highway. "Safer here," Anton explained.

"Better not to mention O'Shea to your Kyiv hosts at all," Boris told Novi in English. "If they don't know how many we were, they won't ask. If they do, they'll ask us where he is, or ask you later, once we're gone. Your story can be that he was only intended to help us get across the border and had to turn around and go to his next assignment. Nothing more. But keep your eyes open; you might not be as welcome as we'd hoped. Call or text me if you run into any problems. In fact, all of us should delete all our contacts. You have Pavel and Iryna's numbers and address memorized, right?" Of course he did.

Anton drove silently and didn't react to any of their conversation. He'd driven through enough checkpoints to know the importance of an empty phone. They sped through the rain on back roads he knew well. They met no roadblocks all the way into Kyiv. Apparently, there was more pressing business elsewhere in the vicinity. The rain may have helped, as a cold night outdoors required a certain amount of motivation.

As they approached the city, Boris tapped a number into his phone. A female voice answered. Boris told her, "I apologize but the delivery is coming by car to your neighborhood. We won't meet you at the train station. We had problems with their schedule." He looked at Bill and Joe, eyebrows raised. "Yes, a bit of a wrinkle but we're okay. We'll meet you at the corner off the high street. Everything else is as planned."

They headed for Podil district, a pretty neighborhood of parks and old, stately apartment blocks. Novi's mental map ticked on as he recognized the area from his study materials.

Father Boris himself had stayed with Pavel and Iryna recently to recon and confirm that the streets nearby were intact, the water running and the hydro grid functioning. This time he and Bill Rudyk would stay elsewhere in the city, both having other business.

Anton drove the group to a quiet corner, just off a main shopping street that seemed incongruously busy and brightly lit for the late hour. "Keep it running, Anton," said Boris as he got out first to stretch his legs, taking a good look around the car and nearby buildings as a trained bodyguard might. Rudyk got out and did the same on the other side. Seeing no threats, they motioned to Novi to join them. Bill got Novi's suitcase while Boris sent another text message.

Around the corner came an energetic, well-dressed woman. She looked about forty years of age, carried a designer bag, and Air Pods nestled in her ears. She stopped to glance around at the buildings and nearby parked cars, smiled at Boris from across the street, and gave a thumbs-up.

She trotted across the street to meet them and offered her hand. Fresh nail polish. Firm handshake. She shook Bill's and Anton's hands enthusiastically. In a perfect London accent, she greeted them in English. "Hi. I'm Iryna. I'm so glad to meet you." To Boris, she bowed her head. "It's a pleasure to meet you again Father, even in these circumstances. Thank you for all your efforts so far. Our people are very grateful to you." Then she turned to Novi and smiled broadly. "Father Mike Kiriluk, yes? 'Novichok'? We'll take the best care of you. Please come with me. Thank you, gentlemen, for bringing him to us safely. Slava Ukraini!"

5

Iryna and Pavel had enough room to entertain a few friends and a spare bedroom in case a guest had one too many. This became Novi's personal space. Two cats came and went, sometimes leaving via an open window to the fire escape. The building was old-school, Soviet era, but solid. Iryna's touches brought charm and taste to the drab bones of their home. She favored ocean blues and greens, a bit of coral here and there.

Iryna had dyed her hair black on the first day of the February 2022 invasion, cut off fifteen centimetres, and begun wearing drab, boring clothes to evade recognition. Both she and Pavel had avoided the trend of getting tattoos, strictly from personal preference. This came in handy now. They had friends being detained in Crimea, and in the Donbas, for no other reason than the fact that they'd had their body art attributed to connections with anti-Russian groups. Sometimes the detentions were merely a pretext for border guards or police to shake these friends down for tribute money, or just an excuse to beat up a few tourists for laughs.

Over the first few days, Novi read the daily papers and watched TV to improve his comprehension while his hosts worked. Their irregular working times allowed for at least one of them to spend the daytime at home with Novi, practicing the local idioms and showing him photo albums of their travels, scenes of the Maidan uprising, and local sights within the city.

One afternoon, Pavel asked casually while looking out the apartment window, "I wonder when the Project will make their move. They seem really professional, but they don't tell us much. Do you get any sense from them?" Pavel was showing Novi tourist photos of places he and Iryna had visited on their last trip abroad, to the Costa Del Sol.

"Same as you, Pavel. I guess they don't want us to have any info prematurely that could change suddenly or get leaked or get us killed."

"Sure. Understandable, I guess. They have to leave room for error and protect their assets at the same time. We're the assets."

They heard the key in the lock, and Iryna joined them. "Ooh! The Costa Del Sol! What a beautiful place. That was one of our best trips, wasn't it?"

Novi admired their snapshots: Stretches of fine sand, movie-star suntans, carefree smiles.

"It's a long way from here now, though. I have a few things to put together for dinner." She excused herself and went to the kitchen sink.

"Want any help, Iryna?" asked Novi.

"No thanks, Father Mike. I'm good."

"Time for some studying then." He retreated to the spare room, closed the door, and opened his laptop.

Pavel's low, urgent voice drifted under the door. "You were gone a long time. Make any stops? I expected you an hour ago." Novi heard the accusatory tone on the other side of the door and froze, holding his breath.

"I was wrapped up in my work, Pavel, you know how I am sometimes. You're the same way when you have a big assignment going on. It's not what you're thinking. It never is anymore. And you should talk!" She hissed back. "You're still out all night some-times. Last week you even came home fresh from the shower. And don't tell me you were at the gym! Your workout bag was right here by the door." She paused.

"I know we're not perfect. But we have a big responsibility right now until we get Father Mike set up and on his way. I'm being serious about it. I wish you'd do the same."

Novi slid over to the bed and sat down carefully, not making any noise. He opened the laptop and with an effort plunged into a new lesson on conversational Russian. He still had one ear open.

An hour later Pavel, Iryna, and Novi sat around the kitchen table before steaming plates of potato pancakes, sausages, and sliced melons. The meal was tasty enough, but the room was silent. A street and transit map of the city lay spread open, three corners held down by their teacups. The cats wove around their legs. Pavel and Iryna took turns, haltingly orienting Novi to their district, the train station, and major sights. They ate as they pored over the map and gamely talked about local highlights. The distraction was welcome.

A loud mechanical wail sounded outside somewhere far away. Iryna's and Pavel's phones pinged once each, then suddenly emitted a harsh, grating dissonant note.

"What's that?" Novi jumped up from the table and banged his knee.

"Air raid sirens and phone notices. Don't worry. Come on, let's take a walk."

Pavel was already on his feet. His face was taut, his words clipped at the edges. He reached into the closet for their jackets. It looked like rain.

Iryna put down a fresh bowl of cat food, another of cold water. "It's been weeks since we've had one of these. Maybe the other side wants to welcome you to town, Father Mike." She smiled thinly at her joke. "Just when everyone was learning how to relax again. Yoy! Let's go."

She put a phone charger into her purse, filled a plastic bottle of water for each of them, and added these to an old yellow backpack. She handed the bag to Novi, rolling her eyes as she did so. "We're supposed to keep you out of sight. We're also supposed to follow the siren rules."

Novi followed them at a near jog through the neighborhood streets to Kontraktova Station. Across the way they could see other people—mothers with strollers and toddlers, small groups, seniors being pushed in wheelchairs—heading the same way.

There were already several hundred people underground. Mosaic faces gazed down from the high walls onto the crowd. On a normal day it would be rush hour anyway, but the station teemed now with the addition of people seeking shelter. The air gradually became warm and humid. Novi noticed a heavy contingent of police. The crowd was surprisingly quiet given the sudden need to assemble here, deep underground. Folding chairs were already being set up. Commuters kept to one side, stubbornly carrying on with their evening routines. A train rolled to a stop. Novi saw that it was nearly full. *Life goes on*, he mused.

"We can thank the Soviets for this, at least." Pavel remarked. "Most of the Metro stations are deep enough to serve as bomb shelters, and each can hold almost a thousand people. Some have been converted into schools. Others serve as storage for water and first aid supplies. The local government and the military have been cooperating well on these measures."

Iryna's phone pinged. The news service had an update. She read a news item aloud. "'All 22 drones shot down over Kyiv. Two cars destroyed by falling debris. No injuries or deaths reported.' So, a good day for the air defense."

Novi didn't realize that he'd been rigid, breathing shallowly and tensing his core muscles, until he began to relax. He took a few deep breaths.

Iryna patted his arm and said, "I don't know if it helps you to hear this, but life's much better in the cities than closer to the front line. We're very fortunate here and we know it. Electricity most of the time, trains and trams, running water. Food in the stores, even live music and art shows. And no censors, random arrests, or political jailings. That is what we fear most from the other side. That is why we must prevail."

Pavel looked down at Iryna's hand on Novi's arm. Novi saw the warning look on his face before she hurriedly brought her hand up and fidgeted with her hair.

Novi continued observing the ordinary citizens in this underground fishbowl. Some worried eyes, a few tired mothers shushing their unruly kids. The overhead PA system eventually came to life and a female voice announced that the alert was lifted. Novi, Iryna, and Pavel climbed the stairs wordlessly, reaching street level and grateful for the fresh breeze. "So, Father Mike, how do you like the sights so far?" cracked Pavel. "I bet you've never had that kind of greeting anywhere else."

"I'm really surprised there isn't any panic. People look calm considering they're all jammed together wondering for how long. No idea how close the rockets are, how many, when it'll stop. When it'll start up again. It's a lot for anyone to get used to."

"Well, we're all used to it now. No real choice anyway," Iryna said. "And everyone knows they don't want to start freaking out or it'll be chaos. Imagine forty-six stations full of panic! We've learned not to show fear in these situations. It doesn't help and it might do harm." She added calmly, "There's a great bakery around this corner."

"I'd better stay out here," Novi reminded them. "I don't want to end up accidentally on camera or something. The Metro visit was one too many."

"Okay. Pavel, can you go in for six croissants? I'll wait here with Father Mike."

"How about if you go? I'll wait with him. You know the owner anyway."

He countered a little quickly, it seemed to Novi.

"Okay, no problem." She opened the shop door and disappeared inside.

Pavel was loquacious. "First time in a war zone, Novichok? Great call sign if so. I'll admit it's been scary here many times in these past two years. We never know what's coming next." His phone pinged. He glanced down and said, "Speaking of which, I have to go meet someone about your next move. I'll go with you and Iryna to get the car."

Iryna returned from the shop with her purchase. Pavel explained that he'd need to go meet an operative with a promising lead on border transit for Novi. She looked at her watch and hesitated a few seconds. Novi sensed something amiss in that pause, nothing he could put a finger on but a vague unease.

"Okay," she said slowly. "The key is at home. Don't be too long, all right? You never know who's out these days."

6

A few days later Pavel and Iryna offered to take "Father Mike" along on an errand. They were tasked with retrieving a box full of essentials for his next steps. Other members of the Project would have assembled these necessities over the preceding few months. The destination was a forest preserve several kilometres outside of the city.

Pavel drove them westward along a busy highway, then turned away from the main road into a narrow two-lane gravel strip elevated slightly above the surrounding fields. A few kilometres further on, they were surrounded on all sides by dense forest marked by occasional broken machinery. There were burned-out tanks, personnel carriers, and a self-propelled howitzer on tracks. Up close, Novichok stared in silence at the rusting hulks. Their size dwarfed the human scale. He felt deeply unsettled by the destructive power they still projected in dormancy.

Novi's mind drifted far into the past, not for the first time. The continuous exposure to his parents' language transported him. It had been almost two weeks since his last memory boost, and he found that emotions, especially nostalgia for remote memories, surfaced too easily. In these periods he worried about being vulnerable to his own thoughts.

On weekends in late spring, like many families of Eastern European background, his family would pack up a bunch of sandwiches, apples, thermoses of coffee and hot chocolate. They would drive about ninety minutes north of the city to their parents' hometown. In Novi's childhood, the rusting machines they climbed on in fields and forests were tractors or combines, not the tools of war. The wild mushrooms were in season in late spring and early fall. The time for discovering and picking them was short. Many of the Polish, German, and Ukrainian immigrants to the prairies dreamed of the springtime for exactly this reason. The mushrooms grew near manure; farmers in the area often let their cattle wander free, within the confines of the fencing that kept them away from the gravel roads. This was scrub prairie, the same land his great-grandparents had risked everything to come to: to live their own dreams, farm their own fields, reap their own harvests. It had been back-breaking labor, gladly done for the simple reward of their freedom.

They were not serfs here; there was no tsar. Each family paid a hundred dollars for a hundred acres. It was second-rate land, full of glacial remains. Stones that broke plows. Shallow topsoil far from the richer river floodplains. This land was more labor-intensive; a strong back and expertise were required to coax a living from this part of the country. But it was theirs. To the north were huge lakes, to the south forests gave way to sweeping flat fields of grain. This was the edge of a vast agricultural heartland. They had only to work hard.

The earlier European settlers had arrived a hundred or more years before then. They wiped out many of the original inhabitants with their foreign viruses, later with their weapons. Finally, they exiled them in their own territory with their European laws. The second wave of immigrants were still better off than many who stayed behind in eastern Europe. Novichok's family land allotment was 150 kilometres north of the city. They had carried their supplies on their backs from the Eaton's warehouse that first winter, 1906. The spur line due north wasn't finished, and the small group of families arriving from Ukraine had no money for a horse.

As children, Novi and his brothers in the back seat took little interest in this history lesson. They liked to shoot cans with Dad's .22 rifle, climb the rusted farm machines, and slide down the pile of gravel at the quarry. In spring, these country road trips were bright, full of sun, fresh breezy air, discovery and exploration. In the fall, the weather might be poor, with rain and a harsh wind lashing their faces as they followed deer tracks, set up targets at the limestone quarry, or built lean-tos for shelter. But repeated often enough, the family story eventually became as much a part of them as the fresh air. Likewise, they appreciated the beauty of scrub prairie in a way that only flatlanders could.

Even as a young boy, Novi took a keen interest in the search for morels, *pidpenky*, and the other species of wild mushroom that were perfect in sauces, dumplings, and soup. His parents showed him all the major tasty varieties of wild mushrooms. They were pleased with their sons when they filled a few grocery bags with this free bounty.

Just as importantly, they also taught the boys which mushrooms to avoid. The amanita would kill you in six days. With practice, a ten-year-old boy could tell the difference. There was disappointment if the forests were too dry, or someone else had gotten there first. The ride home after a bush day was animated, then drowsy. The fresh air was a tonic for their bodies and souls. Their wind-burned faces slept peacefully all the way home. The dog slept across the tired children's bodies. They always pulled off the ticks before the drive homeward.

Today Novi and Iryna were under a sky of blue glass, wandering in a forest, searching for a buried box they'd been sent to collect. She taught him colloquial Russian phrases, and he repeated them back. Most of it was basic conversational talk, much was slang not found in books but handy for blending in. As they wandered in the woods, he found something he hadn't seen in decades—morels growing in the wild a few metres from the rusting heap of a charred armored vehicle. He waved her over to show her the find.

"S*murzhy!*" She was delighted and started to laugh. "I'll make us all some sauce tonight. It goes with anything." They had lunch kits, a few spare plastic bags, and pockets. They were soon on their hands and knees, filling them up with the fungi.

Pavel was spotting for them; he had the binoculars and a radio. There was no sign of any unwelcome activity anywhere in the region, and their intel forecast was for "clear weather." He watched his partner and the laughing newcomer digging in the woods from his vantage point 200 metres away. The familiar nausea of jealousy boiled up suddenly in his guts. They were having a real party out there, crawling around in the forest. Did she think he was blind?

Novi was almost finished picking the last morels when he noticed something else: death cap, Amanita Phalloides, growing a few metres away. This was another unexpected find. Instinctively he put a plastic bag over his hand. While Iryna finished picking another batch of morels further away, he filled a small sandwich bag with the deadly fungi. These he counted, kept separate, zipped the seal, and stuffed into his sock.

Iryna's walkie radio crackled. Pavel. "Hey, is everything okay there? We should move soon."

"We're fine. Novi just found us some *smurzhy,* so we'll have a feast tonight!"

"What about the box?" He sounded irritated.

"Ah. Damn. I'm sorry. We got a little sidetracked." She apologized and meant it. They were never supposed to lose focus when performing a Project task, even on a beautiful day in the forest.

"I'm coming over." He clicked off.

The three of them searched for a birch tree with a carved rectangle on its south side, one metre above ground, trunk ten centimetres in diameter. They were spread out, Pavel in the middle, and the breezy warmth replaced by chilly silence. The box was buried under a few boughs and a thin layer of dirt. It was Novi who found it.

Pavel looked around once more with the binoculars and actually patted Novi on the back. "Good job, Father Mike. Mushrooms and treasure!"

"Thanks, Pavel. Just want to contribute. You guys are doing so much for me already. It's my turn."

They dug up the grey metal box by hand while Pavel explained its presence here, far from the city. "We use these boxes to transmit items between Project people, partisans, and informants. We call them Torbas, or parcels. This one was only placed yesterday so it's easy to dig up. We'll open and empty it in the car. Instructions are to leave it empty beside a post office twenty kilometres away. Another team member will retrieve it and inform Command that the Torba has been received.

"Command already knows this. Every Torba is fitted with GPS. We've found several nests of spies this way, by following the movements of these parcels. Unexplained stops, side trips, delayed pickups are tracked. This surveillance is known to the field workers themselves, but not to outsiders who might come into possession of a Torba. It's a great way of catching infiltrators or transmitting false intel."

Iryna emptied the box into a duffel bag while Pavel drove. They dropped the box on schedule. The ride home was by a different route. They passed a grove of trees, half burned. Several small villages, most houses reduced to barren hulks. A large cemetery, hastily dug in what should have been a schoolyard. The school was now a crater about fifteen metres across. The roadside was littered with occasional rusting tanks and trucks with blasted roofs, flat tires, broken glass. The local people who remained had not yet cleared away all the debris. Many had fled, and others were buried in makeshift plots. The trio rode silently, each inside their own thoughts.

Back at Pavel and Iryna's flat, they admired their catch. Two different Russian passports, two Ukrainian passports, and one Belarusian passport. Michael Kiriluk. Date of birth was changed and listed as ten years more recent. The men of eastern Europe tended to look older than Canadian men; this matched up with life expectancies. Rougher hands, bent backs. More tobacco, less preventive care. His likeness gazed back at him from each piece of ID. One photo showed him with a full head of grey hair. A Russian social services card, a driver's license with a Moscow suburban address. A Moscow Metro pass. A stack of rubles—five hundred thousand. Worth less than last year, but a good pocket decoration. Handy for untraceable transactions. A list of addresses in the Moscow region. Maps: Moscow Metro, Central Moscow, Moscow Zoo. An obscure suburb. A nearby pharmacy. A church. A hockey rink. The Kremlin, Red Square, Novo-Ogaryovo. Floor plans of buildings frequented by the president. Even his schedule from one month ago, with location and activity down to fifteen-minute blocks for an entire week. His transportation and security details. Number of men per security team.

Novi observed, "Someone on the inside—deep inside—must be getting this kind of intel. This isn't guesswork."

A set of keys: a car and an apartment with an address tag. Novi asked, "Is all this prep necessary, or is the Project just really big on planning for contingencies?"

Pavel replied, "There are so many things that can go wrong that they provide for Plan B, C, D, and on. We can always discard what we don't need. It's bad news if we're caught short, though."

The reality of the Project, and his place in it, sometimes washed over Novi in a tidal wave of adrenaline. Seeing the contents of the Torba, and realizing the time, effort, money, and danger involved in assembling such things struck him almost physically. As a pure civilian, he was off every agency's radar. He reminded himself that this was one of his main assets for the Project.

Iryna was a careful and shrewd shopper, coming up to the flat with a whole chicken, potatoes, onions, carrots, cream, and butter. A neighbor had given her a litre of borsch. And of course, morels! With the power off intermittently, she cooked on a small grill on the fire escape, sharing space with the neighbors. They ate like royalty that evening, and Novi fell into a deep sleep. His mind was filled with forest memories. His extra bag of mushrooms lay hidden under the mattress. He'd counted them—twenty. What did he want them for? He really had no idea.

7

Pavel went out to work at the office they shared with other web designers, then made a stop en route home at a nurse's apartment. Lena, a childhood friend of Iryna's, understood his shopping list and gradually poached supplies from her hospital. From the start of this conflict, she had offered her assistance in procuring supplies, coordinating transfer of first aid and basic medications to the front, and to the hospitals and clinics that were still functioning, not yet bombed by the other side. She had hosted injured soldiers on her couch, some even in her bed, if their wounds weren't severe enough to preclude a little morale boost.

Lena had asked to know more about the Project and was willing to be of greater help. Iryna had gratefully declined; the less her friend knew of the Project, the safer it would be if she were to be questioned about it by new authorities in the event of a regime change.

Pavel admired Lena's dark, flashing eyes, her carefree movements, her delicate, calm voice. The stark contrast against her raucous laugh and smutty jokes. She was an amateur musician and singer, entering plenty of talent contests, even winning a few. She collected admirers and boyfriends, trading them with her girlfriends like cards. Some were her soldier guests.

Pavel was Iryna's partner, and therefore out of the running. Lena was well aware of Pavel's reputation and had consoled Iryna many times before on girls' nights. He tried vainly every time he saw her though. Keeping his skills up.

"Hope you didn't have any trouble collecting this stuff. Strictly quiet though, right?" Pavel stood in the doorway, flexing his muscles by instinct.

"No trouble at all. And I'm really careful; I could get fired for employee theft, don't forget," she joked. Nurses were in short supply; she'd practically have to kill a patient to lose her job. Seeing where his eyes were traveling, she added hastily, "How's Iryna?"

"Ah, she's great. We've been signing up new websites for translation services. Iryna had a new idea to set up a money wire transfer site with translation that would pay a small commission for each transaction. A lot of people are transferring money in and out of Ukraine and Russia these days. Traffic is through the ceiling! Big money!"

He didn't mention their houseguest. She only knew he needed the supplies "for a visiting friend."

"Nice! Please say hello to her. Tell her I'll call sometime soon." She handed Pavel a shopping bag full of miscellaneous medical supplies, the things Novi had requested. Two sets of everything, in case he dropped or contaminated anything before he was done.

Back at his apartment, Pavel handed over the bag. Novi looked at the contents and smiled. "This is great, Pavel! Your connections are right on their game. Where should I set up?

Iryna was out buying food and meeting with a client who might have good contacts in Moscow. "You can use the kitchen table and sink. More room. The bathroom counter is too small."

Pavel picked up coffee cups and a newspaper, clearing space.

While Pavel's back was turned, Novi slipped a green pill into his mouth and chewed it up, then went to the sink and washed his hands. It was great to be in a part of Kyiv that still had utilities, at least for now. Hot water was in short supply outside of hospitals, schools, and government buildings. He arranged his supplies: a vial of local anaesthetic, a needle and syringe, disposable scalpel blade, tissue glue, and sterile prep sticks. He donned the gloves, drew up the local, and swabbed the skin over the pouch in his lower left side. Pavel lit a cigarette and stood watching with interest as Novi, grimacing, drew a straight pale line beneath his skin with the Xylocaine on the incision line. He gave the local three minutes to take effect, then made the cut exactly onto the existing scar. He put a finger into the fresh gap and found the zip lock easily. He put one sterile tube of tissue glue back into his pouch with the remaining doses of memory drug and pinched it shut. Then he opened the other tube of glue, applied a thin line to each side of his incision, and squeezed the two edges together, holding ten seconds at each 2 cm interval to give it time to adhere. Finally, he placed a clean linear dressing over the incision. Pavel took a keen interest in the impromptu medical show.

Novi put his dose on the table, then cinched his belt around his ankle and started an IV line on the top of his foot. He raised his foot and rested it on the table. He hooked up the bag of sterile IV fluid Lena had sent along and then injected the dose into the bag and opened the valve to full. The bag began to deflate slowly as its contents dripped into the vein in his foot. Out of sight. A foot IV dot would never be seen by curious soldiers doing a skin search. A bruise or scab on his hand might invite questions.

The memory drug made him energetic, talkative, and insomniac for the next few days and nights. Twitchy, not exactly comfortable. He'd balance it with the pain pills he'd smuggled from home. Half of those were in his other pouch, and he would leave them there until Moscow. The Project team managers had made sure to give him the biggest homework assignments at this time; that was why the Torba contents were made available now. This was study time for final exams. Novi devoured all the reading material and mentally photographed the Moscow maps, the Kremlin buildings, and every entrance and street near Red Square. Schedules and positions of guards from three separate agencies, sample itineraries from the President's workdays. Locations of Army and FSB facilities and offices, numbers of staff in each. Floor plans were less detailed for some of the Kremlin buildings depending on the reliability of the source of intel.

He memorized the numbers and expiry dates on all his false passports and reviewed his own bio as Father Mike to be sure he knew it inside out. The name of the Metro stops at the zoo and in the suburban neighborhood where he'd be lodged in Moscow. The rest of the Moscow Metro in lesser detail. Images, addresses, directions to two churches, an apartment, a pharmacy, and an auto shop. Images of the car he was to use. After some image and number memory work, he switched to language: columns of verb conjugation, tenses, and lists of nouns—masculine, feminine and neuter. He practiced his Russian phrases some more, dozing intermittently when the pain pill took over.

Iryna came home two hours after Novi had finished his IV infusion, done a first round of study, and fallen asleep on the spare bed with the help of his green pill. Joe awoke to hear her arguing with Pavel and eavesdropped silently.

"What was it this time, Iryna? Where were you all afternoon? I need to get out too. There are people waiting to help me set up an exit for Father Mike."

"I'm trying to get Father Mike on his way just like you are. So, I went to see Father Boris. He said that from here, he can help us now that he's back. He has a friend in Gomel. Belarus. A lot of friends, actually. Border guards too." Her tone was somewhere between placating and mildly irritated.

Pavel slapped the table hard enough to cause Novi to flinch fully awake. "So, you have all this initiative without me? Why didn't you ask me along? What the hell's the point of crossing two borders? Isn't one already hard enough? I'm working on this. We can get him directly into Russia. My contact has some soldiers who are friendly to our cause. They don't know who it is we're sending in there, just a guy who could be any operative. All we have to do is wait for the right guys to be working the border crossing."

"How well do you know those people? Are you sure you can trust them?"

"How are you so sure you can trust Boris's? This is my department. Let me work it through. I've put a lot of effort into this. You started what, this afternoon?"

Iryna tried once more, but Pavel wasn't hearing any more of it. He grabbed his coat and began tying his sneakers. He hurriedly pulled on his jacket and took his phone from the kitchen counter. "I'm meeting someone right away about this, as it happens. You've nearly made me late. I'll be out tonight so don't wait up. Bye." And he was gone.

"I'm sorry about that," Iryna said to Novi, who had sat quietly in the next room. "He gets these ideas lately, and I don't know how to do anything to help. His contacts and plans are always 'better' than mine."

"Why not just run with your idea anyway, in case we need a Plan B? We can always call it off last minute and go with his plan." He was fully awake now, his brain buzzing with his boosted memory. "I'm happy to memorize two sets of instructions and contacts. Plenty of room up here." He tapped his head and smiled.

Iryna frowned. Novi had an instantaneous glimpse of her beauty; it registered and flew away. "I need to walk. I'll go get some food from the grocer's. It's only three blocks."

Novi watched her swift athletic stride from the window. Across the street, a grey VW eased into a parking spot opposite her building. He couldn't explain it but felt a sudden rush of fear. He closed the drapes, locked the apartment door and called Iryna's cell from the landline.

She answered immediately. "Father Mike? Is everything all right?"

"I don't know. Probably. A car, a grey VW parked across from the front door just now. Somehow, I feel like I've seen it before, or it's trouble. Just please keep your eyes open and come back soon."

Iryna fashioned an excellent chicken salad from the previous night's leftovers, supplemented with new greens and fresh fruit. She told her story as she chopped and mixed.

"Pavel and I met during the Maidan. He was from Kharkiv. We needed internet experts and a lot of translation. We worked together for months. We were young idealists in an ideal time for that mindset. Change was everywhere and we were intoxicated by it. The *possibilities!* So, of course, we fell in love with each other and our cause. But Pavel—these days, I don't know why he resists me so much. Our relationship is far from perfect. I guess that's become obvious. But I keep focused on the Project and our goals, and Pavel… He just wants what he wants. We have a long way to go before this battle is over. I actually pray in my heart and mind that you, all of us, will succeed in turning this around."

Iryna ate beside Pavel's empty chair. Joe's brain still thirsted for information to digest and absorb.

"Hey, Iryna, how about a lesson on vernacular?" Novi wanted to break the silence and distract them both from Pavel's moodiness and his absence.

Iryna blushed. "I don't really use the bad words, Father Mike. I believe they can bring bad luck.

I know some tamer ones, if you don't mind humoring me." She stood up to put the tea kettle on and began a short lesson about colloquial Ukrainian and Russian terms, harmless enough and helpful for conversational use. Novi's language comprehension continued to develop quickly, and he could converse at nearly normal speed already. The lesson lasted another few minutes as they cleaned up the dishes and the kitchen.

He tried another question. "So, Iryna, what happened to the last Project? We were held off for a long time. They were worried that the memory drug would stop helping me. So far so good, I guess."

She gazed past him to the blue sky outside the window.

"The first attempt failed when the support team couldn't agree on the right time to deploy their payload. He was a British MI6 man we hosted for a month while the plans were finalized."

Her voice suddenly became shaky. To Novi it seemed that she was remembering more than she revealed.

"We got him to within a few days and a kilometre of the target. He was poisoned in his hotel room forty-eight hours before the president was to appear, give a speech, and award patriotism medals in a town square. It sharpened the president's paranoia so much that he doubled the size of his personal security team.

"Nobody could figure out how the other side found him. A few of the team were sent away to join other groups. Two foreigners, a Brit and a Yank, disappeared, and we assumed that one or both had been turned. They were found separately, and weeks apart. The marks of torture were similar and not typically Russian."

There was a long silence.

"Any idea who killed them? Is there still high risk to my being in Kyiv?"

"Oh no, I'm sure not. The Project, Father Boris and his people, have eyes everywhere. Their assessment is that now is the time. You shouldn't worry."

Novi sat down to distract himself with some serious studying—the file on the team in Moscow. He absorbed the material like a sponge: the face, name, and phone number of the veterinarian who had the drug he would be using on the target, in case it became necessary to visit the zoo himself. The face, name, and number of the pharmacist near the apartment, who would assemble the equipment for Novi to access his kangaroo pouches one final time. Once more for himself, and once for the target. The auto repair shop around the corner from a small church in a faded district in the north of the city. And the bio on a man named Father Maxim.

8

Pavel was in better than average spirits the following morning on arrival home. His football pool had paid handsomely, he explained. "Iryna's out for a while and I have some time. Do you feel like coming down to the corner? I need a good cappuccino and I'm out of cigarettes. There's no finer place in the world than Kyiv on a beautiful day. The high street is full of shoppers; we'll be perfectly fine."

"Are you sure, Pavel? I've been told to stay out of sight as much as possible."

"True, but we already saw half the neighborhood in the Metro station the other night. Anyone who wants to know you're here surely already does. And we're only going to the cafe and back. I'll be with you the whole time. Aren't you getting tired of being kept in here like a pet canary? It's amazing out, so let's go!"

Pavel, at his persuasive best, held the door open and locked up behind them.

"You'll feel better just being free outside for half an hour."

They took the stairs down to ground level, exiting the lobby to the right. The street was alive with shoppers, a bustle of energy. Novi felt himself coming alive in spite of his earlier misgivings and began to enjoy the street scenery, people-watching and activity.

Pavel ushered him into a stylish espresso bar. "Good morning, Natalka. Two cappuccinos, for me and Father Mike, my friend. Thank you."

The barista, a well-dressed woman of about thirty, smiled at them—an extra sparkle for Pavel. "Right away, Pavel," she said and set about frothing milk, tapping ground coffee and heating cups. They could have been anywhere.

Pavel patted his pockets. "Damn. I still need cigarettes. I'll be right back." He was out the door in a blink.

Novi woke up shivering. A cold basement, his hands tied behind him. Underwear. Cement floor. *How did I get here? Think!* Daylight in a small high window. *Smells like mice and dust.* His brain switched on, electrified. There was enough light to see stairs, a few shelves, a bare bulb in the low ceiling. His heart rate began to rise as his situation dawned. Deep breaths. Feel the inside of your fingers and toes. Think this through. Stay silent. Let them think you're still out.

The thin mattress under him stank of vomit. Not his, he realized. He checked his limbs and joints. Nothing hurting or broken. He just felt stiff all over. No headache; they hadn't hit him. They wanted him in one piece. *So do I*, he thought to himself. He was thirsty, his bladder full. *How long have I been here?*

With a few movements he brought his bound hands in front of himself, a move the training team had drilled into him. He sat up and saw small puddles of clotted blood on the mattress where his head had been. Then he noticed the sharp burn of lacerations, one behind each of his ears. They'd been looking for chips, he realized. Like a stray dog.

He tried to piece together what had happened. A big hole in his memory chilled him. He and Pavel had gone for a walk. To the local shops. It ended there. He listened for sounds from upstairs. It was silent. His eyes were well-trained to acclimate to the darkness, and he found it easy to browse the contents of the shelves and a small workbench. The rope around his wrists was plastic—thin but strong. Could he bite through it? Maybe. But on the bench he saw a few hand tools and selected a small file. Better than nothing.

He sat down on the mattress and held the file clumsily with his feet. He scraped the rope over the rasp while keeping his hands and wrists away, listening for activity upstairs. It took him a while—how long, he wondered?—to cut through a layer of the rope and loosen it enough to free his hands. Still quiet up there? Good. He hid the rope under the mattress. Long enough to choke someone with. He was running on pure adrenaline, blood whooshing in his ears.

The window was too high and too small to climb through. Play possum and try to confront the captors when they come down? How many were there? Sneak upstairs and hope to surprise them? Maybe they'd be away. Or maybe only one. Would he be armed? Probably.

Fuck. Noise upstairs! A door squeaked, then slammed shut. Novi hid the file under the mattress. He lay down and folded his hands behind his back. He calmed his breathing. *Maybe they don't expect me to be awake yet. Maybe they intended to overdose me? No, I have value if they can get information out of me.* He shuddered, imagining how that might be achieved. *They just wanted me to sleep. For how long? My green pill habit might have saved me. Pavel. Why did he run into the corner market for cigarettes just then? Did he set me up? Does Iryna know? Is she also in danger?*

Surprise would be his best chance to leave this house on his own two feet. Probably his only chance. *Is the basement door locked? Would they be stupid enough to leave it unlocked, or is this a trap?*

The door at the top of the stairs opened. A middle-aged man in jeans and a hoodie grunted slightly. Novi watched through half-closed eyes as he limped down the stairs. *A bad leg, good news.* He carried a metal pail, a plastic cup filled with what? Water? Something rattled in the pail. The jailer glanced at Novi, satisfied that he still seemed drugged, and went back up the stairs, returning this time with a roll of toilet paper and a plate of food. He went to the work bench and placed the items together in a row. He reached into the bucket and Novi saw the cause of the rattling: A loaded syringe, cap off. Now the guard grunted again as he knelt.

Novi opened his eyes wide, frightening the man half to death. His reaction was delayed just enough for Novi to grab the syringe and jam it to the hilt in the man's neck. He forced the plunger to zero and unloaded the whole dose. A lucky shot. As he pulled out the needle a dribble of dark blood followed. Jugular. He grabbed the man's throat and clamped his other hand over his mouth. Another few seconds went by, and the man's body went limp.

The guard was unarmed but had a phone in his pocket. Novi knew not to use it. He undressed his captor. Tattoos everywhere. Novi recognized about half as related to the Wagner Group, and several more with Nazi motifs. He wondered briefly, *Who is this guy, anyway?* He put on the guard's clothes. The shoes were too big, but better than none. He checked for air movement. The dose would keep him asleep for a few hours. Should he kill this man? He didn't know yet. A strange, primal feeling rushed through him now. Survival mode, a pure bundle of senses and reactions. Scenarios played out rapidly in his head against his will. *Kill him. Get used to it. You have to do it soon anyway.* Novi listened for sounds upstairs. Tried to tune out that seductive call to release his innermost violence. All quiet outside his head. And then another voice: *Don't kill him. Just get away from here now!*

He grabbed a screwdriver from the bench and crept up the stairs. There could be cameras or mics, if not people. The kitchen was a mess; food wrappers and takeout trays, sections of newspapers. Empty vodka bottles leaned against the dented refrigerator. A jacket hung on the back of a kitchen chair—key ring in the pocket. Nobody else home, a street somewhere in a village. *Stay quiet*, he reminded himself. No obvious cameras.

The keyring included a car fob. He dared a peek through the front curtains and saw a small apartment block directly opposite. Windows faced the house. Back yard? A concrete wall surrounded a small tomato patch. He grabbed a plastic take-out bag and ran downstairs, his mind making itself up. He would tie the bag over the guard's head and leave. The sedated guard had saved him the trouble, somehow rolling flat on his back. He'd vomited and choked himself out. No pulse. Novi took the syringe and ran back upstairs.

The house was small, one floor. A sitting room, kitchen, bathroom and a single bedroom.

In the bedroom Novi found an open laptop, still plugged in, a paper printed copy of his own face as Father Mike Kiriluk, and a short bio—the same one he'd memorized. A mixed-up stack of hryvnias and rubles, an old police-style revolver and two boxes of bullets on a night table. Half a bottle of vodka. Novi took the bottle, ran back downstairs, and poured a spoon's worth into the guard's open mouth, then wiped off the blood smear at the man's neck. He ran back up again, opening the closet. An oversized jacket hung alongside a small wardrobe of worn-out clothes. He put on the coat and began stuffing his pockets. The money, gun, bullets, phone and laptop. Make it look like a robbery? Sure, if anyone would believe it.

In the kitchen a landline sat on the table. Novi put a dishrag over his hand, took the receiver off the hook and peered through the drapes once more. He had no idea how much time he had. The guard's cell phone sat heavily in his pocket. Was it safe to use? He went into the bathroom and emptied his bladder, put his head under the tap and drank just enough to satisfy his thirst.

There were several cars parked along the street. The fob belonged to a Skoda. Novi found one parked a few houses down. Now or never. He opened the front door and noted the house number, 1611, looking back only briefly. Yellow brick, one floor in a short row of the same. He faked a limp, in case anyone across the street was watching. He clicked the fob button. The lights greeted him, he hopped in and drove away as slowly as his nerves allowed.

The district was almost rural; streets sparse with a mix of apartment blocks, about equal to single homes and frequent open fields. He was settling unconsciously into a trained groove. The tank? Half full. The car seemed fine; he headed toward larger roads. He tried to reconstruct the location he'd escaped from; the information would be helpful. The laptop lay on the seat beside him. He knew the contacts list in the phone would be interesting too. A thought: *Is the car bugged? Does it have a tracker on it? It must*, he decided. The Torba'd had one. He knew better than to drive this car all the way to Iryna and Pavel's place. The phone was cheap, a burner old-style Nokia. It had no location or map function.

The sun indicated that he was going north. After about ten minutes he found an onramp to the E40 and merged into the afternoon traffic going east to the city centre. Afternoon. He must have been out for a little over twenty-four hours. Probably several doses of morphine. Now he noticed that his shoulders and quads felt bruised. The syringe lay on the floor of the car. Novi took a deep breath, took stock. He had a gun, some money. A car he couldn't keep for long, a phone he didn't dare use. He looked at the time; nearly rush hour. What did he need? To unload the car and blend in with the crowd. To get a safe phone. And call—Boris? Rudyk? Iryna or Pavel? Boris. Suddenly a tidal wave of fear, relief and bottomless loneliness struck him. He drove on, crying and wiping his leaking eyes on his sleeves. A side effect? He hoped not.

Novi reached into his mental database for a map of the Metro system, leaving the highway a few minutes later. He found a side street and parked the car, wiping the steering wheel, inside door handle, and keys with a rag from the backseat. The Metro stop was around the corner. Afternoon traffic was thickening, a jumble of vehicles and pedestrians. Better get moving. He got out of the car, wiped the door handle, left the keys, gun, and bullets. He took the phone and laptop.

Nobody paid him any attention as he crossed at the lights and filed down the stairs. A bustling, busy city on an ordinary day. No phone vendors along the way. Damn! At home they were as ubiquitous as cannabis shops. He watched the locals buy their fares from a vending machine, then copied them, fed in his ticket and followed the herd to the platform. Armed guards stood at each end; he'd expected as much. He held himself rigidly, staring at the wall opposite and trying to quell a new sensation of rising panic. The drug? Another side effect?

The train pulled in five minutes later. Novi elbowed his way aboard with the other passengers. At his stop he alighted with several locals chattering excitedly about a coming concert. He envied their energy, their youth. Again, the darkness came. What had they poisoned him with?

At street level Novi heard a man's voice distinctly above the general hum of the rush-hour crowd. "Father Kiriluk! Over here!" He looked over to see a priest waving to him from across the top of a stairwell.

Novi's eyes widened in fear. Friend or foe? The other man immediately said, "Don't worry. Boris sent me. We're watching all the transit stops. I'll call him right now. Stay there." He held up a flip phone, punched one button, and said, "He's here, Kontraktova Ploshcha. Front entrance."

Five minutes later Joe saw Iryna waving frantically from a car window outside. Boris sat beside her. Novi sprinted to the waiting car and jumped in the back seat. Pavel was sitting next to him, his face bruised and his lip split. "Man, are we glad to see you!" Pavel grinned around his injuries, then more somberly, "I feel so stupid. I nearly wrecked the whole thing for a pack of cigarettes."

Iryna explained, "Apparently, we've been watched for some time. They knocked Pavel out and stole you right off the street.

Someone's onto us, and you'll have to be moved. We're setting up a new address, but the security isn't in place yet."

Boris added, "Rudyk and I will be around the corners of the building until then. You're up to it now, right Pavel?"

"Just a little headache," came the reply. "Give me some coffee and I'll be fine."

Boris drove the few blocks to Iryna and Pavel's apartment, knuckles white. "What were you both thinking, to take a chance like that? We haven't put in all this effort to piss it away playing tourist! Pavel, do you remember the last time we got close? How disappointed we all were? Do we want that again?"

Novi wasn't sure of what he saw, but a strange look passed between the two men. A silent inquisition. He glanced fleetingly at Iryna and saw an odd glimmer of recognition as she watched the same silent conversation. Boris's eyes shifted between the road and the rearview mirror, daring Pavel to look away. *A scary guy to work for*, thought Novi. *Like his boss.*

After another uncomfortably silent red light stop, Boris spoke again. "Obviously we need to get Father Mike on his way, and fast. I have a contact in Belarus who might be a great asset if he's still in play. Iryna, it's the name I texted you earlier, keypad coded. I'd like you to work as fast as you can on that."

Pavel suddenly animated himself. "I have two leads directly across the Russian border. Most of it's all set up, and it would reduce border crossings. I'm just waiting for the final date and time options. I've been working on it for weeks."

Novi saw another strange look pass over Iryna's face. Irritation? Contempt? He felt the guard's phone in his jacket pocket, and the laptop was suddenly heavy on his knees. There was danger in this car, between his companions. Suddenly he was very tired. It didn't feel like a side effect.

The silence congealed over the last few minutes of the ride home. Iryna and Novi went inside while the others chose vantage points around the perimeter of the block.

Novi dozed on the sofa for an hour or so but started awake to Iryna shaking his shoulder, her voice low and urgent. "Father Mike! Wake up! Wake up right now! You have to see this!" His mind swam rapidly up, and he surfaced, half refreshed. "What's the matter Iryna? We're okay up here, right? Boris and Bill and Pavel are on guard."

"We're only partly safe. So not safe at all, actually." She held up the guard's phone, the screen showing the guard's contacts, Pavel among them. Pavel. Novi watched as her face changed kaleidoscopically, through rage, fear, and settled finally into deep sorrow.

On instinct, Novi pointed at the ceiling and put a finger to his lips. Iryna nodded silently. A single tear traced a slow arc down her cheek as she tied her running shoes. Novi pantomimed writing on paper, and Iryna nodded. She opened a drawer and took out a few sheets of printer paper, retrieved a pen from her purse, and looked at him questioningly.

He wrote, *They're all outside now?* She nodded again. He wrote, *Your place is probably bugged. I want to show you something. Promise not to react out loud.* Once again, she nodded, more briskly.

Novi led her toward the spare bedroom. She hesitated at the doorway, blushing, unsure of his intentions. He shook his head vigorously: *Don't worry, it's nothing like that!* He lifted the corner of the mattress to show her his prize: the plastic bag full of Amanita mushrooms. She cocked her head, shrugged her shoulders. Her gestures said, "So what? Are you hungry?"

Now he wrote again. *A few of those should be fatal. I have twenty.*

She stared at Novi incredulously, a mixture of shock and an odd sort of admiration. *Where did you get them?* She asked silently. *The forest last week,* he wrote.

Iryna pointed upwards. Novi nodded and they went out into the corridor, then up two flights of stairs. The roof was an amenity, benches and potted flowers adorning a small wooden deck. At the moment, they were alone. Iryna looked out over the neighborhood and found Boris, Pavel, and Rudyk on the sidewalks below as she roamed the edges of the deck. A grey VW Jetta sat half a block further away, windows tinted black.

"I come up here to think sometimes. I've been thinking too much lately. That car has been here most days since you got here. It was outside the Metro station when we picked you up. I think it's trouble. When I told Pavel about it, he told me I worry too much."

"That's the one that parked there a few days back. The car I felt uneasy about. It came to that spot right after you left the flat."

Iryna turned around to face Novi. Her clear blue eyes began to fill, then run over. "It's Pavel. I've tried to tell myself it's not true, that I'm just jealous. But he has a girlfriend who's offered to help him move you. To a place on the border where they'll hand you over. I was so worried when I heard you'd been taken. I wasn't at all surprised to see his name on your guard's contact list. I can't deny it to myself any longer. I'm sorry, Father Mike. I should never have been so selfish. Somehow, I convinced myself that having you here would be good for Pavel and me, that we'd come back together for the Project, and our differences would heal themselves."

She reached into her kangaroo pocket. Novi flinched, still jumpy. She showed him a phone. "It's Pavel's spare. The number is the same as the guard's contact number for Pavel. I just figured out how to open it and I'm showing it to you only once, so you'll believe what I'm telling you. I have to put this back in Pavel's desk before he finds it missing." She keyed in a password and opened a chat in Telegram. "Here. I found this. It's an exchange from last week. I've copied it and sent it to Father Boris. Don't worry about him; he and Bill can handle themselves." Novi's fluency wasn't yet one hundred percent, but he was pretty sure of what he was reading.

Svetlana: That wasn't him. It was a lookalike, a decoy. You still owe me.

Pavel: It's not on me if your people don't know what they're doing.

Svetlana: I really want to love you, Pavel. But you're making it very difficult for me. You have to show me you can keep promises better than this.

(45 minutes later) Pavel: Okay, I'll have him arrive at the crossing you proposed. I just need to know when, and I'll deliver.

Novi froze. He was supposed to stay on living here, in hiding, for the next week. "I know about those mushrooms. They'll kill in six days. First there's a severe stomach-ache for three days, then recovery, then death by liver failure. There are enough mushrooms to kill two to four average adult males."

Iryna asked again, "Kill him? Are they that deadly? Do we really want to do this?"

Novi already knew his answer. They weren't talking about his partner of ten years though.

"It's either that or I get out of Kyiv right now and find my way to Belarus and wing it. I sure can't stay here until Pavel makes his arrangements for me. It makes no sense for me to stay here and be handed over.

"I didn't have a plan for those mushrooms, but I thought that without a gun or any kind of weapon, they might prove useful. I wasn't planning to kill anyone, I swear. But now that we know he's been turned, I don't see any way around using them. Unless you know someone who would do it without even thinking twice. Maybe Pavel has enemies you don't know about."

"What did I ever know about him, anyway? We were a power couple in a very turbulent time. In those days we could have anyone we wanted, and he didn't seem to mind that we played the same game, so long as I limited myself to flirting. The field was huge, and wide open. Then the waters smoothed over, and we stayed together, at least publicly. This city is like Paris for people like us. Or Berlin. We both had our, shall I say, 'outside interests' in those days. But Pavel was less and less committed to me, and to us, every year. At the same time, he has a terrible streak of jealousy and it feels worse all the time.

"I won't say I've been an angel all the time. I've indulged myself too. But Pavel is on another level, and from there he casts stones at me. He does not forgive anything. It's just not in his nature anymore. I'm so tired of it now."

Novi sat silently listening to Iryna as she poured out her heart. He wanted to console her and cheer her up. "Iryna, you know I'm not a real priest, right?" He chanced a smile, and she got the joke. The tears and the laughter came at the same time.

Iryna's logical side began taking over. "If we don't do something about it right away, for sure you have to move. If you move, Pavel will figure out why. That puts me in a bad spot with him. The whole Project would go up in smoke. So, I think it's what we have to do. Father Boris told me he wants you to be in Moscow in one week.

"If we are to use your mushrooms, it must be soon. You say they take a few days to work?" She answered her own question. "Pavel loves a good omelette. I'll make him his last one. It's the least I can do." Her voice dripped with irony. If she had any ambivalence, it was well-hidden. "I'll step up my work with the contact in Belarus. Right now. Breakfast in the morning."

Novi understood her conflict, but he appreciated her commitment to the Project. And like him, she had no other ideas. "There are twenty mushrooms. Use ten and save the rest in case you find another use for them. Cover your hands so you don't get sick yourself."

"Fuck him. I'll use them all!" They went back inside and took the stairs down again to the fourth floor flat. It was a comfortable, whimsical place in better times. A long-haired cat purred and orbited between their feet.

Novi picked up his study materials again: the maps, photos, bios. On a spare sheet of paper he wrote, *I'll keep studying as if nothing has happened. Most of it isn't specific to a single time or place, and there are a lot of duplicated ideas in here. Until you have a clear travel plan for me, we can't let on that we know it's Pavel. I'll keep the Moscow intel away from him.*

Iryna scanned the note and nodded. She gathered up a few more scraps of paper, tore them to bits with emphasis, and flushed them.

Pavel came home at 8 AM, looking rough and complaining about having had no sleep. He had been out all night trying to make his arrangements to move Novichok north to the border. He smelled faintly of vodka, though. Iryna did a masterful job of appearing sympathetic, even contrite, for all his hard work and her seeming lack of support. She offered to make him a fresh breakfast; she had just been out shopping for groceries the day before.

She sang softly to herself as she cracked and whisked eggs, sliced green onions, cheese, and mushrooms. She folded the mixture expertly into the fluffy eggs, threw in a dash of pepper, and put a lid over the pan. The tea kettle whistled a merry note. She poured boiling water onto the bags and covered the teapot to let it steep. Finally, the big surprise: fresh strawberries, a rare treat, with heavy cream. The kitchen smelled wonderful.

Pavel was ravenous. He ate everything on his plate. Novi sat around the corner studying. He couldn't watch in case either he or Iryna gave anything away. She was doing just fine. Pavel mumbled a curt thank-you and left for their website office.

9

Gomel was a mid-sized city, close to the northern border of Ukraine. Because of its location the city served as a primary centre for supplies and strategic and logistics support. Military assets included a network of major highways, rail lines, communication activities, and a large medical school with an active teaching hospital. The country's own president was subservient to the aggressor and made his territory freely available as a training and staging ground. Large numbers of invasion troops were massed together near the Ukraine border in the weeks preceding the initial incursion.

Iryna showed Novi a bio on Doctor Miroslav Yakushev of Gomel. "Father Boris and his network have investigated this Belarusian surgeon thoroughly. They've made contact with him, and he's honored to be asked to help us.

"You have a lot in common with him," she went on. "Studied in America and holds a second degree in languages and history. Fifty-four years old, a widower. Lost his wife in a road accident, and he's lived alone ever since. Collects Western music, mainly classical and jazz, and plays the violin in a local amateur orchestra. The faculty at the State Medical University regards him very highly.

Only his closest friends and advisors know how much he detests this war. He's deeply embarrassed by his own president's role as the invading army's enabler. Before the war he had friends in all three countries. He's really anxious about the possibility of any of them being injured or coerced into fighting.

"In the weeks before the invasion began, the local government compelled Miroslav and his faculty superiors to billet Russian soldiers in their home, give them rides to and from the border, to their barracks, and to training. They wore their boots all over his house, smoked his cigarettes, drank his whiskey and demanded more. He drove them to their mustering points, watched them climb into transports, and then sent their coordinates to local Belarusian partisans. Their locations, size of the convoy, and planned date of mobilization were passed on to the Ukrainian side.

"These sleepers and Miroslav himself were invisible to the military. Operatives tampered with railway signals, sent conflicting messages and commands to Russian Army officers via hacked email accounts, and otherwise made life difficult for the invaders. Supplies arrived late, or not at all. Food, water, ammunition and reinforcements were all jumbled up."

Novi made the connection. "Was that the giant convoy? When the invasion began, a thirty-eight-kilometre-long Russian tank column found itself paralyzed on a single-lane road. It was all over the Western news, how they were sitting ducks, easy pickings for Ukrainian snipers and drones. Soldiers shivered in their tanks waiting for fuel and food rations. Hundreds came back, two hundred in zinc coffins."

"That's right. And Doctor Miroslav's band of anarchists had a big role in it.

Now, more than two years later, there are rumors of a renewed northern front reopening from Belarus. So, Dr. Miroslav is very eager to help the Project any way he can."

Indeed, rumors swirled freely in the air through the campus and in the change rooms of the teaching hospital OR suite. The surgeons debated the wisdom of volunteering their skills as trauma surgeons and instructors versus being conscripted to perform anyway.

Doctor Miroslav's partisan friends continued to cultivate a network of disgruntled soldiers in the Russian ranks. The second wave brought many who didn't believe that they were really expected to go to open warfare against their peaceful neighbors until they found themselves in the back of a truck headed for the front line.

Most of the more recently trained soldiers were country boys from the far reaches of the Russian Federation who preferred soccer, girls, and farm work. They were here out of financial necessity more than any strong interest in geopolitics or war. Poorly trained, they were cannon fodder for frontal assaults. Many lasted only a few weeks, returning east to Moscow as "200s" or as wounded men on the hospital train.

The next four days passed quickly for Novi. With his brain still basting in the memory drug, he devoured his lessons and continued learning colloquial Russian. He had committed Doctor Miroslav's story, the campus and Gomel city maps, regional highways, layout and location of a large Russian Army base to memory. Pavel's absences made it easy to conceal the most sensitive plans from his sight.

Pavel had indeed gotten violently ill from the mushrooms, but after three days, seemed to rally and emerged from the bathroom cleaned up, shaved, and well-dressed. He still looked tired from his recent bout of illness. To cover their tracks, Novi and Iryna had also taken extra decoy trips to the toilet. Pavel thought they all had a stomach virus.

Pavel popped his head around the doorway in greeting. "I'm seeing a contact to set up Novi's border crossing. We might have to drive out of the city for a while, so don't wait up. I'll be home in the late evening. See you later. Bye, Novi."

"Okay, Pavel. Be careful." Novi said. His best poker face was only good for a few seconds. The drug probably helped.

In the kitchen, Iryna gave Pavel a peck on the cheek and he was gone.

Iryna called out to Novi, "I'm starting my next round of calls. We still have to make a living, and it's getting harder to find good translating jobs these days." Iryna pointed to the ceiling, and he nodded. She was making them a fresh pot of tea. "He seems to have gotten over the flu." She frowned.

Novi joined the decoy conversation. "Good thing. I'll need his help at the border in three days." They chatted in both Russian and Ukrainian, verbal lessons to fill in the silence while they wrote down their intended messages. His speech, and his ability to follow and respond in real time, were surprising even to him.

They soon become skilled at writing quick phrases, Novi practising the Cyrillic alphabet on the fly. Now he wrote a longer message: *He should get sick again by tomorrow, the day after at the latest. I hope I'm not wrong about the mushrooms. Either way, I'll have to get away from here. He was talking about moving me out in three days. I need to disappear in two.*

Iryna wrote back: *Father Boris is still in town. He had other business here. I will hear back today about Doctor Miroslav. If it's a go, we can get you packed and away within twenty-four hours.* Over the writing, she asked him aloud, "So aside from the war, how do you like our city? We haven't let you see much of it, I guess."

He saw her laughing eyes, grinned and replied, "I don't know about the sights, but the people have been fantastic. Great hospitality, lovely company. Wish I could stay forever!"

She looked down and wrote another note. *So, we have 24 hours. What would you like to do?* She silently turned the paper to Novi. He looked into her eyes and saw raw hunger.

Iryna silently gathered the bits of paper from the table, put them in an aluminum pie plate, and set them alight with a cigarette lighter. She turned the deadbolt lock and walked slowly toward Novi. Her eyes held him captive. She took his hand, and he stood up, allowing her to lead him to the guest bedroom. She stopped just inside the doorway, turned and whispered into his ear. They were almost touching. "I promise I won't feed you anything poisonous." Then she leaned into him and their bodies connected in one fluid line from lips to knees.

They were all hands, grabbing at buttons, zippers, hair, skin. Panting, shaking, underwear on the floor. Iryna pulled away for a second, put a finger to her lips, smiled, and pointed to the ceiling. Bugs. She felt him rising between her thighs and slid her flesh back and forth on him in rhythm with her heartbeat.

He nudged her gently back onto the bed, pulled her knees apart, and knelt on the floor. He licked her playfully a few times before closing her inner lips in his mouth. She grunted, she panted, she bucked her hips against his mouth with the pillow over her face. The ecstasy washed over her in waves, subsided, and returned even more intensely. Once her second wave of delight receded, he stood briefly, kicked off the bunched clothes at his ankles, and slid himself effortlessly into her. They found a new rhythm and pressed against each other until they reached the same explosive climax together. The only difficult part was staying silent.

They rested side by side, gazing at each other in happy bewilderment. Novi had to resist the urge to laugh out loud. He had a fleeting thought: *I can always blame the drug.* After a few minutes, Iryna got up and went into the bathroom while Novi got dressed. They had work to do now; they could play again later. *Roof?* he wrote. She nodded. They climbed the stairs with tired legs.

Iryna used a borrowed Project burner phone to contact Father Boris at a local Kyiv parish not far away. He had told her of strife between two large church factions. The older institute was suspected of sheltering operatives of the Russian Orthodox Church. The Canadian priest was staying in Kyiv to gather intel that would eventually lead to the destruction of a large part of the opponent's propaganda apparatus.

Iryna explained the Pavel situation in a series of vaguely worded text and Telegram messages. In a fury, Father Boris rang her directly. "What are you saying, Iryna? Where is Pavel right now? How much of the Torba did he see?"

"Father Mike kept the Moscow parts to himself. We all saw the contents, but Pavel never had time alone to photograph or read any of the sensitive materials. He only saw the generic stuff up close. Maps, driver's licenses, passports, money. And honestly, he's hardly been here this whole time. I never know where he is."

Father Boris used another secure phone to connect with Doctor Miroslav. The situation was discussed over landlines. Various nouns were substituted to get the message across while confusing any listening ears. Novi would leave Kyiv with Father Boris, the Weatherman, and Torba materials.

Iryna and Novi spent much of the night undressing each other, exploring, tasting, enjoying, and wanting more. The inevitability of the next day drove them on; they would probably never see each other again. Novi's recent memory boost yielded a pleasant side effect: it energized him to keep up his side of their *pas-de-deux*.

Iryna woke Novi at sunrise; he'd finally dozed off halfway through the night. She had gazed at the ceiling all night in a hazy state of grateful bliss. He woke easily; this was day six since the drug, and day ten since arriving in Kyiv. Pavel had been away two nights in a row and hadn't answered any messages. She made them coffee, knowing that it was Novi's preference. His suitcase was ready at the door. They went silently up to the roof. The neighborhood was beginning to glow pink with the sunrise. From up here everything was expectantly tranquil, an early day full of possibility and promise. The birds chirped and chased each other. They could have been anywhere.

"I guess this is goodbye, Father Mike. Thanks for being such an interesting guest. I wish there had been more time to show you real life here."

"Maybe someday, Iryna. I can't thank you enough for everything—the lessons, the *smurzhy,* your kindness. I know you have a lot to think about. And I know it was hard for you to learn about Pavel and make the choice. The world might thank you someday. I'm thanking you now."

Surprising them both, he grabbed her in a bear hug and began to cry.

"It's been such a strange time. Nobody knows if or how this will work out. You've been dedicated the whole time. Thanks again, for everything."

Two blue cars waited on the street, a Ford and a Toyota. Father Boris and a driver were in the first, Bill Rudyk with a driver in the second. It was 0630h and the sun had risen, but the sky was still a beautiful pink. They tossed Joe's suitcase into the trunk and drove off. Novi sat in the back seat behind Boris and the driver, a local who knew the streets and highways from his pre-war life as a cabbie. The other bag in the trunk belonged to Boris. They would travel together again.

Novi didn't look back. He knew Iryna was inside, crying as she packed her own things hurriedly. The cats would be hiding in a closet.

The two-car convoy drove quickly through Chorna Hora to the E95. It was a three-hour drive to the Belarussian border, another hour to Gomel. Boris's phone rang. He heard a few words and spoke a few more. As they passed through the city toward the outskirts, Boris made a quick phone call. A filling station appeared along the roadside, and they exited into the parking lot. Both drivers watched as a grey VW sailed past, but in the second car, Rudyk pulled out his binoculars and saw the VW slow down and stop on the shoulder of the road.

They waited ten minutes beyond refilling their cars and spare jerry cans, emptying their bladders and drinking coffee made freshly by a smiling, matronly woman at a kiosk beside the station. The VW hadn't moved, so Father Boris made another call, this time from his second phone. All five men returned to their seats and the cars were moved behind the filling station. The bags were transferred to different cars, a green Skoda and white Daewoo.

Novi wondered suddenly how Iryna was doing. Had the VW come from her apartment? "Father Boris. Can you call Iryna, or check on her somehow? Those guys followed us around the neighborhood. What if they go back there?"

The priest pointed subtly, without raising his hand, toward the VW about five hundred metres further along the road. "Keep watching," he said softly.

Amidst the rushing wind of cars passing along the highway there was another, higher-pitched ambient sound. As the group sipped their coffee, Boris lit up a cigarette and offered the pack around. Rudyk and both drivers accepted gratefully. Boris held out an ancient Army issue lighter.

The whirring sound soon revealed its source. A small drone, about fifty centimetres in diameter, descended rapidly and stopped directly above the VW. The passing traffic eased, and there was a brief moment where the roadway was otherwise empty. As they watched, it suddenly dropped onto the car and the whole thing disappeared in a ball of fire. The car exploded, a door blew off. A hand reached out feebly through the opening, a burning head leaned sideways, and a man fell to the road. The passenger door opened, another hand hung loosely and then dropped.

They waited another half hour, through the arrivals of fire brigade, police, and a tow truck. Calls went rapidly in and out of Bill's and Boris's mobile phones. The identity of the two men in the car was now known. Neither of them was Pavel. This was bad news. Boris had seen no other option, though, since going further out of Kyiv would have revealed their direction and intentions.

Pavel would be well aware that Novi wasn't sticking around to follow his plans for entry into Russia and would go after Iryna. Novi looked at Boris again with pleading eyes.

Boris sent a text and reported. "Iryna's okay. She's with a friend named Lena, far from her neighborhood." He held up a photo on the screen as proof: Iryna with a weary smile beside another strikingly pretty young woman. A nurse she had known for several years. They stood among a team of uniformed men.

The coffee woman came out of her kiosk with a crescent wrench, pliers and screwdriver, ignoring the sirens in the middle distance, and calmly began removing the plates from the vehicles they were leaving. She smiled at Rudyk and tossed her ponytail invitingly. He blushed and said to the others, "Boris has his contacts. I have mine. What of it?"

He, Boris, and the drivers chuckled as the fire brigade sprayed a fresh round of foam into the burnt hulk on the shoulder ahead.

Novi stared at the wreckage. Boris saw his discomfort and laid a hand gently on his shoulder.

"This is what we do. What we *have* to do. Remember this. It's a kind of baptism into another faith. An eye for an eye, and more. Did those two guys kidnap you? Quite possibly. If it wasn't them, you can bet they knew the people who did. Were they just out for a drive and some fresh air? Hell, no. They were following us. Why? You can guess, so can Bill, so can I. We'd all be right. So don't mourn those guys, Novi. Just pray for them."

"Thanks, Boris. That helps. Maybe this trip is stressing me in ways I haven't grasped." Or it's the drug, he told himself inwardly. His thoughts turned to Iryna and Pavel. How could she be so close to him for so long, and never really know him? Who really knows anyone else? How do people trust each other? Such frightening ideas. Coming from the drug? Novi had to push his mind back into the present. Li Fu's techniques came to him. He calmed himself, felt the inside of his skin, breathed deeply.

Traffic had picked up and was squeezed into one lane to pass by the wreckage. A police officer became an instant checkpoint, asking drivers for licenses, destinations, travel plans and so on. The two cars joined the queue, Father Boris and Joe with their driver first, lowering the window.

Novi sorted through his selection of passports a minute ahead of time. He handed over the Ukrainian one with the closest photo resemblance. He hid the Russian and Canadian documents under the seat in front of him. Father Boris had typed a message onto the screen in his phone. The policeman read the message and said aloud, "Absolutely Sir! You will find the border crossing very easy. Thanks for letting me know."

They drove on through Chernihiv, across the rolling hills north of the city, past green plains and fields of wheat and sunflowers, the big gold-crowned heads saluting the sun. Further north they entered marshes and wetlands. Flocks of ducks paddled on the ponds; thickets of trees flew by their windows. Their escort car, with Bill and his driver, occasionally sent a text to Boris's phone. Nothing to report, just checking in. There were no more followers all the way to the border. The crossing into Belarus was effortless. Boris's mention of Doctor Miroslav was their passport.

10

Miroslav showed Joe, Boris, Bill, and their drivers his piece of the world proudly. He lived alone and kept a pretty garden of vegetables and flowers. He was well-connected to the local Baroque chamber orchestra, playing with them regularly. He operated food drives for the needy of his local church parish, sponsored annual cleanup days in the city's largest park, and taught surgery as a full professor at the city's State Medical University.

In spite of his many large circles, living alone helped the doctor choose his closest friends carefully. He often entertained visitors, some from south of the border. He kept spare license plates in a tool shed, and these were applied swiftly on his guests' arrival. He had fresh SIM cards for their phones. A group of friends who worked for the national telecom company swept his house regularly and found no trace of surveillance gear. They applied free service to the SIM cards the new arrivals had installed in their phones and added blocking software to all the accounts so there would be no fear of information leaking to the other side from them.

Miroslav took a keen colleague's interest in Novi's medical background. "You say you do minimally invasive procedures? We have a few faculty who have these skills also. Several were conscripted and sent to the Russian base hospital. They help with trauma surgery and reducing blood loss. It wasn't their choice though. For them it was 'either go and help out or forget about keeping your position here at the University.' Lucky for me, I'm too old now to be dragged out there. I'm told that the base has a nice full-service hospital, though. Guess they plan to be there a long time. Damn them."

"This is where I keep my memory now," Novi joked, showing the surgeon his incisions. He looked around, saw that the others were setting up air mattresses in the study, and added, "I have a form of dementia at an early stage. It was just beginning to show when I started taking this new drug. I don't know where I'd be right now without it."

He explained the injections of mind-boosting drug, the problems with body temperature storage, the procedure of retrieving it from his kangaroo pouches every two weeks. Novi described the side effects of sleeplessness, jittery hyper awareness, and unpredictable emotional reaction that followed his dosage for a few days afterward.

"You don't worry that you're losing your own self? Does it take the anxiety of making a terrible decision from you? Do you feel responsible if you do something I might call unethical? Because this is an interesting moral question: if your actions are dictated by a chemical, whose actions are they really?"

This was exactly the kind of thing Novi loved to debate, right up there with hockey and politics. The two men moved into the study and joined the rest, still deep in conversation. Miroslav retrieved a hidden prized bottle, missed by his uninvited guests earlier in the year: Crown Royal Canadian whiskey.

"Have you ever heard of this stuff? I haven't tried it. It's been awaiting the right time. Tonight seems perfect!"

Novi, Bill and Father Boris exchanged knowing looks and Bill deadpanned, "Yeah, we have this back home. It's not bad, I guess."

Boris countered, "What do you mean, 'not bad'? It's terrific stuff! How in the world did you come by that?" He studied the label. "It's thirty years old!" Better have it tonight, or it might get too old to drink!"

Novi couldn't resist a poke at Miroslav's argument. "If I perform a criminal act while under the influence of that chemical"—he pointed to the ornately shaped whiskey bottle—"is it the drink or me who should go to jail?"

Bill Rudyk put his hands over his eyes and feigned a headache. "Ugh. Stop, you guys! If I listen to any more of this, I'll never want to drink again!"

They all laughed and held out their glasses. The banter was a welcome relief from the morning's departure from Kyiv and the killing Boris had ordered up as easily as one might get a meal from Skip the Dishes.

They sat down in Miroslav's dining room. Portraits in ornate wooden frames gazed down on them from the walls. Maimonides, Vesalius, Shevchenko, Dostoyevsky. Dvorak, Tchaikovsky, Beethoven and Bach. His heroes. Novi was again struck by a sense of kinship with their kind and well-read host.

Father Boris offered grace before they ate. "Heavenly Creator, you know our world, our hearts and our struggles. Hear the pleas of the suffering, strengthen the hands and the resolve of the brave, and hold us all to the balance of right and wrong. We ask this in your holy name. Amen."

They enjoyed an excellent dinner of roast beef, *pyrohy*, garden vegetables, and cognac. The food had appeared almost magically, prepared by unseen friends and delivered earlier that day. The providers had no advance knowledge of the identity of Miroslav's guests. As they ate, the talk turned to next steps. Miroslav had met and befriended several disaffected soldiers during the initial Russian buildup of troops and machinery near his city. They had, in turn, introduced him to some of the officers who had voiced displeasure with the higher command. Now Miroslav's connections were tightly bonded.

"I know several of their middle officers personally. Many of them and their men are desperately unhappy to be here. They know full well what happened to the first wave of the invasion in 2022. Many would run away if they could. They're crowded into tents. Training consists only of deprivation or unloading supplies and equipment from supply trains. They have no clear idea of what's planned for them. The higher officers aren't much better off.

"The wounded get patched up here if they're not too seriously injured. The worst ones get loaded onto the return train going back east, to a big base outside Moscow. The mild cases go straight back to the front, just east of the Russian border toward Sumy. Active soldiers, fighting men, would be missed if they ran off, so they're guarded and counted like cattle. Or sheep. Many want only to go home to their families in the far republics of Mother Russia.

"Medics and chaplains have a bit of freedom as they're officer class. I have met two chaplains who are due to be rotated back to Moscow. They're heartsick about what's been perpetrated in the name of their church, and they're willing to help us. The next train leaves in two days. It's a stroke of luck. I've sent these two men a message to gauge their interest in deserting."

Miroslav's plan was to swap the chaplains for Novi and Boris, keeping the head count normal, and have them travel back separately shortly after to rejoin their new assignments. He needed to confirm that they were still willing to give up their seats and to stay with the doctor for a few days. They spent most of their time raising the spirits of wounded young men who had found themselves far from home. Some with life-altering injuries, missing a limb or an eye. Others with terrible moral confusion when they learned what was being demanded of them.

Miroslav and Boris went out for a walk around the garden after dinner, taking turns chatting with the two chaplains on Miroslav's phone. The Russian chaplains agreed to come by for a visit, meet the two men who would replace them, and learn from them directly why they needed to take the train ride. They were stationed close to Gomel and could be there within an hour.

A green jeep-like army truck pulled up as the sun began to set. Miroslav had suggested moving their two-car convoy, partly to make room on the drive and also to avoid the cars being unnecessarily seen by anyone not essential. It was a matter of habit. Two men in black climbed out, both younger than Novi and Boris had expected. Mid-thirties perhaps. They wore big silver crosses and lanyards with photo ID around their necks. The men inside looked at each other in dismay. Photo ID! They knocked on the door and were ushered in by a smiling Doctor Miroslav.

"Brothers! Welcome again. I have some friends here to meet you. Bill, Vitaly, Boris, Mike, Andrei. Come and meet our divine helpers. Yuri, Petro, these are my guests. Boris and Mike are going to Moscow for some extra work."

Miroslav poured them each a hefty glass of amber liquid from his bottle of cognac. They accepted gratefully and took deep sips, sighing appreciatively.

Miroslav said, "Brothers, thank you for offering to be of service. Let's go to the parlor and sit where we can be comfortable. Comfort is a luxury in times like these. We may as well enjoy it whenever we can." He addressed Boris and Novi directly. "I'd like to ask the others to keep busy setting up space to sleep, and to take a look around the streets nearby. We need as much privacy as we can get, just for a while."

Boris intuited another level of sensitivity for what was coming and left the room for a minute. As he returned and took his seat, they could hear the others putting on their shoes and jackets, Bill covering his shoulder holster and checking his weapon.

The door closed quietly, and Novi silently assessed the remaining guests: Boris, Yuri, Petro.

Yuri said, "Not every Russian, even among the Army, agrees with this attack on a peaceful neighbor. Many don't agree with much of anything about how our society treats those who have the courage to speak up or to live their lives differently from the president's wishes. Petro and I have taken vows to serve God, and to serve our Motherland. But we have also taken vows to protect each other. To serve each other."

Now it was Petro's turn to speak. "And to love each other. We struggled with learning and accepting our true selves for years before we met. I denied myself to myself. Like Saint Peter three times denied his Master.

"We came to the priesthood for the same reasons: We couldn't believe that a just and loving God would turn His back on so many good souls for no reason beyond whom we love. What kind of world, what kind of God, would punish anyone for love? We both realized that regular family life, with wives, children, homes and jobs, would be a nullification of our real selves. We met in the seminary, learned how identical our thoughts and feelings were. We graduated, went our separate ways, and found each other here again, in war. It is the happiest part of our fate. We are two among many who wish only to be of service in the world. Our position has allowed us to be mischievous without killing. Our contribution has perhaps been helpful in reducing the amount of death and injury to the people on both sides of this terrible situation. We truly hope so."

He reached for Yuri's hand as his voice began to quaver. "Neither of us wants to return to Moscow. We have seen the things you have read about. Things too terrible to describe done to human beings by human beings who listen to orders. Orders received and given by other human beings. We will be sent back to a front line where the killing has intensified. We have been ordered to make the young men believe that they are doing the work of God. The hypocrisy is too much for us. The shame is far greater than the president's view of us and how we live. So, you are welcome to take our places on that train for whatever purpose you have. Miroslav is a great man, and he has assured us that if you succeed, this war may end sooner than if you do not ride that train."

Yuri added, as he squeezed his partner's hand, "We are as well-connected as any local Russian Army members in Belarus. You will need to pass security to get aboard the train. We can get new ID tags made for you tomorrow and have you ready to ride to Moscow in a car full of wounded and distressed soldiers who need the comfort of your presence. You must play the part: hear confessions, forgive sins, pray with the men. It's an all-night ride. There will be no border or customs, but you must be ready for this trip. In your hearts and souls. Can you trust us?"

Boris gazed out the window onto the garden. Sparrows frolicked in the trees, and robins looked for worms in the grass. The setting sun shone onto the world and made long shadows. Leaves whispered to each other at the edge of the garden. Novi saw a tear fall silently down Boris's cheek and disappear into his black beard. He looked at his feet and saw his own vision blurring.

How life must be in Russia for these men and for so many others, he thought. Just living was its own act of courage. He felt humble and unworthy beside them. "Boris, I don't know about you, but this is exactly why we must continue on and do what we have been asked to do. Gentlemen—brothers—I hope you can make me a great fake ID. I'm one hundred percent in for this. Teach me quickly what I need to know. Boris is a pro; I'm an amateur. But I learn pretty well on short notice."

The younger men were visibly relieved. In their world, such confessions as theirs demanded personal conviction and bravery. They had taken a huge risk merely to declare who they were. Their plight was not lost on their listeners. They all understood why the others had been sent outside.

11

Boris's phone pinged with a message. He put down his glass, lit up a cigarette and opened the message. His eyes widened. He looked at Novi and seemed to see right through Novi's eyes and into his soul.

"Holy shit! Pavel's dead. He was found comatose in a car in Kyiv. No cause known yet. My medical friends suspect poisoning but don't know the agent yet. Any ideas, Novi?"

By now Novi had finished off a glass of cognac and almost another of Miroslav's Crown Royal. His face flushed, and he felt sweat begin to bead his face. He took three deep breaths and composed himself. For a split second he thought about playing dumb and trying to lie his way past this. He could think of no advantage in doing so. He cleared his throat.

"Pavel and Iryna were having a running disagreement about how to get me into Russia. He kept insisting on using a contact he knew and going straight into Russia in the company of some soldiers. Iryna found out that he was being used by a Russian woman. He set us up on the train. Matt O'Shea was taken because he looked like me. Because Pavel told them who to look out for."

He looked at the others. "Pray for O'Shea, guys. His sin was looking like me. God only knows where he is, or if he's even alive. The only good thing here is that he'd never be able to tell them exactly where we are now, or how we're going into Moscow."

Boris asked gently, "So, how did you do it, Novi? Some medical thing?"

Novi took a deep breath. He related the story of their trip into the forest, the Torba, and the mushrooms he'd remembered from childhood. The Torba, it turned out, that had been planted by Boris's partners in Kyiv. How Iryna had cracked Pavel's phone and found him out. How she made the omelette. How he and Iryna pretended to have a stomach flu to mask the first round of the poison's effect. Finally, Iryna's help getting Novi ready to flee the city, alerting Father Boris, and thus finding Miroslav as a safe harbor on short notice.

The others listened silently until Novi had finished. It was Petro who said, "All right, Novichok! First lesson is how to hear confessions." He got a good laugh, and the tension was broken. Novi spent the rest of the evening practicing the rituals and committing his lines to memory. In Russian. He put down his whiskey glass and asked for water.

He remembered going once, almost twenty years ago, to St Peter's Basilica in Vatican City. He was on a tourist trip to Italy, with a companion who would one day teach him a harsh lesson about the pain of betrayal. In a fit of guilt, hope, or religious fervor, he'd gone to the confessional in the Pope's own parish.

It was like nothing he'd had seen before. Rows of bingo-hall tables had been set up. One whole side was staffed by Italian-speaking priests, the other tables showing little flags to signify the language spoken by the priest staffing the table. German, Korean, Tagalog, Spanish, French, and several others. The first English-speaking priest waved Novi over. He sat directly across from his interrogator, who looked straight into his eyes. He felt naked, exposed, already shamed, and doubting the wisdom of going through with it.

Novi began, "Father, forgive me for I have sinned. It has been about five years since my last confession. In that time... Well, the main one is that several years ago I left my wife."

The priest recoiled. His head turned sharply away as thought he'd been struck physically. "I see. And have you taken another woman?" Novi's girlfriend watched from several metres away. A knowing smile played faintly on her lips. Novi, now flustered, stammered, "Yes, Father, but not until after..."

The priest jerked his head again, the other way. As if Novi had slapped him. The priest spoke with a flinty low voice. "I cannot give you absolution. You must see your own parish priest. Go now!"

And that was it. Novi sat stunned for a minute, but he was out of quarters, euros, or whatever currency the dead machine in front of him would accept. The priest remained fixed in position, facing the far wall. Novi felt foolish, and then suddenly nauseous. He got up to leave.

It had now been eighteen years since his last Confession.

Yuri took photos of Novi and Boris with his personal phone and sent them to a friend of Miroslav's who operated a photography studio. There was no accompanying text. Miroslav used his own phone to send a text explaining the purpose of the photos. This friend ran a healthy side business creating illicit passports for those who wished to flee quietly across the border to Poland. He had access to a nice library of documents—like Russian Army ID—that proved useful to Doctor Miroslav's mischief-makers.

The whole group laid low for another day and night. Miroslav and Novichok (the whole group loved the irony of that call sign) enjoyed some rambling philosophical discussions. Boris and the others made plans for the return of Bill Rudyk and the drivers to Ukraine. The same border crossing was open to them, and they were eager to get back to Kyiv. Bill would go back into hiding, and the drivers Andrei and Vitaly would go home to their families and await their next orders from the Project.

Yuri and Petro's photographer friend was highly skilled. Her fake ID for Novi and Boris would have made any teenager proud back home. There would be no database on the train, no way for a commanding officer to ascertain that these men weren't who their ID claimed them to be. The ID tags were a perfect match for the ones Yuri and Petro wore, aside from the substituted images of Novi's and Boris's faces. It was a matter of pure luck that Novi's face hadn't seen a razor in almost three weeks. Beards were part of the uniform for the Orthodox priesthood. Boris, of course, came pre-equipped.

Petro and Yuri were hardly alone in the camp as objectors to the "Special Military Operation." Rumors filtered back into the camp, the body bags returned in refrigerated trucks, the wounded unloaded from vehicles of all types. Some were ferried straight out to civilian hospitals for major surgery. Yuri knew several junior officers who would be on the train back to Moscow. While they weren't close enough to know his life story, they shared his opposition to the war. They were indifferent to the trade of one pair of priests for another. Anything that would keep them alive and whole was fine.

Once again Novi clicked the pieces of intel into the mental picture in his mind's eye. His memory pathways were so well-used that adding more factual material was almost automatic. Knowing the size, layout, conditions, and appearance of the next destination helped him keep oriented in each moment and reduced the chance of being thrown by surprises. Where the base was located, whose name to give as an entry reference (Sgt Luchenkov, 112th Infantry, rotating out for rest alongside his wounded men). How many soldiers. Where to find the rest of the clergy (and whom to avoid, since they looked nothing like the men they were replacing).

The camp was situated in a series of fields along a stretch of E10 highway, surrounded by farmland and about a kilometre from the road itself. A rail line nearby had been linked to a spur line and troops, food, supplies and ammunition were brought here almost daily, offloaded into heavy trucks, and driven south.

Just a few days into the Special Military Operation, some of the cars on each train became "200." Early in the campaign, the cold weather had helped prevent the bodies from decomposing, but now, more than two years later, the fighting had locally resumed. In the summer nature didn't help maintain air quality. There were 12,000 men stationed in the encampment, row upon row of eight-man tents and prefab barracks that held 4 officers each. Each quadrant hosted a command centre with electricity, Wi-Fi, meeting and briefing rooms, wall maps, and large-screen TV.

The soldiers slept in tents on the ground and had been doing so since the first men arrived in January 2022. Services were centralized within the camp. Plumbing and heat were only available at the hygiene stations, one for every two hundred men. There would be about sixty of these still functioning. The plumbing was hurriedly patched into the city's regional infrastructure, the hydro connected to the local grid with maximum speed and minimum care. There was a cloud of stink about fifty metres wide surrounding each of the hygiene stations.

At one end of the camp stood a large modular field hospital. It was equipped with running water, diesel generators, an imaging and triage centre, and two operating theatres running continually. Originally intended to be temporary, it had become a semi-permanent building over the past two years.

The entire site was now converted from a training facility to an active rearguard battle station. About two hundred men were in hospital with various wounds. Amputations, head and facial injuries, burns. Some were blinded by shrapnel, a few paralyzed by spine injuries.

Others were hollowed out by the sounds and the terror until they couldn't fight anymore. The top brass had no patience or treatment for shell shock. These unfortunates were assumed to be malingering and singled out for special duties. Emptying out the cisterns below the rows of latrines. Hauling buckets of waste, deliberately overfilled by leering non-coms. Shining the officers' boots. Burying the medical waste from the field hospital, the amputated limbs, and occasionally a body or two if the 200 train was too full or losses occurred in the field hospital. Feeding the soldiers whose injuries made it impossible to feed themselves. Cleaning up their waste when they couldn't get bedpans fast enough.

These tasks were felt, by the generals and colonels, to be therapeutic. Exposure to war heroes would show these mamas' boys what real men could handle. Or at least, incentive enough to prompt a speedy recovery and a return to the front line. Of course, these weaklings weren't given any access to weapons or any assignments that might allow them to drive vehicles. There was no escaping, only waiting for the order to be shipped like cattle to the next assignment. The front line had returned with a vengeance.

Yuri felt that their best chance was to go straight to the train, stay there, and await the arrival of the injured men who would be their travel companions. The train would fill tonight with the injured, the shattered but still walking—and the spiritual and nursing help they would need for a nine-hour train ride to Central Command outside Moscow.

12

The Russian service vehicle resembled a Jeep. Petro and Yuri retrieved it from the garage where it had been kept out of sight. Boris assured them that he could drive it and took a few laps around the block with them to prove it. It was a four-speed manual. There were no doors, a canvas roof, open sides. In another context it would have been great fun to play around with. Here it was part of Boris's and Novi's disguise.

Yuri, Petro, and Boris had taught Novi enough of the sacrament of Confession that he felt comfortable with administering it if necessary. Still, he was apprehensive about hearing the battlefield sins of men he'd heard shocking stories of depravity about.

Would he meet these perpetrators, or were they already moved on? Were these the hardened, trained, willing soldiers? Or the soft, untrained, misled cannon fodder? Yuri and Petro didn't know which sort of fighter the train was carrying back to the capital.

Where did the rationalization that "I was following orders" end and personal responsibility begin? The only common factor among them was that they had been injured, some seriously. These were young men who in another world might have been farmers, fathers, athletes, husbands. Here they were sick, maimed, damaged goods. What awaited them in the civilian world? A hero's welcome in the hometown, then a drop off the cliff of hope. A harsh life, limited career choices in a crumbling and isolated economy. Meagre army pensions. Abundant vodka and cigarettes.

The lucky ones would have a wife who could stay with a man with no hands or one leg. These would be men in rage, or men spent and broken, lives amputated like their limbs in just a few short months of service. What would happen to their attitudes toward the Special Military Operation?

Novi and Boris rode silently toward the base, their false credentials dangling beside their silver crosses. Which was heavier?

Boris again sensed the distress of his traveling partner, an older man inexperienced in this arena. Boris was blessed with a deep understanding of what made people who they were. This was the man who led a double life back home. A source of solace and comfort to his parishioners. They had no idea how many people he'd killed. Neither did he. Boris would shepherd Novi carefully through the next day. He had a meeting planned for Novi and himself with a Russian Orthodox priest in Moscow.

They drove south in silence for several minutes along the P-150, leading toward Ukraine's border, the same crossing where Boris's text message had opened the gate as if by magic. They listened to their own thoughts, the tires, the wind. Novi was getting more apprehensive with each passing kilometre.

Boris knew there would be talk. It came after about ten minutes.

"How do you do it, Boris? You never seem to get into a flap. People can always reach you when they need to. It was an accident that Pavel turned out to be on both sides. Iryna was really in a panic when she searched you out. In no time, you gave us Doctor Miroslav. And he gave us shelter, contacts, everything we need to take the next step. Is this the usual way these things work out? Because it feels to me as if we're bouncing around like pinballs, between good and bad luck."

Boris thought for a minute, lit a cigarette. Inhaled and exhaled. His pauses were when everything happened. He offered one to Novi, who declined.

"I knew even as a kid that my life would be different from the way other kids grew up. I felt different. I thought about different things; never gave a shit about whether some girl liked me, or if my family could afford a better school.

"Our family moved a lot. My father was military. Our life was random. My mother didn't miss him when he was away. I'm sure she hoped many times that he wouldn't return from a deployment, or that one of her other friends would take us away from the base. When he was home, they fought like cats and dogs. My sister and I were always afraid of something. Of him coming home, of him not coming home. Of their fighting, of their silence. Of moving again, of staying.

"I retreated into reading. The bases always had great libraries for a kid with my interests. I got hooked on war, and the place of war in history. I would have been labeled a nerdy kid, but I was bigger and stronger than just about everyone in every school. So, nobody messed with me. I had girlfriends in high school, but I was too full of some sense of urgency. Moving around a lot, never sure whether I'd have a close friend, I got to be good at anticipating best and worst cases. I'm a born planner, I guess." He laughed at his memory.

"Eventually, I chose the priesthood, or it chose me. I was sixteen when 9/11 happened. I wanted a place to derive belief from, a sense that fallible humans weren't at the controls. It was a way to preserve traditions, belong to something and believe in something so much bigger than my own small concerns. So, I read religious texts. The Bible, the Koran, the Gita. Books on Buddhism, the lives of saints. I wasn't satisfied even then, but those stories—wandering, seeking, belief—showed me my path. I chose Christianity by default; it was how I was raised and much easier to explain to my family than joining the Hare Krishnas or something. My belief in a higher creative force is unshakeable. For me, the fault in specific religions is that they all insist that they're the only ones who've got it right. That automatically sets up conflict. The sermon you heard was an aberration in a dark hour. I'm usually much more peaceful!" He smiled.

"Soon after I received my Holy Orders, I saw what was happening in Crimea and offered myself as a translator, driver, whatever they needed. I wanted to see the old country; my parents had been very strict about us learning the language and not just enjoying the food. Here was a chance to serve and learn.

"The US military and CIA were all over Ukraine at the time, gathering intelligence. They put me to work, connected me to CSIS, filled me up with bravado. I was a clean slate for them and had a perfect cover. Ukie priest! Fluent in both languages. A decent physical specimen, and still young enough to be of service perhaps for decades. Then I met Carter, and I realized… *this, this* is where I need to be. Travel, excitement, the thrill of going behind the curtain to make real things happen in a real world. To make positive change without being outed. My identity—non-American, an ordained priest—made me even better suited to the things they asked me to do.

"I have been forced to kill people in order to protect myself or a mission. I prayed about it, I sweated buckets about it. When it actually happened for the first time, it was like… nothing. The fear was way more intense than the experience. I was just a few years out of seminary then, full of an energy I didn't really understand. If I'm to be honest with myself, I still don't know what motivates me to keep doing it. But right now, in this time in history, I can't stop. I'd never forgive myself if I left a gap and trouble leaked through it.

"I love inspiring my parishioners to do good things, to be better humans, to care about each other and the world. The war makes that part of my life easy. Everyone is on the same page, we all feel kinship with Ukraine and want to see justice done, our country and its traditions survive. Has Ukraine been perfect? No, but neither has anyplace else. So, it's a different kind of clean slate.

A testing ground for proving that individual lives and freedoms matter enough to fight back with everything in our power. It's gratifying to see so much support for them from the West, or the Free World, or whatever they call it these days."

He went silent for a while, lit another cigarette, and gazed at the vehicles ahead. Ordinary people doing their ordinary things on an ordinary, cloudy late summer day. It looked like rain might come. Now he was back in work mode, all business. "We'll have to limit our interactions as much as possible with the regular soldiers. Try not to speak too much, just introduce yourself as Father Yuri and ask them how they're doing, or how they're feeling. Listening is better for them and for you. Keep your Russian passport handy at all times. If someone asks to see it, try to deflect. Don't forget, the passport is for Father Mike! Chances are pretty good they'll just tell you about where they came from, or what happened when they got injured, or how worried they are that life won't be the same for them. Don't offer any medical advice. Don't offer to hear confessions unless they ask. It might be something awful you'll wish you never heard."

They had arrived at the gate to the base. Boris looked at Novi and said superfluously, "I'll do the talking."

13

Cameras on shiny metal poles were aimed at the doors and license plates. Two armed men stood at the window, Russian insignia on their shoulder patches. One aimed a rifle at Boris while the other inspected their tags. Boris had assumed a pleasant half smile, almost as though he were greeting worshippers. If he was feeling at all nervous, he was hiding it like a pro, thought Novi.

"We're with the hospital train. Went to town to see the cathedrals. Leaving for the capital this evening."

The guard wasn't interested. He was looking at photos his girlfriend had sent to his VR Kontakte account. They weren't the sort of thing he'd care to show a priest, so there was no conversation beyond, "Okay, come through. Go straight to your own detachment's motor pool, park the vehicle, and board the train. No detours."

"Thank you," replied Boris. He guided the vehicle forward along a two-lane trail through the forest to a large cleared area another half kilometre on. At the far end of this cleared field, beyond rows of identical tents, were a series of low prefab buildings that served as mess halls, offices, logistics, warehouses, armories and strategy meeting areas. There were rows of equipment; tanks, APCs, trucks, flatbed trailers for carrying shells and other pieces of weaponry. The lot was immense and held something close to two thousand pieces. At the far end, beyond the field hospital, was a pair of locomotives linked together and painted in the olive drab of the army.

A white letter Z was painted on the front engine, apparently by hand. The engines were connected to a train of twelve passenger cars and ten freight cars. The last two of these were marked with "200" in black numerals. They were edged with a small rind of frost at the corners.

Boris parked their truck at the end of a long line. They got out and fetched their bags from the back. Miroslav had reminded Novi to leave his original suitcase with extra passports built into the sides in Gomel. No regular soldier would be seen wheeling a piece of Western luggage around the base, or onto a train. They walked briskly, side by side, toward the train, just a hundred metres away. Novi's heart hammered wildly the whole way; Boris looked calm as always. Novi breathed deeply while they walked.

In Russian, Boris kidded with him, "See, Novi? This is easy stuff. You worry too much."

Novi laughed nervously, not at all comfortable with where they were. The train was unguarded. A great piece of luck. More time to get oriented. They walked the length of the first three cars, finding them empty. The carriages were outfitted with brackets to hold stretchers in place, hangers for IV bags, a nurses' station for the medics to write notes in charts. Each car had capacity for twenty soldiers, plus space for medical or nursing personnel.

Novi slipped a green tablet from his pocket and slid it under his tongue. He knew he'd feel better in fifteen minutes. He reminded himself to breathe deeply and relax. Departure time was in one hour. They sat on a bench seat and gazed out the window. A few minutes of reverie were snapped by a voice behind them.

"Welcome aboard the Moscow Express. Sgt Vassily Luchenkov, 112th Infantry. At your service."

They turned to see a jolly-looking, bearlike man towering behind their seats.

"Father Yuri told me there had been a change in his travel plans. He's been a great help with my men's nerves, and I owe him one. My own men will be on another train, so his absence will not need explanation. I've arranged things so none of these men on this train will miss Father Yuri or Father Petro or wonder about your ID not making sense. Nothing makes sense around here anyway, right?"

He laughed out loud heartily.

"I'm not even a real soldier. Many of us here were something else a few months ago. Yet here we are. Lucky to be alive and in one piece. I don't think you'll have much to do. We're riding all night, Moscow in the morning. I'll get one of my men to bring you food. This isn't luxury travel. Today it's ham and buckwheat. Same as yesterday. It's a weekly special because it's the same shit every day all week."

He chuckled again, delighted at his joke. Novi and Boris couldn't help but smile at his infectious good nature.

"Best to use the latrines behind the tents before we leave. The plumbing on these trains is usually blocked within the first hour."

Novi considered this more carefully than he might usually, then nodded toward Boris. "How about it, Padre? A quick break, and then a hot meal."

The three men stepped off the side door to the ground, watching for rough spots and followed Luchenkov's direction as he flagged down one of his corporals. The busy men around them paid no attention. The short walk was uneventful. Inside the stall, Novi slid another tablet from his pocket and chewed it up, holding the paste under his tongue. He sat a few minutes and went out to meet Boris.

Back on the train a young private held two tin plates of warm buckwheat covered by thick slices of ham. Better-than-average army food. He saluted and left; they outranked him. Novi was suddenly famished and sat down on the bench seat of the rail car.

Boris held up his hand. In his best Russian he said, "Wait, Novi. Do you know if the cook even washed his hands?" He sniffed the plate, turned a slice of ham over. He seemed satisfied. "Guess we'll either eat and survive or not, or not eat and go hungry. If this has been messed with, we're dead anyway. They would never let us off the train alive. Supposedly only the sergeant knows we're not Yuri and Petro. It's all up to him."

Boris said a small silent prayer over his food and dug in. Novi watched for a minute, marvelling at the other man's confidence in his decisions. Then he began stuffing kasha into himself. The train began to fill up, stretchers first, borne by careful junior men. Some occupants were sleeping, others staring up at the sky or curiously gazing around. Some missing limbs. Some with bandaged faces, either burns or shrapnel. Loading was quick and efficient. They were to leave by dusk. The able-bodied and the medics came last. The steps were withdrawn, and the train began to lumber slowly out onto the main line from the side track. A soft breeze blew in through the open windows over the faces of the train's occupants. As they picked up speed, windows were slid shut.

Novi and Boris were seated surrounded by wounded men, some apparently drugged for the trip. An unexpected piece of good luck. But one man near the back of the carriage grunted and grimaced when the car bumped over the rails. He was missing both legs below the knees. His dressings were stained with fresh blood. The medic in Novi couldn't tolerate the legless man's groans. He stood up and lurched his way to the end of the carriage. Boris was engaged in a lively conversation with another injured man who had a bandage over one eye. Novi summoned up his freshly acquired Russian, rehearsing his lines as he held the handrails. He did a rapid mental calculation of the calendar, another of the tablets in his pocket. A small battle played itself out in those few seconds. Should he part with a dose of his precious opiate? To this stranger, technically an enemy? His estimate told him that he could spare up to four pills without interrupting his own needs. He debated the risk of blowing his cover, the soldier blurting out anything. The man groaned again and began to cry. Novi sat down next to him, pulling out a tablet in the same motion. "Hello, soldier. I see you are in pain. When did this happen?"

"Yesterday," gasped the wounded man. "I don't remember it well. I think it was a land mine. They just stitched the skin shut and put me on this train. I don't know what else they'll do. If I need another operation, or what. But right now, it hurts terribly. I wish I'd never come here. I wish I could die, it hurts so bad. And who needs a man with no feet?" He began to weep loudly. "Fuck all of this! What a fucking mistake! The idiots who are in charge are nowhere near this mess."

Novi took the man's hand and squeezed it between his own. He stared hard into the younger man's eyes, imagining himself as Father Boris might perform this. As a ritual, a sacrament, between two human beings on opposite sides of something neither understands, yet so alike in every other way. Their hands separated, and the soldier saw the green tablet. He looked at Novi with questioning eyes. Novi put a finger to his lips.

"This is a small sacrament of mercy. The Lord loves us all. He will heal the wounds of your heart and give you courage. This will quiet your pain for now. Take it and sleep, soldier. You have earned it."

The suffering man looked at the pill in his hand, once more at Novi, and swallowed it with a sip of water from his canteen.

"Good," said Novi. "Now tell me about your life. Where do you come from? And your family?"

The soldier relaxed visibly and began to relate details of his life. He was from a farming family in Yakutia, a brother and two sisters. Tough land, an injured, alcoholic father. Sisters both younger and still in school. Little prospects for a better life, so he joined the Army for travel, money and experience. Left the younger brother to figure it all out. Like half the guys on this train. The other half were the younger brothers. None were from Moscow or St

Petersburg. As he talked, his eyelids drooped, and he was soon asleep. Novi was relieved. Six to eight hours of calm. Nobody had seen his sacrament.

Novi stood up, feeling more confident in his ability to be a presence for these other men. He smiled and nodded as he moved back up the carriage. A weary-looking man with a bandaged eye smiled back, and Novi sat down.

The man asked, "If I've killed someone, and I was following orders, whose sin is it? Mine, my commander's, or both of us? I don't say I have killed anyone, but I operated a tank and fired rounds. Maybe I killed someone. I'll never know."

Novi pondered a few seconds, and replied, again trying to think as Boris might, while sparing his words. His Russian database was fine, but his accent wasn't perfect. He glanced ahead at Boris, who was apparently praying with a small group of men. "The fact that you even consider guilt and sin in your situation tells me that you have a good heart. When this is over, dedicate yourself to doing good for your community, and you will know peace. If you have harmed or killed anyone, in this extraordinary circumstance, I am sure God will forgive you. All you have to do is ask with sincerity. If you are truly sorry, you must also find a way to avoid doing it again."

The young man looked at the floor. His voice shook. "I never imagined that I would be here, wondering if I've killed someone I've never seen. I joined the Army to serve my country. I thought this meant helping with rescues, disasters, and patrolling borders. Defensive stuff, but not offence. Never this! Our group all have the same story. We believed the lie that we were fighting evil. Now we have dead and wounded. So have our neighbors. Who will forgive this? I'd be happy to go home and forget this whole thing."

Novi smiled sympathetically. "There are many people of power and influence. They are not the same as us. We have little say in the course of events. We are ordinary people, and we follow the rules we are given. It is they who must bear the responsibility for the harm that is being done. This is just my own opinion, and I know that it does not align with the official sympathies of the Patriarch. Like you, I am a simple and ordinary man. I wish you good luck and a full recovery." Novi stood and stretched his muscles. He shook the young man's hand and carried on to sit next to Boris.

Boris stayed in character while scanning Novi's face for signs of worry, or of things not going well. Seeing none, he suggested that Novi take the first nap. The medics arrived just then with a tray full of medications and loaded syringes. They topped up IV fluids, gave antibiotics and pain shots, handed out pills: to sleep, for motion sickness, for mild pain. They paused briefly beside the man at the back, who had received Novi's tablet. He was sound asleep, so they stepped past and into the next carriage.

As the evening wore on, men fell silent and drifted off to sleep. Novi nodded off almost immediately and began to see dreams of his medical training. The old man who had a seizure and arrested while Novi was discussing risks of a procedure with him. The man went on to have a fatal heart attack and died four days later. A high-risk baby, born without a pulse. The horrified eyes of the father above his mask as Novi caught the thrown baby, tossed by a desperate obstetrician, in mid-air. That baby did well. The kids on the oncology ward who stayed with Novi and fought along with him to stay alive. His favorites all succumbed in his last week. The big saves on call, the racing through underground tunnels, up flights of stairs, to code blues and premature deliveries. Beneath these images ran the same current: that he was training his whole life for one final procedure. He felt it even in his sleep.

At sunrise the train slowed, then clanked noisily along on a side track. The train was surrounded by low buildings rather than tents; a huge military base from the look of it. Novi felt Father Boris's elbow on his ribs and started awake. The rest of the carriage was still asleep. Novi looked at Boris and saw him sending and reading messages from his phone, a burner that Miroslav had given him at the last moment.

Boris spoke nonchalantly, as if remarking on the weather. "We have accommodation in the city for a few days. We're to meet Father Maxim in Gorky Park. An Army vehicle will take us there. Luchenkov can't accompany us from here. He's connected us with a driver. We'll tell him we have two days off as tourists until our next assignment. No deviation. We need to stay in uniform. When the train stops, we go straight to the latrines, then get some water or tea, and go to the motor pool. I know the way. Follow me and don't say anything unless you're directly asked. We want to get out of here fast." He muttered all this in tense, clipped syllables, but softly enough that nobody else could hear him. His black beard hid his lips; anyone more than a metre away wouldn't even know he was speaking.

Novi asked him if he'd slept at all. Boris grinned and shook his head. They moved to the rack and retrieved their duffel bags as the train slowed to a crawl and then stopped with a jerk. The wounded man at the back of the carriage was fully awake and groaning again. His face was flushed, his face shiny with sweat. Novi could guess from the other end of the carriage that he was sliding into sepsis. Nothing Novi could do about it now. Boris and Novi slipped quietly out the doorway and stepped onto the platform.

Boris's newest contact was waiting at the motor pool. They had to clear out of the encampment. They walked briskly to the right, showed their badges to a hungover-looking young recruit, and were directed to the third truck in a long line. At the wheel was an impatient middle-aged man in camo gear. He looked as though he'd been recycled and thrown right back into duty. He had a cheap glass eye that stared straight ahead and the left hand gripping the wheel was missing two fingers, the remains stained yellow.

"Luchenkov said I was to get you to Gorky Park. He didn't say what for. I trust him but I don't know your asses from Adam. I owe him one, that's all. Let's get out of here!"

They said nothing. They took their seats, bags on their laps. The driver backed out and took off at speed toward the front gate. He waved his badge at the surprised guard at the gate. The guard cranked up a wooden gate, adorned with the orange and black letter Z, and they were on the road away from the base. Novi reached into his pocket and found a tablet of comfort. He surreptitiously slipped it under his tongue as Boris, riding shotgun, tried to make small talk with the driver.

"The camp looks bigger than the last time we came through here. New men?" He asked innocently. He held out his packet of cigarettes; the driver took one without looking down and lit it with Boris's lighter.

"Yeah. More big plans. We don't know anything. It's the mushroom treatment. Keep us all in the dark and feed us bullshit. I don't think even the officers know what they're doing around here. New guys keep coming, they get on the trains, load up with ammo and food, and disappear. The COs tell us how everything is just great, but we never see those guys again." He puffed hard on the cigarette and relaxed somewhat. "So, what's in Gorky Park that you need to see so damn urgently, huh? Are you guys tourists or what?"

Boris spoke for them both. "We're chaplains, that's all. Not cut out for fighting. Our boys came back for medical help. A fellow priest said he'd show us around the big city, get us places to stay in a monastery here. We're tight for time. Our next train to the south leaves in 48 hours. My buddy here, he's a bit spooked by all this. We need some rest."

The driver seemed satisfied by this and finished his cigarette in silence, flinging his butt out the window. He turned onto a larger road, then again onto a ramp, and then the A101 going toward the city. Novi decided to try for sleep and soon dozed off. The wakefulness after taking the memory drug had faded days ago; he would soon need to repeat the procedure. The tablets in his pocket were few, and he needed to open both his surgically implanted pouches soon. Their driver woke him after a half hour or so, proud to show them sights as they advanced further into the historic central city. The sky had clouded over, and soon a light rain began.

They passed dense forests of apartment blocks, bright cafes, and stores. The driver took a short detour to show them Novy Arbat, then turned away from the deeper city core to avoid traffic. They could see the huge glass towers of the International Business Centre a few kilometres ahead. Novi listened with his language ears tuned to pick up the man's accent and casual phrases, sifting for mannerisms of speech he could use if needed. His map memory was perfect; he recognized the Garden Ring Road as they turned south. One more bridge, another turn, and they were at one of the great park's many gates. Boris gave the driver another cigarette. They pulled out their duffel bags and the Army truck drove away.

The rain had increased. They walked hurriedly into a small shop just outside the park entrance, a tourist trap displaying umbrellas in the window. A middle-aged woman behind the counter saw their uniforms and badges. She immediately came out to greet them, asking what they needed. Novi and Boris pointed to the array of umbrellas beside the postcards, T-shirts, candy, and knickknacks. They both selected dark blue. Novi paid with his stack of rubles while Boris tapped at his phone. The woman tried to refuse payment, calling them heroes and thanking them profusely. If she only knew, thought Novi.

They crossed the street and entered the famous park, headed west toward the river. Father Maxim would meet them at the Rosary Garden in the park in ten minutes. He was watching for two men with blue umbrellas. Novi knew it was time for goodbyes, and suddenly he felt an awkward rush of emotion.

Novi spoke, his Russian fluent and rapid: "I need to thank you for everything you've done to get me here. You gave me the moral okay to do this, you connected me to the team in Canada. They gave me back my memory, my mind, my life. This has been the scariest experience I've had since I don't know, maybe ever. You got me across countries, over the hurdle of my faith in myself, and now here. I feel alive. I can't repay you, only thank you.

"If this goes wrong, it won't be any fault of yours. And I'll do my very best to succeed. I want to survive this if I can. Survive and go home to my family. Only right now do I understand how I miss them. I appreciate the fact..."

He began to cry.

"...The fact that you saw my potential and brought me back to life."

The rain was coming down harder now, and Novi was relieved to have an excuse for his wet face as they passed a few strolling people along the path.

"I'll never forget you, Father Boris. In case this doesn't go as planned, please tell my family that I loved them, and that I really wanted the best for them. My poor wife especially." He paused and collected himself, then asked, "Now what about you? Where do you go from here?"

Boris smiled and gazed across the river. "I have other business in this city before I go home. I have people to meet here, locals who are sympathetic. They don't know of you or our Project. I have other plans to work on with them. You don't need to know. I hope we will meet again, back home. Promise me you'll start going to church!"

As they walked into the garden, a stocky man in black priest's clothes approached from across a circular path. He carried a blue umbrella too. He wore a broad smile, and his bright eyes twinkled over a bristly grey beard. He stuck out his hand and greeted them cheerfully, "I'm Father Maxim. Welcome to Moscow."

PART III

1

Novi had memorized more addresses and stories. This man, Father Maxim Volyanov, was a genuine servant of his flock of believers. A reflective, compassionate man of fifty years with a sharp, inquisitive mind, he blended into the crowded streets of different neighborhoods with ease. He might visit the pharmacy, the mechanic who repaired his aging Lada, the barbershop or the grocery without raising an eyebrow beyond a shy "hello." He attended the sick at home and in hospital, making himself available to listen to their troubles—difficult marriages, problems with alcohol, disappointments in their careers, disobedient children. All the trials of modern life. His ears filled and emptied like the tide, and he prayed to rinse himself of what he heard from his trusting congregation.

Father Maxim played host to new and visiting priests from other parts of the Diocese and from outside the Moscow area. He housed a new colleague every two or three months and had done so for several years. Father Maxim had never married; this made him an object of idle curiosity and occasional gossip. Most of the neighborhood accepted the fact that he was seriously devoted to God and the church and had no time or space for family concerns of his own. Father Maxim had been careful in seeking out like-minded people in his own parish. He remained unknown to the authorities but well-connected to the Project.

He had two mobile phones in the names of deceased parishioners. Not every guest in his parish house was a colleague; over the past several years, he had also had visits from members of the Ukrainian Orthodox church, and from various organizations with more worldly interests in his extensive base of support. These men were of a steely discipline. They followed a more pragmatic belief system, one that mirrored his own. Their late-night talks motivated him to offer assistance when he heard what they felt needed to be done.

Novi had read up on Father Maxim, but the priest was eagerly curious about his latest houseguest. They chatted all the way home on the Metro about different neighborhoods of the city, parishes they had worked in (all a cover story on Novi's part). They confirmed his invented history, the one that would be necessary if Father Maxim were ever to be asked by the authorities about this visitor. They talked about parishes in distant parts of Russia: Kamchatka, Buratia, Siberia, the Urals. Novi had learned much of this information from National Geographic articles, old newspapers, and online travel magazines. His Russian was by now advanced enough that he was confident on the Metro but still kept his voice low, in case his accent was too obviously foreign to the ears of the other passengers.

Maxim's housekeeper created a hearty meal of borsch, potato pancakes, caviar, and cabbage. She left quietly, as she always did when a new arrival came to visit. The two men talked about everything: the politicization of the Russian Orthodox Church, the progress of the president's war and the response of the West. The decline of the Western position from moral authority to primary self-interest and fading primacy in the Third World. The parallel loss of religious influence in modern life and world affairs.

Father Maxim, as an ordained theologian, was surprisingly candid in his assessment of the failure of religion to lead, at least in the West. Partisan strife, adherence to outmoded ideas in an age of equality, birth control, gender rights, and more. He was even up to date about the abuse of Indigenous peoples, including Canada's. Novi was impressed by his objectivity, his ability to accept that the Church owned responsibility for its own condition, and that of the societies who required moral guidance.

For Maxim, this was a major occasion. He was hosting not a colleague, but an outsider from the West. Someone who shared his values and thoughts from halfway around the planet. He would serve his best vodka. Homemade, a gift from thousands of kilometres east.

"Maybe my institution is a dinosaur," he joked, refilling their glasses. "Still, it was a very big one, and for a very long time. But time changes everything. We adapt or we die. The old ways of unmerited respect are gone. So let us earn it back."

They clinked glasses and drank.

"You may wonder why a priest would get involved so closely in this business. For me it wasn't a choice. I believe in a just God, yes. But I also believe that everyone must right a wrong when it's in their power to do so. I have a wonderful group of supportive people who trust me to do right by them. My own needs are simple, my life is simple. The simplicity itself helps me to be calm for those I serve, and this is by far the best act of service I can think of. To help stop a war from getting any worse. I have thought and prayed for many hours over this. Even if it means death must be part of the plan? Death of one, or more death of many? A simple equation. And using the name of the Church? And of God Himself? I feel grateful to be chosen for this."

His face was tense and flushed.

"I envy your skills and your resolve. I trust that you have the will, the personal force, to kill. I believe I could do it, but I've never been tested and hope never to face such a dilemma. I will pray every day for your safety and success. Now it's getting late, and we have errands to run tomorrow. Olga has fixed up your room. You will be very comfortable. Sleep well."

Maxim saw Novi to the doorway and went on down the hall. Novi's mind began to race; he shouldn't have had that second glass of vodka. He recited the next steps, counted them off. Target date was only a few more days. The priests and spies had moved him like a chess piece—*a pawn?* he asked himself drunkenly—across four borders and through a nation at war. He needed to trust them now. One more dose of the memory drug before showtime. Meet the next enabler, plan entry and get ready for the final act. Extraction, if the whole thing fell apart too soon, or if by some miracle he could be retrieved from the palace before the accusations and bullets flew.

His bowels squeezed and his heart thumped. *Deep breaths, relax,* he told himself. He opened his travel kit, took a pain pill, and a sip of water. *You've come so far. Trust these people. They want what you want. Believe it.* Maxim had been kind enough to provide him with his own toilet next to the bedroom. Perhaps he understood how this might feel. Novi actually said a silent prayer of thanks for his progress so far and fell into a heavy, drug-addled, and drunken sleep.

He awoke with the birds the next day. The sun had returned, and their neighborhood in north Moscow was freshened by the previous day's rain. Olga the housekeeper had again assembled a hearty meal: blini, sausages, eggs, and a huge silver samovar of tea. She apologized for the absence of fresh fruit. Such things were becoming scarce. It was her closest approach to a political statement. She was over seventy and liked her quiet, comfortable life just as it was. Widowed, her children living overseas. She was devout and prayed daily in the church, with all the other babushkas. As she had done the day before, she greeted the two priests, then withdrew to give them privacy.

Maxim dug into his breakfast with vigor, stopping every few minutes to offer new information. Today, he said, they would visit a friend, a mechanic from the neighborhood. This mechanic had the other key to a car, the twin of the key from Pavel and Iryna's Torba. They rode in Maxim's Lada, just five streets away. Joe recognized the street names from the map in his head and recognized the car instantly from a photo in the Torba.

Maxim stayed back in the office while Mikhail the mechanic took Joe out for a test drive. Mikhail was a bald, barrel-chested man of fifty-three, with huge greasy hands and a severe limp. His hearing was poor; too much time spent close to artillery fire. He was a funny, dry-witted guy. One who had learned to take everything and nothing too seriously. On meeting Novi though, he became almost reverential. As they eased the car from its parking spot Mikhail told Novi his story.

"I was a soldier, five years in Afghanistan as a motor pool mechanic. I can fix anything with a motor and wheels. But I got wounded from shrapnel, and my brother was killed in the same ambush. I've seen and heard enough about the glories of the past, Mother Russia and all that shit our president pumps into our heads. Those sycophants on TV make me puke. Mother Russia took my brother away and he's not coming back. I told my kids to stay home and find normal careers."

The car was a Lada from the 1990s, vintage by North American standards but a common sight on the roads here. It was old, rusty, and nondescript. But the mechanic kept it in perfect running condition, and it was equipped like a getaway car: high-performance powertrain, fresh tires, a new clutch. And some extras: Kevlar panels in the doors, bulletproof windshields and side windows. These were special order, he laughed.

They went through the local high street where Mikhail pointed out the pharmacy, a grocer next door, and a medical clinic. The traffic was light; fewer people spent money on fuel as the price rose after missile strikes on production facilities. Mikhail directed them onto a large motorway, and Novi realized that they were going into central Moscow, about half an hour away. Suddenly he felt like a tourist, and at the same time had the adrenaline rush of seeing these famed sights: the bold skyscrapers of the financial district, the domed St Basil's Cathedral, the vast expanse of Red Square, the Arbat, the White House. Mikhail was showing him something he hadn't expected: the local Muscovite's pride in a great metropolis still bustling and largely insulated from what the rest of the world knew was happening.

The power that had conjured such brute force was in the beating heart of this legendary, historic city. And these people, shopping, eating, taking photos, strolling, were oblivious. There were small signs of something being not quite right—several of the finer storefronts were boarded up or papered over. Novi understood what Mikhail was telling him wordlessly: "We are people too. Please do not forget that we are more alike than different."

They drove back into Mikhail's neighborhood and stopped on the high street at a small rectangular brick building with a simple sign, the one Mikhail had pointed out earlier. "That's Artemy's apothecary. He's married to a girl from Sevastopol. Her family was displaced by the Crimea takeover in 2014, so he's one hundred percent with us."

"How so?" asked Novi.

"The president's security for the Sochi Winter Olympics were drawn mostly from Special Forces. Sochi is a short distance from Crimea, and it was easy to deploy the same men for a new assignment after the Olympics. A master stroke of chess—check by discovery. The minute the Games ended, the real purpose of the security force became clear. As you know, chess is very popular here. Our leaders play for the biggest stakes.

"Crimea was a great public relations score at home for our president. Historic naval bases were captured in days. The people of Russia celebrated a triumphant return of the region to the Motherland.

"But not everyone in Crimea was thrilled by the outcome. The Tatars, the Indigenous people, were displaced and disadvantaged yet again. Artemy's wife's family have Tatar blood. Their distant relatives were sent to the gulag back in Stalin's time. The Turkish and Greek ethnic communities were also uprooted after decades of peace. Depending on the information source, the percentages of Russian-speakers were more than, less than, or about half of the population. Even among them not everyone supported the return of Crimea to the Russian Federation."

Artemy Matyushev the pharmacist had been discovered by a team of recruiters who picked up leads from the local churches, professional societies, or social media platforms. These platforms increasingly came under surveillance, riskier now than before. Everyone remotely affiliated with the Project had an out-of-country VPN and got their news, intel, and instructions by means hopefully beyond the eyes of the government in Moscow.

The pharmacist had access to all the basic medical supplies Novi would need, and also to Naloxone, the antidote to opioids. Better yet, he had made a friend who worked as a veterinary director at the Moscow Zoo. The veterinarian had slowly amassed a large quantity of Carfentanil through the chemists that supplied this Zoo and others in the Federation's largest cities.

Artemy had no love for the president's regime and had been an easy convert to the Project. A tall, thin man with remarkably thick glasses, a scholarly and quiet manner, his fretful wife kept a close check on him and their two teenage boys. Average family, nothing worrisome or flashy. Absolute secrecy was required as his wife still had many relatives in Crimea. His family thought he belonged to a chess club.

He depended on his store for his family's livelihood. His pharmacist's credentials could vanish overnight if any authority body took exception to his politics. His in-laws could vanish too. Like so many ordinary people in Russia, he simply wanted to get on with his life; politics were a source of irritation but not a major interest. His wife wanted her family to be free of anxiety, and he wished them all to live peacefully.

Peace had vanished from view, and he felt cheated of the calm, orderly life he'd always considered to be the reward of his studies and efforts. The family attended church every week as ordinary parishioners, not teachers of the Catechism or anything notable. Their parish happened to be that of Fr Maxim Volyanov. The priest who quietly but vehemently opposed the current war, and war in general.

Mikhail sat in the car while Novi went inside. On Mikhail's instruction, he asked for a package of "diabetic supplies" and the tall, thin pharmacist handed him a white paper bag. The pharmacist spoke little but told Novi to return in three days for a prescription that needed filling. Novi hadn't mentioned any such prescription. He asked about the hours for visiting the Moscow Zoo, and the pharmacist replied that the zoo was closed for maintenance. With all their coded instructions understood, Novi left and got back in the car, feeling the dizziness of another surreal moment, sensing how close they all were to making history. Or to being rounded up for questioning.

They stopped for fuel at a different garage, and Novi paid with rubles from the Torba. He drove them back to Mikhail's garage without asking for directions, the clutch set nicely for fast shifting. He knew that he was due for a final dose of the drug before showtime but his recently stored memories were firmly planted.

Back at Mikhail's auto shop, they headed for the small office beside the repair stalls. When they opened the door there was another man waiting inside. Dmitry was a tall, well-built young man of about thirty with athletic grace and a big smile. He was fair, good-looking, and might have been a model. Except that he wore a uniform: the Kremlin's Guard. Dark colors, patches at the shoulders, nothing showy or obtrusive. But unmistakable, and just like those in one of the files Novi had committed to memory. The president's own personal security team.

Novi couldn't hide his shock or his fear. He gaped at the soldier, wondered if he were to be arrested now? How much did he know? Was it all over? He looked from one face to another, dumbstruck and fearful. They sat around the desk, smoking and drinking from mugs of strong tea. He turned pale, began to sweat. Father Maxim saw his discomfiture and decided to rescue Novi from an impending panic attack. "Father Mike, this is Dmitry. My nephew."

2

Novi took a deep breath, exhaled slowly, relaxed and composed himself. "I'm sorry. I didn't know what to think. I figured you were here to kill me, or arrest me, or all of us."

"Sorry Father Mike! I should have come in civilian clothes, but you handled the surprise like a champion! Wish you could see your face though. Anyway I'm here to introduce myself. Obviously we couldn't tell you anything about me until you were across the border and safely in the city. Imagine if they'd gotten *this* bit of info from you in questioning. I'd be in the basement at my place of employment by now. I've only heard about what happens down there.

"Soon we'll begin the final phase of your training. I'll be your only contact once we get you inside the building. My time is tight; we don't get much opportunity to mingle with anyone outside the office. I'll be at Maxim's tomorrow night. I have a seventy-two-hour window every two weeks. We'll do some studying. Oh, and be sure to take your medicine. We have a lot to cover."

Novi gaped at the younger man in amazement once again. He addressed the group, "Can I ask how in the world you were able to get a Project member so deep into the Kremlin? I'd have thought that would be impossible. I mean no disrespect but none of you seem like insiders or anything."

They all laughed at this, enjoying Novi's astonishment. Mikhail spoke up, "Do you remember Pavel and Iryna? Your helpers from Kyiv?"

Novi flushed at this. How much did they know? "Of course, I'll never forget them. It's too bad about Pavel though."

Mikhail grimaced. "What's too bad is I didn't get a chance to really fuck him up. Power tools, a crowbar, something. He nearly wrecked the whole thing. I'd love to meet the people who figured him out in time. Anyway, hacking goes both ways. Iryna made up a bio about Dmitry's very promising career in the police, then in the FSB. All fiction, packaged up beautifully. Official letterhead, signatures, references, the whole dumpling. Then she fed it to the right agencies at the right times, based on the intel they received about personnel losses. To COVID, to the Special Military Operation, to desertion. The first wave of FSB were either fired, put in jail, or both. They needed good people and they needed them fast. We gave them our best."

Now he grinned proudly at the uniformed younger man beside him. "Dmitry is my nephew too. See how handsome he is! Same genes, or some of them. Maxim and I are brothers and Dmitry is our sister Anna's oldest boy. Anna moved to Kyiv many years ago, married a wonderful guy—a banker, and they lived in Dnipro. Until his bank was blown up, that is. He was at work, and in a minute, he was gone. Now she's in Copenhagen putting her life back together. Her daughter is an army medic. We don't get to talk much these days but it's just one more reason we want to see this plan succeed.

"Dmitry's swept the garage for bugs, and Maxim's house too. That's why we can speak freely here. Even better, he's in charge of his foursome of guards, knows all their schedules. Only their Captain ranks higher. They rotate senior guards out when they reach thirty-five. No old bastards like us. Lightning fast, skilled in martial arts, good with a pistol. District Jiu-Jitsu champ. And an improv actor like Zelensky!" He laughed out loud, slapped his thigh at this irony.

Dmitry was calm the whole time and showed no emotion at the tribute his uncle paid him. Maybe he was staying in character or practicing his acting chops, thought Novi.

"Nice, Uncle, thank you. Novichok, you will take your next dose of the memory drug tomorrow, two weeks after the last one. Correct?"

Novi nodded.

"Then I will bring you paper copies of the floor plans to the office the president uses most often. The big room, oval table, high ceiling. I'm sure you've seen it on TV. Plans for that room and the ductwork leading there via the ceiling. We'll go over the list of what you'll need to carry in, and you can tell me how we can best make our delivery. Tonight, make a list and review it with Uncle Maxim. I'll look after getting you into the building. You'll need to be able to crawl to the right spot. The room will be ready, but I won't be able to help you once you're into the ducts. It's about one hundred metres, on your belly. The ducts are large enough for you; I've seen them myself. Once inside, you'll have to get into position and wait for about four hours. Empty bladder. No food or drink. My superiors have let me in on the timing of a visit from important allies of the president. The president will almost certainly make them wait an hour. And these allies hate each other. It's a contest to see who's more loyal. A strong boss can do that I guess."

The others turned as one.

"You mean..." Maxim stammered, "All three at once? How will it be possible? They'll be at least five metres apart!"

Dmitry smiled. "If you were either of those two, what would you do first? The room has cameras everywhere. They know this. They'll rush to his aid, then call for help. Our friends at the zoo have been able to obtain a double dose of Carfentanil for this eventuality. Father Mike, Novi, I hope your brain is well-prepared for this. It's an unexpected surprise but just imagine the importance of taking out two of the most likely people to fight over the throne. This is a state visit. That's why we're certain they won't use a body double."

Novi was beginning to feel a mild dysphoria. He was sweating again, a bit anxious, nauseous and wishing he could get up and move around a bit. Then he realized: Methadone. The opiate clock in his brainstem had wound down. He was two hours overdue. He hadn't anticipated the length of today's errand. "Gentlemen, is there a toilet I can use? Mikhail, I need to get something from the car. May I use your key?"

They looked at him sympathetically. In their own way, they were all taking risks and had endured various hardships along the way. But the sweating, pale Novichok was growing more restless by the minute and they knew this meeting must be adjourned. They just didn't know which drug he needed more acutely.

3

The next day bright and early, Novi awoke with the birds, stretched and took a spoonful of Methadone. He longed to go for a walk, blend in, and see the neighborhood as the local Muscovites saw it. A home, familiar and reliable. He began to feel homesick, nostalgic and lonely. This was counter to the side effects he'd been told to expect, back home before this trip began. Withdrawal! He was two weeks past the last dose, and due today. This was a discovery of its own, and he should report it to Dr. Young back home. He suddenly realized, as if a curtain had been pulled aside, that he might never see his family, his wife, his home. Any of it. The few friends he hadn't lost touch with. His brothers. His mother. God almighty! Was he losing his nerve, his cool? So close?

There was suddenly so much he wanted to tell everyone. His wife. How he loved her without knowing how. His mother, who was losing her own path back to her memories. His kids, who hadn't asked him for this. Something was wrong inside his head, and he realized that he urgently needed the steadying hand of the memory drug. He was shaky and felt a millimetre from losing his resolve. He took his usual aspirin and cholesterol pill. His remaining supply of each was two weeks. Would he outlast them?

He opened the other bag—the "diabetic supplies"—and inspected the contents. Local anaesthetic 20 ml, sterile prep 50 ml, 5x5 cm gauze, 10 ml syringe, 18 and 25 g needles. Tissue glue, two vials of 3 ml each. Number 11 scalpel blade. And this time, 4.0 Vicryl suture in case the tissue glue didn't hold. Eight vials of 0.4 mg Naloxone, the reversal agent for Carfentanil and Methadone. A PICC line kit, more reliable than a regular IV. The second "prescription" was to be filled later today at the neighborhood pharmacy. He would need to wait until everything was assembled or do the procedure twice and hope the tissue glue would hold.

He put the bag away and went out to the front parlor where Fr Maxim liked to sit and read. The Bible, the papers, whatever was handy. Olga was already there. The breakfast oatmeal and ham smelled delicious. She poured him a mug of tea.

"So, Father Mike, do they not feed you so well back home? I come from Kamchatka, and we were always very kind to our priests in my day."

Novi froze. Was she calling him out or just teasing him? He thought fast. *Answer a question with one of your own. Throw on some flattery and serve hot.* "I can't help myself when the preparation is so spot-on, Olga. How long has it been since you were there? And which was your parish?"

She closed her eyes in memory. "My husband died twenty-four years ago in a mine accident. The kids were already gone, so I had no reason to stay. Father Vadim at Christ the King—bless him— he found me this position in Moscow. I've been in this parish for twenty-two years."

Novi was relieved. "I spent only two years there in St Anna's. I guess we wouldn't have crossed paths. Wonderful people, though. Very kind and decent." *Close call*, he thought. He'd passed this one without tripping up.

Or so he thought. The old woman smiled sweetly, but her face hardened suddenly. Her wrinkles deepened. She seemed to enlarge, becoming powerful before his eyes. She handed him a black priest's cassock, the inner vestment. She showed him the reinforced pockets, the extra arm holes, and said, "This will hold a 100 ml IV bag and tubing. Your car key goes here. If you wish to carry it, your gun goes here—double-reinforced. Clips beside it. All plastic zippers. Dmitry said you might not be able to take metal inside with you. He'll know tonight. This might help distribute the powder if the room is too big or you can't get close." She held up a small battery-powered fan.

He was dumbstruck.

"You can stop kidding now. Father Maxim told me exactly who you are. My husband actually died in a police station when he went to report some unusual activity near the mine. We never found out what he saw, but it was enough for them to kill him and cover it up. I miss him every day. Do what you're going to do for him, and for me."

She began to cry. "I was back home last year. So much pain. Every family has lost sons, grandsons, husbands. The recruiters come for them like crows. The women in the villages are destitute. A man was killed in the Special Military Operation. They paid his widow off with a bushel of carrots. For her man's life! Is that all a good man is worth to those bastards? They don't recruit in Moscow or St Petersburg. Do you wonder why? God bless you, Father. I'll pray that you will be a good killer. Come and have breakfast."

Father Maxim appeared in the doorway and saw the cassock. He nodded his approval. "I see you've met each other for real now. Good. We can all speak freely. Olga and I can assist you with your own treatment later, after you've received everything from the pharmacy. The pharmacist has been very helpful and tells me the zoo is back to regular operation. His friend has what you need, a double supply even. I'll pick it up for you so as to keep your footprint small. Dmitry will be here for dinner and your final round of studies. Olga and I will leave you to it."

They ate a quick but delicious meal, and Father Maxim left. On his return, he handed Novi a smaller bag than the last one with the store logo on it—white paper and Cyrillic lettering. Novi assembled his gear on the kitchen table and washed his hands at the sink. The others watched curiously as he donned the latex gloves, painted the prep solution onto his skin, and drew up the local while the paint dried. He pinched up the skin over the first incision, drew an expert straight line along the incision with the local, needle buried to the hilt, and repeated the steps on the opposite side while the local took effect. Then he incised the scars, right then left, felt for the Ziploc seals and opened up both pouches. The priest and his maid had never seen anything like this before; he joked about seeing it done on YouTube once. They looked at him blankly, then Father Maxim made the connection to the local equivalent on VKontakte. They laughed politely.

Novi put the memory drug down on a sterile paper sheet, then showed Olga how to pass the plastic vials that held the Carfentanil without breaking sterility.

He put the final duplicate doses of memory drug into the left pouch. On the right, both vials of Carfentanil, double wrapped in silicone rubber, and a small drinking straw to blow the powder around the room. He was liking Olga's pocket fan better. He palmed the sterile bag of green pills out of view while distracting the others with a request for more prep solution. He taped the edges of both incisions together with Steri-Strips.

Next, he prepped the inside of his left arm and pinched his skin with local. Made a small nick, poked the juicy blue vein there, and put a wire 20 cm through the needle. He undid the belt he used as a tourniquet, swapped the needle for a dilator and then a PICC line trimmed to 45 cm. Felt his pulse, nothing amiss, and put a plastic lock over the exit site. Olga and Father Maxim watched curiously but said nothing. Finally, he injected his memory drug dose into the rubber port on a fresh 100 ml IV bag and hung it on the back of a chair. Olga brought him more tea, and he sipped quietly as the drug dripped into him.

The infusion was done in thirty minutes, as always. He began to feel that detached wakefulness, a sense of invincibility. His earlier sense of nostalgic sadness evaporated. He was in the *moment*, like a Zen master. Olga's phone rang; she answered in monosyllables with a rough voice. "Dmitry is on his way. He will bring the itinerary. The palace meeting is on Thursday at 1000h."

Today was Tuesday. Novi's pulse quickened. He told himself it was the drug.

Dmitry came in carrying two coffees from the All Taste fast food chain, the one that had supplanted McDonald's. He offered one to Novi, who accepted gratefully. He wasn't a tea fan.

Dmitry was brisk. "Okay, there's a small service road where some of us guards park our cars, at the edge of the Novo-Ogaryovo complex. We're encouraged to use it, as it reduces the possibility of strange cars too close to the president. It happens to be close to where they've been refurbishing the air-conditioning. The president is paranoid about stale air ever since COVID and has ordered this rectified. The work is almost complete, and they've been opening access to the ducts right about where we like to park. So, I'll carpool on the big day, and Father Mike, you'll memorize the route to drive your Lada—the sporty one—to these parking spots. I've been using it for months, so it won't be unfamiliar. There is a gatehouse. The guard there is one of us. He knows the car. He'll turn off the camera and open the gate before you even stop.

"I have another friend who directs the security cameras, sometimes without any supervision. He will aim away from the parking spots for fifteen minutes, starting at 0545h. You'll park, put on your priest's robe, and exit the car dressed as a priest. Hide the robe en route in case of any hitches. Here are some photos of the wall of the outer building beside the parking spots. Notice anything?"

Novi looked hard. "Just these panels. They look new, and the rest of the wall is old brick."

Dmitry smiled, "Good. Those are fakes. Look again."

This time, Novi saw a smaller group of four rusty metal grates. "These? Can I fit in there?"

"Absolutely. I tried them myself while my friend kept the cameras turned off. You can fit in there and he will have a fifteen-minute blind spot for you to do it. The screws are already out. You have to crawl in. They sprayed for rats a week ago; it should be fine."

Now Dmitry pulled out a series of large paper sheets and a roll of tape. He spliced the sheets together and they saw a blueprint of the facility's ductwork, plumbing, and electrical conduits.

"The meeting room's in the basement, two levels below ground. You have to climb and crawl through the system. The ducts are big enough for an adult thanks to the target's insistence on fresh air. Sixty by forty centimetres. At least four hours before meeting time, get into position, maybe have a nap. Once in place, you can prep your brain however you see fit. There are no real windows in the target's meeting room. There is a huge table, two doors, and tons of guards. One of those guards is me. My foursome will clean up the room—literally—with sanitizer. The table, chairs, phone handles, light switches. Then we'll be back with metal and heat detectors and a sweeper for bugs. It is imperative that you choose the near right corner of the room. That's the quadrant the president likes best; it's closest to the door in case he's attacked by anyone he's meeting. It's also closest to the air duct you'll be using. That's my quadrant. I'll have disabled my metal and heat sweepers, so I won't detect you. The whole room is under camera watch, and I don't think I can disable those or ask my friend for help with them. The guests are two chief allies of the president, as you've heard. We know he'll keep them waiting but we don't know for how long. Based on previous patterns, an hour is the maximum."

Novi was still absorbing the blueprints, memorizing the turns he would need to make while inside the duct system. Straight ahead twenty metres, down one level, right five metres, straight ahead again seventy-five metres. Two floors down meant that if he survived, two floors up on the return trip.

Dmitry saw the part of the map Novi was staring at and explained. "We've got that covered, don't worry. Two of the air conditioner repair crew are Project guys. They built in a gymnasium rope. You can use it both ways, up and down. And there are twelve ladder rungs on the right as you enter, left as you leave. Assuming you get to leave, the exit is the same as how you entered. The car is fast as lightning but looks totally ordinary. You've driven it before. Any problems with it?"

Novi shook his head.

"Good. So once the target enters the room, best plan is to begin spreading the powder. With the super-powered air handling units, it may be difficult to get enough concentration of the agent in one place. My contacts in the trade will arrange to slow down the fans to half speed for the first fifteen minutes of the meeting. I understand Olga has given you a pocket fan. Let me see it."

Novi fished the fan out from his robe pocket and Dmitry turned it on. It hummed softly but wasn't silent.

Dmitry noted, "If the meeting room is quiet enough, the target and his friends might be able to hear it, especially if the air duct acts as an echo chamber."

Novi replied, "I think it's a great idea. Reduces the risk I might poison myself with my blowgun idea, and a fan won't run out of breath before spreading powder around the whole room."

"So long as it doesn't clunk against the side of the duct. You also have an IV in your arm and have to open the pouch one final time while you're up there. Olga, can we have some flour?"

The old woman went into a pantry and returned with a bag of flour, a sifter, and a tablespoon. She poured a spoonful of the flour through the sifter, then picked up some of it with the spoon. She then poured the spoonful over the sink with the fan blowing. The flour flew sideways, away from the fan, and drifted onto the countertop, then to the floor. They eyeballed the distance, about two metres.

"Success," they all said in unison. They went back to the blueprint. The distance from the air duct to the target was about three metres, and two metres from ceiling to the tabletop.

Novi had a thought. "If the building fan is being slowed down, maybe we don't need to add to it."

Dmitry replied, "There will only be one way to find out. We can't really guess how the agent will disperse. If the building fan is off, you'll probably need that one. Olga, how old is this pocket fan? And how long will the batteries last? We sure don't want to have them run out at the wrong time."

"That thing saved me when I went through the change! Well, another like it, I mean. Batteries last for hours. That has new ones; I just put them in yesterday."

Novi looked over the city road map one more time, clocking his route through the maze of roads from his suburban neighborhood to the vicinity of the palace, and then the second set of maps, of the Grand Kremlin Palace and environs. His pulse continued to race.

"Okay, so let's say I've delivered the powder and it's effective. Who comes into the room first?"

Dmitry answered. "My team, wearing hazmat suits. Even when they're intact, the suits can admit small particles of poison, radioactive materials, et cetera, so we all know not to spend too much time in a hot zone. My guess, knowing those guys, is they'll be happy to pick up the targets and get them out of there as soon as they can. The good news is the suits take a few minutes to put on.

"If the response is slow, you'll have more time to back up. If not, back up as fast as you can and reverse position. If you make it to the car, watch out because the area will be crawling with police, military, everything. Drive slowly and be inconspicuous. If someone chases you, and it looks like you'll get stopped, do whatever you think will save you. The car is fast, but you can't outrun a radio. You might have some Carfentanil left. This is when you may have to say goodbye to us all." He stood up, reached into his shoulder holster, and drew a Glock. "I hope you're a decent shot at close range. The main thing is to keep your wrist stiff to fight off the recoil. The safety's here. On and off, like this. The clip holds fifteen rounds. I don't think it's wise to bring it into the ducts above the target room, just in case someone else's detector picks it up, or it smells like powder and they have dogs. If they use dogs that day, and they might, I'll have to figure out some way to confuse their sense of smell. One of the Project guys works with the dogs. He's hoping to sedate them all with their morning meal. We're not sure yet if he'll be able to do it without giving anything away. Best to leave the gun with the car in case you need it in getting away. We'll tape the handle and steering wheel, gear shift and so on, so no fingerprints are left behind."

Novi was still in the druggy state of energetic euphoria he had learned to enjoy so well. He had no fear; he wished to be able to just go do it all right then. "Dmitry, you said that's your car. They'll catch you too."

"Don't worry. It was reported stolen three months ago and nobody claimed it. It's technically not mine, and I've never parked it in this exact spot. The permit is made out to the last registered owner. She's been dead some time, and nobody really knows whose car it is anymore. I have no fingerprints or any other evidence to link me to it."

"Suppose I can't get out of the ducts," said Novi, as he counted down the possibilities.

"Well, they may find you in place or somewhere in the ducts. You'll be killed if you're caught alive. If you think you can hide up there for any length of time, try it, but my sense is that they might tear the building apart as soon as they figure out what's happened. Your default should be to get out of there fast."

"I'd rather die peacefully. I'll just shut off my IV and take a deep breath of the remaining powder."

Dmitry nodded, and so did Olga. They'd heard enough legends about the maniacal skill of the basement staff at the Kremlin. "We also want you to take that deep breath. Because if they keep you alive long enough, they may come for us, and the rest of the Project next. So, it's nothing personal, but if you're caught alive, stay silent or die quickly."

"And if I'm not found but can't leave the ducts?" His pulse revved, a bit faster than usual, a giddy thrill overcoming what should have been dread, or at least the rational fear of a tight-rope walker. He had no net and knew it. The drug eliminated his fear of what was to come. But not the thrill.

Dmitry replied, "Wait until you see a chance to climb back out. You might get to the car. If not, or if it's been removed, remember you're dressed as a priest. You might be able to bluff your way past the police or guards on the street. If I haven't heard from you, or the car isn't there, I'll look nearby, or send Olga, Maxim, or someone else they won't recognize to wander nearby. In that event, you're to walk straight north at every traffic crossing, every option point. Anyone associated with the Project will ask if you're diabetic. We used that as the password for your pharmacy drop, right?"

"Right. Okay, let's go over all the steps for showtime."

"0430h, wake up. Light meal."

"Potato pancakes, Olga, please?" Novi smiled at the old woman. He felt an intense affection for her, for how her entire life had played out, and led her to this place to be part of their adventure.

"Of course, Father Mike. It would be a bigger honor to make you another batch the next day. What will be will be. I hope they're not your last."

Dmitry continued, "0500, connect IV to PICC line, Take a dose of oral Methadone and IV Metoprolol. Load and check pockets: fan, eight doses pre-drawn Naloxone, two pre-loaded clips, gun, car keys, phone, sterile gloves. Hair bonnet, N95 mask. Drive to car park site, edge of the palace. Arrive 0545-0550. Park; put on the robe. Leave gun, clips and phone under floor mat. Grate will be loosened. Pull it straight out, climb in and pull it into place behind you. We expect that you will have fifteen minutes to get inside and into position. Remember, it's one hundred metres and two levels down. About seven metres per minute, and as silently as you can manage. The drops are at twenty and twenty-five metres from your point of entry. The ladder steps are on your right side going in, left side coming out. There's a rope for you to hold at each drop. You have to do this in the dark as much as possible."

"I'll let my eyes adjust to the dark as soon as I get into the ducts. I have good night vision. Is there any activity I might encounter or need to be aware of?"

Dmitry showed him two points on the blueprint. "There's a guard room here and a bathroom next to it. Both are one level down, between your twenty and twenty-five metre marks. The ducts have big branches into both. So, you need to move quietly. That's why Olga made you the big robe—to keep warm and to muffle noises."

"Okay, so I've reached the meeting room. Nap time for four hours. Alarm set for 0950 hours. I wait for the guests, give myself one dose of Naloxone, then open a vial of Carfentanil?"

"Right. Wait until the target sits down and is clearly in range, not about to stand up and run. Then you can spread the powder. Once he tastes it, he may still be mobile for thirty seconds or so. See, doc, I've learned a bit of your trade too! He can be saved by Naloxone for up to five minutes after he stops breathing. My job will be to confuse everything, waste time, and slow down the response team. Looking like it's accidental, of course. I'll have a hazmat suit on, and they may not even recognize me in it. I'm hoping, anyway."

"Dmitry, that makes me think: what about your immunity to our powder? How will you be sure that it doesn't get through your suit, knock you out, or… kill you? Let's give you an IV too. Or can you think of a different place they might need you, the video room, or somewhere that isn't right where the air is dangerous?"

"Damn, you're right. And I have to go with my team, or they'll suspect I knew something beforehand. I've practiced lying about it in questioning a thousand times."

Novi asked Olga, "Can you find out from Maxim whether he can get us another IV and more Naloxone? And some Metoprolol, 5 mg ampule, two please. I think I'll take some too—I'll write it down—for Dmitry. To help us keep our heart rates and shakes down." And to Dmitry, he added, "We'll put an IV in your foot, above your shoe where you can reach it easily. Do you get a bathroom break? You can run in there and inject a vial each of Naloxone and Metoprolol. They'll last an hour. Have it drawn up, ready to plug in. That's in case you have to go into the room, and there's no excuse you can make. Keep a mask in your pocket too."

Olga was making a short list and writing the pharmacist's number down from memory. *No dementia there*, Novi thought with a pinch of envy. He went over each step of the plan with Dmitry once more, then repeated the steps himself with no prompting. He then went to sit in the next room, repeating the steps until they became grooved into place. In his mind, he pictured the parking spot, the air grate, himself getting inside the ducts.

"Knee pads. A little dental mirror. Best if these things are black. And spare sterile gloves. Extra saline."

"Okay, good. This is exactly what we need to be doing now," said Dmitry. He wrote the items down. "And other Project members will be creating a diversion on the other side of the palace from where you'll be operating. Their cue will be the disturbance in the main meeting room."

"A box cutter in case I get too close to someone? Or to pry open a grate, window or anything."

"Sure hope not, but a good idea. You'll be non-metallic if you leave the clips and gun in the car. Let's do that. I'd hate for one of my team to beat me there and sweep your part of the room. Box cutter it is."

Dmitry dictated, and Olga wrote it onto her list next to "potatoes, bacon, eggs, onion, garlic, sour cream."

Novi silently rehearsed his movements, surroundings, timing. He looked as though he were hypnotized but was actually in deep concentration. He could almost feel the events of the next day taking shape and wondered idly whether the memory drug possessed any hallucinogenic effects.

Olga went into the next room and called Father Maxim to ask him to call back on the house's landline. Dmitry had cleared the house phone, but cell phones were another matter. She passed on the short list of new items and groceries. He was at an old-age home near the shops and would bring home the remaining items. He asked her to call ahead to their pharmacist, Artemy, who had been so helpful so far. She did this also from the land line.

Maxim arrived an hour later with the remaining supplies from the pharmacy. Meanwhile Dmitry and Novi continued learning the blueprints and running through their plan, looking for leaks and oversights. With each iteration, the leaks were plugged until no gaps within their control remained. If they found out about any change in the president's schedule for Thursday, everything would be put on hold or scrapped altogether. Maxim's hands shook slightly as he put the white paper bag on the kitchen table.

"Any last ideas? What kind of shoes will you wear, Father Mike? Soft soles, remember. You need to be silent."

"Sneakers, Father. A great name for the purpose. Mine are black."

4

Olga woke Novi at 0400, as planned. She had a steaming plate heaped with potato pancakes, a bowl full of sour cream, and caramelized butter and onions, exactly as he'd asked for yesterday and dreamed of overnight. He sprinkled pepper on the sour cream and stirred it in, a childhood habit. No coffee though; he had decided against too much liquid and a full bladder. Did he want a catheter? Not really; what if it got in the way somewhere in the ductwork? Four hours of dehydration wouldn't overload his bladder. He'd done many longer surgeries in his life.

For someone in his situation, he felt surprisingly calm; the evening Methadone and side effects from his memory drug lingered. He went to the WC to relieve himself and apply contact lenses. Glasses might fall off if he got sweaty. His hands were steady. He came back with clean hands and began his ritual of laying out supplies with Olga's help. He was aware of finality today; this may well be his last procedure. His nurse was this stoic, loyal stranger. He was suddenly grateful for her and for everything he'd felt, everyone he'd loved, and everything he'd learned. The feeling washed over him and was instantly gone. Out of his control.

He donned the cassock, loaded the other pockets with the fan, dental mirror, pen flashlight, the bag of IV fluid and eight vials of naloxone, already drawn up. Everything fitted perfectly into Olga's pockets. She had done it all by guesswork. Bless her. She pressed an N95 mask into his hands and he stowed it in yet another pocket, then took off the assembled outfit. No point telling her that it didn't work properly with a beard. Novi hugged her emphatically.

"Thank you for everything you've done, Olga. For all of us. Say a little prayer for me. Remember, potato pancakes again tomorrow!"

The old woman's eyes began to well up in spite of her hardness and years of struggle. She held his face as a mother might and admonished, "You better come back alive! I can't go over there to help you, so be careful. Who'll eat my pancakes?"

The Lada was around the corner, a short distance from the house. Pre-dawn birds chirped happily, the velvet blue-black sky nearly cloudless. Father Maxim had gone ahead to be sure of clear weather in the other sense. An open fuel door meant all-clear. Novi closed it and got in, started up and drove with the lights off to the second corner. Maxim waved from the steps of his church.

Everything around Novi was dark. There was no traffic, and he knew nobody was on his tail. He found the motorway and slid into the sparse traffic headed west of the city. The radio was tuned to a pop station, unrecognizable tunes sung in Russian. He recalled the shock of being stripped of the joy of music a few short months earlier and realized he was unconsciously humming along to a bouncy song. He didn't want to concentrate on the lyrics though; they might create a mood. He was all business now.

Novi got off the highway two exits ahead and used the side streets imprinted on his memory to approach the parking spot. He was exactly on time, the sky lighting up ahead of the coming sun. He rolled through the open gate, parked at 0505, put the gun and clips under the driver's seat, and took a deep breath. He pulled on the cassock and felt all the pockets and compartments. Dmitry's friend had the camera on another channel; this was his window. Overhead, a small group of sparrows chased a crow from a nest.

Novi put on the latex gloves he'd brought along and locked the car. He had only one key, and it fit snugly in one of Olga's stash pockets. Dmitry carried the spare. The old rusty grate was easy to remove, as Dmitry had promised. He was inside in seconds and tied a string with distance markers every five metres to the grille once inside. The first metre was fishing line, invisible from outside.

There was more dust than he expected inside the ducts. A lot of cobwebs too. Dmitry's map showed that the first ten metres was old construction, decades for sure. Novi hoped the newer ducts would be less dusty. Fewer spiders would also be nice, as he squashed one with his gloved hand and wiped the guts on his cassock. He could safely use the penlight for the first several metres and then needed to rely on the indirect lighting from the rooms below. He took a peek at his watch to gauge his rate of speed. He was crawling carefully, military style, using his arms and riding on his elbows. Thank God for Olga's sewing, he thought. He'd wanted lightweight clothes, but she'd known better. The AC was turned up high, and the duct was cold and getting colder as he passed small side channels that fed more dry, cold air into the system.

He came to the first drop. Risked a peek with the light, saw the first step and the rope. It was tight and awkward, but he was able to curl into a ball and lead with his left foot, balance with the rope, and let his weight down gently. Twelve steps in the dark, feet first. He flashed back to the base in Winnipeg. They'd taught him these physical moves, had him lie in the dark for long periods with no food or water. Novi thanked them silently now.

When his feet hit the floor of the duct, he checked it to be sure it would take his weight soundlessly. No problem. The newer section was cleaner, but he was covered in dust. Just as the musty smell registered, dust flew into his eyes on the breeze of the AC fan. His eyes watered ferociously; he squeezed them shut to rinse out the dust. No luck; he felt his heart rate rising. He got one hand into position for balance and used it to pinch out one of his contact lenses. Aware that it would have his DNA on it, he popped it in his mouth and swallowed it. Murphy's law; it stuck in his throat and now his mouth was drying as he fought down a rising wave of panic. He desperately wanted to cough in spite of the Methadone still attached to his diminished remaining receptors.

Ten deep breaths. Count blessings. The eye without the lens in place was adequate for vision even if he had no depth perception. *No big deal*, he thought. He wasn't driving or playing hockey. No rats in here so far, only a few spiders. No bad smells. The duct was huge, and he could move comfortably. Lots to be grateful for here, so onward.

The urge to cough passed. At a T intersection he heard voices on his left. A faint fluorescent glow. The guards' lunchroom and lockers. The voices were indistinct. He couldn't make out what was being said. Except for one voice, louder than the rest, who complained to his fellows about his pay packet being two weeks late. He couldn't hear the soothing reply, but the voice was familiar: Dmitry!

He felt a surge of energy almost as intense as the rush of the memory drug. Seventy metres to go. Up ahead was a right turn. The duct became dark again as he turned the corner. His left eye, with the contact lens still in place, had settled. He squinted with alternating eyes to see his watch or the middle distance. He chanced a peek at his watch. 0530h. It would be several hours of silent waiting once he reached the planned rest stop. With luck he could doze.

His heart fluttered when he found himself directly above a washroom. He timed his movements to the sounds of a toilet flushing and the sink tap gushing water. A flatulent operative broke wind while his colleague griped. When the dryer fan turned on, he crawled as silently and quickly as he could and traversed the grille without being heard. Beyond the right turn was the second drop, built the same way as the first. He was better prepared this time. He got his leg into position using a side duct. The rope was as expected. He found the steps with his penlight. Counted down again. Twelve steps.

Again, he tested the floor of the duct. It held his weight without complaint. *Pretty good sheet metal worker*, he joked to himself. He moved ahead on his elbows. Thirty metres to go. He checked the distance line and his watch. His shoulders were really burning up now. The military crawl was for younger, fitter people.

He realized that his counting was jumbled. His focus was drifting as his shoulders stole his attention. He recognized it and took a few more deep breaths. In, out. In, out. Seven seconds each way, as he'd been trained to do. Better. He pushed himself the last stretch and then he saw it. The huge room, with a big oval table. Faux windows to simulate a location above ground. It was directly below him. The grille was near right corner just as Dmitry had shown him on the blueprint.

Seeing the meeting room was unsettling. It had been featured many times in news updates. White walls, gold trim, an AC vent in the wall beside the president. Novi felt a surreal tourist's awe, like seeing the Eiffel Tower or the Tower of Pisa. But mass murder was plotted here. His pulse began to race. History would be made in this room in just a few hours. Time seemed to collapse around him as a newsreel of atrocities blended with images of meetings conducted in this very spot and played themselves on the inner screen of his memory. He took a sip of Methadone from a syringe he'd kept to one side separate from the Naloxone. Soon his medicated brain began to slow down. His four-hour sleep break, just like back in school. He set a vibrating alarm on his watch for four hours. A few more deep breaths and he was out.

5

Novi awoke with a start, feeling dizzy. His resolve and focus came back like a slap of cold water. He'd slept in the duct work above the false ceiling for four hours straight. The last dose of Methadone was a double, and while it kept him calm, too much would reduce his alertness. He'd titrated perfectly and his timing was ideal. He shut off the vibrating wristwatch alarm five minutes before it was due. Adrenaline began to take over as he heard the voices in a hallway nearby. One was Dmitry.

He calmed himself. Ten slow breaths. The Carfentanil was just beneath his skin, impervious and only dangerous if he mishandled it. Review the tasks: first, reload his own opioid receptors with Naloxone this time. The PICC line was just above his left elbow, easy reach. This would put him into withdrawal, he knew, but in ten minutes the president would be two metres directly below him. So close now, and no room for second thoughts. Second task: retrieve the vials of Carfentanil. He fished them out from his right pouch. Now he lay motionless again.

Dmitry entered first, followed by three others Novi hadn't seen before. They weren't in any of the files he'd seen. Or maybe it was his facial recognition again. Wasn't the dementia drug supposed to fix that? He almost wanted to laugh out loud. Most likely, they'd been rotated out. Or perhaps Dmitry was able to request a new group of partners.

"Everyone, take a quadrant," Dmitry said, pulling out his heat sensor and metal detector. He sounded nonchalant, and his hands were steady, courtesy of Novi's prescribed beta blockers. He positioned himself below Novi and waved his disabled sensors slowly over the walls, up toward the ceiling, and over the floor.

Another of Dmitry's helpers was to have interrupted the camera feed and inserted blank footage of the room empty with a false timestamp proving it to be sealed. Everyone knew there would be cameras and bugs in this room. Novi knew it too. The bugs were harder to deal with. They really had no idea how many there were, or if there were any near the ceiling. One was known, in a jar of pencils and markers on a table beside the big battle map.

The map had seen better days; multiple redrawn lines and arrows intersected each other. Numbers at the margins were crossed out, replaced by lower numbers. That map would hang in a museum someday, the pictorial truth of futility and death the president had unleashed. Angry red *X*s belied the changes made hurriedly to try and stem the losses and the bleeding. The president hadn't seen this particular map yet. If he did, there'd be nowhere to hide. The security crew had debated this a few days earlier: where do we keep it for quick reference? One of their lieutenant generals, A. V., had already gone missing last month, soon after the president, teeth clamped together in rage, had softly pronounced, "I'd hoped for better news this day, general. Please stay after the meeting."

In case the message wasn't getting through, he'd been found eviscerated, hanging from a tree in the courtyard where the operatives took their tea and smoke breaks. His guts were piled neatly on his combat boots. His wife would receive the standard telegram about the lieutenant general's misfortune in the midst of a special military operation. No pension for this one's family; he'd fucked up too badly to be worthy. The president was full to his back teeth of stories of failure, excuses, poor morale. The security crew knew that part of their job description included disposal and cleanup. Dmitry, raised on a farm, was more immune to the mess and the smell, a big part of his appeal among otherwise very hard men. He had cemented his place in the team in this way. He pressed his advantage on occasion to keep from being too obviously quiet.

Dmitry decided to berate one of the security detail. "Hey! Visitors will be here in 5 minutes with the minister. Get moving or we're all in deep shit."

One of the other uniforms was gazing absently at the map, maybe looking for the closest spot to his family's village, or just imagining anywhere far from here. He recovered himself and quickly spread the updated version, specifically crafted every forty-eight hours for these meetings, on an easel. The original factually correct map was hurriedly rolled up and threaded into a tubular case. Nobody mentioned its existence aloud. Bugs. This map was slid into a spot between the radiator and the wall where it wasn't visible. The story it told was not favorable. The substitute was a watered-down euphemism, drawn and maintained by syco-phants to keep the boss happy.

Almost on cue the door opened wide. The next team of secu-rity strode in, looked around the room. They were all dressed in black. Huge sides of solid beef. Shoulder holsters. One put down a pot of tea. *How much easier this could be if we brewed that tea*, Novi thought. Another placed three cups for the president and his guests. These were the elite, impenetrable, incorruptible core of a huge security network. They all worked in teams of four. Men only. Each trained in at least two methods of martial arts and fully experienced in the use of knives, handguns, and anything else that could be used to kill. Always armed. All required to retire at age thirty-five. To keep the force nimble, fit, and unable to stay long enough to form any alliance aside from unwavering support and fear of the president.

The table was long, and the president was known to have a habit of taking the seat closest to the door in any room he entered. Novi was two metres above and to the right of the chair the president would occupy. The new security team looked around. One picked up the cup of pencils and markers, looked inside, and replaced it with a satisfied smile. Another looked briefly at the map, shook his head, and swore softly.

The largest, a huge solid wall of muscle, kicked him fiercely. "What the fuck is that? We know our president will turn this around. Are you on this team or what? Remember Andrei? Get your fuckin head on straight, brother! And remember this—THIS is the real map, right? The reality for the president. Nothing else. Or he will lose his temper, and I'll ask him to start with you."

He looked at the uniforms as they prepared to leave.

"Who's got a cup? Anyone? Fuck. Who hired you anyway?"

He took the president's cup, poured it about a quarter full, and gave it to Dmitry. "Drink up, friend. *Na zdrovye.* Let's go!"

Dmitry, as much as anyone in this room, knew the risks of sipping tea around here. The Project had once hoped to turn the chef's underlings. Tea would have been a useful vehicle. He feigned caution, gave the beefy man a pleading look, then drank the serving in one gulp. Pretended to be stricken with fear. Then surprised, even pleased and relieved to have survived it. For now, anyway.

"Thanks, captain. It's good. More?"

The captain froze for a second, then laughed heartily. Dmitry was a favorite. "No, but you can rinse that out at the bar. Don't tell the boss."

Novi saw this small drama play out from his perch in the ductwork. He felt enormous affection for Dmitry too. Dmitry, who had gone over the building plans several times, always patient, fully aware that the team could have no holes, squabbling, rivalries, egos. He was a born leader and had become a friend in just days.

He had found a pharmacist with underground contacts all over Moscow and beyond to procure the necessary medications to keep Novi alert, calm, and coherent. And the plastic knives, vials of tissue glue from cosmeticians' spas, a quiet supply of opiates and naloxone. Dmitry had understood, with his paramedic's training, the critical nature of having Novi in just the right headspace at the right times. As a former soldier, he knew how and when to react. As importantly, when not to.

Now Dmitry dried off the teacup, placed it on the tray beside the samovar and the other matching cups, and called his team to the door. He was giving the performance of his life. He and Novi both knew they might never meet again on this earth. Novi felt the bittersweet tang of melancholy suddenly—for all the friend-ship, all the love, all the guilt and joy he'd known along the way—and silently asked for forgiveness from all who had been on the sharp end of his arrogance. His mean childhood violence. His petty grudges. He longed to tell the people he'd hurt that, in this extremity of his life, He'd learned something. He was sorry. He knew that he might live only a few minutes more, and that the history books may not be kind. It would all depend on who was writing them. And on whether he, Novichok the second team point member, succeeded.

The security group withdrew to the doorway, their captain satisfied with the room. He found much of this preparation to be theatrical and unnecessary. The whole compound had been swept completely for bugs, other than the FSB's own, every month for years. Nothing had been found since before 2014, when he'd joined the Service. Poison in the tea? Forget it. We poison the other guys, not the other way around. Still, it was important to put on enough of a show for those junior to himself in case anyone got funny ideas. Dmitry showed promise; maybe he could be a captain someday. The others seemed to him like dead wood, taking orders without any curiosity. Generally, perfectly suited to this line of work. Too much curiosity might make a man think too much, get the wrong ideas.

They were very well-paid in this group by military standards, and they had prestige. Girls were impressed when they heard stories about the president. The boys on the team all got laid regularly. They could grab what they wanted from the shops or skip out of some of the better restaurants just by flashing their badges. With the president's recent changes to the law, demanding absolute fealty to the state, the security forces guys really came into their own. Nobody dared challenge them over a disputed girlfriend or on occasion even a nice car, watch, or motorcycle. Life in Moscow was good for the personal security boys. Really no need for curiosity. Or a conscience.

There was a knock on the door. To amuse himself in this extreme situation, Novi imagined names for the people in the tableau vivant below. Big Beef opened it, and the minister of defence strode in, posture rigid, his face tense. His loose jowls reminded Novi of a basset hound. "Listen up, everyone! There's been a change of plan."

Novi suddenly began to sweat: should he start trying to back up? Get away before he was found out? What if they were about to change rooms? Where was Dmitry?

The minister resumed. "The seats will be reconfigured here, and the camera staff will set up to record this important summit meeting for national television. This will prove to the people that our objectives are being met." Novi's heart slowed; there would be no change of venue.

The minister himself longed for this to be objectively true, but the men in the room knew that the truth on that other, hidden map was very different. Having esteemed guests would be a much-needed image boost. Novi watched the team's confusion with mild, detached relief. The room was still being used, and he was positioned nicely. A change of room would have been disastrous—and might indicate that someone in security was onto the plan. Dmitry was helping the cameraman set up his lights and reflectors. One of the black clothes detail was assembling a microphone stand beside each of three upholstered chairs, with the placebo map on the easel as a backdrop. The minister was pacing around the room and looking in corners, at electric sockets, and ventilation ducts.

Novi was just around the corner of an elbow in the man-sized duct he'd occupied for the last few hours. Suddenly he wanted to piss himself. After several hours of purposeful dehydration, his kidneys still made enough urine to give him the urge. Through his small dental mirror, he saw the minister glance up at his duct, then away, as he carried on around the room. Satisfied with the video preparations, the minister turned to the cameraman.

"The president, our president, will be here in this room, in that chair. Our message today is one of victory for our nation, and for our president! Do you understand? The people need to see strength, charisma. The greatness of our nation, our cause, our heroes. I am merely a servant to the nation. But our president is everything to us! Make him look good. Great. Like the leader that he is! This footage will be historic. Give these moments all the respect they deserve."

The cameraman was well aware of the reviews his latest opus had received; he didn't need to be told his job today. One of the uniformed security group had visited his apartment after the last video was analyzed by the Western media. The president had looked pale, badly lit, twitchy. The minister had appeared tired, depressed, desperate.

The cameraman went out to drink away his worries after the show. The visitor had informed the cameraman's wife that his next piece of work needed to be of higher quality, or he may soon be out of work. Or worse. The poor wife had called her husband in terror. They had three young kids. They couldn't afford much; they certainly couldn't afford unemployment or panic. He'd sworn off the vodka that night. No more drinking on the job. This room had no natural light; there were no windows underground. The side umbrellas with indirect light would flatter the president's cheekbones; less glare would reduce or eliminate the need for makeup. The president detested makeup for any shoot. His intense homophobia was known worldwide.

The minister needed some color; he looked half-dead from stress or lack of sleep. He'd been dreading this performance for the last few days. The command to produce a new set piece for the people had come indirectly, not from the president himself. The minister of defence sat on one of the red-and-gold armchairs and the cameraman applied some foundation while he studied the notes he would speak from: the enemy was being driven further back, another town had been taken. Our bravest and best were carrying the battle fiercely, proudly forward. It was the will of God. It was our destiny.

In reality, the minister knew something else: the mothers' action group was demanding the return of their sons' bodies for a decent burial. Another battle formation had been ambushed by clever use of drones and decoys. Among that group were another general and two lieutenant-colonels. A large cache of ammo, two helicopters, and twelve tanks had been destroyed. Incursion into Russian land, sacred land, had occurred. Another command control HQ was gone. A regional centre had been lost back to the enemy, and the mobilization of new recruits had driven many of the nation's young men straight into the welcoming arms of the dreaded, satanic West.

The minister's life was becoming increasingly difficult. His wife and children had asked for months now when they would receive permission to leave for their villa in Italy. The minister knew that if he let them go, the president would find out soon after and would take that as a vote of non-confidence. The minister's wife was now refusing to sleep with him. As if he'd be able to perform anyway, such was his stress. She shrieked her rage and disappointment whenever he was permitted to leave the palace and see his family. He felt more at home among his men.

Suddenly there was confusion in the meeting room. The leader of the black-clad team was telling the minister that he would not be appearing on camera with the president; the chairs were being rearranged. The special guests would arrive soon; he would pour the tea and leave.

He knew what this meant. He argued, he pleaded. They were unyielding. "Fine then, let them choke on their fucking tea!"

He was led from the room by the security team, their guns drawn. He had just been demoted. He wasn't going to see the villa in Italy, and neither would his family. More worthy, more important guests were coming to take his place.

Novi, watching from the duct, knew what he was hearing: the death-throes of a man who'd taken his position for granted, now headed for the basement level where the practitioners of the president's favorite spectator sport awaited. He felt no pity.

The guests arrived and were shown to their seats at the far end of that massive table, about five metres away from the president. They sat patiently, like children at a class photo, while they were subjected to the grooming and makeup routine. Novi didn't dare to angle for a better view. He watched it all through the dental mirror, filling in the blanks with his imagination. He checked his supplies while the confusion continued. Carfentanil. Fan. Straw, just in case. He felt for the Naloxone syringes. Checked his watch. The guests would wait for the president to make his appearance. They sat obediently and stared at the table. Allies but not friends.

The president entered through the door, held open by Dmitry. He took his customary seat near the right side. Again, Novi had that sense of being a tourist. But something else: the adrenaline thrill of voyeurism. Nobody in the world knew where he was in that moment. Just a few metres away sat one of the most recognizable people in the world. Who couldn't see him! Who didn't know what was about to happen! The rush was beyond any excitement he'd ever felt.

The president looked small, pale, tired, and pathetically human. The makeup man approached and the president unleashed a stream of abuse. Novi hadn't learned half the words he used, but they were effective. The makeup man backed off hurriedly and left the room, closing the door behind him.

The cameraman got his shots lined up and moved out of the frame. He also left the room to operate the camera remotely, and the door was closed again. It was Showtime.

6

Something was wrong. Novi smelled smoke. Burning tires? Suddenly he saw thick black plumes billowing from the air vent behind the president. For an instant he lay bemused in a dissociated sense of detachment, wondering where it might be coming from. In the next moment he realized that it surrounded him too. His eyes began to sting suddenly. Now he was fully engaged, all senses on high alert and his inner alarm bells pealing. His eyes watered fiercely, and the remaining contact lens floated off. He blinked and it was lost. He clawed at the tapes securing his incisions, then took a deep breath and pulled the clotted margins apart with a groan. The Carfentanil was right there. He popped both vials into a pocket of his robe and slid his N95 mask up.

The memory drug must stay warm! Two plastic vials, five milliliters each. Hurriedly he sucked on the port of the IV bag, put the first vial in his mouth, swallowed it, and chased it with a small sip of saline. Then the second. He tried to keep swallowing, his throat drying rapidly in the smoky air.

Big Beef burst through the door, pushed the president to the floor and drew his weapon. The president crawled on all fours away from the vent, keeping his head down and gasping every few seconds for breath. The smoke thickened, Big Beef now looking into the air vent at waist level. Novi realized that his breathing was shortening, growing ragged. Dmitry was holding his composure but stifled a cough. Novi began hacking uncontrollably. The president looked up at Novi's ceiling vent, and his face slackened in astonishment.

One of the men from Dmitry's team rushed in with a ladder. Big Beef trained his weapon on the ceiling. The team-mate pulled the grill off. Novi, bleeding and coughing, put his hands out to be seen. His eyes met Dmitry's for an instant.

The president's face now turned to stone, his eyes cold blue beads of malice.

The fan sped up noticeably, the air circulation system pushed into overdrive by an unseen operator. The whole room filled briefly with smoke, then cleared rapidly. The only one who was unable to go to ground was Novi. Everyone else—Dmitry, the special guests—had crowded around the president on the floor to shield him from harm.

When the air cleared, Big Beef's security team surrounded the ladder under Novi's vent. Weapons aimed at his heart and head. Big Beef roared up at him, "Get down here now, you son of a bitch. Hands on the ladder or I'll kill you right here and now!" To the president he lowered his head. "I am truly sorry, Mr. President. We received intel only a few minutes ago about a plot on your life. We were warned about a rat in the ceiling. And here he is!"

The president put a restraining hand on Beef's arm. "Forgot your training, captain? We want to know more about our visitor. I have learned much from rats in my lifetime. Don't kill him so soon. Please, help him down here. And do *not* let him hurt himself. I'm sure we have much to discuss."

Big Beef nudged one of his team. "Get a partner, hold that ladder steady, and make sure he can't hit his head." To Novi he barked," Hands right onto the ladder handles. That's right. Now feet. Move it, you scum!"

The whole group—president, guests, and guards—stared in bewilderment as the dusty black hem descended to the top rung of the ladder. A *priest*? Novi had trouble keeping his hands visible while finding his footing. His eyes continued to water. Big Beef growled. "Don't try anything funny, you bastard. Are you a priest? Who the hell are you? Rasputin? Talk fast or start praying!"

Novi inched down the rungs carefully, trembling head to toe, trying to think. He now stood in the centre of the circle of men, ringed by rifles, with his hands in the air.

The president stepped forward to stare straight into Novi's eyes. For Novi, it was like seeing into a well with no bottom. He shuddered inwardly, a feeling of contagion. "Come here, visitor. What brings you to interrupt our business? In my own home! And a priest, no less. What would the Patriarch say?" His voice was firm but gentle. Even in his dire state, Novi found it persuasive, strangely soothing.

Dmitry stepped forward with his disabled metal detector, waved it over Novi and pronounced, "No weapons Sir." Novi's eyes looked to everyone else like a plea for mercy. Dmitry sensed the beginnings of a faint hope.

"Strip him." Ordered Big Beef. Dmitry stepped forward to comply, Beef's sidearm aimed squarely at Novi's head. The whole assembly—vassal guests, security, the president, Novi—were gathered at one end of the room. Novi glanced around himself. The air fans blew at half-speed. Dmitry understood immediately, they would all get a taste of Carfentanil if they stayed clustered here. He pulled off Novi's N95 mask, dropped it at his own feet, and yanked the robe over Novi's head, leaving Novi standing in his underwear. The incisions gaped, bleeding at the margins. They had been opened only the previous day, and now Novi had just clawed them open again. The PICC line hung exposed from Novi's left arm.

The president connected the dots. Now his voice rose. "You're the one my godson warned me about! You killed him, didn't you? My turn now, scum. I know all about your little group. As soon as we conclude here, I'll deal with them for good."

Dmitry tried to buy time and saw a flicker of light in Novi's eyes. "Sir, what's this all about?" He pulled out the syringes from the black robe, holding them up for his commander.

"Let's ask our visitor. Talk fast, you bastard!" Big Beef slapped Novi hard across the face. His nose began bleeding profusely.

"Fuck yourself. With both fists!" Novi shot back. Big Beef slapped him again. Blood sprayed onto the president's suit as he stood right beside the two, enjoying his ringside seat. "Okay! It's—it's Novichok. I was sent to poison the president with his own favorite drug."

Now Dmitry held up the wrapped Carfentanil. He was catching on. "And what's this, you piece of shit?"

"Cocaine. To help me stay awake."

"And why did you come with your own intravenous? Are you some sort of drug addict? Disgusting."

"They put me up to it. They said I'd never have to worry about getting enough safe drugs." Novi gasped, improvising neatly into the gaps Dmitry opened for him.

The president's voice was barely a whisper, his face pale with rage. "You personify everything I despise about your corrupt West. Weak. Cowardly. So overconfident that you can't perceive your most glaring weaknesses. How infuriating it is for a great warrior nation such as mine to play second fiddle to you people. They send a drug addict to kill *me*? *You're* the best they could find? I guess that's no surprise.

Once I was cornered by a rat. Now I have cornered a rat myself. And I have learned to always be decisive, to do what must be done. You killed my favorite godson. A wonderful man. I will savor the pleasure of avenging Pavel myself."

"Thanks for making my day, Mr. President. Your favorite godson? Now I know for certain that killing that rat was the right thing to do. He deserved to die more painfully. Like you, he was a liar. Unworthy of trust or respect by real human beings. Good riddance. No regrets."

The president's rage softened his voice to a whisper. He pointed with a shaking finger at Dmitry's hand. "Give me that drug. Novichok. I've yet to personally see it in action. I've heard it's quite a show." Big Beef put his weapon on a nearby table, stepped behind Novi, and grabbed his left arm in a shoulder lock. He motioned Dmitry over. The rest of the security team kept their weapons trained on Novi.

Dmitry knew that anything less than immediate compliance was useless. Novi's eyes traveled to the Carfentanil ampules and back. Dmitry understood. He screwed the first syringe of Naloxone onto the PICC line, opened the valve, and offered it to the President. With unrestrained glee the President pushed the dose into Novi.

Novi made a show of fighting back as hard as he could, his face bloodied and his shoulder almost dislocated in the iron grip of the big guard.

"Again! Do it again!" the president shouted. Dmitry fired in a second dose. Novi began to sneeze. His eyes watered, he gasped and sneezed, and his limbs began twitching. His pantomime of Novichok poisoning may not have been fully accurate. It felt a lot like opioid withdrawal.

Dmitry held up a vial of Carfentanil. He had a dose of Naloxone on board already and his planned diversion coming any time now. "Captain, let's really mess him up!" He checked to be sure that he was upwind of the group, and without waiting for a reply, he held the vial in front of Novi just as Novi wound up and sneezed again. Dmitry held his breath, then coughed out into the cloud of powder floating past him. Being at the edge of the clustered men, he dodged the whole thing. The building's fans did the rest, the powder drifting to the president, the guests, and minions.

Dmitry coughed again, doubling over to grab for the robe. He felt for the IV just above his ankle and emptied another dose of Naloxone into himself. He jammed the rest of the syringes into his uniform pocket.

The president was too surprised to react immediately. Big Beef, his team, and the two special guests didn't see any threat from the powder in the air until it was too late. The president's face went blank, but his right hand went instinctively to the inside of his suit, fumbling for his shoulder holster. The gunslinger's walk. He fell headfirst to the floor. The others were close behind.

Dmitry grabbed Big Beef's gun from the table and fired twice through the guard's head. With an executioner's practiced hand, he fired a single round into each sedated man's head. He stopped at the president, looked at Novi, and handed him the gun. "It's why you're here, Novi. He's probably already dead."

Novi's hand shook. Nerves or withdrawal? He gritted his teeth and looked down at the president, curled up on the floor. But the president twitched and suddenly the hand came from inside the suit jacket with a small handgun, aimed at Novi. The president's eyes opened, unseeing, a pure instinct. Novi had just enough time to fire once into the top of the president's head. That brain. Then something animal burst out of Novi's soul. He fired five more times, his hand now steady, while he screamed curses.

Dmitry gently lowered Novi's hand. "That's enough. Let's get out of here."

In the far distance, a loud explosion shook the building. The cameras stopped blinking, and the ceiling lights flickered out. More dust fell from the duct. A team of men rushed in wearing hazmat suits and respirators. Their leader wore a body camera; he stopped briefly to rotate himself and give the camera a full view of the carnage, zooming in on the dead president. There could be no coverup when the footage was uploaded to the world. In the glow of their headlamps, they pulled Novi and Dmitry from the room. They pushed a cabinet against the door from outside. The president, his vassal visitors, and Big Beef's team bled silently on the floor.

In the next room the hazmat team got to work. They found Dmitry's IV and added more Naloxone, then did the same for Novi. Dmitry was falling asleep; he revived quickly and smiled up at Konstantin. "Great work! Let's get away from here."

Into his walkie, Konstantin barked, "Plan Delta. Plan Delta." He ushered Novi and Dmitry through the anteroom, past a row of hazmat suits, to a rack full of AK47s. "Dmitry, one for you and one for me. Novi, here's my Glock. Keep moving!"

Konstantin led them to a stairwell with a disabled lock and up two flights of stairs.

The lock at the top was disabled, the door hanging partly open. He showed them a ventilation grill, partly opened. The lights stuttered as the backup generator kicked on. The overhead camera was dead, its glass eye shattered. Novi realized where they were and bent down to the grill. The screws were already out, and the grill came away easily. Konstantin's team had done their job thoroughly.

"Get in! Hurry. Go left and stay straight ahead. It's about seventy metres." Novi urged the other two. His voice was raspy, his eyes running and his nose still bloody. All three of them were buzzing with adrenaline.

In the background, the electricity went out again, part of the unseen team's efforts to provide them a head start.

Dmitry and Konstantin dragged and shoved Novi onward through the duct to the grill beside the parked Lada. Novi was fully into withdrawal now, shivering and cramping. They kicked out the grill and ran for the car, Dmitry at the wheel, and Novi in back. Konstantin held his rifle tensely at the window looking for any sign of ambush. Novi took a big mouthful of Methadone while Konstantin made a quick call.

"Plan D. On our way. Bring more Vitamin N. Throw away the phone!" He yelled to Mikhail. Dmitry knew every shortcut, side, and back street and drove the fine-tuned Lada like a stuntman. They could hear the sirens approaching the palace now. In the rearview mirror a plume of black smoke rose behind them. Another diversion.

Once on the motorway Dmitry slowed down to highway speed and began to relax. The radio played bouncy Russian pop music. The weather report was mundane, a bright sunny Moscow day. The news would come on later.

In another half hour they were back at the garage. Mikhail immediately took off the plate from the Lada's bumper, chopped it to pieces, and replaced it with one from an old wreck in the yard. The serial number had already been ground off. He would start painting it now. The spray gun was primed and ready. Ukraine-flag blue.

Novi, Dmitry and Konstantin were treated to a cold outdoor shower standing over a grate to remove any traces of Carfentanil. Novi kept the water away from his incisions; he'd had no chance to glue them shut. The first hour dragged as he waited for the Naloxone to give him back his needy brainstem. His swollen nose stung fiercely under the stream of cold water. Mikhail donned a painter's respirator mask and rinsed the black robe over the drain in his garage, then hung it to dry. Novi started an IV on Konstantin and gave him the last dose of Naloxone as a precaution.

Mikhail donned a mask and gloves, rinsed the cassock over the drain in his garage, then hung it to dry. Artemy the pharmacist had called trusted colleagues and now arrived with three patients' worth of Naloxone to last over the next twenty-four hours if needed. He'd brought skin prep and tissue glue, bandages, and a gift: ten tablets of 10 mg Oxycodone. He shook Novi's hand with both of his own, tears in his eyes.

Artemy gave Novi a ride to Father Maxim's home. "If my wife can see her family one day it will be because of your bravery. We can never thank you enough. Still early days but we're grateful no matter what."

Olga was cooking at Father Maxim's house. The potato pancakes smelled wonderful. Birds sang near the window. Outside, the sky darkened, a forecast for unexpected rain later. Novi was greeted at the door by Father Maxim. He had a concerned look on his face. As the door closed, he embraced Novi and asked, "Are you okay? I can only imagine how you must feel."

Novi's mind swam in a pond of discomfort, tension, confinement, and darkness. It was a blur at the moment. He knew he had completed the Project's mandate and was safely among friends. No immediate danger. "Fine, I guess. We had to make adjustments. We all did everything the way we should, and still there were improvisations."

"But we killed. You killed. You need to confess. God will forgive you, and all of us. We have only to believe." Father Maxim put on his stole, crossed himself three times, and began, "Bless me Father, for I have sinned. Now you, Novi."

Novi, who had not been in a confessional since being evicted from one, repeated after the priest, "Bless me, Father, for I have sinned. It has been eighteen years since my last confession." The words began flowing from him automatically as the sacramental memory, part of his being from early childhood, disinterred itself and took over.

"In that time the sins I have committed are killing other human beings, lying to my family, skipping church almost all the time..." He paused and took a deep breath before he could continue. "Being unfaithful to my wife." His voice began to fail him. Another long pause. His emotions began to well up from far in the past. "Being envious of those who seem happier or better off than I am. And in my youth, being hurtful to everyone around me when I couldn't understand myself or my life. Being ungrateful for all the blessings I've taken for granted. I am sorry for these sins, Father, and I resolve to do better."

Father Maxim crossed himself again three times, and said firmly, "Your sins are forgiven. For your penance, say one Our Father. And promise to be a better man."

Novi also crossed himself and stood to full height. He didn't realize he'd been crying the whole time.

7

A wave of panic washed over the city. VKontakte overheated, overloaded, and shut itself down within ten minutes of the first leaked whisper. Much of the populace had been steeped in the brew of propaganda that had poured forth from the Kremlin over the past decade. They had long been conditioned to believe the president's version of events, that Ukraine was a Nazi state that needed their fraternal love to return to decency and a rightful role as subordinate little brother. These were in the majority and immediately blamed Ukraine.

Security in Moscow the next day was as tight as anyone had ever seen it. Checkpoints were set up everywhere. Downtown businesses were closed. All motor and Metro traffic was halted in a ten km radius around the Kremlin. The palace outside the city was even more heavily guarded. Homes were searched, occupants were questioned, many at gunpoint or in secure rooms with the cameras turned off. All airports were closed, all borders sealed by order of the prime minister as second-in-command, now the top dog.

RTI, Tass, and other press organs of the Kremlin reported breathlessly on the President's sudden death. Almost immediately came the commentary by hawkish politicians and news anchors demanding immediate deployment of nuclear weapons to bomb Kyiv into the last century, or the next. London, New York, Paris, and Berlin too. Those murderous bastards! Fucking Nazis! Scum!

The world's communication satellites beamed the death of the president into every time zone. Billions were transfixed by their screens. The online services showed the same image, with local variations: a passerby looking through a window at a screen displaying newsreel imagery of the president's public life—reviewing troops, riding horseback, a judo match. The print crawl underneath told the story.

The Ukrainian president was contacted for comment. Zelensky steadfastly proclaimed that his people had no prior knowledge of the president's fate. He insisted instead that the president had gotten off easy, rather than face the war crimes court and rot in solitary confinement. His story never wavered. His face began appearing in sidewalk window screens too.

The Russian security agencies knew their fearsome reputation would be badly tarnished by an assassination. Especially this! Right in his official residence, of the man everyone feared. They were fucked, and they knew it. Their creative wheels turned. The scapegoat was already in custody. They could invent the full story later while the minister was held incommunicado. His family's passports were confiscated. They missed their Italian vacation. The press was merciless, as were no doubt the president's specialists in the basement below FSB HQ at the Kremlin.

Gangs of thugs roamed the streets of central Moscow. The half of the populace that had supported the president were hunted down by the mobs who'd despised him. The Arbat, reduced to a shadow of its usual extravagant self, was awash in flipped cars, broken glass, and later, in blood. In the outer city and farther afield ordinary families bought water, toilet paper, canned food, vodka, and buckwheat. They sat in long queues and filled up their cars and trucks even as police blockades left them with nowhere to go. A full tank was an investment. The ruble crashed as citizens waited hours to clear their savings accounts. This was disorder on a scale both personal and widespread. The forests of apartment blocks on the periphery of the city centre housed many of the less fortunate. The destitute lived in parks or along the riverbank. They were a handy outlet for the rage of all those young men.

Anonymous, the hacker group, previously pushed into the shadows by the prospect of fifteen years of hard labor, were emboldened now. They took to the internet to declare that they had never believed the story pushed on TV. Net Voenne. No War. Indeed. They ramped up their cyberattacks and brought a new level of confusion to the proceedings. Russian banks were disabled, airports and train stations were idled, and the internet itself became wildly unpredictable. Even the president's state funeral broadcast was interrupted with peace messages and images of ruined Ukrainian cities, mass graves, wounded and dead children. The soundtrack was the Ukrainian national anthem playing on repeat. The facial recognition cameras sprinkled around the city core were disabled by hackers.

This was how the war came to Moscow. The factions burned each other's homes and cars, the police declared a curfew and routinely enforced it fifteen minutes early to shake the coins loose from fearful stragglers. The hospitals began to fill. There were no available ambulances.

An old friend of the president's watched the news in disgust from his dacha outside Saint Petersburg. He grieved his friend but was pragmatic. Business was suffering. He made some calls. He ordered the few remaining generals on location in the Kremlin to publicly declare that the minister of defense, acting in retaliation for his loss of status and in fear of his life, had acted alone to poison the president. He hated that guy.

The army declared martial law and began rounding up FSB operatives. The FSB retaliated with kidnappings and defenestration. The FSB had a trump card: they still controlled the palace and its security. They bargained for the release of their weakened, tortured officers from basement lodgings in the Kremlin. None were in any condition to lead; most could barely walk. The Duma was surrounded on the outside by the Army, and the building was under siege from within by the FSB.

The military was rudderless, the minister imprisoned, and the office locked. The FSB, personal security apparatus, and remnants of Army command began drawing up their own succession plans. Rivals before, now they were blood enemies. Car bombings and disappearances reached epidemic numbers. Generals and their families retained off-duty soldiers and police as bodyguards.

In Ukraine, the news was met with jubilation. Along the Russian side of the border, local gangsters and chieftains began their own regional campaigns and dug up the bones of long-buried feuds. Army captains and majors formed their own teams. Some carried on with their assigned battle orders, while others struggled for control of towns and regions. The general result was a disjointed offence effort, a loss of discipline, and easy pickings for the Ukrainian side. Pro-Russian politicians appointed in Kherson, Mariupol, and the Donbas began disappearing or surrendering to inform on their colleagues and buy their lives back from the abyss.

Novi was fed generously by Olga. She had even somehow found him coffee beans, a French press, and a grinder. She had begun squirreling away necessities months earlier to avoid suspicions that might arise if she were seen stocking up a week ahead of the assassination. She kissed his hands and told him over and over what a hero he was.

Novi's memory served too well. The day replayed itself to him by day and haunted his dreams at night. The cramped duct was tight when he needed to turn around. Dark. Dusty. Cold. Withdrawal. The bottomless void of the president's eyes most of all.

He'd felt no tension, fear, or remorse. The drug had succeeded in making him robotic for the necessary period of time. As the three-day euphoric wave of its initial effect wore off, he felt only a bit more tired than usual. He had to remind himself to check the toilet for the next day or two. He was mightily relieved to recover his last two vials of the memory drug. He washed them in vodka and iodine, then reinserted them into his kangaroo pouches.

Father Maxim was tasked with the plan of Novi's escape from Russia using a landline in a nearby parishioner's home. Novi and Olga didn't see him much for a week.

Dmitry, Mikhail, and Artemy were incommunicado of course. There could be no congratulations, reunion, or friendly banter. Everyone understood why. Rumors of a house-to-house search campaign had surfaced on the expatriate VPN group chats. There were always rumors in Moscow. Gossip was one of the foundations of any society, but an equal partner to fear and power in this city. The urgency mounted with each news report of an arrest made, a false lead resulting in a house search. Neighbors turned on each other, just as they had learned to do in the Soviet days. Nobody was safe.

With his mission accomplished, Novi's thoughts turned homeward. He sat at dinner one night with Father Maxim, Olga having gone to forage for food and eavesdrop on the neighbors' conversations. The TV news played footage of jets flying over Poland and Finland. The TV map of the Polish border pricked at Novi's conscience. He told the priest, "I'm starting to feel really homesick. Now that the work is done, I have time to worry about my family. I'm sure they're worrying too. The news stories here are all bravado about air force flights over Poland and Finland. I wonder what they're seeing back home. I bet it's scaring them."

Father Maxim saw his distress. "Need a line for a short phone call? That's no problem. Give me a bit of time."

"Thanks, Father. I need them to know I'm all right and there's no danger to me in Warsaw. I'm already a few days overdue."

Maxim had friends in many useful places; the call took place on a Lithuanian VPN line the next day. Novi was relieved to tell his family the white lie that he couldn't do a video call because the internet wasn't reliable or stable enough for it.

"Hi Daddy!" chirped Sam, his daughter. "You've been gone exactly three days too long. When are you coming home already? Will won a soccer tournament. Mom says hi."

"Hey. That's my news! You can't tell my news. Hi Dad. Is Poland nice? Did you meet any kids our age? Are you coming home soon? Mom was getting worried. She tried your phone, but it said 'no service.'"

"Hi, kids! Yes, Poland is very beautiful. The food is amazing! All my faves. But it's really busy at the border. A lot of people need help. Some of them are sick and don't have a doctor or nurse to look after them. So, I've been mostly working. Only I don't know much Polish. I learned the swear words though. Someday we can visit. I've made some friends."

Sara joined in. "Hi, Joe. Has it been a good experience? I know you wanted to do your bit, and I hope it's been what you wanted. Are you eating well? Health okay?"

Joe smiled inwardly. If she only knew. He promised himself to become more present for his loved ones, all of them. Especially his wife. Sara, who had patiently heard all his complaints, his stresses, even when her passion for him had grown cold under the ice water of COVID, work, and every sling and arrow they'd thrown along the way. Even in their imperfect marriage, they had some bonds that were unbreakable. He heard it in her concerned voice. He was reassured and loved her again right then.

She continued, "The news here is all about the president this, president that. Has it affected the border or your work there? Are you safe?"

"Oh yeah, not much has changed here since then. More smiling faces maybe. The people are trying to go home in bigger numbers, but otherwise it's just the same. Lots of flu, untreated infections. Stress, mental health. Those are the big problems. We don't know how lucky we are sometimes. That's what I've learned here.

"The transport situation is messed up pretty badly, though. And with this assassination thing, the airports are clogged with extra security. I hope I'll be home in a week or so, but I can't even guess when for sure. When I find out more, I'll let you know."

That seemed to satisfy them. Novi hung up with a sigh, remembering that he still had to face the reckoning of his dementia when this was over. Time would be precious. Could his mission success be parlayed into a life's supply of memory drug? Assuming its effect didn't fade. He wanted to call his mother too but knew that too many minutes might trigger suspicion. That would have to wait. He would add her to the list of calls to make from Warsaw.

Maxim came home one late night ten days after the assassination with news: "Novi, you'll have minimal trouble exiting Russia to Belarus. The border is largely held by pro-Russian soldiers, local governors, and partisans. They only need to see a Russian passport. I've devised a plan. Here's a letter for Father Mike on behalf of a friend in Gomel. It's written on Orthodox Church letterhead, two copies. He asks you to provide temporary parish help while Professor Miroslav's local priest recovers from back surgery.

"Just show this letter at checkpoints and at the Belarusian border along with your Russian passport. Keep a copy hidden in case you need to use the same trick twice. If this doesn't suffice, you could offer a gift. They'll happily accept a few thousand rubles, a carton of cigarettes, or some vodka. This will get you as far as Gomel, anyway. Transit from Gomel into Ukraine will be a bigger challenge. Miroslav is working on that. One step at a time, I guess."

Maxim made another visit to Artemy's pharmacy. He and Olga helped Novi set up his gear, and he opened his incisions once more. The one on his left was getting red around the edges; Artemy had anticipated this and sent along an antibiotic ointment.

Novi sat on a kitchen chair and felt the alertness bringing him alive again. Maxim gave him some study material: road maps, current as of yesterday, where the checkpoints were least numerous, the police presence less dense, the weather clearer. He had paper copies too. The internet was spotty, service still shaky. Any map app on a phone was unlikely to be usable.

The Project team was still actively collecting information. A riot was being planned for the next day. Antiwar and prowar protesters were both to march close to Red Square. Both sides would have provocateurs in their midst. Extra police presence would be required downtown. Many of the force's most aggressive were already salivating. Fewer would be manning checkpoints beyond the suburbs. Novi sat with his thoughts, meditated the map contents into place in his head. Its interior by now was a butterfly museum of images, pinned to the wall of his history. He had Miroslav's phone number and an approximate arrival in the mid-afternoon. With no hiccups, the trip was nine hours. He expected hiccups.

Olga had cleaned the robe for him and taken out some of the incriminating pockets. Curiously, she had left him the spaces for his gun and ammo. He would say, if anyone asked, that the Church had issued it to him for his own protection. His other clothes were ready too. His toiletry kit was awaiting the toothbrush. Always the last thing to pack.

One final task: she sat him down in the kitchen. While Father Maxim watched with a grin, she applied grey hair dye, smoothed it in, and put a plastic cap on his head. He would match the appearance on his second Russian and Ukrainian passports.

The rioters began crowding into the district around Red Square at dawn. The police radioed for backup shortly thereafter. This left them spread thinly in the suburbs, just as the Project had planned it. Novi sat at the kitchen table with Olga. She held one of his hands while he sipped tea from the cup in his other. They both had tears in their eyes.

"None of us ever knows what our life will bring. I'm so, so happy that I could live to see my country given a chance to be free. And to help such fine men as you and Father Maxim." She held his face in her bony, wrinkled hands, wept profusely at this bittersweet goodbye.

Novi couldn't talk; he knew his voice would break.

Father Maxim embraced him, kissed his cheek, and told him, "I'll pray for you and all of us for the rest of my life. None of us will forget this."

He got into Maxim's car for the short ride to Mikhail's garage. The Lada was a nice shade of blue, but the mechanic was skilled enough to make it seem like an old color, rust spots still showing through and none of the dents hammered out. He'd even driven it through the puddles of rainwater in the potholes behind his service garage. Gas stops would be unnecessary. Mikhail had added a separate fuel tank, and another twenty-litre red jerry can sat on the rear seat. In these days of sudden inflation extra fuel was a common sight.

Novi would again stay with Miroslav. Novi's coffee travel mug was from Stars, the rebranded ersatz Russian Starbucks. He had a bag of apples, and another containing potato pancakes and a little pot of sour cream. With the pepper mixed in, the way Olga had seen him do it.

He threw his suitcase into the trunk and started the car. Mikhail was crying openly. Tears and snot streaked the oil and grime on the mechanic's face.

"Don't worry, Mikhail! I'll look after your baby well."

Artemy had stayed away to avoid any extra trips to this part of the neighborhood. He didn't like goodbyes anyway. His wife had asked to send a note to Novi; her gratitude would be eternal and more. The pharmacist had worked more of his miracles; Novi's pouches held another vial of Carfentanil alongside two doses of memory drug, tissue glue, and ten more tabs of Oxycodone. Two tabs for the road. He couldn't carry them openly across a border.

He reached the edge of the city without incident. Half an hour outside the ring road, he was stopped by a soldier working alone and laboring under a ferocious hangover. He had only to show his passport and the letter from Father Maxim. It barely registered as the disinterested young man waved him through. The cameras were still disabled. There would be no record of the moment the president's killer skipped town.

Novi was alone, but not lonely. The drug acted as his friend and navigator. His mind had been busy for months now. A road trip with a big cup of coffee sounded like the perfect way to start sorting out his inner closet. There was so much to throw away, more to keep. How long would he retain the ability to choose?

Once out of the city, the ride was uneventful, relaxing even. Mikhail had provided an unexpected luxury: pirated satellite radio, Russian version. That catchy, bouncy girl's tune played every hour. He was tired of it and found some Dvorak on a classical station. The roads were in decent shape, the coffee was excellent. The weather cooperated nicely. Some bands of light rain misted his Lada; the sky was mostly cloudy. A good day to travel. Large flocks of birds swarmed against the sky. There were no crows.

Pretty little villages gave way to drab ones the farther out he got from the city. The land looked good though. His prairie eye could tell a healthy crop, and it looked like a good harvest was coming for the farmers. "If they aren't busy burying their sons," he mused aloud to himself. "It could so easily have gone the other way for me. Guns to my head, powdered drugs in the air, kidnapping. Still, here I am, alive and in one piece. So random." A resigned melancholy settled over him. He fiddled with the radio, couldn't find anything to soothe the wound that suddenly opened in his soul.

Three hours later in a field beside the highway, a murder of crows picked at a dead, decaying farm animal. Joe felt a sudden rush of pity for the carcass. He blared the car horn as he passed and the crows ascended in unison, a black cloud of particles, high into the air. "Leave it alone, you fuckers!" He shouted out the open window.

His vision darkened and he suddenly saw himself instead in that field, the dark cloud of crows calling each other to the feast, his own wracked body twisted and dead in the stubble of cut hay, waiting to be claimed by the earth before the crows could do their horrible work. Their beaks and claws shone metallic and bright, circling hungrily overhead...

A kilometre further on, he pulled over into a side road, turned the car to face the highway for a faster getaway if needed, and emptied his bladder, breathing deeply to calm his sudden terror. Another coffee would have been welcome. He added the jerry can's twenty litres to the tank and resumed his ride.

He passed through another checkpoint near the Belarusian border. Dead bugs were plastered to the windshield, and the car looked as though it had been the same color forever. He wasn't especially worried; he had good paperwork, a story, and a destination. Father Maxim had prepared for every contingency. In the glove box was a cell phone, connected to service in Moscow. Novi had memorized the number and those of some of the contacts. Only a few contacts were entered, under names like Father Leonidov and Father Pavel Grywynsky. Barber, Cleaning Lady, Doctor, each with its own name attached. Most names were pulled from an old hard copy phone book. Only one belonged to anyone from the Project. Professor Miroslav Yakushev.

The lone soldier at the checkpoint was more diligent than the hungover specimen on Moscow's perimeter. He read the letter carefully, his lips moving in tandem. He scrutinized the passport, wrote the number down. Novi's bowels started to cramp. He looked in the rearview mirror and saw corn fields. Nobody else in the makeshift guardhouse beside the road. No sound of distant traffic. His hand moved to his lap from the steering wheel.

The soldier was twitchy, saw the movement. His eyes fixed on Novi's. "Who's Professor Miroslav to you?"

Novi felt the hairs on his neck rising. His mouth went dry. "Nobody I've ever met, Sergeant. I was assigned by my prelate to go and relieve a priest in Gomel. He has a bad back; he needs an operation. The professor is a parishioner."

The soldier still was not convinced. "Aren't you too old to take orders? Why don't you have your own parish by now? Do you like boys or something?" He was a country boy, went to church regularly, and had never seen a priest this old as a subordinate.

"No. I... I have a problem with vodka. They won't give me a parish of my own unless I can stay sober for a year. It'll never happen. I'm dying for a drink right now. Can I go?" A great lie, and it also explained the sweaty face and shaky hands.

Now the soldier was more sympathetic. But he was practical too. "So, then, I'll let you keep one of those bottles. I'll have the other." He put out his hand and Novi gave him the bribe.

"Thank you, Sir. Thank and bless you." He started the car and drove slowly away. The soldier took a picture of Novi's plate with his phone. Novi's hands shook. He was exhilarated again, as he'd been inside the palace air ducts. He wondered what his chances would have been if the soldier had forced his hand. The adrenaline paired nicely with the gradual fade of euphoria as his body metabolized the memory drug.

He had seen the soldier taking a photo of his license plate and knew it would be time stamped. He would need to stay within the speed limit until the border, now only a half hour away. The soldier didn't seem to have a radio. Maybe the cell service here was spotty. Novi turned his on and saw that he had none. Great news. He pulled over for a minute to shift the gun up under the passenger's seat into the springs. It was loaded, safety on. He put the clips there too on a hunch. Better to give them only one place to find anything they shouldn't.

Two soldiers guarded the border crossing. Novi showed the letter, his Russian passport, and recited his rehearsed story. The vodka version was very credible. He congratulated himself, smiling inwardly. He'd been wise to take his green tablets earlier on the ride. They asked him to open the trunk. Just his suitcase in there. The first soldier opened it, threw socks and underwear around, and dumped the contents into the trunk. Novi's heart rate began to climb as the second soldier reached under the seat. The first questioned him about his parish, destination, and the bottle of vodka on the passenger seat.

His partner grunted. He was kneeling on the passenger side. "Hey, Father, what's your home parish again?"

Novi was suddenly blank. He didn't know; it was a hole in his Swiss cheese. He only knew enough, in that moment, not to give away Father Maxim. He gave the first answer that came to him, from a map he'd memorized. "Immaculate Heart of Mary. Voronezh 31, Donskoy District."

The guard stood up, holding Novi's gun. "Exactly what sort of church is this, Father? Hey?"

His partner, seeing the gun, drew his own and aimed it straight at Novi's heart. "What the fuck is this? Hands up you bastard! Now!!"

Novi fought against his panic. The thought flashed through his mind: *I've made it through something bigger already. Keep cool.*

The second guard patted Novi down, tugged at the robe. "Take it off right now." He kept his gun on Novi as he pulled the robe over his head.

The two now regarded the man in front of them not as a priest or a traveler, but as an enemy. They made him remove his underwear. He stood naked and barefoot on the pavement. He pleaded.

"My prelate gave that to me because he said traveling alone wasn't safe. I don't even know how to use it!"

No tattoos. Not much muscle bulk. The reddened incisions caught the first guard's eye. "What the fuck is that?"

"It's my hernia operation. See, on the other side there's another. We don't rest when we're ill. God always has something for us to do." He hoped to show them that they were on the same side of something—disarm their suspicion.

The first guard handed Novi the gun. The second kept his trained on Novi and looked at his partner in surprise. "What the fuck are you doing, Comrade?"

Number One said, "Show us. This should be fun. Can you hit that fencepost across the road?"

Novi took the gun in his left hand, looked at a side toggle button, and asked, "Is this the safety?" The sight of a naked man demonstrating his inadequacy at target practice would have drawn quite a crowd, but they were at a quiet part of the border. Novi fired the weapon at the fence with his left hand, missed badly, and dropped the gun in the process. It went off again and the round hit the office booth.

Number Two was furious. "Hey, that's enough. Do we keep this guy or not? Let's not fuck around like that anymore!"

Number One looked at Novi in distaste. "Do you wanna keep him? Look at him. He's fuckin pathetic. I'll flip you for the gun. It's a nice one."

To Novi he barked, "Your weapon is hereby confiscated. You can't handle it anyway. Fuckin amateur! Hurry up before I change my mind. And that vodka? That's evidence too. You shouldn't drink and drive!"

"My apologies, captain! Thank you! Bless you!" He grabbed his clothes and shoes from the pavement, got in the Lada, and drove away as quickly as care allowed. He left the soldiers flipping a coin for the gun.

8

Novi and Miroslav alternately laughed and shook their heads in amazement as Novi told of his day's journey, the checkpoints, and the border guards. He'd been able to keep his identity secret—had avoided killing one man and being killed himself.

"What's with the grey hair? Did your time in Moscow do that to you? I can just imagine how it must have been!" Miroslav teased as he poured them each a tumbler of cognac. "This will reverse the aging process for at least an hour or two. To peace." He toasted, and they clinked glasses.

"Now let me be serious. I've been researching the region's border crossings. Most are closed, the rest guarded by a combination of soldiers—mostly Russians and Belarusian border agents. They won't accept requests for free passage anymore, I'm afraid. Any personal favors could get someone into a lot of trouble. Things have changed around here since you performed your task.

"My friends have sent me drone footage and locations to consider." He opened a laptop and showed Novi an aerial shot of a rural two-lane road, with a guardhouse at one side and another larger building about fifty metres from it along a single lane of dirt track. The sides were fenced with razor wire, and gates hung over both ends. The metal was shiny, the whole site appearing to be brand new. "I've done a lot of thinking about your re-entry into Ukraine. I've figured out a story for you. Suppose you're working for Patriarch Kirill, and you have to get intel to his minions in the

Orthodox Church in Ukraine. There's a monastery in Chernihiv. Imagine that you have word on deportations of the bishops. It's been a rumor for weeks now. You're bringing them new ID packages so they can escape, just blend into the general population. You can't send anything by the internet or email. It's too risky and transmissions like this are being intercepted all the time. That's why you're going in person, to bring in hard copies in your role as a priest in their military. It's perfect! At least the guards will consider it. You'll no doubt need to improvise a bit, but this will buy you time to figure out your next move. You can take a file folder filled with paper. If they want to look at it, drive right through the gate while they're distracted. It's just chain-link fencing. Looks like they got it from a farmer or a hardware store."

Novi counted his assets. The element of surprise: a meek-looking priest. A fast car with bulletproof panels and windows. The gun Miroslav begged him to take along. "I asked my contacts about this, and they all told me you'd be a fool not to take it if you have the choice. It wasn't easy to make this hardware appear on request. I'll feel better if I know you're on equal terms with the border patrols. Your task isn't over unless you get home."

No road was ideal; Novi would cross at Miroslav's recommended smaller border point further east and then join the E95 further south. After all the adventure and chaos of the past few weeks, Novi still had his engrained apprehension about border crossings. He slept poorly but felt fully energized in the morning as Miroslav poured a full cup of coffee into an insulated road mug. "So, this is it, Novichok. It's been a privilege to help you both ways. My life has been more interesting ever since I first met Father Boris! I wish you safe travels home to your family."

"Many hands make light work, doctor. Thanks for all your help. We all had important roles to play." Novi took the coffee mug, his suitcase and an apple and they headed outside to the surgeon's little garage where the Lada awaited. The two men shook hands and

Novi put the car in first, waved once, and drove out of sight. He stopped to fill the car and jerry can with gas, paid with Belarusian rubles, then turned southward.

The day was misty, the sky a smudged newspaper grey. To Novi it felt cinema- perfect for crossing a border. He rehearsed his story as the Lada rolled slowly to the window of a small hastily built hut. A paunchy uniformed guard with a tense frown and Stalin moustache appeared at the window. His uniform was Belarusian. "State your business. Where's your passport?"

Novi saw a second man in soldier's fatigues coming along the other side carrying an AK-47 loosely slung over his shoulder. His own weapon was cradled in Olga's tailored pocket, just below his left armpit.

"Military. Russian Army Chaplain." He held up the Russian passport, his image a perfect match for his face, scruffy beard, and dyed hair. "My orders are to deliver new ID materials to the Chernihiv local clergy. Zelensky's supposed to be deporting them all. They work for our side, and we need them in place. So, new identities for the bishops."

The soldier with the assault rifle was now beside the border guard. He looked like a puppy, thought Novi. Scrawny, poorly fed, and pimply. Novi saw two Border Services trucks parked about fifty metres ahead beside a closed second gate. A straight line, no turning options between the first and second gates. To both sides, razor wire coils stretched for several dozen metres. Two trucks, maybe four more men. Where were they? Novi knew from the maps and drone shots that this road ran straight ahead through farms for several more kilometres before turning right to join the main highway. Was it mined? Were there more guards? The farther into the south, the more likely that they would be Ukraine's.

The tumblers in Novi's mind calculated madly. Army ID in a different name. Show them? Hope they don't notice? No. No way. Distract one of them? How? Ah! An idea!

"I've already been issued my own new ID, if that helps." He held up the Father Yuri tag with his original photo. "See, a different name, hair color, everything. I have twenty more in back."

To Stalin Junior, he said, "I have to get this info to my colleagues before they're rounded up. Who should I tell them is holding their fate in his hands?" And to the kid with the rifle, he said, "I outrank you, if that uniform is genuine. So, I'm ordering you to let me pass." The flustered guard and soldier looked at each other. Stalin nodded to the kid to come nearer.

Novi saw his chance. He reached under his arm and shot the kid's rifle from under the cassock. The rifle dropped. Novi shot once more, past Stalin Junior's head, taking out the security camera in a sizzle of electricity. He stamped his foot to the floor, let out the clutch, and drove through the chain-link gate at the end of the fenced border enclosure, ducking as the gate snapped, and pieces flew over the car roof. He shifted quickly and flew straight past the second guardhouse. The men inside were still getting their keys out and grabbing weapons when the Lada hit one hundred kilometres per hour. He heard shots pinging harmlessly off the rear window.

The straight line of the rural road gave Novi an edge in getting up to full speed, two hundred kilometres per hour. The guards would be on enemy turf if they wanted to try and detain him now. He drove another five minutes flat out, not daring to look behind him, and then finally checked the mirror. Nothing. He slowed and turned west toward Chernihiv.

Damage to the town was clearly visible from the road. He stopped the car, got out, and walked a few streets. There was almost nothing remaining of the school; the athletic field was a mass grave populated with markers and crosses. Overhead, some robins and sparrows chirped and played. The wind was gentle, and blue sky was just peeking through the heaviest clouds as they slid silently away on the breeze. As he returned to the car, he realized: Russian plates.

He had no tools to remove them and decided to chance getting into Kyiv and then ditching the car. He tore two pieces of black cloth from the cassock and tied them around the plates. Better than nothing.

Half an hour farther along the road a police car carrying two officers, passed him at speed and then slowed directly in front of him. No choice but to stop. The nearer officer barked, "Put your hands out the window! I wanna see them NOW!"

Novi began to feel that queasy cramp building in his gut.

In Ukrainian he called back, "I'm not a threat. I can explain."

The second cop replied, "You *will* explain. Get out of the car. I want to see your hands out front at all times." The cop's gun was out, the partner was calling for help on the radio. "Kneel down and lean against the car. There. Good. Don't move or you'll get hurt." The cop tore off the black cloth while Novi tried to think his way around what he saw coming. "Russian plates! You motherfucker!" He kicked Novi savagely in the ribs and screamed, "If you move, I'll shoot your balls off."

Novi lay shaking on the roadside shoulder. Two more police vehicles screamed along the road and stopped beside him and the first police car. Ominously, one of the new vehicles was a panel van. He didn't want to go in there. The new cops patted him down, felt inside the cassock, had him lift it over his head. No tattoos. They told him to get on his knees and start praying.

"O-ho, what do we have here?" One of the cops had reached under the driver's seat, finding the gun. "Do you know how much time you'll get just for this?" The next two officers came out with full body armor, helmets, and AK-47s.

"Cuff him, for fuck sake, you idiots!" screamed the biggest and loudest, obviously the ranking officer here.

They yanked Novi to his feet. His stomach clenched. He farted, and one of the cops kicked him in the ass. "You think we don't have manners in Ukraine? Us Nazis?" he roared.

The top man spoke again to the back of Novi's head. "Your story better be good, friend. I've killed lots of Russians scarier than you."

His team nodded silently; they hated to see him get this worked up.

"Put him in the van. Tow the car. Take all his possessions. Meet us at HQ. Move it!"

They scrambled to obey. A bad day now could easily become a bad month for the whole division. Novi was helped roughly into the back of the van by two officers. They put a blindfold on him. The van eased onto the highway, lights on. Two officers stayed back with the Lada. The road was jamming up with curious motorists, gawking at the priest being arrested and wondering what sin he'd committed. Some who spotted the license plate already knew.

The ride was silent for a while. One cop relented a bit. "Calm down, Father. I'm sure you have some perfectly rational explanation for coming to visit us. Right?"

His partner chuckled. Then he went tense. "I hear your Patriarch wants to kill us all. True or false?"

Novi decided to try reason. "Guys. If I were really a Russian operative, why would I drive here, toward Kyiv, with that car? Lada. Russian plates. Would I be that stupid? Or suicidal?"

"Our specialists will ask all the questions that need answers at HQ. Your job will be to answer them fully, completely, and honestly. Your next ten to twenty years depend on it."

Novi thought back, decades ago, to his oral Royal College surgery exams. How he'd felt as though his life hung in the balance. He tried to prepare, to go back in time to that mode of pressure and draw calm from it.

After getting off the motorway, there were several turns, traffic noise, and finally, a full stop. The car door opened. They dragged

Novi to his feet and marched him forward. He heard an elevator door open, and a hand shoved him in. The door closed, and Novi felt the elevator go up, not down. A good sign? One of the cops yanked off the blindfold. Alpha ordered, "Take him to Intake One. Five minutes."

Two officers ushered him into a windowless room and cuffed his ankle to a metal table leg. His suitcase was there, unopened. He thought quickly, mentally listed the contents. Nothing he could be busted for. The Oxycodone tablets were in his belly pouch, along with the last doses of memory drug, a gram of Carfentanil, and a tube of tissue glue. Why hadn't any of them thought to give him Ukraine plates? Because they would have gotten him detained in Belarus. Of course. His bowels were tightening up again, and he was beginning to sweat. He hadn't had any opioid for almost twenty-four hours. He longed for a tablet now.

Alpha Dog opened the door and entered with two men. One was in uniform, the other in a military T-shirt and camo gear. They displayed guns in shoulder holsters. Alpha addressed Novi, his face five centimetres away. He reeked of *kubasa*.

"We're going to open your bag. You're going to tell us about each item." To the ceiling he shouted, "Camera on!"

A blue plastic hemisphere came to life and began to blink once per second. Novi breathed in rhythm with it and tried to relax.

The military man hoisted the case onto the table and popped the latches. He spilled the contents out. Novi had just folded and neatly tucked everything into place that morning at Father Miroslav's. The soldier wasn't interested in the clothes. He felt around, found what the Belarusian border guard had missed in his excitement over the gun: A zippered side pocket. Russian rubles, the Moscow map, the Russian and Ukrainian spare passports, Russian driver's license.

Alpha was intrigued. "What the hell? What have you been up to? If you need time to think, I can keep you for a month with no charges. And that's if I play by the rules."

Novi knew he was in too deep to dig himself out with logic, wits, or anything of the sort. He weighed his options. What was Pavel's standing with them, now that he'd likely have been exposed posthumously as a traitor? Should he ask them to bring in Iryna to bail him out? Was she known to them? Were any of these men working both sides? He could blow her cover if she was deployed in some other capacity. If she was even in the city.

He decided to gamble his identity. "Can I talk with your highest-ranking officer? And one other witness? I'm not armed. And I'm not a threat to anyone here, or in this whole city."

"Who are you, Taras Shevchenko? I think I've heard everything now."

The others laughed. Novi's guts heaved again. He needed a bathroom. "And I need a toilet right away too. If you were in my position, you'd understand. Or it's gonna get messy in here, and we'll all have to suffer with it."

They were flummoxed. This guy had some nerve. Maybe he had something they actually should hear.

One of the officers unlocked the ankle cuff and jerked Novi to his feet. "Okay. let's make this quick. I don't wanna have to clean up shit. Especially Russian shit. We've all had enough of it."

He walked Novi down the hall at gunpoint, stood outside the stall, heard him grunting, flushing, and standing up. The door opened. He thanked the officer. They could deprive him of food or water instead, he thought.

They fastened his ankle again. Another man was in the room, in plain clothes. He also wore a shoulder holster and an impatient scowl.

"I wanna see what's so important that I get dragged over here at lunchtime. My boys have filled me in. You're driving a Lada with foreign plates. You enter our country from Belarus. You're a priest or claim to be. You're armed. My guys found extra passports, both Ukrainian and Russian. Has anybody stripped this fellow down?"

An officer said, "Not completely, captain, but he has no tattoos or anything else that would link him to any known groups."

His superior raised one eyebrow and looked at the rest of them. They hurriedly pulled off the cassock and took off Novi's shoes.

The captain resumed. "Okay, friend, what's your story? What could be so very important to take me away from lunch? And it better not be good. It better be fuckin' incredible."

Novi cleared his throat. "I have another passport. Bring me a knife and I'll show you."

The captain snapped his fingers. The military man took an army knife from his khakis and gave it to the captain, who handed it to Novi. They all took two steps back. Alpha aimed his pistol at Novi's chest. The captain said, gently, "Try anything and you won't leave his room on your feet."

Novi nodded. He turned the case over and cut out the little curtain inside that held his used socks and underwear. He felt for a metal seam and slid the knife in. With a few strokes, the prepared part of the seam gave way. He put the knife down and pulled out his Canadian passport. He held it up for the captain.

"So, what? You're a passport forger? Big fuckin deal. You *yollups*, you dragged me away from lunch for this shit? Night shifts for all of you." He shook his head. "Holy mother of God." To the military man, he asked, "Can I come work with you? It has to be better than trying to manage these imbeciles."

But the military man wasn't listening. His eyes were fixed on the fake priest. He knew exactly who Novi was. He and the captain stepped out into the hallway. The others heard the muffled exchange through the metal door. The military man was saying things in a low voice, and the captain was having trouble keeping his voice down.

They returned from the hallway. The captain got on his knees and undid the ankle bracelet himself. He straightened to his full height, almost two metres. He offered his hand to Novi.

"There has been a misunderstanding. I'm sure you have dealt with this situation once or twice. My men are diligent and were following orders. Simple as that. You're free to go. Take your time, collect your things. I'm sorry to say but your vehicle has already been impounded. It may be a few days before we can get it to you. Will you have a local address?"

Novi looked at the military man and took a chance. "Iryna's place. She can keep it. It will serve her well."

"Do you need a ride anywhere? We can take you somewhere in the city, or the train station?"

"How about Iryna's?" Novi asked.

"Done," said the military man. "I'll take you myself."

Novi filled up his case, taking his time to fold everything and put it into its correct place. "Can you call her ahead and ask for diabetic supplies plus? She'll know."

He'd guessed right. Military man pulled out his mobile, opened his contacts, touched one button, and waited. "Iryna. Major here. Boris's friend. I have a houseguest here. Asking for 'diabetic supplies plus.'" Novi could hear the squeal of delight on the other end. The same sound he'd heard when they'd discovered the morels on a sunny day in the forest. He smiled.

He brought flowers and chocolates along; the military man knew where to find such things. She was waiting at the end of Lena's street—a different neighborhood, different apartment block. There were uniformed men at the street corners. She ran to the car, embraced Novi, kissed him, and hugged him again. She was crying. "Oh, Father Mike, I really never thought I'd see you again. This is the greatest birthday I've ever had! Major, you have no idea how happy this makes me! Thank you."

The military man helped Novi pull out the suitcase. They shook hands formally. Then the major slapped Novi on the shoulder. "Well done! You've helped us all immensely. I hope it's enough to carry us through the rest of the year. From there, we can win this. Thank you."

Novi and Iryna went inside. The need for secrecy was still there, but she was leaving Kyiv. To Odesa, away from the capital and its memories. The apartment was piled with boxes from her old place.

"Wait here. You can't be seen anyway. Any requests? I'll go get some groceries."

"How about *smurzhy*?" he asked with a grin.

Lena the nurse arrived with supplies for Novi. She had procured a small bottle of Methadone to keep the shakes off. About three days' supply; she couldn't manage more

They all cooked together; he served as sous-chef. She made chicken Kyiv—what else? And a white cream sauce with butter, spring onions, and mushrooms. A salad with produce from a community garden at the end of the street. They drank a precious bottle of Bakhmut sparkling white wine. How long until the wineries would return to life?

Iryna sat next to him on the sofa. They had half full glasses in their hands. She put her head on his shoulder, and her body gradually settled into the gap between them. The contact with her made him come alive again. He felt euphoric, youthful. On his other side, Iryna's friend sat slightly apart. But as the wine settled in, and the old romance film on TV pulled them in, she also moved closer. He felt even better.

Novi woke up in Iryna's bed with the sun streaming in through the thin curtain. They were tangled with each other and the sheets. "See, Father Mike, your morals are stronger than your instincts!" she teased. He'd stayed dressed. The mission was over, he'd survived, and his fondest memory of the whole journey was enough for him.

Lena made coffee while the others took turns in the washroom. They drank it hot while they scanned Iryna's laptop for train tickets to Warsaw. Novi was going home.

9

Joe's arrival home was greeted ecstatically. The whole family came over for a backyard BBQ. He regaled them with stories of the Polish capital, the crowds, the chaos. They were more subdued as he related the stories of suffering he'd heard from the people fleeing for their lives. He had to concentrate to avoid any mention of leaving Poland for points further east.

Sara had fretted the entire time for Joe's safety. He could see the relief in her eyes, the dark rings he'd never noticed before. Because he hadn't bothered to really see? They hadn't been apart for this long since getting married, but she'd managed well on her own with the kids, house, and everything that they entailed. She had grown and changed too. She was more direct with him, more able to speak her mind and her heart. To tell him what she needed in her life. They had long talks, serious talks, and made real peace with each other. Life was short and complete happiness elusive. They would seek it together.

But there was so much more to say; Joe lay awake at night silently composing his full confession. The pills, the blackmail, the mysterious Carter, Father Boris. His dementia diagnosis. The trade-off of the memory drug for his skills as an assassin. Training, Iryna, Pavel, the Russian Army camp. The day of the assassination itself. His dangerous return trip. He'd never envisaged the conversation or how she might feel, if she could believe it at all.

NOVICHOK

He had two doses of memory drug left. On schedule, he went to the base from the side door of the YWG terminal and submitted himself to another battery of tests. There were no red flags in his stress or emotional scores. As expected, all his medical testing came back in normal range. They did another functional MRI pre and post memory drug administration. There were differences, the same ones as before he'd left for the Project mission.

Dr. Giguere supervised all his testing. "Hi, Joe! Welcome back. You made it, and with flying colors. The test results are really encouraging. Looks like the drug still works for you. But before you start to lose its effect, we've had a meeting about it and feel you should come off it while you can. We can rethink it sometime down the road."

Joe looked at her, surprised. "What are you saying here, doc? Come off the drug? If it stopped working, that makes sense, but this?"

Her eyes welled up suddenly. "They didn't want me to tell you this yet, but remember Dr. Young? My mentor? He stayed on it too long. And now…" she faltered, "and now he's dead. He killed himself last week. He'd been on it, and on the beta version, a total of four years. I invented this and it killed the man I admire most. I won't allow it to do this to you, Joe. I'm really sorry. Maybe when we know more about the duration of effects, maybe tweak the dosage schedule, but for now, no way. Those last two doses; you'll notice they're numbered. Right?"

Novi recalled the previous evening, dosing himself in the home office at 2 AM, and realized that she was right. The usual kick, the heightened alertness—the high was diminished. "You cut the dose, didn't you?" Joe was getting hysterical. "So, what about the last one I still have? Huh? Right here!" He pointed at his left pouch. "That's a half dose too, isn't it? I was gonna negotiate for a lifetime supply of this shit, but you're telling me it's poison? *Now* you're telling me? Dr. Young sold me on this. *You* sold me on this! I trusted you.

What a fuckin' mistake! I heard a saying once: 'No good deed goes unpunished.' Well, here's the proof. So, what will happen to my mind? My career? My family? Hey, doc? Look what I did for us all! Give me that drug and let me find out for myself if it harms me. Dr. Young's brain isn't mine. Hello? Scientific method?"

"I know what you're thinking, Joe. I swear to you I didn't plan it this way. The peptides are tricky, and this is uncharted water. Remember? We said all that. So, please don't punish me for *my* good deed! Back then it was the best thing we had, and you were all in. I know you're furious but please see both sides. You might not be here right now if not for that drug. We don't know and we can't know. We have newer versions in testing but not ready for human use yet. My promise to you is that if we can start another human trial, you'll be Patient 1."

Joe had calmed himself down; Li Fu's lessons had many applications. "Work fast, doctor. My time is gonna get really tight. I have to go."

Inevitability cast its long shadow over Joe. He knew the final memory boost would soon wear off, leaving his mind stranded. After more than two years of artificial stabilization, he had no idea what to expect. He racked his brain for opening lines, ways to create a time window, how to tell the story to Sara with minimum hesitation.

The kids had left for school. "Sara, let's go for a walk. It's a nice day. The leaves are full color. Do you have a lot of work today?"

"Nothing that can't wait, I guess." He had her jacket ready. She steeled herself. *Something's coming.*

Unconsciously, Joe steered them toward the riverside trails. They walked silently, Joe working up the nerve and trying to decide how to start. Sara, halfway between amusement and mild irritation, sensed his discomfort. She let him struggle for just a few minutes and then rescued him as she always did when he was tongue-tied. "Okay, Joe, here we are. What do you need to say?"

"I'll start at the end. The rest of this might make more sense. The preface is that I love you, whatever else happens, or has happened, or hasn't. I haven't been a great partner. I know it. And the window is closing fast. We diverged and I took the easy way to keeping my head on straight. Work more. What else? COVID really drove it home. But now I have a progressive form of dementia. I don't think I'll be able to function for very long. My trip to Poland went a lot further and I need you to know what actually happened."

"Joe, you've had your adventure, done good works in a new part of the world. And that's great, it's fine and I'm glad you're home. But can we stick to the facts? I don't know how you would go from doing aid work in Poland to dementia so quickly."

Silently Joe lifted the bottom hem of his T-shirt to show her the incisions he'd opened and closed dozens of times. When she pointed and her eyes turned to question marks, he resumed. "Remember when I had my knee fixed? A few years before COVID? I got hooked on the pain pills. A colleague turned out to be a dealer. She was under watch by someone. They got my name, and I was blackmailed. 'Wanna keep on working here? Then do this procedure for us.'

"I did some work on a chemist who was on the run from Russia. I was passed along to this spy ring, or I don't know what you'd call it, when the Ukraine war began. I'd already been diagnosed with dementia. Remember my friend Krishna, the neurologist? He gave me a year or two of reasonable quality living, then a few years in a diaper. The spy leader offered me a chance to join a very small drug trial. An experimental injection that needed storage at body temperature. This drug restores memory and allows for hugely accelerated learning.

"They gave me the drug, and it gave me a chance to keep on functioning. The catch was: they wanted someone to get close to an assassination target. And then perform the deed. At the same time, they trained me. That's when I went 'up north' every month for the past two years. Remember when you saw me testing out a procedure tray at 2 AM? I was just about to start cutting my incisions open to give myself another dose." He pointed to his scars. Then he rolled up his sleeve to show her his PICC line scar. "This was where I put in a line to keep myself from being poisoned while I was doing the job they sent me for. It was in Moscow. You would have seen it in the news."

Sara's face registered skepticism, outright disbelief, then the wide-eyed clarity of recognition as parts of his story clicked into her own recollections. His absences. Her suspicion of another woman. His late nights in the home office. "You mean you killed someone? You have dementia? You're doing operations on yourself?"

He told her more, omitting the names. The recruitment. The spy priest who had shielded and guided him. Gently, he told her about the woman in Kyiv who had sheltered him while they poisoned her partner, and the time they had shared in that brief intersection of their lives.

"Please understand that I'd just survived a kidnapping, orchestrated by her abusive partner, and I was heading into an assignment with a fifty-percent fatality rate. It's not something I'd done in all our years of marriage." He carried on, telling her about the detour through Belarus, the loyal team of helpers in Moscow, the day of the event itself. How the drug blunted his emotions but left him feeling unstable. Leaving Moscow, his escape from Russia, the arrest in Kyiv.

"I'm of no use to them now. They've withdrawn the drug beyond the dose I have with me right now. They tell me it'll kill me if I stay on it. My memory will fade a month from my last dose to whatever it would have been without their intervention. I suspect that's great for them. I wanted you to know what to expect, as far as I can predict.

"I've had the advantage of knowing all this for over two years and living it. You're hearing it all at once for the first time. We can talk about it anytime you want. I know it's a big bomb to drop on you. I never meant the parts of this that are hard for you to know.

His voice grew hoarse with emotion and the effort of getting all this out before he lost his nerve.

"I don't know how to tell the kids about the dementia part of this. They never need to know the rest. I'm sorry to leave you to figure it out." Now he was weeping openly. "I'll help as much as you want me to while I can. For starters we should get some help from a professional. For all of us. It's gonna be a rough next few months."

Sara was silent for a long while. When she finally spoke, Joe fleetingly wished he'd stayed quiet.

Her voice was molten with rage. "You selfish son of a bitch, Joe! This beats choosing your career over us all. It beats every self-absorbed boring anecdote, every time you went off to work without saying goodbye. Every time you made a change to your work schedule for the sake of some colleague or patient but couldn't do it for a family birthday. Like mine, for instance.

"You kept this to yourself? For over two years! We could have had a scrap of real life before your lights go out. And you made the choice to go off and do whatever you wanted. A killer, of all things! Christ, Joe. Dementia, my ass! You've been out of your mind *all* this time, I guess. I'm so glad you told me now! Should I help you with the funeral arrangements? Fuck you! Do it yourself while you still can."

Now her breathing slowed as tears poured down her cheeks, and she sobbed loudly. Joe walked silently beside her. When he reached for her hand, she pulled it away and moved to widen the gap between them. He kept his own tears silent; he had just enough sense to know that this was her time, not his.

They stopped at a favorite bench facing the river. On the far bank a small herd of about twenty deer grazed placidly among the shrubbery. They sat, each at their own end of the bench, staring blankly ahead. "I thought they'd fix my dementia. The drug they gave me worked really well. I wanted to bargain for a lifetime supply. But I could feel my mind going haywire now and then. It turned out to be unsafe for me to keep taking it. I have one more reduced dose, and then I'll be wherever nature leaves me. No more memory drug. It was a gamble. They just told me last month that it isn't going to work out the way I'd hoped it would.

"My thinking was: get this miracle drug, live longer with my brain still working. Hell, live longer, period. More good time to spend with you and the kids. They paid better than the usual up north week.

"They've also guaranteed lifetime security and income for you, education for the kids. Relocation if you want that too, after I'm... after I'm gone. New identities if you feel they're necessary. There's an email address, gordiehowe@project.ca. They respond quickly.

"I know it's not exactly your idea of consideration, but I was thinking of you and our whole family when I signed on with them. I need you to understand that. And a big part of this is that I couldn't tell you about all the spy stuff, the drug, the mission, without putting you all at risk. If there'd been a leak of some kind, possessing knowledge of what I was involved in could be fatal. They were very clear about it."

"Oh yeah? So why tell me now? So spy people can come for me too?"

"Because you need to know what's about to happen. Sara, I'm gonna start dying. Very soon. And I can't hold it back without their drug or anything else. What would you think if I hadn't just told you, and you woke up at 3 AM to see me burning up the stove, or leaving doors open all night? And our children? They need to have counselling of some kind soon. I don't know how long I have."

There was a long silence. Joe knew her well enough to stay silent while she processed. After several long minutes, she reached for his hand. When she spoke, her voice faltered. "I don't know,

316

Joe. I hoped this would bring you back to me. I had a bit of time to myself, and it was good, it was healthy. I thought a lot about how our life should be and what we need to improve on. For ourselves individually, as a couple, and as a whole family. But now you say you're going away from me and there's nothing either of us can do to stop it. We lost so much time that we can't get back. And now all this. It's a lot to absorb at one time.

"I will say I'm proud of you for actually taking your dream in your hands and making it happen. For yourself and for the benefit of so many people. I'm really shocked that you could hide something like this from me for so long! You've never been any good at keeping secrets. I don't know *how* you managed this one." She shook her head slowly, a bemused smile on her lips.

"I keep this mental snapshot of you as the idealist I knew once upon a time. I know I haven't been perfect either, and we've both found ways to make our lives harder than they needed to be." Her eyes welled up again, and she began to shake with her sobs. "I appreciate that you're telling me about this, even this late in the game. Hopefully I'll have time to process it all before you get really disabled. Let's just promise each other to make the most, the very best, of what we do have. I'll try to remember you as a hero, Joe. A real hero."

They were back at the house. "If you want to see it, in case you have any doubts, I could use a hand. Today's my last dose." Joe pointed at his incisions and made a cutting gesture.

"I'll help you get set up, but I can't watch that. You know I was never the blood-and-guts type."

Joe went into the bathroom, washed his hands, then cracked open the sterile procedure tray, showing Sara how to arrange it on the desk, pour the antiseptic, and hold up the bottle of Xylocaine. He picked up the syringe and she shuddered. "I'll go take another walk." She laughed nervously as she left the room. Joe looked down and began the procedure.

A month later, he was reviewing patient charts while the kids slept upstairs. Paperwork was so grooved onto his cortex that he could perform it accurately even now. But it took him twice as long as it had six months ago. Sara was out with some friends from the gym. Or it was yoga. He got tired, took a break and opened his email. The hydro, water, and credit card bills were unpaid. Damn, he'd forgotten again. His morning routine was getting progressively sloppier; he forgot his phone or his ID badge at least twice a week. Both were as essential as air for him to function properly in the hospital.

He rode his bike past the church on the way to work. Which way was he supposed to turn to get to the hospital again? Half the time, he didn't know. He enjoyed the ride anyway, but it took longer every week. When he arrived, he opened his computer and realized he'd missed a meeting and forgotten a dentist's visit. He didn't care. He hated them both anyway.

10

Three months later Joe lay in a bed at a long-term care institution an hour and a half from home. It was located in the same tiny hamlet where his parents had been raised—a coincidence. Part of a new policy to ease congestion in places closer to the city. Joe had been pleased by the symmetry of this final assignment, and it absolved Sara of any guilt about not taking the kids to see him while she adjusted to the new reality of her life.

Mint green chipped paint. The walls were half-covered with taped information sheets about new seasonal viruses, handwashing reminders, visiting hours, safety and behavior rules.

A private room at least. Family photos on the wall—a few of Joe in better shape, in better days. As a young man. With his family, with his parents. The village ladies who staffed the facility recognized Joe's parents in the faded photos. There was an open window, late autumn leaves faded and nearly all gone. From the position of the man in the bed, the bare branches were beyond sight. His nurse smiled cheerfully; it was part of her job description. "Joe, you have a visitor! What's your name again, hon?"

A tall man in a well-tailored blue suit said, "Carter. We know each other from work."

"Oh, okay. I'll leave you to it. If he gets agitated, just pull the cord on the light. We'll come help him settle."

Carter waited for her to leave. Out of habit, he looked around the corners of the ceiling. No cameras. He leaned over Joe and whispered, "I know what you did, Joe. We're all really proud of how you performed. A hundred and fifty percent effort. Congratulations on a job well done."

Joe lay in a diaper. He'd lost weight. A crusted feeding tube protruded like a snake from below his ribs. He couldn't speak clearly anymore. "Emmy Ug? Emmy Ug?"

Carter recoiled, feeling contaminated by the weaker man's condition. He was embarrassed by his own inability to grant the request. He faked it badly. "I can't understand you, Joe. Your family is being taken care of financially. I wanted you to know that. We're watching them from close by. They will face no repercussions. We're providing them lifetime security. We owe them, and you. Do you understand me, Joe?"

The man in the bed lay quietly. His brown eyes bored into Carter's, the ferocity out of keeping with the rest of his state. Carter was discomfited by the directness. He stared back, trying to apologize without words. The patient now had tears in his eyes; they pooled and ran down onto the pillow and sheets. "Omiss? Bomiss!"

Carter was shaken. "Yes, Joe, I promise. Just came to see how they're treating you. Looks pretty nice here, eh? Whaddaya think, boss? Hang in there, okay, buddy?"

He got up and left the room. He stopped to compose himself in the men's room and left in a hurry. He went through a drive-thru and got a large coffee. Then he drove back to the city. He caught a regular flight from YWG to YYZ. To his wife and kids. He needed to hug them. They were still several hours away.

He fought the traffic along the 401, turned north onto the 416. There was a big roadside food court. He grabbed a burger, then found he couldn't eat it. He wrapped it back up and put it on the empty passenger's seat. He drove with the radio off. There was too much noise.

Two more hours and he was home. He turned into the driveway in a nice subdivision in Kanata, not far from where the Senators play. He hugged his wife as she came to the door. This wasn't characteristic; she hesitated a few beats and tentatively hugged him back. The teens in the family room were plugged in, zoned out, and hooked to their phones by the eyeballs. Everything here was status quo.

"Well, I'm back," he said.

11

—

2025

Now it was late winter. The roads were slick and the drive out to see Joe was tricky, sometimes impossible. There hadn't been a visitor in some time. Parking lot capacity was reduced almost half by plowed banks of dirty snow. The sun slanted from low in the sky, nearly twilight at four PM. The clerk at the front desk looked up to see the silhouette of a tall man in a long over-coat, a blue suit partially visible underneath.

Carter knocked his boots together to shake off the snow and took three steps to the desk. He re-introduced himself to the smiling receptionist. "Any visitors lately, Marge?"

"Just the family, about a month ago." She replied. "So sad. It seems to upset the children so his wife can't see him often. And there's the winter driving. Joe's a favorite though. He was a doctor once, and we look after him as our own. I guess you knew that, of course. You're from work. Go on in and see him. He should wake up for a while, anyway. He sleeps so much."

"No other visitors? Everyone at the hospital in the city knows him."

"I guess it's the drive at this time of year. He'll be happy to have some company."

Carter signed the guest ledger and went down the hall. He leaned in close, almost intimately as if to tell a secret, and smiled. The man in the bed sensed a presence in the room and opened his eyes. Even in his dim understanding, he smiled with his eyes. A visitor! A friend. Someone who had been important to him once. Who? What? The shelves of his memory stood bare like the trees outside, even with the exercises the therapist had taught him while she could.

Carter could hardly contain himself. "Hey, Joe, how's your Arabic?" he asked.

www.ingramcontent.com/pod-product-compliance
Lightning Source LLC
LaVergne TN
LVHW052323210925
821619LV00005B/92